CRITICAL ACCLAIM FOR
LEIGH GREENWOOD'S
FERN:

"I loved *Fern*, but I absolutely loved Fern! She's fabulous! I really think this is an incredible job!"
—*Romantic Times*

"*A powerful yet sensitive tale, Fern* adds a deeper dimension to this magnificent and colorful saga that began with *Rose*. Leigh Greenwood just keeps getting better!"

—*Affaire de Coeur*

"I loved *Rose*, but *Fern* is even better!"
—*Rendezvous*

"Gentle persuasion and passionate loving stirred with the tender, loving pen of Leigh Greenwood present the reader with an unforgettable, high-caliber read!"
—*Heartland Critiques*

DRESSED TO KILL

"Why are you so afraid to admit you're a female?" Madison said.

Fern stared at him, flabbergasted. She didn't move when Madison advanced on her, not stopping until they were only inches apart.

"You've got a body men pant after. You tease us by parading about in your pants, but your clothing also forces us to keep our distance."

Fern stepped back; Madison stepped forward.

"Are you too ignorant to know you drive men crazy, or do you dress like that because you like to see us with our tongues hanging out?"

Fern's mouth opened, but no sound came out.

"You know you're more dangerous in pants than a dress." He stalked her as she retreated before him. "You can go where other women can't, cause havoc other women never dreamed of."

"I don't...I never—"

"But there's a problem," Madison said.

He was so close she could feel his breath on her skin. She held her ground, determined she wouldn't run away. She didn't want to admit he frightened her, but he was so close he was practically touching her. It made her limbs go weak.

"I'll bet no man has ever held you in his arms or kissed you."

The *Seven Brides* series by Leigh Greenwood:
ROSE

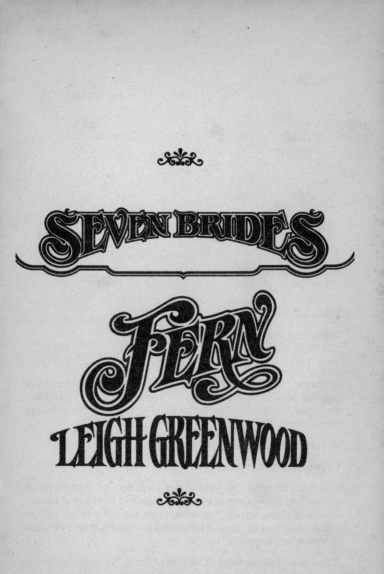

SEVEN BRIDES

FERN

LEIGH GREENWOOD

LEISURE BOOKS   NEW YORK CITY

A LEISURE BOOK®

Published by

Dorchester Publishing Co., Inc.
276 Fifth Avenue
New York, NY 10001

Copyright © 1994 by Leigh Greenwood

Cover Art by John Ennis

The name "Leisure Books" and the stylized "L" with design are trademarks of Dorchester Publishing Co., Inc.

Printed in the United States of America.

Chapter One

Abilene, Kansas—1871

Fern Sproull rounded the corner of the Drovers Cottage, spurs clanking, her fists tightly clenched. She skidded to a halt when she saw George Randolph standing on the porch in a deep study. "Piss and vinegar!" she muttered angrily. Then tilting her head at a defiant angle, she walked straight past him into the hotel.

"How long has that skunk been here?" she demanded of the man behind the desk, stabbing a slender index finger in George's direction.

"Keep your voice down," Frank Turner implored.

Only then did Fern notice that the windows had been thrown open to catch the breeze. George Randolph had probably heard every word she said, but she didn't care. It was about time he knew what she thought of him and all the rest of his clan. It infuriated her that people like the Randolphs thought money gave them the right to do anything they liked.

Even kill.

"It would ruin me if he and the rest of the Texans took their business to the Planters Hotel," Frank explained.

Fern leaned against the desk. "I wish they'd all go back to Texas and stay there."

"You might as well say you want to take the food out of my children's mouths."

"Why couldn't he get killed by lightning or run over in a stampede?" Fern complained, ignoring her friend's objection.

"I thought it was Hen Randolph you hated so much. George ain't done nothing."

"I can't stand any of them." She directed her words toward George, but he showed no sign of having heard her.

"If Hen killed Troy, they'll find out at the trial," Frank said.

"George will try to buy him off."

"You can't buy people in Abilene," Frank assured her.

"Half this town has already sold out to Texas cattle," Fern declared, pointing her finger again, this time at Frank. "The governor postponed Hen's trial until their fancy lawyer could get here. Now he's moved it to Topeka."

"How do you know it's a lawyer he's waiting for?"

"What else could that telegram mean? Besides, why else would anybody be coming all the way from Boston? You might have known nobody in Kansas or Missouri was good enough for them."

"Bert had no business showing you that telegram," Frank said, a frown creasing his brow.

"He was just trying to help. We got to stick together against outsiders."

"That kind of loyalty will get you both in trouble one of these days."

"Not likely anything I can't handle," Fern said with a confident squaring of her shoulders. "I've a good mind to tell George what I think of him and his murdering brother."

"I wouldn't if I was you," Frank advised. "That kind of talk is none too popular. I ain't the only one who makes his living off the drovers."

"Then you'd better start looking for another business. It won't be long before the farmers and respectable ranchers drive all the Texans out of Kansas. But not until after we hang Hen Randolph."

"Ain't nobody seen who killed your cousin," Frank pointed out gently. "I ain't saying it weren't Hen Randolph, but you got no way to prove it. And you know this town won't hang no Texan unless you got dead proof. Folks are afraid they'll take their business to Ellsworth or burn the town down over their heads."

"You're nothing but a bunch of cowards," Fern said angrily.

"No man likes being called a coward, Fern, especially them that is. There's a lot of Texans here right now, so unless you plan on staying away from town—"

"I mean to stay right here until I get a good look at that lawyer."

"—you'd better watch your mouth. If you don't, you'd better watch your back."

"You think George Randolph would shoot me?"

"No. He's too much of a gentleman, despite all you say about him, but that don't hold for everybody from Texas. When there's trouble, they stick together like they all had the same last name.

Not that he needs any help," Frank said, gazing at George. "I hear tell he has six more brothers, each one meaner than the next."

"I don't care if he's got a hundred and six," Fern declared. "Hen Randolph will hang. You have my word on it."

The Kansas Pacific engine belched thick clouds of black smoke into the pristine Kansas sky as it slowed in its approach to Abilene. Inside the only passenger car, James Madison Randolph sat erect in his seat.

"Don't be fooled by its rough appearance," said the only other passenger, a talkative man with whom Madison had been trying to avoid conversation since Kansas City. "Charley Thompson only laid out our little town about a dozen years ago, but already it's one of the most important in the state. Someday it'll be the most important city in Kansas."

The man had introduced himself as Sam Belton, the owner of the largest land office in Abilene. Madison tried to ignore him, as well as the nearly overpowering noise and stench emanating from the stockyards that bordered the train tracks on the south, but failed on both counts.

"Of course, a lot of people are only interested in making as much money as they can while the cattle boom lasts," Belton continued, "but we got a lot of good solid citizens here who hate the cattle trade as much as I do. One day there's going to be farms as far as you can see."

Madison didn't have to study the countryside to know that farming would be a very chancy occupation. One glance had been sufficient to tell him it was as barren as anything he had seen in Texas.

But Madison had no thoughts to spare for Kansas or its future farmers. George would be waiting at the station, and with him questions that had gone unanswered for eight years. From the moment he stepped on the train in Boston, Madison had been dreading this meeting.

Madison reluctantly rose to his feet as the train came to a halt. He looked at his clothes and frowned. Travel had ruined his appearance. That and the heat. Kansas was nothing like Boston or Virginia, but it was depressingly like Texas. His three years in that state had been a nightmare he preferred to remember as seldom as possible. Preferably not at all.

Don't think about it. Just do it. Then your debt will be paid, and you can get back to your own life.

"You'll want to put up at the Gulf House," Belton told Madison. "It's not the most popular hotel, but the Drovers Cottage is full of Texans. We don't mind taking their money, but nobody wants to sleep with them."

The look Madison gave Belton caused him to leave the train without further comment.

Madison didn't know what he expected of Abilene, but he had thought there'd be a railroad station at the very least. Instead, he stepped out onto a bare piece of prairie as big as a military parade ground that separated the tracks from the buildings of the town.

His luggage landed at his feet.

The heat soaked up by his black suit made him feel twenty degrees hotter. He picked up his bags and headed toward the first building he saw. The words *Drovers Cottage* were printed in huge letters across the front of the three-story hotel. It offered shade, rooms, and, Madison hoped despite Belton's remarks, some modicum of comfort.

Fern felt her stomach do a double flip. The most gorgeous man she'd ever imagined had just stepped off the train. Sinking down on the open windowsill, she gaped at him, her mouth as wide open as her eyes. She'd never seen anything like him. He didn't even dress like an ordinary person. His clothes would have caused him to stand out in any gathering. In Abilene, they were sure to make him an attraction all by himself.

She was used to rough men, dirty from their work, coarse because of the way they lived, strong because they had to be. They were clean only when they came fresh from the bath. Then they moved about as though uncomfortable with their unaccustomed state.

There was nothing uncertain about this man. He looked strong and determined, like a young bull surveying a new territory he meant to make his own. He also looked polished and slicked down. His coat fitted his broad shoulders as tightly as her gloves fitted her hands.

As he stood there, gazing disdainfully around him, the remaining strength drained from her limbs. This man looked enough like George Randolph to be his double. He had to be another one of the Randolph clan.

But even as Fern felt anger cause her ebbing strength to return, she couldn't resist taking one last, lingering look at this Adonis who had caused her heart to skip several beats. If it had been another time . . . if he had been another man . . .

But he wasn't. He was a Randolph.

Reminding herself of Troy's murder, she resolutely hardened her heart. This man was her enemy. He had come to mock justice.

She meant to see he didn't succeed.

Madison's forward progress was arrested when his near double stepped off the porch. George. It unnerved him that they should look so much alike. There had always been a strong resemblance between them, but he had been a teenager when they'd last seen each other, George a man. Now it was like seeing himself in a mirror. It brought his past rushing back on him with incredible force.

The tangle of strong and conflicting emotions unsettled him. He had told himself he wouldn't feel anything. He hadn't wanted to feel anything. But one glance at the older brother he hadn't seen in ten years and he felt far too much to sort out in the short time before they came face to face.

Chagrined that his stride should have faltered, that he should have felt a vague desire to retreat to the train, Madison forced himself to step forward again.

They met in the middle of the wide, dusty expanse of barren ground. Two men alone.

"I told them you were alive," George said, staring at his brother as though drinking in every detail of his appearance. His words sounded like a sigh, the release of a long-held breath.

Madison hadn't expected George to fall on his neck with joy, but neither had he expected the first words out of his mouth to drive home, with the penetrating power of a steel-tipped lance, the agony of George's years spent wondering if he was alive.

Guilt. Too heavy and hot to deny.

Guilt because he had known that George would worry, because he hadn't written. Guilt for the fear that his family might somehow destroy the new life he had built for himself.

"I knew you'd come back."

They hadn't been reunited for a full minute and already George was trying to draw him back into the family imbroglio that had nearly suffocated Madison years before. He felt it as if it were a hand in the small of his back pushing him along.

All the self-recrimination drained away.

"I haven't come back, George. I'm here only because Hen is in trouble."

"He was in trouble when you ran off and left Ma and the rest of them in that hell-hole without a man to protect them. Why come back now?"

Madison could feel his temper, never very far below the surface, pushing up, threatening to explode.

"Look, George, I didn't come back to argue over what I did eight years ago. If you don't want me here, I'll leave."

"Of course I want you here. Why do you think I came to meet you?"

"You have a damned funny way of showing it."

"Maybe it's because I can't decide whether I want to hit you or hug you."

Damn. George always had a way of twisting his guts in a knot.

"I guess you'd better hit me. I don't think they'd understand anything else in this town. Besides, it'll make you feel better."

"I guess they'll have to try," George said, as he stepped forward to throw his arms around his brother.

Madison stiffened, refusing to return the embrace. He didn't want George thinking he was giving up a single inch of his hard-won independence. He wanted to be welcomed, but on his own terms.

"Why didn't you write?" George asked as he released his brother and stepped back. "Everybody thought you were dead."

"You didn't. Why?"

"We're too much alike. I would have felt it."

Madison started to deny that—it seemed incredible that anyone could think he was at all like a man who was content to live on a cow ranch in southern

Texas—but he couldn't, not when looking at George was almost like looking at himself.

"How did you find out about Hen? I could hardly believe my eyes when I got your telegram."

"It was in a company report."

"What kind of report?"

"I'll tell you some other time. It's not important now. Tell me about Hen."

"What good will that do?"

"I'm a lawyer. I've come to prove he's innocent."

As soon as the words were out of his mouth, Madison realized that Hen had been fourteen years old when he left Texas. Madison knew even less about his younger brother than he knew about George.

He didn't know any of his brothers anymore. He hadn't realized until he had stepped off the train, not until the awful Kansas landscape brought back the reality of the Texas brush country, that he had been thinking of them as they used to be in Virginia. There, living in a large mansion with a dozen servants, it would have been impossible for a Randolph to commit murder. Here, in this savage land, anything was possible.

Including murder.

"Let's go inside," George said as they started toward the hotel. "You can't be used to this much heat back East. I thought you fancy swells wore white when you went to the tropics."

"*Fancy swells* might," Madison replied with some asperity, "but this is not the tropics. And I prefer to be thought of as a gentleman rather than a swell."

A trace of a smile lightened George's expression. "Prefer what you like, but everybody here is going to call you a swell. At best a tenderfoot. Nobody would believe you spent three years living in a dog trot."

Madison had tried to pretend those years never

happened. There had been times when he felt like an animal, fighting and clawing just to stay alive.

"What are you doing in Kansas?" Madison asked. "It's a long way from south Texas."

"I came to look into some investments."

"Investments? With what?"

George cocked his head and eyed his brother.

"The Circle Seven is one of the biggest and most successful ranches in Texas. We've spent most of our money buying breeding stock to improve our herds, but we've had to sell off the old stock to clear the range. The profits have been so good we've been looking for ways to invest the extra money. Once we start selling our improved stock, we'll make even more."

"The Circle Seven? I thought it was the Running S. Did you buy a new ranch?"

"No. Rose thought we ought to have a new name."

"Rose?"

"My wife."

"You're married!"

George seemed amused by his surprise. "You have a nephew, too."

"Another male Randolph," Madison said, his expression sardonic. "Wouldn't the old man be pleased."

"Probably, but Rose was sorely disappointed. She's firmly convinced a girl would be the making of us all."

"How did you find anybody willing to marry a whole clan?"

"She answered an ad for a housekeeper. Got us all shipshape in no time. It was just about the death of Monty."

Madison felt a chuckle rising within him. "I'd like to meet the woman willing to take on six Randolphs."

"Seven. I've been expecting you any day now for five years."

The chuckle sank and dissolved. Madison was slowly realizing that the past was not dead. For George, it never would be.

"I ought to talk to Hen."

The animation faded from George's eyes. "It can't be this hot and dusty in Boston," he said.

"It feels exactly like Cape Cod on a July afternoon," Madison replied sarcastically, angered by his brother's unexplained change of mood.

"You have a house there?"

George's putting him off irritated Madison. He wasn't a child. If there was something he needed to know, Madison wanted to hear it now.

"No, but Freddy's family does. I usually stay with them."

"Your friend from school?"

Madison nodded.

"Who works while you play?"

"Nobody works much in the summer. It's too hot in the city."

"Cows need tending year round," George observed, "whether it's hot, cold, raining, snowing, sleeting, or hailing stones as big as a hen's egg."

"That's why I choose to be a lawyer rather than a rancher."

They had reached the hotel porch and were about to climb the steps when a youth shot through the doorway and came to a halt directly in their path.

"One of you wasn't enough," he barked, glaring at George. "You had to bring in another one." He jerked an angry thumb in Madison's direction. "Well, it won't do any good. Hen Randolph murdered Troy, and he's going to hang for it. So you," the irate youngster rapped out, rounding on

19

Madison, "might as well get on that train and head back out of town."

With that, the youth turned and stalked off toward the stockyards.

"Who was that foul-mannered young ruffian?" Madison asked, glancing over his shoulder at the retreating form as they ascended the steps to the Drovers Cottage. "If he talks like that all the time, I'm surprised some of your cowhands haven't reduced him to Kansas dust."

"There's not a cowhand in Texas who would lay a hand on that *ruffian*," George replied, a hint of a smile on his lips.

"Why not? I was tempted to dust his britches myself."

"Because that *he* is a *she*," George answered, his smile broadening. "Underneath all that dust and sheepskin resides Fern Sproull, only daughter of Baker Sproull."

"That's a female?" Madison exclaimed, spinning around to get another look. Only then did the full enormity of the pants and the swaggering walk sink in. "Good God! I'm surprised she hasn't been arrested."

"According to local gossip, she's always been like that. Since the other young women don't seem anxious to follow her example, nobody gets upset about it."

Madison looked at his brother in some surprise. "When did you start listening to gossip?"

"Unless you mean to talk to yourself, there's little else to listen to. After Boston and New York, you'll find us very short of newsworthy events." They had reached the hotel desk. "This is Frank Turner, owner of the Cottage."

Frank nodded anxiously.

"I'd like a room," Madison said, "the best you

have. As good as that may be," he added dubiously, looking around the lobby with distaste.

"I've already reserved a room for you," George said.

"Will I be awakened in the middle of the night by a crying nephew?"

"Only by roistering cowhands or bawling long-horns," George said as he led the way to a narrow hallway that ran the length of the Cottage. "Rose and I stay at a house in town. She isn't up to keeping track of a three-year-old in a hotel. She's waiting in your room. She wants to meet you." A particularly satisfied smile settled on George's face. "She likes to protect me. She's never sure when someone, especially one of my brothers, will try to take advantage of my better nature."

"She doesn't know the Randolphs very well, does she?" Madison laughed mirthlessly. "We don't have a better nature."

"Actually, she knows us rather better than you would think." George knocked before he opened the door.

Madison entered to find a small woman sitting erect in a chair by the window. His eyes grew wide when she rose to meet him. George's wife was very pregnant.

"What do you mean, dragging your wife all over this benighted wilderness when she's . . . she's . . ."

"Going to have a baby," Rose finished for him, her gaze going from brother to brother. "George told me I'd recognize you at once, but I never thought you'd look almost as much alike as the twins."

Madison muttered a hurried apology. "I'm terribly sorry to be so outspoken, but if you've been married to George long enough to get that way, you know none of us has any manners."

"I've been married to George long enough to get

21

this way twice," Rose answered forthrightly, "and I find that the endless capacity of the Randolph men to adapt and change continues to surprise me."

"A diplomat," Madison remarked. "I guess she'd have to be to survive."

George gave his wife a look that caused her to sputter with laughter.

"Have I said something wrong?" Madison asked. He hated it when people laughed at him. It made him feel stupid. His father used to do that when he wanted to punish him.

"Remember to ask Monty about her first two days on the ranch," George said.

Madison didn't know anything about women having babies, but he guessed Rose shouldn't be standing. Boston matrons went to bed the minute they learned they were pregnant and didn't get up until they were fully recovered. Rose looked like she was about to pop, and she had been trailing around after George through this trackless wilderness.

"Have a seat," Madison said, and dropped into a chair, hoping Rose would do the same.

She did.

"How did you talk George into letting you come on such a long trip?" he asked. It wasn't the question to ask a woman he'd just met, not even his sister-in-law, but he wanted to know.

"I didn't tell him," Rose answered. "He wasn't pleased when he found out. He still hasn't forgiven me. I practically had to tie him up to keep him from turning around and taking me right back home."

The picture of this tiny woman tying up her hulking husband amused Madison, probably because he'd wanted to do the same thing when they were boys and George's greater size and strength had given him an insurmountable advantage when they wrestled.

"I didn't take her back because she agreed to rest as much as possible," George explained. "That's why she's waiting here rather than meeting you at the train as she wanted." He helped his wife to her feet. "Now we'll leave you to get settled. I'll come back in an hour. We'll have dinner after we've seen Hen."

Chapter Two

"He came in on the afternoon train," Fern told her father as she set his dinner before him. Her agitation caused her voice to be too high. "I should have known they wouldn't settle for a local lawyer."

Baker Sproull started eating without waiting for his daughter. "I heard he hasn't seen his family in years," he said, his mouth full. "Maybe he doesn't care about his brother."

"I don't know about that," Fern said as she set the rest of her father's meal on the table, "but he's here to get his brother off. You can see it in his eyes."

Black eyes, Fern remembered, eyes as dark as night and as deep as never. His handsome face had remained calm. In fact, he had looked vaguely surprised that she had had the nerve to speak to him. But only vaguely, as though nothing could throw him completely off stride, certainly no one as inconsequential as Fern Sproull.

24

Fern

She'd teach him to ignore her. She hadn't worked her whole life to win the respect of the male community to let some slick-talking Eastern lawyer ooze into town and ruin it for her.

He probably thinks everybody in Kansas sleeps on the ground and talks to cows more than people.

Well, let him. It would make it all the better when she showed him how wrong he was.

"What's he like?" her father asked.

As if the man's appearance were more important than what he was here to do. But then her father had never gotten upset over Troy's death. He said Troy had been asking for it; if it hadn't been Hen Randolph, it would have been somebody else.

"He's practically the double of George Randolph," Fern told her father as she served a plate for herself, "but not as big-boned. Even if he wasn't the spitting image of his brother, you couldn't miss him. He dresses like nobody you ever saw. I swear there wasn't any dust on his boots, even after walking from the train. Probably isn't any dust in Kansas brave enough to land on him.

"He wore a plain black suit, but you'd never believe how it fit. It looked like someone made it just for him. I swear I thought his collar would choke him. It was up to his chin and stiff as a board. He won't find anybody in Abilene to do his collars that way. Or his shirts. You could practically hear it pop when he moved. And his hair is as black as his eyes, thick and wavy. He's tall, but he seems even taller because he looks down at you like some eagle. He'll make a powerful impression when he stands up to talk."

"You shouldn't have been hanging around eavesdropping on his conversation," her father said.

"I didn't eavesdrop. I walked right up to him and told him I meant to see his brother hang." She poured some coffee into a chipped mug, laced it with a generous helping of thick cream, walked over to her place at the table, and sat down.

"You shouldn't have done that," her father said, looking up from his plate long enough to indicate his empty coffee cup. "What's he going to think of you?"

"I don't care," Fern replied, setting her meal down and going to refill her father's cup. "I wanted him to know right from the start he isn't going to get his brother off just because he's from Boston."

"He might," her father said. As soon as she set the coffee down, he handed her his empty plate. "There's not many folks around here that would hang Hen if the railroad was against it. You know he's connected with the railroad, don't you?"

Fern walked back to the stove where she ladled more chicken and dumplings onto her father's plate. "You can't mean people would knuckle under to him just because of the railroad?" she asked, realizing even as she spoke what a powerful ally the Randolphs had on their side.

"I didn't say they would. Just said they might. Besides, this is a whole lot of trouble for a no-account like Troy. Don't hardly seem worth it."

Fern set her father's plate in front of him and sat down to eat her dinner. "You didn't feel that way last year when our cows started dying from Texas fever."

"And I won't if they start dying again, but I expect this'll be the end of it. They'll most likely go to Ellsworth or Newton next year." He seemed to lose interest in the conversation. "Cut me a slice of cake before you get settled," he said.

"That's not the point," Fern said over her shoulder as she got up and walked over to the cake keep.

"Yes, it is," her father contradicted. "Nobody but

a born fool like Troy would get into a fight with Hen Randolph, not knowing he's got a bad temper and a fast gun. Insulting his pa was bound to make him mad as fire."

"But to kill Troy," Fern said, coming to the table with a thick slice of seven-layer cake with plum preserves spread between the layers.

"I don't hold with shooting people, but I don't hold with insulting their parents, either." Baker pushed his plate aside, handed Fern his empty coffee cup, and reached for the cake. "Troy was a cocky, loud-mouthed, bullying son-of-a-bitch. None too honest either. I never would have let him work for me if he hadn't been kin."

Fern returned to the table with her father's coffee. She sat down and took a sip of her own, but it was cold, so she got up to throw it out and get some more.

"How many times have I told you about wasting good cream in coffee and then throwing it away?" Baker complained as he pushed away from the table. "I could make a couple of dollars a week with what you waste."

He got up and went to sit outside where it was cool. Fern was left to eat her meal alone.

She didn't care what her father said. Killing wasn't right. No more than it was right for Texans to bring diseased cattle into Kansas when it was against the law, killing off the farmers' expensive blooded cattle, trampling their crops, eating their hay, and drinking their water.

And it wasn't right for a self-important tenderfoot to come slithering into town expecting to evade the law just because he had a smooth tongue, a big job with the railroad, and dressed like somebody out of a Sears & Roebuck catalog.

If he thought having a shatteringly handsome face

was going to make any difference, he was sadly mistaken. Kansas women appreciated a good-looking man, but they wouldn't make fools of themselves over him.

Fern absentmindedly smoothed her long, dark-blond hair. Troy had tried to get her to cut it. He said it would ruin her throw if it came down while she was roping a steer. Her eyes sought the picture of her mother sitting on the table next to her father's chair. In a way she couldn't explain, her hair made her feel more feminine. She couldn't give up this one link, weak as it was, to the mother she couldn't remember.

"Hen's not one to talk very much," George said to Madison.

They were headed toward the jail. Madison was trying to think of this case as nothing more than a legal problem to be sorted out with calm good sense, but the closer they came to the jail, the more insistent was the refrain that rang in his head.

This is the boy you abandoned.

No one had ever said those words to him. Still, he couldn't free himself from the silent accusation. It lurked somewhere just beyond the edge of awareness, always ready to spring into his conscious thoughts in an unguarded moment.

"He never did talk much," Madison replied. "Even Ma had trouble getting more than two consecutive sentences out of him."

As he walked along the noisy boardwalk, dodging cowhands and farmers headed for the beckoning lights of the saloons that lined the street, he knew his brothers would never understand why he'd left. Nothing would absolve him in their eyes.

"Maybe you'd better give me a quick rundown on what happened," Madison said.

"There's not much to tell. Hen went out riding, south toward Newton. We've had some trouble with a farmer out that way, and he wanted to see if he could find another route into town. When he got back, Hickok arrested him for murdering Troy Sproull."

"Sproull? Is he any relation to that female who practically attacked us?"

"Her cousin."

Now Madison understood why she was so angry. She probably thought he had come to cheat the gallows. He had, but he intended to prove the gallows had no claim to Hen. "What kind of evidence do they have?"

"A man named Dave Bunch says he saw Hen riding toward the deserted Connor place. He says he recognized Hen's horse. When he heard a shot a few minutes later, he turned back to see if Hen needed any help. Troy was dead when he got there, and Hen was nowhere in sight."

Madison felt a twinge of uneasiness. Thousands of men had been hanged on less solid evidence. He had to assume Dave Bunch was lying or mistaken.

"Anything else?"

"Hen and Troy got into a fight the night before over something Troy said. Hen threatened to kill him if he said it again. It was about Pa."

Of all the memories Madison wanted to put behind him, those of his father came first.

"What has the old bastard done now? I was half hoping some Yankee would shoot him."

"One did. He was killed in Georgia."

Oh hell, he hadn't meant it. He hated the old man, but he didn't really want him dead. Not that way.

Madison had stayed away all those years, refusing to make any contact with George, for fear the old bastard would come after him. He was no longer a helpless youngster, but some parts of his life were just too painful to be opened up again.

"If Pa's dead, what could Troy Sproull have said to get Hen so riled?"

"There's some story going around that Pa stole a Union payroll in Virginia. I don't know how Troy got hold of it, but he started taunting Hen about Pa being a thief."

"Did Pa steal it?"

"I don't know. I never saw him after I left to sign up."

Madison would never forget that day. No sooner had William Henry Randolph's two oldest boys disappeared than he had announced that he was going to volunteer, too. He didn't seem to care that he was abandoning his family, that his wife was devastated, or that his five youngest sons were paralyzed with shock. He just left.

Their mother never recovered.

"Hen beat up Troy," George said. "Hen told him Pa was a liar, a cheat, and probably a thief as well, but nobody had the right to call him that but his own sons."

"That was all? Even in Kansas, you need more reason than that to kill a man."

"Everybody thought it was enough when Troy turned up dead with Dave saying he all but saw Hen pull the trigger. We've got to stop in here."

George turned into the Alamo Saloon.

"What for?" Madison asked.

"You seldom find the marshal anywhere else."

Marshal Wild Bill Hickok, dressed in fringed buckskins, his shoulder-length black hair parted in the middle and a pair of pearl-handled guns at his waist, sat at one of the tables engrossed in a card game. He looked none too pleased at being interrupted.

"Haven't you talked to that boy enough?" Hickok asked when George told him he wanted to see his brother. "Can't have much more to say."

"This is my brother Madison," George told the marshal. "He's come to handle Hen's defense."

"Don't look like it'll do much good as long as Dave Bunch sticks to his story."

Madison could feel his irritation growing at this cocky man who seemed to have such contempt for him and his family. He had seen many men of small character corrupted by power. He imagined Abilene's marshal was just another one.

"We'd like to see him anyway," George said.

"Suit yourself," Hickok said, reaching for the keys. Much to Madison's surprise, he handed them to George. "But he ain't said *boo* to nobody for more than a week."

Once they were outside, Madison asked, "Does he give everybody the keys?"

"It saves him breaking up the game," George said.

Either Hickok respected George too much to think he'd help Hen escape, despised him too much to think he would succeed, or didn't care. Madison decided to take a little time to get to know Marshal Hickok.

The jail was a small frame building. Abilene had appointed its first marshal the previous year, and so far they hadn't needed anything else.

Hen's cell was really a room with bars on the door. A bed, table, chairs, and even a lamp for reading made it more comfortable than a conventional jail cell. Hen was lying on the bed when George opened the door. He didn't move except to turn his head so he could focus his gaze on the man standing behind George.

His fixed look intensified as recognition set in,

31

and Madison could see the muscles in Hen's body draw into tight knots. Hen sat up.

"What the hell are you doing here?" he demanded. His voice, barely above a whisper, was tight with rage.

Several rejoinders hovered on Madison's tongue. Having been a Virginian at Harvard during the war, he had survived too many confrontations not to be able to turn them off with a light remark, a biting retort, or a question of his own. That would have told both Hen and George they couldn't reach him, couldn't hurt him.

But he hadn't traveled all the way from Boston to hide behind subterfuges. In the last several hours, many things he thought dead or buried had reared their ugly heads, their vigor undiminished by the passing of so many years. He had thought himself hardened against emotion, shielded against accusation and innuendo. But he was discovering that where his family was concerned he was as vulnerable as he had been ten years ago.

"I came to help."

"How long do you plan to stay this time?" Hen demanded, his bitterness undiminished. "Long enough for the hanging, or will you leave in the middle of the trial?"

"There won't be any hanging."

"And how do you plan to arrange that? George won't let me break out. He'd bring me back if I did."

"I'm a lawyer," Madison explained. "I intend to prove you didn't kill Troy Sproull."

"So the runaway comes back all dressed up as a fancy lawyer to help his poor, ignorant brothers," Hen sneered.

It took all of Madison's grit not to waver. Neither George nor Hen had forgiven him. Could he expect any better from his other brothers? If not, what was he doing here?

"What makes you so sure I didn't kill Troy?" Hen demanded, obviously trying to goad Madison into losing his temper.

"I don't believe the boy I knew could turn into a killer."

Their father may have lacerated their souls, turning them into savage, angry men, but Madison wouldn't believe that any of his brothers could commit murder. He had to keep that foremost in his mind. What his brothers felt about him, what he felt about himself, wasn't important now.

"How would you know? You weren't around to see me grow up, to see what I became."

Madison wondered how a voice speaking barely above a whisper could thunder in his ears with the force of a cannon.

"Ask anybody who knows me, even George. I'm a killer. I would have killed Troy if he'd said another word about Pa."

"Don't be pigheaded, Hen," George said.

"Why did you bring him here?" Hen demanded of George. "I'd rather you'd shot him before he reached the edge of town."

"He means to help—"

"I don't want his help," Hen said, his eyes shining like cold, blue diamonds. "Get him out of here, or I may murder him."

Madison turned on his heel, a red haze of anger clouding his brain, a sick feeling in his gut causing his stomach to tie up in painful knots. He had expected Hen to be angry, but he hadn't been prepared for such fury.

No, hate. Hen hated him with the same intensity Madison had hated his father. He knew what that felt like, the depth and the intensity. Nothing would change that, not even proving Hen's innocence.

Madison paused outside the doorway of the jail. He looked about him at the rough, raw town. Streets ankle deep in dust, which would turn to mud at the first rain; the stench and noise of the stockyards, which had nearly overpowered him when he stepped off the train; false-fronted stores hiding mean, low buildings full of coarse, common goods; soft light spilling into the streets from a dozen saloons; the shrill cacophony of a piano combined with voices singing off key; the bark of drunken laughter; men living each day on the brink of eternity. He didn't begrudge them their moments of pleasure, but he couldn't understand them.

His brothers had become men like that. He couldn't understand them either.

Yet he had to try, or he might as well go back to Boston and forget he had a family.

He noticed a young man swaggering toward him, and his anger and frustration were diverted by the unknown cowboy. With an unpleasant shock, he realized the "young man" was the young woman who had accosted him on the steps of the Drovers Cottage.

He felt his interest quicken, his attention narrow. He watched her approach, bemused by his response to a female who should have set his teeth on edge instead of arousing wry amusement and great curiosity.

She certainly was an unusual-looking female. She wore her hair pinned up under a wide-brimmed, flat-crowned hat. Her flannel shirt, butternut pants, and high-heeled boots were indistinguishable from those worn by the dozens of cowhands who must be holding cattle on the countryside.

She was a tall girl, bigger-boned than most, but she had covered the telltale aspects of her figure with a loose sheepskin vest. It must have taken years outdoors on horseback to give her that tanned complexion and swaggering walk. Only the most discerning eye would have guessed she had entered the world as Fern rather than Ferdinand.

She wasn't at all the kind of female he was used to, yet he found himself wondering what could have turned her into such a rebel. It couldn't have been anything insignificant. If anybody knew that, he did.

But even as he wondered what chain of events could have produced such remarkable results, he remembered that Fern Sproull wanted Hen dead.

Her walk seemed to slow. She had recognized him. Now it quickened, and she exaggerated the swagger ever so slightly.

He stepped forward into her path. It would be fun to watch her try to decide whether to walk past as if she'd never seen him or to acknowledge his presence. He liked to make his opponents uncomfortable. It threw them off their game, made them make mistakes.

It gave him the advantage.

Chapter Three

"The men of this town are braver than I thought," Madison said when she drew near.

"What do you mean by that?" she demanded. She had started to walk past him, but now she stopped and turned toward him.

Madison assumed a languid pose. "Most people don't feel comfortable when other people go around pretending to be something they aren't. It's the old wolf-in-sheep's-clothing dilemma. If I remember correctly, it bothered King David when he was still a shepherd boy."

His attack was clearly unexpected, but it didn't faze her.

"I'm surprised you've read the Bible," she shot back. "I didn't think your type espoused any credo beyond getting what you wanted."

Nice snappy recovery. Her understanding of what was expected of a woman might be all backwards, but her head wasn't filled with straw.

He took a minute to straighten his coat. He wanted to draw attention to the difference between his clothes and the local haberdashery.

"We evil types have to read all the good books so we'll know what you good types are up to."

"Well, you can read the *Good Book* all you want, but it's not going to save your brother."

Clearly Miss Sproull wasn't intimidated by his dress. He'd have to employ another tactic.

"Why doesn't your father buy you a dress? A nice calico can't cost half as much as those boots you're wearing. As for that gun, that ought to buy you a whole wardrobe full of frilly dresses."

"I wear exactly what I want," she snapped, obviously caught between a desire to leave him standing and an equally strong desire to give him a tongue-lashing he'd long remember.

So this wasn't a case of a daughter being forced by circumstances to dress like a son, Madison thought to himself. She had chosen her wardrobe. Now why would a girl do that? In spite of himself, she intrigued him.

He looked at her more closely. He didn't think she was unattractive, but it was difficult to evaluate her appearance under the handicap of her clothing, worn and ill-fitting clothing at that. Still, it was clear she had a splendid figure. She might cover the swell of her breasts with a loose vest, but from the waist down her body was as clearly outlined as a mountaintop at sunrise.

No woman he knew would parade around like that. His mother would have fainted.

But Madison didn't feel faint. In fact, he found his pulse quickening. He was accustomed to a coquettish smile or a fluttering eyelash, but he found the allure of trim hips and long, slim legs even more captivating. It must be pure animal lust. Nothing else could cause such a reaction. He certainly couldn't appreciate such a female with his mind.

Madison smiled. "It ought to pose something of a problem for you, being one thing but wanting to be taken for another."

"Not at all," Fern replied, her chin tilted at him in defiance. "It's been so long since I proved I can do anything a man can, nobody thinks about it anymore."

Madison decided there was a little too much challenge in her voice and stance. She was clearly proud of herself, but he had a vague suspicion she wasn't entirely pleased that no one thought of her as a girl. Correction. Woman. He didn't know much about her yet, but one thing he did know. Fern Sproull had ceased to be a girl some time ago.

His smile broadened.

"Then along comes some dude, a city slicker, a tenderfoot, and you have to prove it all over again."

The tilt of her chin increased.

"What you think is of absolutely no consequence."

Madison chuckled inwardly. She didn't like him, not one single bit. But he liked needling her. He especially liked the way her eyes flashed.

Madison resumed his languid air. "I seem to remember you had a lot to say about my brother's innocence."

"He's not innocent," Fern said, hopping on the word as if she meant to exterminate it. "Dave Bunch saw him—"

Madison's entire demeanor changed. He came vibrantly alive, aggressive and combative. He practically charged her, stopping only to avoid knocking her down. Fern jumped back in surprise.

"Mr. Bunch is reputed to have said he recognized my brother's horse," Madison said, assuming his most intimidating manner. "Now, unless you believe horses can pull triggers, and that my brother is responsible for the actions of his horse, you don't have much of a case."

She glared at him. She had very fine eyes. Hazel with a bluish-gray tint. He wished it were still daylight. He wanted to be more sure of the shade.

"You must think everybody in Kansas is an idiot," she shot back, "just waiting for some self-important know-it-all to come tell us what to do."

She was spilling over with things to get off her chest. Not a bad chest at that. But he had to keep his mind off her body. He was here to help Hen. It was okay if he whiled away a few hours satisfying his curiosity about this quixotic creature, but the shape of her legs, the swell of her breasts, and the color of her eyes had nothing to do with that.

Fern refused to let this Randolph intimidate her. She also refused to admit he was so handsome that she had trouble remembering why he had come to Abilene. She kept telling herself she hated him, that she wanted to see him run out of town. But it would have been a lot easier if she could have closed her eyes.

"We know what to do with killers," she said. "We also know what to do with a stuffed gunny sack made up to look like a man."

"Are you going to trample me under your pretty little feet?" Madison asked. He moved closer and flashed an ingratiating smile.

"We're going to ride you out of town with a fire under your tail." She hoped she sounded fierce and confident. She felt completely unnerved.

Smiling even more broadly, Madison brought his face down until their noses practically touched.

"You know, if my sister had talked like that— if I'd had a sister, that is, my family being only boys, which I assure you was a great hardship to my mother, the poor woman not really being up to handling a household of eight men, not that any female is up to handling that many men, or one man for that matter, females being delicate by nature and not given to being able to put up with the riot and rumpus of seven boys—"

"Piss and vinegar!" Fern hissed. "Would you get to the point? I wouldn't be surprised to learn you win your cases by driving your opponents insane." *By smiling at them, causing them to lose every thought in their heads.*

But no man had ever done that to her, and she didn't mean for Madison Randolph to be the first.

"As I was about to say," Madison said, sounding injured in spite of his smiling eyes, "if you'd talked that way in Virginia, you'd have had ladies fainting away by the parlorful. And that would have made you very unpopular. It's very difficult for a woman to get in and out of her stays. And of course the first thing you do for a fainting female is to loosen her stays. But then you wouldn't know that, would you?"

"I imagine you know far more about feminine apparel than I do," Fern said, giving ground.

"From the looks of it, a sheepherder knows more than you."

Madison could tell she hadn't expected that one. He could see the anger flame in her eyes. It made the blue disappear leaving nothing but gray, like ashed coal, a cool, dull surface but burning hot underneath.

"Is there some reason why you're blocking my path?" she asked. "I'm sure your forked tongue gets plenty of exercise in Boston. It's sure sharp enough."

Not bad. This woman would bear further study. Clearly there was more to her than a pair of dusty pants and a sheepskin vest. Besides, despite her clothes, she was more fun to look at than horses and cows. Maybe he'd tell her so, but only if he found just the right moment.

He smiled, genuinely this time, hoping to reduce the tension between them.

"Well, actually I was wondering if you could tell me how to find the scene of the crime."

"Why don't you ask your brother?"

"George is rather preoccupied at the moment." He knew she meant Hen. "His wife could present him with a baby any minute, and he is understandably loath to leave her side."

She looked at him as if to say *I don't know what you're trying to do, but I don't trust you.* Aloud she said, "The Connor place is a long way from here. The only way to get there is by horseback."

"So?"

"You'll have to ride."

"I didn't expect you would offer to carry me."

"On a horse."

"You mean I could ride a buffalo if I want? What fun you get up to in Kansas."

Fern couldn't decide whether he was being sarcastic or if this was his idea of humor. "Anybody in town can give you directions. Or take you out there if you like."

"I'd rather you take me."

"No."

"Why not?"

"I don't want to. Besides, why should I help you get your brother off?"

"You wouldn't, but it's been my experience that at least one significant detail always gets overlooked. I assumed you'd want to be around in case I found anything."

Fern told herself she should have nothing to do with Madison Randolph, but she couldn't let him go to the Connor place alone. She didn't trust him. She respected the native shrewdness of Kansans, but she wasn't naïve enough to think a big city lawyer didn't know a few more tricks than Marshal Hickok. Whether she liked it or not, she had to keep an eye on him until after the trial.

"When do you want to go?"

"How about tomorrow morning?"

"You'll have to meet me at my father's farm."

"I'll be there at nine o'clock. I know a road is too much to hope for, but you do have a path leading there, don't you?"

"Follow the south road," she said, glaring at him. "Take the left fork about a mile out of town. We're another two miles farther on."

"I suppose it's too much to hope for a mailbox."

"Why should we have mailboxes?" She knew he was having fun with her now. "Surely you don't think we can read."

Fern started walking away from him, a decided swagger to her stride. "If you're not at the house by nine o'clock, I won't wait," she called back over her shoulder. "I can't spend all day playing nursemaid to a tenderfoot. I've got some bulls that need castrating." She stopped and turned back to face him, one hand on her hip, an unmistakable challenge in her eye. "That's one job I'm real good at."

"I guess I'd better wear a thick pair of chaps."

She wondered if he really knew what chaps were or if he'd read about them in some book.

"Until tomorrow." He waved.

She turned on her heel and walked off.

Madison stood watching her for a moment, then burst out laughing. He rather thought she'd got the best of the exchange with her remark about the bulls. He'd better stay on his toes. He couldn't let it be said he'd been bested by a woman from Kansas who didn't know enough to be sure of her own sex, even if he was quite positive about it. Wouldn't Freddy love that.

But Freddy and Boston seemed so far away now, almost as though the last eight years had been a dream and Texas was the only reality.

Madison shook his head to dislodge that fearful thought. He didn't know whether it was Kansas, his brothers' cold reception, or this most unusual female, but nothing had gone as he had expected.

Fern paused, the coffeepot in one hand, her cup in the other. The sound of Madison's laughter still rang in her ears. It had rung there all night, keeping her awake, aggravating her, making her wonder why he had laughed at her, making her angry that he had, making her furious that she cared.

She poured her coffee and carried it over to a heavy earthenware jar. As she stirred thick cream into the steaming black liquid, she berated herself for talking to him. She shouldn't even see him again.

But she was going to take him to the Connor place this morning.

She would have been lying to herself if she didn't admit she felt a kind of simmering excitement. She might hate the reasons that brought Mr. Randolph to Abilene, but it was impossible to hate Mr. Randolph.

"You're moving mighty slow this morning," her father said as he finished his breakfast. He drained his coffee cup and stood up. "You'd better hustle about or you'll never get your work done."

"I'll get it done." She took a swallow of her coffee and decided it needed more cream.

Of course, being from Boston, he probably thought everyone in Kansas was hardly better than a savage, that all he had to do was show up and they would release Hen automatically.

That was one expectation he wouldn't see fulfilled. Boston might be important to Bostonians, but as far as the people of Kansas were concerned, it was just another town and its citizens no different from anybody else.

The door slamming behind her father brought Fern out of her trance. She walked over to the table and sat down. She wrapped her hands around her coffee cup and stared into space.

Of course all the men in Boston couldn't look like Madison Randolph. If so, every female in the country would move there.

Fern had long been aware that the Randolphs were unusually good-looking men. The ladies of Abilene had talked of little else after three blond, young, and single Randolphs had ridden in together one day four years ago. Fern wasn't too fond of blonds, but she did agree that George Randolph, who came the next year, was the best-looking man she had ever seen.

But that was before she saw Madison. When she looked into that ruggedly handsome face, it was hard for her to remember he was the villain and she was supposed to hate him. Even when he needled her.

The door opened and her father stuck his head inside. "You going to castrate those yearlings this morning?"

"No. I promised to take that Randolph fella out to the Connor place."

Maybe he was just laughing at her. It would be like him. He had a real high opinion of himself. And it was more than carefully tailored clothes or the way he dressed. It was the way he walked, the way he looked about him as though he could barely tolerate being here.

Well, she had a few surprises in store for him. Nothing too severe, but Mr. Madison Randolph was going to return to his snug, comfortable, self-satisfied Boston knowing he had come up short in matching strength, skills, and wits with a mere female.

"Just yesterday you were mad as hell he was here at all," her father said. "Why are you taking him about like a hired guide?"

"He says he's looking for evidence," Fern said, "but there's no telling what he's up to. Besides, I mean to see he comes back a mite roughed up."

"What are you planning to do?" Her father's voice sounded sharp, distrustful.

"Nothing much."

"I don't believe you," he said, his harsh gaze unchanged. "The last time I saw that look in your eyes, you slipped the Stuart boys Indian whiskey."

"They shouldn't have made fun of me."

"All they said was they hoped you never took to wearing dresses. And since you'd die before you'd wear anything but pants, I never did see what there was to get upset about."

"That wasn't all they said."

"Maybe not, but you seem to have a way of getting fellas on the prod. You gotta quit fighting with every man who shows his front in Abilene, especially the drovers and their hands. It makes it damned embarrassing for me to have to go around

45

apologizing for you all the time."

"You don't have to apologize for me."

"The hell I don't. How do you expect me to sell to them if I don't, especially at my prices?"

"I don't do anything I don't mean to do."

"I know, and that makes it all the harder to convince them otherwise. I guess you're going to prod that lawyer fella whether I want you to or not."

"I just want to teach him a lesson."

"I don't trust you when you start teaching people lessons. You get one Texan mad at you, and they'll all be on your back. It could ruin me."

"Nobody's going to ruin you, Papa," Fern said.

"Don't go too far. His brother's the one who killed Troy. This other fella had nothing to do with it."

Fern didn't respond.

"It was your idea to lead him around, so you make sure he gets back in one piece."

She still said nothing.

Sproull's expression darkened and he came a couple of steps inside the house. "Don't you let me hear of even one tiny accident."

"You won't hear a thing," she assured him. And he wouldn't. Madison Randolph would never tell anybody about what she was going to do to him.

Her father didn't look convinced, but he turned and stomped from the house.

Fern tried to ignore the fact that her father was more worried that she might do something to hurt his business than that she was going on a long ride with a stranger and that something could happen to her. In all the years she had worked her fingers to the bone to please him, taking care of his herd and his house, cooking his meals, always hoping to win some word of praise, he'd never shown a sign of affection for her. She sometimes wondered if he felt any.

Fern

He's always been that way. He's not going to change now. Besides, you're partly to blame. You get furious if anyone implies you can't take care of yourself. That's what got you so angry with the Stuart boys.

Madison Randolph made her just as mad.

He looked at her as though he didn't quite believe what he was seeing. And all because she didn't wear a dress. It would serve him right if everybody in Abilene gawked at him just because he dressed like a fancy dude.

But it wasn't the way Madison looked at her that upset her. It was the way he made her feel. She didn't feel things the way she wanted, the way she'd been teaching herself for as long as she could remember. Everything felt strange and uncomfortable, and she sure as hell didn't like it.

Her whole body felt different. She felt awkward; she felt flushed and hot; she couldn't stand still. Even her brain didn't work right. Instead of thinking of ways to put him in his place, she found herself wondering what thoughts lurked behind those black eyes, or dwelling on how very tall he was. She was a tall woman; she wasn't used to feeling small, but she did around Madison Randolph.

And that wasn't all. Instead of concentrating on ways to get rid of him, she found herself wondering how long he was going to stay in Abilene, what he liked to do for fun, what he thought of the young ladies of Boston, if he was married or engaged.

But it was useless to wonder about Madison Randolph. Whatever he was really like, he wouldn't stay in Abilene longer than he absolutely must.

Fern got up to throw out her cold coffee. It only took a minute to wash her father's breakfast dishes and put them away. She usually ate a good breakfast, but this morning she had no appetite. That was something else she could blame on Madison.

She picked up a brush and began working the tangles out of her hair. It was a waste of time—she intended to pin it up under her hat—but it always helped her to think.

She wondered how he meant to get from town. A buggy, most likely. She'd probably have to saddle his horse for him. She doubted he could do it himself. But he had to ride to the Connor place, and she had no intention of letting him choose his own mount.

If he apologized, she'd mount him on Blue Wind. The mare had a mouth like leather, but even a Sunday school teacher could ride her. If he acted like he had the day before, she would saddle Shorty. He would start bucking just about a minute after Madison got in the saddle. Not very hard, but enough to toss a tenderfoot like Madison Randolph over his head. It would give her a great deal of pleasure to see him lying in the dust.

But what if he really got hurt?

She wanted to hurt his pride, not his body. She couldn't blame him for wanting to get his brother out of jail.

Through the window she saw her father round the corner of the barn. He was taking pork, butter, and eggs to sell to the drovers who arrived every day from Texas starved for fresh food after two months on the Chisholm Trail.

He jumped down from the wagon and stuck his head in the door. "Don't spend all morning hanging around waiting. If he doesn't show his front inside of ten minutes, get on with your work."

"He'll show up," Fern said. "His kind never misses an appointment."

Not that she thought that was bad. After all the times she had waited for her father, or some other man, only to have him say he'd forgotten, or got busy talking, she would appreciate it. But she was irritated that Madison should be the one to be punctual.

Of course she didn't know he was punctual. That was just a guess. He could be hopeless when it came to keeping appointments.

But he wouldn't be. He wasn't the type.

Thirty minutes later Fern found herself pacing back and forth in front of the barn. She told herself it wasn't time for him yet, that she was too busy to worry about him, but she couldn't keep her mind on her work.

Just as she started to catalog all the terrible things she was going to do to him, she saw a rider in the distance. A short while later she recognized Madison. It couldn't be anyone else. Not even his brother could present such a lean, immaculate appearance.

The second thing that caught her eye was the horse. Madison was riding Buster, the best horse in the Twins Livery Stable. The big bay gelding was Tom Everett's favorite horse. He didn't hire him out to just anybody. He was a strong animal and not always easy to manage, but he seemed to be going easy enough for Madison.

The next thing to catch her eye was the way he rode in the saddle. Absolutely erect. He looked extremely handsome in his city clothes, but she couldn't imagine anyone who looked less as if he should be on a horse. She could think of several men she might call handsome, but they weren't a spot on this dandy. It was a pity he was a Randolph.

But he could ride. Not that riding a horse along a clear trail at a canter was anything to write home about, but it was the way he did it, with negligent ease. She didn't know how or where he'd learned, but he was used to being on a horse. Just how used she meant to discover soon enough, but for the time being she had to revise her opinion of him. He might dress like a useless dandy, but he didn't ride like one. Maybe he wasn't one.

But he had to be. He was from Boston, wasn't he?

Whatever he was, she'd never find out by standing around arguing with herself. She mounted up and rode out to meet him.

Chapter Four

"We're going to have to travel fast," she told him, making certain not to look into his eyes. His forthright gaze disconcerted her. "Follow me."

He didn't move. "I thought I had arrived on schedule." He consulted his elegant gold timepiece. "I have two minutes to spare," he said, returning the watch to its pocket.

"I have a lot of work to do today."

"Ah, yes, those unfortunate bulls whose future you are determined to blight."

A bubble of laughter stirred in Fern's chest; she choked it back. It wasn't her habit to go around laughing all the time. She had noticed that the people who were most respected always looked somber or actually spent a large part of their lives frowning. She had achieved her perpetual scowl only after considerable effort, and she didn't intend to let this dandified lawyer bring it to naught.

"Steers gain weight," she snapped. "And bulls cause trouble. Even a lawyer from Boston ought to know that."

"Yes, but it has never been my ambition to gain weight."

"You prefer to cause trouble?"

"Are those the only two choices you're offering?" Madison asked.

He brought his horse to a stop alongside hers. They were only inches apart. She was sure he'd done it intentionally so she couldn't avoid looking directly at him.

"I'm not offering you any choices."

"How disappointing."

She was certain he meant something different from the words that came out of his mouth. Maybe he was flirting, but she couldn't be sure. His wasn't the direct way of Western men; neither was it the formal manner she thought would be favored in Boston.

Her chest constricted at his nearness. Even her breath seemed to shudder as it left her lungs. She told herself not to be stupid. He was baiting her. He'd like nothing better than to confuse her.

Now he was smiling at her, but there was something unfamiliar in his gaze. She didn't know what it was, but it made her uneasy. She felt intimidated. It infuriated her that he would try to overawe her, even more that she would allow him to succeed.

"Do you always talk nonsense?" she asked.

"If you were a man, you wouldn't consider castration nonsense. Do you know what they do to men in Turkey, the ones they use in the harems?"

"I don't know anything about the habits of heathens," Fern stated, "and I don't want to. If you want to see the Connor place, follow me. If you want to stand around talking about outlandish people in places I never heard of, you can go back to town."

She dug her heels into her horse's sides, and he bounded away. He was a swift, short-coupled horse, one more suited to cutting work than long rides across the prairie, but she felt more at home on him than on a big brute like Buster.

She was surprised to find Madison at her elbow almost immediately.

"I gather you don't approve of foreigners."

His comment made Fern painfully aware of her threadbare education. She had learned as much as she could, but she was certain that Madison knew more about everything than she did. That made her feel even more intimidated. And angrier.

"I have no doubt you know much more about foreigners than I do, especially barbaric ones, so I shall leave it to you to decide whether I would approve of them or not."

"How can I do that when I don't know anything about you?" he replied. "For all I know you might approve of castrating men."

"Do you always talk about such awful things?" she demanded, twisting about in the saddle.

"I'm not the one taking a knife to those poor bulls," he pointed out. "The way you mentioned it so offhandedly was quite callous. I would have thought that even here in Kansas, women would have had that kindness of heart, that gentleness of spirit that—"

"You didn't think any such thing," Fern contradicted, rounding on him once more, much to the confusion of her pony who was at a loss to interpret the continual stops and turnings, particularly when there were no cows about. "You were just looking for anything you could say to annoy me."

"It seems I've succeeded."

"You certainly have," she replied, turning her

horse back up the trail and digging her heels in again. "If you want me to take you to the Connor place, stop talking and ride."

Once more she set out at a gallop, and once more he was at her side in a matter of moments.

"You don't have to run from me," he said. For a moment she almost thought he sounded apologetic. But that was impossible. Men like him never apologized for anything.

"I wasn't running. You just made me mad."

"I won't do it again. Is this what your prairie looks like?" he asked, looking about. "I thought it was supposed to be as flat as a spinster's chest and as dry as her humor."

"You are a truly disgusting man," Fern said. "Isn't there anything you respect?"

"Truth."

His reply nearly floored her. She had expected him to mention power and money. He exuded both.

"Everyone respects truth," she replied.

"That's where you're wrong. Most people are afraid of it. They actually depend upon lies, or at least false appearances, to protect them. The truth would ruin most of us."

"I should have expected something like that from somebody like you," Fern shot back. "You don't know anything about real honesty."

"What kind of person am I?" he asked. He looked at her with a penetrating look that unsettled her. "And why don't you think I know anything about honesty?"

The retort on her lips withered and blew away. There was something different about him now. The bantering look had left his face. So had his smile. Even his eyes seemed to have lost their glint of laughter. He simply looked at her.

Fern

This was a trick, the way he unnerved his opponents, got them to say or do something without thinking. *Well, he's not going to do it to me. Nothing's going to keep me from telling him exactly what I think of him.*

"I think you're a slick lawyer used to getting the kind of verdict your rich clients want."

"And?"

She swallowed. "And I don't think you much care how you get it."

There, she had told him. But even though he now knew he couldn't intimidate her, she didn't feel better.

"At least you're not afraid of the truth all the time," he stated and dropped back to ride behind her.

What did he mean by that? She had never been afraid of the truth. That was why she'd started acting like a boy in the first place. She couldn't remember when she first realized her father didn't want a daughter. She supposed she'd always known it.

She did remember when she decided she didn't want to be a girl. It was at Betty Lewis's thirteenth birthday party. Fern had showed up in pants as usual. All the other girls wore dresses. Betty's was prettiest of all. Some of the girls whispered and pointed at Fern. They laughed when Betty opened Fern's present. Even Betty giggled. Fern had given her a pair of leather riding gloves to protect Betty's soft hands.

Betty didn't ride. She was afraid of horses.

In the following years, the chasm between Fern and the other girls had grown wider until they ceased to include her in their activities. She had become an outsider to her own sex. She had to face the plain truth. She didn't belong.

And she'd been facing the truth ever since.

*   *   *

"There it is," Fern said, pulling up before a deserted sod house built into the side of a ridge along a tributary of the Smoky Hill River. "Troy's body was found inside."

"And you say this happened at night?" Madison asked. He dismounted and allowed Buster's reins to trail on the ground. Fern wondered whether he knew he had just ground-hitched Buster, or whether he was too stupid to think about it at all.

She decided that whatever Madison Randolph was, it wasn't stupid. He must know, but how?

"Sometime after midnight, according to Dave Bunch. It was pretty dark that night, but there was enough light to see. There always is on the prairie, even when it's real cloudy."

Madison didn't answer. He walked inside. The house was abandoned, but in remarkably good condition. Three sides and the roof were made of blocks of sod cut from the prairie. The fourth side had been dug out of the side of the ridge to help keep the house cool in summer and warm in winter.

"Did anybody find a lantern?" Madison asked, emerging from the house.

"Why would anybody want a lantern?"

"You couldn't see an albino elephant in this place at night without one. It's hard enough to see into the corners with the sun blazing down."

She'd never thought of that. She'd only visited the house during daylight. She slid off her horse and entered the soddy. She couldn't see anything until her eyes adjusted. The only window was so covered with dust and cobwebs it admitted virtually no light.

"What was he doing out here?"

"I don't know. He used to live here when he

worked for us, but he moved into town when he left."

"Could he have been shot in town and come here to hide?" Madison asked.

"Maybe, but that would mean Hen followed him and shot at him again. Dave said he heard the shot just minutes after he saw Hen."

"He said he recognized Hen's horse. I haven't heard anyone say he recognized Hen himself."

"You try getting anybody else to ride that crazy horse. If there was anybody on him, it was your brother."

She could see Madison making a mental note to check that out. He would get a nice surprise there. Hen's white stallion was almost as notorious as Hen himself. Not only was he an evil-tempered beast, the jagged black markings on his rump and hind legs were impossible to miss.

"Did your cousin tell anybody he was coming here?"

"Nobody had seen him since that morning."

"When did the marshal actually find him?"

"About an hour after Dave rode in."

"Did anybody notice whether the body was stiff?"

"I don't know . . . come to think of it, somebody did say he was awfully stiff. They put it down to it being night and so cold."

"Were there any marks on the ground, footprints, signs that something had been dragged across the floor?"

"Why should anybody look for those things? Troy was dead, and everybody knew who killed him."

"Did anybody actually see Hen fire the shots?"

"No, but . . ."

"Then you didn't know any such thing, and your marshal conducted a very sloppy investigation. I'm sure you could have done better yourself."

"Since that wasn't meant as a compliment, I won't take it as one."

Instead of paying attention to her, he scrutinized the ground, climbed the ridge, and scanned the prairie all around.

She didn't know what he expected to gain by insulting everyone in Abilene, but he would soon find that Marshal Hickok, for all that he was as lazy as a cat, wouldn't take kindly to having his actions criticized. Not that this man would care what Marshal Hickok thought. Never in her life had she seen anybody so cocksure.

Still, she had to admire his tenacity. She didn't know whether he really believed that his brother was innocent—she didn't see how he could in the face of the evidence—but clearly he was determined to leave no stone unturned to prove his innocence.

Fern found herself wishing that someone felt that strongly about her.

She immediately chastised herself for doubting her father's affection, but the feeling wouldn't go away. There were times when she wondered if he cared about her at all except as a pair of strong hands to help run the farm. He never asked her how her day was going, never offered sympathy if she was feeling out of sorts, never offered her a hand when he was idle and she was still busy.

Odd that she should feel certain that Madison would. He was so ruthlessly efficient, you wouldn't think he had time for anything except business. But he had put aside his work to come out to Kansas to defend his brother. Just once it would be nice if somebody would do something like that for her.

Madison emerged from the cabin.

"You ready to go?" Fern asked.

"I'm not finished yet, but you can go on if you need to. I can find my way back."

"I'll wait." She had to know what he was doing.

She didn't understand why he should have such a powerful effect on her. It would be much easier just to dislike him, to hate him even.

But most disturbing of all, she wanted him to notice her. Not the way other men noticed her. She wasn't interested in showing him how well she could rope or ride or perform any of the dozens of other skills she had worked so laboriously to master. If not that, what? She found herself tugging at her shirt, unsatisfied with its fit. She even felt dissatisfied with her pants. She would have to see about getting some more. These were old and worn.

She wondered what he thought of her looks and found herself pulling the brim of her hat lower. She hadn't really looked at herself in the mirror for months, maybe years, but she knew that sun and wind had turned her skin unbecomingly brown.

He probably didn't think of her as a woman at all.

She began to fidget. She was tired of standing about doing nothing. She wasn't used to it. She wasn't used to being ignored either. She wasn't used to being upset, and she wasn't used to feeling inferior. She wasn't used to worrying about what somebody else thought about her, and she wasn't used to worrying about what she looked like.

"I've got to be going," she said. "You're just wasting your time."

He turned in her direction, his gaze gradually focusing on her. "Do you dislike truth on principle, or do you dislike it because it doesn't fit your prejudices?"

"What do you mean?" she asked, stung by his accusation.

"You don't care about anything except seeing my brother hang. Not what happened that night, why Troy was here, or if there might be another explanation for what was found."

"I do care," she protested, knowing her protests were useless. He would believe what he wanted. "And what makes you so certain your brother didn't kill Troy? You can't say he never killed anybody."

"Hen wouldn't have gotten into a fight if he'd meant to shoot your cousin."

"But he'd threatened to kill him."

"I know, but everybody will tell you Hen never shot anybody who wasn't trying to steal our cows or hurt someone in our family."

Fern opened her mouth to contradict him, then realized that the only instances she had ever heard about were exactly as he said.

"You have no evidence," she said

Madison's confidence did not waver. "I know Hen didn't kill your cousin. So I asked myself who might want to kill Troy and have Hen hang for the murder? It would have been easy to arrange. George says everybody knows Dave Bunch passes by here on his way home. Somebody wanted him to hear the shot and see a horse that looked like Hen's."

"You're making this up," Fern said, beginning to feel a terrible pressure inside her. It made her furious to think Hen might escape punishment for a cold-blooded murder.

"Nobody could see inside that cabin, not to shoot a man in the heart with a single shot. You could empty two guns in there without hitting anybody. On top of that, the body was stiff. According to Dave Bunch, he went straight to town for Marshal Hickok as soon as he knew Troy was dead. That would mean they got back here in about an hour. If Troy had been killed by the shot Dave heard, the body would still have been warm. That means Troy was killed earlier, probably somewhere else, and then brought here. The shot Dave heard was fired into the air."

"That's preposterous," Fern protested. "You've twisted everything so it will look the way you want it to."

"No, I'm just looking at the facts. You and everyone else *assumed* my brother killed your cousin and you just slapped him in jail. If anyone had bothered to look *before* half the town trampled this area under dozens of hooves and footprints, I bet you would have found a clear set of prints for a fourth horse, the horse ridden by the killer."

"Nobody's going to believe a word of this," Fern said, confident that the men she knew would believe Dave Bunch over Madison Randolph. "They'll know you're lying."

But Madison pressed on.

"Somebody was already looking for a way to kill Troy when he and Hen had that fight. That was simply the opportunity he needed. Who else had Troy been fighting with? Who disagreed with him, distrusted him?"

Her father.

He and Troy had had dozens of arguments, many of them witnessed by half the town. Worst of all, her father had fired Troy about a month before the Randolph herd reached town. Troy had gotten a job with Sam Belton selling farmland to homesteaders, but he had let everybody know he had a score to settle with his uncle. If people started to listen to Madison, suspicion would turn to her father. And he didn't have any witness to his whereabouts all that night and part of the next day.

"You're just trying to throw up a smoke screen," Fern said, "to confuse people so they won't know what to believe."

"Who are you trying to protect?" Madison demanded.

Fern tried to appear confident, but she couldn't. Her father was all she had in the world. She knew he hadn't killed Troy, but if Madison started telling people about his theories, they would begin to remember that her father hadn't been very interested in trying to find Troy's killer. She had to stall Madison until she could warn her father.

"I'm not trying to protect anybody," Fern insisted. "And I'm certainly not afraid of anything you say."

"I can see it in your eyes," Madison replied. "You're so afraid your teeth are chattering."

"I'm not afraid," she shot back. "I never have been."

"Then why are you so afraid to admit you're a female?"

Fern stared at him, flabbergasted. She didn't even move when Madison advanced on her, not stopping until he was only inches from her.

"You've got a body that men must pant after. You tease us by parading about in pants, but your clothing also forces us to keep our distance."

Fern stepped back; Madison stepped forward.

"Are you too ignorant to know you drive men crazy, or do you dress like that because you like to see us with our tongues hanging out?"

Fern's mouth opened, but no sound came out.

"I don't know what kind of woman you'd make, but you make a damned sorry man."

The attack was so sudden, the words so unexpected, that Fern found herself unprepared for the impact. It went straight through the armor of years, penetrated the hard veneer she showed to the world, and exploded the dark veil she had kept drawn over a secret so painful she'd locked it away even from herself. And now she sensed it there, waiting, obscure still, but frightening.

"You know you're more dangerous in pants than a dress." He stalked her as she retreated before him. "You can go where other women can't, cause havoc other women never dreamed of."

"I don't . . . I never—"

"But there's a problem," Madison said.

He was so close she could feel his breath on her skin. She held her ground, determined she wouldn't run away. She didn't want to admit he frightened her, but he was so close he was practically touching her. It made her limbs go weak.

"I'll bet no man has ever held you in his arms and kissed you."

"I don't want anybody to kiss me," Fern protested. "I wouldn't let—"

"For all your teasing and tempting, the other women are way ahead of you. They know what it's like to feel a man's embrace."

She felt his arms go around her. She fought against the tightening band, but she was powerless to keep it from closing around her.

"They know what it's like to feel the pressure of a man's body against their own, to feel his touch on their skin."

The circle closed around her until it crushed her against him. The shock of such intimate contact aroused the deeply buried memories, black and frightening recollections that blurred Madison's face.

"They know what it's like to be kissed."

Madison's lips took Fern's in a gentle, lingering kiss. A small part of her was aware of his gentleness, of the willing response of her body, but the terror in her mind blocked out everything else.

Fighting with all her strength, Fern tore loose from Madison's embrace. With a muffled sob, she pulled herself onto her horse and galloped off, her eyes so filled with tears she couldn't see where she was going.

Chapter Five

"Stop!" Madison called. But even as he shouted after her, he ran toward his horse. He knew she wouldn't come back. At this moment, he was the last person on earth she wanted to see.

He cursed his uncertain temper. He had become so annoyed with her refusal to even try to look at the facts of Troy's murder that he had spoken in irritation, meaning to shock, but not to injure. But somehow his words had penetrated her defenses and found some unsuspected pain, some deep wound. In order to keep the wound hidden from the world, perhaps even from herself, she had virtually denied she was a woman.

She probably couldn't remember the last time she'd cried. He was certain she had never run away from anyone. He was equally certain she would never forgive him for being the one to make her do so now.

He had expected her to be furious at him. The look of shock and fear before she'd leaped on her horse had stunned him. He'd never expected her to cry.

He really did think she would make a better woman than a man. He really did think she'd like being kissed once she let down her defenses, that the young men of Abilene must have been panting after her for years without having the courage to tell her so, but he had no right to force himself on her. Certainly not to hurt her feelings.

He hadn't meant to. He was beginning to admire her courage, her willingness to accept the consequences of her actions, even in an odd way her social rebellion.

But taking her into his arms had nothing to do with growing admiration. It had more to do with her long, shapely legs, well-rounded bottom, and the tempting mound of her breasts. She exercised an attraction over him that flew in the face of his beliefs about himself.

Even more bewildering, she seemed to act like a lightning rod to some ambiguity hidden deep within himself.

He should leave her alone. He had hurt her, and she would want to recover in private. He could apologize to her when they both felt more composed.

But he never slowed his stride. It took him a moment longer to mount—he had never learned to fling himself into the saddle as she had—but Buster reached full stride in just a few seconds. It was a lot like riding to the hounds, with Fern the terrified fox. Only the terrain was flat and brown—there were few trees, no fences—and it was far more important that he catch up with her than any fox.

But it wouldn't be easy. Her mount ran like the wind, and she rode with the unconscious skill of someone who had lived in the saddle practically from the time she was able to ask for her own pony. But Buster was a strong horse, long-striding and blessed with plenty of stamina. Her cutting pony would soon tire, and then he would overtake her.

The taste of her kiss, tinged with the flavor of coffee, lingered on his lips. The faint aroma of fried ham and strong soap clung to a shirt softened and worn thin with wear and washing. He could still feel the firm softness of her body as he'd held her close.

Every part of him had absorbed something of her, and it left him shaken and confused.

Fern looked back. When she saw him in close pursuit, she whipped her pony across the shoulders, turning him away from the trail into open country.

Here the prairie became dangerous, deceptive. Folds and dips opened up before them without warning. She led Madison over ground that had been criss-crossed by streams, carved and chiseled as the water of countless thunderstorms sliced across the earth, gouging a path through the soil, wearing away the soft stone. Up banks, down ridges, around bends, over muddy streambeds they went, Madison exerting all his strength to coax the maximum speed from his mount, calling upon all his horsemanship to keep up with Fern.

But as Buster's powerful strides closed the distance between them, Fern started taking terrible chances. She would throw her pony on its haunches and turn at a full gallop before Madison could get his own mount slowed down enough to turn and follow her. She would leap a dangerous ravine or scramble up a treacherous bank. Never in his years in Texas had Madison experienced a ride such as this, not even the time bandits had caused him to flee for his life. He had a tremendous admiration for her riding ability, and he'd tell her so if he survived this mad chase.

It didn't take him long to realize that Fern wasn't heading back to the ranch. She was taking him into rough country, far to the east of Abilene. He had to keep up with her. Though this was no time to be considering such things, he knew his pride would chafe under the necessity of admitting he had been outridden by a woman and left to find his way back to town.

Just as he thought the chase would go on forever, Fern turned to look over her shoulder. At the same moment, her pony stumbled going up a small rise. Fern catapulted from the saddle and over the edge of a stream bank onto the stones below. Her body skidded for about five yards before coming to a halt.

She didn't move.

Madison flung himself from his horse before it stopped. He leaped down into the creek and, slipping on loose rocks and jumping a sluggish trickle of water, raced to the motionless Fern. He slipped his hand inside her shirt next to her neck. A pulse, strong but rapid, relieved his most immediate worry. She was alive. But the fall had knocked her unconscious.

Now she lay helpless, probably injured, miles from home. And it was because of his temper. If only he hadn't stopped her in the street last night; if he hadn't forced her to take him to the Connor place; if he had kept his opinions to himself . . .

He stared at her lying unconscious and felt heartsick. Despite her bravado, she was a lonely young woman, injured by something in her past, terribly afraid of it, and touchingly lovely in her vulnerability.

He had to get help. He probably shouldn't move

her, but he couldn't leave her lying in this streambed. He carefully checked her arms. Neither seemed to be broken. It seemed odd to be examining a woman's limbs. With Fern unconscious, it was almost as if he were taking advantage of her. For the first time since he had met her, he was grateful for her male attire. Even on this deserted prairie, many miles from another human being, he would have been reluctant to raise a woman's skirts, even to make certain she had no broken bones.

Her legs weren't broken, but what about her collarbone or ribs? Madison hesitated. Nothing in his experience had prepared him to examine females. Still, he couldn't move her until he had made at least a partial examination. Unbuttoning her shirt, he was shocked to find she wore a chemise of fine lawn trimmed with lace next to her skin. It was so delicate, so utterly feminine, it seemed incongruous alongside her sheepskin vest. Clearly, Fern was not happy in her assumed role. It must have taken some terrible experience to make her hide behind an impersonation so foreign to her nature.

Slipping his hand inside her shirt, Madison ran his fingers over her lower ribs. He couldn't tell for certain, but he didn't think any were broken. He wasn't nearly so quick when the examination brought his hand into contact with her breast. He found himself unable to concentrate on her bones. The soft give of her breast was much more compelling.

Her sheepskin vest was a better disguise than he had suspected. Who could have guessed her breasts were so full, so firm? He felt heat flood through his body like water through a sluice gate. Not even his most intimate moments with Lillian Claiborne had caused his body to respond so quickly. And there was no woman in the world more feminine and alluring than Lillian.

Madison cursed himself for his lack of self-control. He ought to be thinking of getting her to a doctor, not her breast, her skin, or the soft curve of her lips. He snatched his hand from her body. Still muttering under his breath, he quickly rebuttoned her shirt.

It worried him that Fern hadn't regained consciousness. He also worried about the bruise forming on her forehead. He hadn't seen it at first, but it had darkened quickly. He didn't know how many other bruises might mark her body. And he couldn't find out. Not here. He had to get her home to her father.

He knelt down and slipped one hand behind her back and the other beneath her legs. She didn't weigh as much as he had expected, but carrying her along the rocky streambed and up the steep bank to the prairie above proved a difficult task. He was thankful to find a cattle crossing.

Madison quickly discarded the idea of mounting her on her own pony. He was a good horseman, but he couldn't support her and control two horses. Straining his every muscle, he lifted her into his saddle and mounted behind her. Breathing deeply from his exertions, Madison put his arms around her, leaned her against his chest, took up the reins, and urged Buster forward with a squeeze of his knees.

Her horse followed of his own accord.

Madison didn't dare move out of a fast walk. He had no idea how a jarring trot might affect a concussion or broken ribs. He also worried that she might have suffered an internal injury. As the minutes rolled slowly by, he wondered why he'd never bothered to learn more about the human body.

Fern

If you're going to make a practice of driving people into a blind panic, you ought to be prepared to deal with the consequences.

But he hadn't done it intentionally. He had been so worried about Hen, so hopeful of finding another explanation for what happened the night Troy Sproull was killed, he hadn't given any thought to how his words would affect Fern.

Yet now, as she leaned against him, her breath even, her pulse strong, he asked himself what could have caused this strong-minded woman to hide her femininity under men's clothes. He wondered whether she was covering herself up because she was ashamed of herself, or because she didn't want to attract male interest. Either way it didn't make sense.

If she had done it to avoid attention, she had made a tactical error. He couldn't imagine a more surefire way to attract the attention of cowboys starved for feminine companionship than to dress in pants.

The longer he rode with her in his arms, the more his awareness of her body increased until he could think of little else. Worried as he was, his own body responded to her nearness, to the feel of her warmth pressed against him.

Never before had he been so acutely aware of a woman. Their bodies touched along most of their length with nothing but thin material preventing their flesh from coming into contact. There were moments when Madison felt that even that hardly counted. The heat generated between them might burn away this fragile barrier at any moment.

He rode with his arm around her middle to hold her in the saddle. Every time she fell forward, her breasts pressed against his arm. Despite trying to concentrate on Fern's possible injuries, his entire consciousness focused on the feel of her breast.

And his body trembled from waves of pure lust.

Nor could he forget the shapeliness of her calves or the gentle curve of her thighs. Never had he been so intimately familiar with the body of a woman he couldn't fully see or touch, and it imposed a severe strain on his self-control. He kept imagining what she would look like without her clothes. Just the thought caused him to grow so hard he ached.

An hour ago he had thought of her as an amusing curiosity, someone with whom he might while away a few dull hours. Yet now she caused him to writhe on the spear of his own desire.

It disgusted him that his physical nature should so easily gain control over his brain. It horrified him that at times he had wished he hadn't any control at all. He had observed enough of the animal side of men's nature to know it often caused him to do things that had a calamitous effect on his life and career. It was a matter of principle with him that he never let this happen.

His relief when the Sproull farmhouse came into view was almost physical.

"Hello in there," he called. "Anybody home?"

No one answered. He rode up to the house and peered in through the window. No one was inside. He rode over to the barn, circled it, calling all the while, but no one answered.

Her father wasn't home.

He couldn't just toss her on the bed and ride off. Even if her father came back soon, Madison didn't know if she would let him take care of her. He had to take her to Abilene.

But even as he turned Buster toward town, he felt the warmth stir in his limbs once again. He cursed. He didn't know what it was about this woman that affected him so strongly, but the sooner he put some distance between them, the better.

Fern

*　*　*

Madison had almost reached the outskirts of Abilene when Fern groaned and stirred awake. When she twisted around to look up at him, he could see the pain in her eyes.

"Don't move," he said when she tried to wriggle out of his arms. "You've been hurt."

"What happened?" she asked, still struggling to escape his embrace.

"You fell off your horse."

She stopped struggling and turned her unbelieving gaze on him. "I *never* fall off my horse," she declared, wincing with pain. "You must have done something to me."

A flash of anger prodded Madison's temper, but he tamped it down before he could utter any more ill-chosen words. His anger sprang from guilt; he could only atone by accepting the responsibility for what he had done.

"I said something I shouldn't. It made you too angry to watch where you were going. Your horse stumbled and you pitched forward into the creek. I wouldn't be surprised if you have a deep concussion as well as a few broken ribs."

"How do you know?" she asked, her eyes wide with trepidation.

"I checked."

"You handled me?" she asked, anger and fright mingled in her voice.

Madison didn't know why her reaction should irritate him so much. He couldn't expect her to like being handled by a stranger.

Yet it made him furious.

Because she made him feel guilty. And after struggling so hard to control his physical desire, he felt he deserved a little credit. If she guessed what he would have *liked* to do, she probably wouldn't wait to see

73

him hang. She'd shoot him herself.

"I touched you as little as possible."

"How dare you touch me at all!"

"What was I supposed to do? Ask a passing gopher? Forgive me if I didn't follow the proper etiquette for a woman who dresses, acts, and expects to be treated as a man. You'll have to explain it to me sometime."

"I don't want to see you ever again," Fern exploded. She pushed against his chest, then groaned with agony.

"You may have some broken ribs," Madison said, sympathy and concern battling with anger and guilt. "Stay still until I can get you to a doctor."

"Take me home," she cried.

"I did, but your father was gone."

"Take me back this minute."

"When is he supposed to get back?"

"I don't know. Maybe tonight. He's gone to sell to the drovers."

"Who'll take care of you?"

"I can take care of myself."

"No. You need a doctor to look at your chest to see if you really are hurt."

"No man is going to *look at my chest!*" Fern exclaimed. "Let me down right now."

But when she tried to break his hold, her face crumpled with pain.

"You wouldn't make it five yards. You'd collapse in the street."

"That's none of your concern."

"Ordinarily I would agree with you, but somehow it would get around town that I was responsible for your fall. Next thing you know, people would be saying I took you home and left you to die. By tomorrow every man in Dickinson County would be after my blood."

"It wouldn't do them any good. I'm going to get it all."

Madison surprised them both by laughing. "Why don't you just relax and let me take you to a doctor? Which one do you normally see?"

"I haven't seen a doctor since I was born, and I don't intend to start now."

That shouldn't have surprised him. She was just the type to refuse to admit she needed any kind of help.

"Pick one."

"If you don't let me down, I'll scream."

"For someone wanting to be treated like a man, you sure are quick to use a woman's trick," Madison said.

"I'll use any trick I can to get away from you," she replied. "Now let me go."

For a moment, Madison was tempted to do just that. She wasn't his responsibility. But the pain in her eyes wouldn't let him.

"I will make a compromise with you. I'll take you to my sister-in-law. If she says you're okay, I'll take you home. If she says you're hurt, you're going to see a doctor."

He expected her to keep arguing. Her capitulation convinced him she was suffering a lot of pain.

"At least allow me to ride my own horse. I may let her examine me, but I won't be carried through town in a man's arms, particularly yours. I'd rather have all my ribs broken."

Madison was tempted to break her neck, but he decided it might be a little rough on George to have two brothers hang at the same time.

"Can you hold on to the saddle horn?" he asked.

"Of course. What kind of mollycoddle do you take me for?"

"Why don't you just answer my question?"

"I can hold on," she said, subdued.

Madison slid from the saddle. Without his support, Fern swayed, but she managed to stay erect. "It'll be easier if you stay on Buster. I'll lead the horses."

She didn't like that arrangement, but she was finding that without his support, the pain was much worse. The increased discomfort took the steel out of her resistance.

"Don't take me through the middle of town," she managed to say through teeth gritted with pain. "I won't be paraded around like a circus freak."

"How am I supposed to get you there without using the streets? I'm not a magician with a magic carpet to transport you. I doubt whether Buster or your pony would ride on it if I did."

"For a grown man, you talk more foolishness than anybody I ever met."

"I'm sure my professors at Harvard are chagrined they allowed me to graduate first in my class."

"I don't mean you're stupid," she said, "just that you say stupid things. I know you do it just to make me mad." She paused for a moment. "I guess I can't blame you. I never said anything nice to you."

Surprised, Madison turned and looked up at her.

"Even though you are the most miserable, low-down piece of rotten cowhide I ever had the misfortune to come across, I probably shouldn't say so."

Madison swallowed. "Being such an extremely poor specimen of humanity, it would surely be unreasonable of me to expect your approbation."

"There you go again," she said, "always—"

She never got to finish her sentence. Two dogs dashed across the street practically under Buster's feet. He came to a stiff-legged stop, causing Fern to be thrown roughly over the saddle horn and onto his neck. This broke her grip on the saddle horn. She slid off the horse's back into Madison's arms. Her cry of pain as she fainted banished all anger and uncharitable thoughts from his mind.

Ignoring the stares of everyone he passed, Madison hurried along the street until he reached the house George had rented. A fence surrounded the yard.

Two little boys played on the porch. "What's your name?" Madison called out.

"Ed Abbott," the bigger boy responded, looking scared.

"Open this gate, Ed. Then run inside and get your mother. This lady has been hurt."

"Mama's gone," the boy stated. "She said I was to stay on the porch and not talk to strangers."

"Get Mrs. Randolph then," Madison said.

"She's taking a nap."

"Then wake her."

"Mama said not to," the boy replied.

Madison fought down a desire to throttle the child.

"Open the gate," he barked.

"No."

Madison wondered if the entire state of Kansas had banded together to thwart him. He had navigated the treacherous waters of New England society with far greater ease than he had endured twenty-four hours in Abilene. He bent down far enough to grasp the latch. Opening the gate wide enough to insert his toe, he kicked it open with his foot.

"Miz Randolph! Miz Randolph!" Ed screamed. The younger boy merely stood watching, a carved wooden wagon in his hands. Rose came through the front door as Madison climbed the porch steps.

"What's wrong?" she asked. "Why is Ed yelling?"

"Fern Sproull was hurt in a fall from her horse," Madison explained, ignoring Ed. "She's in a lot of pain."

"You ought to take her to a doctor."

"I wanted to, but she won't go. I can't leave her at home because her father's gone."

Rose looked at Fern more closely. "I don't like the look of that bruise. Bring her in."

"I'm afraid she might have some broken ribs, too."

Rose led the way into the house and to a small bedroom with a minimum of furnishings. "Has she been unconscious since the fall?"

Madison smiled in spite of himself. "She was conscious long enough to give me a good blessing out just a few minutes ago. Some dogs startled her horse. She fainted when she fell off." Rose looked up, startled. "I caught her," Madison added.

"If she has any broken bones, I'm calling a doctor whether she likes it or not." Rose stared at Madison. "Well, what are you waiting for? You're going to have to get her out of those clothes. In my condition, I can't do it."

Madison felt heat rush over his body like a blast from an open furnace. He couldn't undress Fern in front of Rose. He didn't know what George would have done, but Madison knew that he would be mortified with the plain evidence of his lust.

Chapter Six

"She'll kill me if she finds out."

"Then I won't tell her."

She would find out. Women always found out the very things they shouldn't. At least he could take off her boots. That shouldn't give rise to any future desire to fill him full of bullet holes. But after he removed her boots and set them in the corner, he still faced a fully clothed Fern.

"Come on," Rose said impatiently. "I can help a little, but I can hardly bend over without falling."

If Rose fell, George would kill him. If Fern found out he'd undressed her, she'd kill him. Either way it didn't look like he had very long to live.

But there was no one else.

The moment Madison leaned forward, his hand extended to deal with the buttons on Fern's shirt, he felt his body begin to tighten. *It's absurd to become so excited over the thought of touching her. You're just going to remove her shirt. You're not going to touch her breasts.*

Suppressing a strong desire to rush out and buy a ticket for the next train out of Abilene, Madison quickly unbuttoned Fern's shirt. Leaning across her body and averting his eyes from the twin mounds of her breasts, he slipped his arm under her and lifted her up just enough to ease her arms out of the sleeves.

The shirt wouldn't come off.

"Her hands are caught in the sleeve," Rose told him. "Hold her while I unbutton her cuffs."

Madison lost all ability to concentrate. His face was practically buried in Fern's breasts. He lowered her back on the bed.

"I'll lift her *after* you've unbuttoned her cuffs," he said, taking a deep breath to clear his head.

"You act like you've never touched a female," Rose said, a trace of a smile on her lips.

Madison didn't answer. If he didn't say anything, he wouldn't incriminate himself. But his body could. He fought down the surging desire while Rose had her back to him.

As soon as Rose unbuttoned the second sleeve, Fern's shirt slipped off easily. But Madison wasn't done yet. He still had to remove her pants. He heaved a fatalistic sigh.

Rose, amused by his predicament, watched.

Even as he undid the buttons to Fern's pants, Madison could feel a scalding heat surge through his loins. Wrenching loose the last button, he tried to pull her pants off by the legs.

Rose couldn't completely hide her smile. "You can't snatch them off," she said. "They're as tight as a second skin. Here, let me help."

Taking several slow breaths to calm his thumping heart, Madison slid his arm under the small of Fern's back and lifted her gingerly. Rose helped him work the pants slowly over Fern's hips.

Very slowly. The longer he held her, his face close to her stomach, the longer his hands stayed in contact with her upper thighs, the more agitated he became. Finally, with a strong pull, Rose brought the pants down to Fern's knees. Madison stepped around Fern, and with a quick pull they were off.

He clutched the pants in front of him. He only hoped his expression didn't reveal how deeply he had been affected.

"Now her shift."

"No!"

"You can't leave her in it," Rose argued.

"Yes, I can," Madison declared, adamant. "You can bandage her in or out of it, but I'm not touching it."

Rose grinned. "Don't tell me you're—"

"Don't say it," Madison said, struggling to recover his accustomed gravity. "In the course of this day I have endured enough at the hands of that . . . Fern . . . to give me gray hair. I'm sorry she got hurt, but if she had let me take her to a doctor, none of this would have been necessary."

"I can't bandage her chest over her chemise," Rose insisted. She sat down on the side of the bed, her back to Madison, and began to run her hands over Fern's rib cage. Madison heaved a sigh of relief and willed his body to return to its normal state.

It was fortunate he succeeded. Before Rose had finished her examination, they heard the front door open. Moments later a heavy tread approached the room, followed by the rapid patter of smaller feet.

"What is going on here?" Mrs. Abbott demanded, bursting into the room, Ed right behind her, suspicion and outrage making her gaze dart from Fern to Madison.

"You're just in time to help Rose take care of Miss Sproull," Madison said, backing toward the door. "She's had an accident and refuses to see a doctor."

"She must be undressed," Rose said. "She may have some broken ribs."

The sight of Fern lying unconscious on the bed completely transformed Mrs. Abbott's stormy countenance.

"Poor dear. Here, let me help," she cooed as she shooed Madison and Ed out of the room. "It won't take a minute."

Much to his relief, Madison found himself outside a closed door. He turned to Ed, who looked unhappy to have had his complaint so hastily shoved aside.

"The next time I come to your door, let me in," Madison said sternly. "And there's no need for all that caterwauling and running about. What kind of man will you grow up to be if you yelp at every little thing? Why don't you act like that other little boy?" Only then did he remember the second child wasn't in the room. Madison looked on the porch. The child still played with his wagon.

"See," Madison pointed out, "he's not jumping up and down, yelling like a cowhand trying to turn a stampede."

"He never yells," Ed said.

"Admirable child," Madison said. "He'll be a captain of industry someday, just like his father."

"His father don't captain no industry," Ed told him. "His father's Mr. Randolph."

Madison stared. This little boy with black hair, black eyes, and unflappable demeanor was his nephew. He didn't know why he hadn't realized it before. The child looked exactly like Zac in that picture Ma had taken just before the war.

It gave him an odd feeling to know that this child

was George's son. George had always seemed so sure of himself, so secure, so much bigger than life. This child was like another part of him, a nonthreatening part. Madison knelt down before the little boy.

"Hello."

Madison didn't know what he was doing practically sitting on the floor, but the child intrigued him. He didn't seem the least bit afraid or particularly interested. He just stared back at him.

"You're not my daddy," he said finally.

Now Madison understood why he had stared so hard. None of his other uncles looked like George. Madison looked enough like him to be his twin.

"That's right, I'm your daddy's brother."

The little boy held out his wagon to Madison. "You want to play with it?"

"No, you keep it," Madison said, smiling at the thought of what his friends would say if they could see him sitting on the floor playing with a toy wagon. He started to stand up, but knelt back down again. "What's your name?" he asked.

"William Henry Randolph," the little boy announced with unmistakable clarity.

The shock caused Madison to sit down on the floor. George had named his son after their father.

Fern watched Mrs. Abbott tidy the room and give the bedclothes a twitch to straighten out an invisible wrinkle.

"Are you sure you're strong enough to be sitting up?" Mrs. Abbott asked. "It's a miracle you've got nothing broken."

"I'm fine," Fern replied, doing everything she could to keep the pain that racked her body from sounding in her voice.

"You really ought to lie down."

"It's better when I sit up." Each breath caused

stabbing pain, but she felt as if she were drowning when she lay down. "Where is Mrs. Randolph?"

"She's seeing to her little boy. I can get you what you need."

Fern wasn't comfortable with Mrs. Abbott. The women of Abilene had disapproved of her ever since she could remember. Even now she could see a censorious look in Mrs. Abbott's eyes. It seemed to say that if Fern hadn't been out with a man all by herself, something no decent woman would do, this would never have happened. Mrs. Abbott's disapproval became even more evident when she spied the pants and shirt folded neatly on the top of the dresser.

"I wanted to thank her for taking care of me."

Rose hadn't judged Fern. There was bound to be some strain between them—they couldn't avoid it with Fern determined that Rose's brother-in-law would hang—but it wasn't a personal rejection, and that made a difference. Fern could handle disagreement. She'd faced that all her life. But the sting of rejection never seemed to lessen. After all these years, she should have been able to ignore it, but each time was like the first.

"I'll tell her you want to see her," Mrs. Abbott said, giving the crocheted dresser scarf a last straightening before she left the room. "But she may be some time. She's seeing to her family. She's a wonderful mother to that little boy, but that's nothing to the way she dotes on Mr. Randolph."

The moment the door closed behind Mrs. Abbott, Fern collapsed against the mound of pillows and let the pain take over. She would pretend it didn't hurt when Rose came in, but right now it was easier to give in and admit it hurt like living hell.

Piss and vinegar! You're lucky you didn't break your neck.

Fern

It was stupid to have run away from Madison. He hadn't said anything others hadn't said. Yes, he had.

Why are you so afraid to admit you're a female?

Usually she'd have no trouble denying such an accusation. She was expected to do a man's work, so why shouldn't she dress like one? That was the reason she gave everybody. She kept the real reason closely concealed in her heart. Yet somehow Madison had figured it out in one morning.

Or had he? Maybe he had used those words by accident. She would pretend he'd never said it, and maybe he wouldn't mention it. If he did, she would deal with it then.

But he had taken her in his arms and kissed her.

Maybe he could pretend that had never happened, but she couldn't. Even now, despite the pain from her cracked and bruised ribs, she could feel his body pressed against hers, her breasts crushed against his chest, his lips covering her mouth. Just thinking about it caused the panic to come flooding back.

But before the panic, she remembered feeling something else. It had been only a moment between the shock of his embrace and the onset of fear, but she remembered it very clearly. It had been excitement and pleasure, comfortable and familiar, as though she had found something she had lost.

But the joy of discovery had been swept away too quickly, gone never to return. Madison wouldn't kiss her again. Surely she didn't want him to.

A soft knock on the door was followed by Rose's entrance. Fern marveled that anyone so swollen with child could move with Rose's grace. Fern marveled even more that she could look so happy, contented, and radiantly healthy under the circumstances.

"Mrs. Abbott said you wanted to see me. Is the pain worse?"

Fern smiled as bravely as she could. "At times, but it's not too bad now. Besides, I'm used to it. When you spend half your life in the saddle, you're bound to get a few hurts. I've been recovering from one thing or another most of my life."

"Are you comfortable? Do you have enough pillows? You're smiling, but there's a lot of pain in your eyes."

Fern realized that Rose must have given up her own pillows, probably those of her son as well, to make her comfortable. She couldn't not like a woman who would do that for a stranger, especially one who could be considered an enemy of the family.

"I guess I ought to be glad it wasn't worse," Fern said, trying to look cheerful, hoping she didn't look as miserable as she felt. "Troy would say it served me right for riding like a Yankee dude."

She felt a flush of embarrassment rise in her cheeks. She hadn't meant to mention Tory.

"Not that I mean to say Madison rides like a dude. I'm the one who fell off my horse. How *did* he learn to ride like that?" she asked, curious. "I was sure he'd come out to the ranch in a buggy or a wagon. But he rode like he's spent most of his life in the saddle."

"Ask him," Rose said. "I'm sure he'd be happy to tell you. It would be a change from all the worries he has over his brother."

"I doubt he'd want to talk to me," Fern said, her gaze in her lap. "Even if I did ask him, which I won't."

Rose looked at her, a question in her eye.

"We got off to a bad start," Fern confessed. "Now we can't seem to get on the right track."

Fern hadn't realized until she felt herself relax that she had tensed, ready to defend herself against

Rose's expected reproaches. She was further surprised when she felt the need to explain that everything wasn't Madison's fault. Up until this moment, she had been convinced it was.

Rose smiled. It was an easy, warm, friendly smile, one that invited Fern to relax, one that promised she would not be judged . . . even if she deserved it.

"The Randolph men are noted for their strong opinions and their willingness to state them without the least encouragement," Rose said. "You just have to stand up to them. Once they know they can't buffalo you, they're actually quite gentlemanly. Even sweet. They can positively spoil a woman."

Fern couldn't imagine Madison spoiling her. He was more likely to ignore her.

"I was going to try to show him up for a tenderfoot."

"And now you find the shoe on your own foot," Rose said. Her expression was noncommittal, but Fern could see a humorous gleam in her eyes.

Fern nodded.

"I don't know what Madison has done since he went to Boston," Rose said, "but he grew up around horses and spent three years in south Texas chasing longhorns."

She should have guessed. It was stupid to think men like George and Hen would have a brother who couldn't ride.

"If you give him a chance, I think you'll find he can be quite the gentleman."

Fern felt the constraint return. "Not with me. I mean to see that Hen hangs. Madison means to get him off."

Fern wasn't surprised to see the friendliness leave Rose's expression. A terrible sadness seemed to settle over her, as though Hen were her own child.

"I'm sorry about your cousin. I lost my mother

and father, so I know how you feel. But I've lived with Hen for five years, and I know he didn't kill your cousin."

"He's killed other men," Fern pointed out. "Everybody says he's the most dangerous man in Abilene, including Marshal Hickok."

"I know. From the time he was twelve, he's had to be prepared to kill to survive. But inside he's just as gentle as George."

"I don't think we'll ever agree on that subject."

"No, I doubt we shall, but I hope it won't prevent us from agreeing on others."

Rose was making an overture; she was reaching out. Much to her surprise, Fern found she wanted to respond. She didn't know why. She never had before. Maybe because Rose was the first woman who hadn't tried to change her, who didn't try to make her ashamed of herself.

Fern was also curious about Rose. She was the only woman in a world of men. She had not only survived, she had thrived and was obviously happy. Everyone respected her. More importantly, she could be herself.

Fern had survived, but she hadn't thrived. She wasn't happy, either. She still had to fight for the little respect she got. And nobody liked her the way she was. Not even her own father.

But what intrigued Fern most about Rose was her own suspicion that though Rose was a very attractive woman, her apparent success owed very little to her beauty.

Fern had to discover her secret.

"Are these your clothes I'm wearing?" Fern asked. She had been uncomfortably aware of the lace-trimmed pink nightgown from the moment she regained consciousness.

"I'm sorry I don't have anything to fit you," Rose

said, "but you're so much taller than I am."

"It's not that," Fern said, fingering the soft, thin material. "I don't feel right using your clothes."

"Don't give it a second thought. I have dozens of gowns. When you get to be my size, it's about the only practical thing to wear."

"I don't feel comfortable in gowns. I never have."

"I wouldn't feel comfortable in pants," Rose said. "I guess it's all in what you're used to."

"Can't I wear my own clothes?"

"Not until you're better."

"I don't think I'll ever stop hurting."

Fern was surprised she could make such an admission to Rose. She wouldn't have to anyone else. Not even her father.

What about Madison?

Maybe. It might not be so hard to admit a weakness to him. He certainly wouldn't offer her unwanted sympathy. She smiled. He would expect her to blame him. She wondered what evidence he'd produce to show it was really her fault.

That reminded her of his theory that somebody else had murdered Troy, and her smile vanished. They would always be at cross purposes. If Madison got Hen off, she'd never forgive him. If Hen died, he'd never want to see her again. The best thing for both of them would be for him to get on a train back to Boston and for her to go home and stay there.

"You can't sit there and say nothing," Madison said to Hen, his patience exhausted. "It's your neck that's on the line."

Hen didn't speak. He just stared at Madison.

"And there's no point in glaring at me like you hate me," Madison said. "You don't have to like your lawyer to talk to him."

Hen turned away. He seemed to prefer looking at the wall.

"You don't have to forgive me for leaving when Ma died, either."

Hen didn't turn around, but Madison could see his back stiffen.

"Maybe you're right. Maybe I was a coward to leave. Either way, it doesn't matter now. Keeping you alive does."

Still Hen didn't turn around or speak.

"Okay, have it your own way. You always were so damned sure you were right and everybody else had to be wrong. Well, you listen to me, William Henry Harrison Randolph. Doing what you despise, trying to be what you aren't, isn't always right, especially when it turns you inside out and bleaches the life out of you. There's a lot that's good about you, but you're too hard and unforgiving. You hate far better than you love. You hold grudges easier than you forget. You stick to your principles more readily than you understand how those principles might destroy another person's life.

"You can think I did the wrong thing. Sometimes I agree with you. But I'm not dead inside," Madison said, thumping his chest. "I can still feel. And one thing I feel real strongly is that you didn't kill Troy Sproull. I intend to prove it, because I'll be damned if I'll let you hang.

"And you know why I'm going to make sure you stay alive? Not just because I can't stand by and see my brother die for something he didn't do. And not just because of the pain it would cause the rest of the family, especially George.

"It's because I want you to walk out of that courtroom knowing you owe your life to me. I want you to know that the despised brother who deserted you when you were only fourteen is the only reason you're alive. I want you to be forced to thank me. And you will. You'll hate it, but you're so damned stubborn you'll make yourself do it, even if you choke on the words.

"And you know what I'm going to do when you finally say those words? I'm going to tell you to go to hell."

Silence. Hen didn't say a word. He didn't move. He just sat facing the wall. Madison left the jail.

When he reached the street, he was so angry he was shaking. He hadn't expected his brothers to welcome him with open arms, but he hadn't expected this unending reproach. Rose was the only one who seemed to be glad he had come.

It would serve them right if he got back on the train and never left Boston again.

But he knew he wouldn't leave. The same feelings that had made him leave Boston, which had forced him to risk seeing his brothers again, would force him to stay in Kansas until they had reached some kind of settlement. He understood now that that was why he had come. Hen's trial was merely the impetus. If it hadn't been that, it would have been something else.

It surprised him how much his brothers' rejection hurt. He had never felt alone before. Not *really* alone. He had had Freddy's family, but he'd always felt that his own family would be there if he needed them.

Now he wasn't certain.

He shrugged. He'd think of something, he always did, but not tonight. Right now he'd better see how that rebel in leather and sheepskin was getting along.

He told himself he wouldn't be going if he didn't feel guilty. He told himself he wouldn't feel so concerned if it hadn't been his fault. He told himself a few other things, all of which were true, but none of them changed the fact he was going because he wanted to see her. Try as he might, he couldn't forget the feel of her body pressed against his, of his lips on hers, of the softness of her breast as she leaned against him.

He told himself not to worry that she fascinated him so. It wouldn't come to anything. This feeling of kinship, of a common bond, was just an illusion. He would go back to Boston in a few weeks and forget all about her.

"She was very lucky," Rose told Madison. "She could have been killed."

Madison had found George and Rose sitting together on the front porch when he reached the Abbott house. William Henry played close by.

"I tried to stop her," Madison said, pulling up a chair.

"From the little bit I've seen of you two," Rose said, "I imagine there was as much provoking as placating."

"I seem to have that problem with everyone lately."

"I gather you had no success with Hen," George said.

"He won't even speak to me."

"I'll go see him," Rose said.

"It's no use," Madison said. "He's still angry about my leaving."

"I don't care what he's angry about," Rose said, getting slowly to her feet, "it's no reason to refuse to talk to you when you're trying to defend him. Keep an eye on William Henry, George. He can sneak off almost as fast as Zac."

George started to say something, but Rose didn't pause.

"This is the most stubborn, hard-headed family

I've ever met. I can tolerate it most of the time, but not when it could cost Hen his life."

"Wear a shawl," George said. "It gets cool at night."

She entered the house.

"Aren't you going to stop her?" Madison asked.

"Do you think you can?"

"No, but—"

"Neither can I."

"I don't understand," Madison said. George had always been able to control everybody, even his father on occasion.

George smiled, rather complacently, Madison thought.

"You wouldn't," George said. "Not after living with Ma and Pa. I wasn't sure I could understand either. I wouldn't have tried if Rose hadn't forced me. Now sit down. If anybody can make Hen talk, it's Rose."

Rose came out of the house. "Is there anything you particularly want to know?" she asked Madison.

Madison didn't understand how this petite woman could make a stubborn man like Hen cooperate when his own threats had failed.

Probably the same way Fern has captivated you.

But Madison wasn't willing to admit to that just yet.

"I need to know where he rode that night, who may have seen him, and exactly where he was at the time Troy Sproull was killed. If I could prove where he was, nothing else would matter. Failing that, I've got to figure out who did murder Troy. I'll need to know everything Hen knows about the man, even the smallest detail."

"I'll do my best."

"How is she doing?" Madison asked, nodding his head toward the house.

"Go see for yourself," Rose answered, her expression lightening. "You'd better stand in readiness, George. If the last twenty-four hours are any example, it shouldn't take more than three minutes for the fireworks to start."

Madison had started to get up, but he sat back down. "I'm not going in there if she's going to start yelling at me."

"I don't know what she's going to do, or what she did, but you owe her an apology."

"Me? I didn't push her into that stream." Madison had admitted his guilt to himself, but he didn't like hearing it from somebody else.

"Maybe not physically, but you drove her to run away. Now go in there and talk to her. She feels guilty, too. Will you be here when I get back?"

"If she doesn't chew me up too badly."

"Does he always talk about women like this?" Rose asked George.

"He didn't used to."

Madison threw up his hands and went inside. As long as everybody was determined to have a piece of his hide, he might as well let Fern have her share.

Chapter Seven

Mrs. Abbott looked up from her needlework when she heard the door open. "Where are you going?" she demanded.

"To see Miss Sproull."

"Not in my house. I don't permit men to visit ladies in their bedrooms."

Madison bit back the retort that came to mind, reminding himself that George and Rose were staying here.

"I'll leave the door open, and I promise not to approach the bed," he said, striding past.

"Mr. Randolph! Mr. Randolph!" he heard Mrs. Abbott calling to his brother. Either Rose or George must have found a way to allay Mrs. Abbott's fears, because no one came after him.

He raised his hand to knock on Fern's door and realized he didn't know what to say. How do you say you're sorry to someone you've been intentionally aggravating? It didn't seem fair that he should have to take all the blame, but he knew the fault was his. Feeling guilty made him angry, and his mood wasn't very contrite when he knocked on her door.

"Come in."

She didn't sound too sick. Maybe he could make a quick apology and leave. He felt in need of a good stiff brandy.

Madison came to an abrupt halt the moment he stepped through the doorway. If he hadn't known he was in the right room, he would have sworn he was looking at a stranger. The Fern he knew wore pants, a baggy shirt, and a hat. The woman in bed wore a very attractive pink nightgown and allowed her long dark-blond hair to fall becomingly over her shoulders. Big blue-gray eyes stared at him, somewhat apprehensive, somewhat accusing. She seemed to draw within herself when he stepped into the room.

"How are you feeling?" he asked. It was a dumb question. She had to be feeling like hell, but he couldn't ask the question he wanted answered: How had the tomboy he'd helped undress turned into the woman in the bed?

Fern could feel the heat of embarrassment engulf her body until it reached her toes. This man had undressed her, had handled her body. She would have pulled the covers over her head if the pain of even the smallest movement weren't excruciating.

"You took my clothes off, didn't you?" She shouldn't have asked him—she didn't want to know the answer—but she couldn't help herself.

"What makes you think . . . Why should . . . Why does it matter?"

"Why does it matter?" she echoed. "How would you like it if some woman knocked you out, put her hands all over your body, then took off your clothes?"

"I didn't knock you out," Madison responded testily.

She felt that Madison had violated her privacy. She felt almost as vulnerable and defenseless as she had that night so long ago, the night she had tried so hard to forget.

"At least I didn't touch your chemise."

Fern flushed a deeper shade of crimson. No one, not even her father, knew about the lace-trimmed chemises she had ordered directly from Chicago. It mortified her that after trying to appear so hard-nosed, after bragging she could do anything a man could do, after demanding she be treated like one of the fellas, that Madison, of all people, should know her secret. It made her feel like a fool. A silly female. A pathetic fraud.

"Besides, it's your fault as much as mine," Madison said. "Do you always pull crazy stunts when you get angry?"

Fern would gladly have hit him if she could have lifted her arms. She also was a little frightened of him. She never felt in control when he was around. She didn't act like herself; things didn't happen the way she wanted. If she didn't put some distance between them, he might try to kiss her again. Even worse, she might want him to.

"I try to fall off my horse every time I find myself alone with a tenderfoot," she snapped. "They tend to get depressed, what with being so helpless once they're out of the city. Carrying me into town gives them something to do, makes them feel useful."

"You sure gave a convincing performance," Madison said, his temper rising.

"I do my best for Boston lawyers with a penchant for forcing themselves upon helpless females.

Besides, if I hadn't run away, I might have been so overcome by your good looks I'd have compromised myself."

"It takes two to be indiscreet," Madison replied, too angry to weigh his words. "You don't tempt me that far."

Madison regretted his angry response as soon as the words were out of his mouth. He felt all the more like a heartless bully when he saw the hurt in Fern's eyes. She seemed to have a unique ability to make him forget even the most basic tenets of civility. Then make him feel bad about doing it.

"Look, I didn't come here to argue with you," he said, struggling to get a grip on his temper. "I just wanted to see how you were doing and apologize for what I did. I have a nasty temper. It doesn't take much to set it off, and I've discovered an abundance of fuel in Abilene."

Damn! When was he going to learn to shut up before he put his foot in his mouth?

"Then you shouldn't have come here. We don't have one law for Texans and another for everybody else."

Madison could feel the last thread of his self-control snap.

"Miss Sproull, I sincerely hope that one day in the very near future you are accused of something you didn't do. I hope there isn't a single man, woman, or child in Abilene who believes a word you say. I want you to sit in that jail thinking the hanging rope is your certain end. Because then you'll know what you've done to that boy."

She opened her mouth to speak.

"And don't prate to me about justice. You're only interested in vengeance. Otherwise you wouldn't close your mind to anything that might throw light on the events of that night. You'd sift through every piece of evidence, every clue, over and over again until you *knew* what took place that night."

"Nobody can know what happened."

"The killer knows."

"But that's Hen."

Talking to her was like talking into the wind. Trying hard to keep his expression from showing his frustration, he said, "Suppose I can prove Hen wasn't anywhere near the Connor place that night."

"You can't."

"But suppose I could. Do you hate Texans so much you'd rather see Hen hang and the real murderer go free?"

He could see the battle going on within her. If she said she wanted Hen to die no matter what, she condemned herself.

"If you can prove he was somewhere else that night," she said, struggling with each word, "I'll do everything I can to help you find the killer. But—"

"Good. Now you'd better get some rest. We have a lot of work to do before the trial."

Mrs. Abbott was standing outside the door when Madison stepped into the hall.

"She's all yours. Her temper is a little frayed and her integrity is stretched to the limit, but her virtue is unsullied."

Mrs. Abbott's gasp, a sure sign of her badly violated sense of propriety, made Madison feel better. Now he only needed to beat Hen senseless, and he might even feel cheerful.

George looked fed up when Madison reached the porch. "I hope she came out of the interview in better shape than you. If Rose finds her with an elevated temperature, there's going to be hell to pay."

"That's the most obstinate, irritating female I've

ever met," Madison said, pointing toward Fern's room.

"That's how Rose described your brothers when she first came to the ranch. Are you sure those words aren't more applicable to you than Miss Sproull?"

"If you had any idea what that girl said—"

"I know exactly what she said," George interrupted.

Madison looked blank.

"It's July. The window is open. Half of Abilene knows what you said. I don't know what happened to you in the last ten years, but you weren't brought up to treat women like that, even when they irritate you. How many more times are you going to cause me to be ashamed of you?"

Madison thought he would explode. Why in God's name had he ever left Boston? He might as well have been facing his father all over again, his needling, his snide remarks about Madison's cleverness, making light of his interest in books, of his friendship with Freddy, making him feel small and unimportant.

He never expected it of George. George had been the one who tried to protect him, to explain him to his father, the one who tried to make him feel better when his father had left him shattered and shaking after one of his blistering tirades. Madison had thought he could depend on George at least, but it was obvious he couldn't.

"I don't give a damn whether you're embarrassed or not," Madison said, so angry he had trouble keeping his voice steady. "I mean to prove that Hen didn't kill Troy Sproull. Then I'm going back to Boston, and you'll never hear from me again."

He turned and stalked off the porch, down the walk, and into the street. He wanted a stiff drink, and he was going to the noisiest, roughest, most dangerous saloon in town to get it. If Abilene lived up to its reputation as the wildest town in the West, maybe he could spend his time dodging bullets rather than hiding from his thoughts.

Fern wished she could have bitten her tongue off. She hadn't intended to drive Madison away in a rage. This whole mess was more her fault than his. Yet the minute he stepped into the room, she had felt violated. That had put her on the defensive. And when she felt defensive, she became belligerent. That was how she reacted to all men.

She wondered why somebody hadn't pointed it out.

They have. They just stopped a long time ago because it didn't do any good.

"I tried to stop him," Mrs. Abbott announced as she burst into the room. "It's not proper for a man to visit a woman in her bedroom."

"He just came by to see how I was." Piss and vinegar! Now she was defending him to Mrs. Abbott!

"It is *not* okay," Mrs. Abbott declared, her sensibilities injured. "He may have meant to be thoughtful, but he was quite rude. Some people think just because they went to a fancy school and wear fancy clothes they can act like a king or something."

Fern didn't have fancy clothes and she hadn't even finished grade school, but she had been acting like bad-tempered royalty for years. She couldn't blame Madison for doing the same thing.

"He'll probably behave better when he's not upset."

"If he comes around again treating me worse than a black slave, he'll have plenty of reason to be upset," Mrs. Abbott declared. She gave the bedspread such a vigorous straightening that Fern feared for the seams.

"Has Mrs. Randolph returned?"

Mrs. Abbott's countenance cleared as if by magic. "I don't think so. It's quiet on the porch. She's never around but what that little boy is calling her name every half minute. Mr. Randolph positively dotes on her. You'd think it would ruin her the way he spoils her, but she's just as bad about him. It's hard to believe a man could be so besotted with a woman as big as a cow about to drop her calf."

Fern didn't want to hear how George spoiled Rose or adored her despite her present condition. She felt sadly neglected and unwanted, and hearing how George worshiped his wife didn't do a thing to lift her spirits. On the contrary, it showed her one more thing that would never happen to her.

Mrs. Abbott seemed to have decided that the entire room needed rearranging after Madison's disturbing visit, even Fern's clothes, which caused the woman to grimace in disapproval when she touched them.

"And she's such a little thing," Mrs. Abbott continued. "So graceful despite being big enough to have two babies. It's no wonder every man in town treats her like a queen. I never saw a more gracious lady."

You might as well say I have all the charm of an outlaw steer, Fern thought to herself.

Mrs. Abbott began rearranging everything on the table next to Fern's bed.

"But she doesn't sit around preening herself in the mirror. No indeed. If I didn't stop her, she'd do half my work. And her paying me to take care of her. Do what I will, I can't stop her taking care of my Ed. You won't find that kind of consideration every day. No, you certainly won't."

Mercifully, before Mrs. Abbott's veneration for Rose could drive Fern to the screaming point, the object of her adoration returned.

Fern

"You're looking a little drawn about the eyes," Rose said, giving Fern a rather searching look. "I gather your interview didn't go well."

"I should think not," Mrs. Abbott declared, fire once more in her glance. "How could any decent female feel comfortable with a strange man in her bedroom? And shouting at her all the time."

Rose looked inquiringly at Fern.

"He was put out about something I said," Fern told her, unhappy at having to confess her folly.

"Him put out!" Mrs. Abbott exclaimed. "Humph! You wait until I see him again. I'll put him out a bit more."

"I don't think that's such a good idea," Rose said. "We want him to concentrate on clearing Hen of those murder charges. Making him furious isn't likely to help."

"I'm sorry, but I can't have him violating my house."

Rose tried to repress a smile but wasn't entirely successful. "I don't think he meant to do that. Could you warm some milk? I think Miss Sproull should go to sleep."

"Coming right up," Mrs. Abbott said. She straightened a dresser scarf she had straightened twice already and gave the room one more glance before finally departing.

"I trust he didn't upset you too much," Rose said.

"It was more a case of me upsetting him," Fern admitted, so glad to be relieved of Mrs. Abbott's censorious presence she was willing to tell Rose practically anything she wanted to know.

Rose gave her a long, penetrating look. Fern felt as though the protective layers surrounding her soul were being peeled away one by one.

"Do you have to hate him so much?"

"I don't hate him," Fern exclaimed, shocked to realize she didn't hate him. She'd thought she did. She had intended to. "I just don't want him getting his brother off." She couldn't explain about being undressed or about the chemise. Not even to Rose. "But I don't hate him. I don't think anybody could."

"Yes, they can."

"Why? He's thoughtless and positive he's the only one who has any brains, but he's not really mean. He just doesn't stop to realize how what he says affects people. And he hates being here. Everything about Kansas irritates him. Especially me."

"He probably finds it even more difficult to be with his family," Rose said, her gaze still rather clouded. Now she was the one straightening dresser scarfs. "In fact, I would like you to do me a favor."

"Of course," Fern said. After what Rose had done for her, it would be churlish to refuse any request.

"This may seem a strange thing to ask, but could you try to be nice to him?"

Fern opened her mouth to speak.

"I won't expect it of you if you can't, but could you?"

"Why?"

"I don't feel I can explain that just now, but things are much more difficult for him than you know. I have a feeling your being nice would mean a great deal."

"But surely you, his brothers . . ."

"There are times when family can be more of a problem than a solution."

Fern swallowed. "I'll try," she said, wondering how to go about being nice to a man whose instinctive reaction on seeing her was to growl and start tearing up the ground, "but I can't guarantee he won't close his eyes and groan the next time he sees me."

Fern

Rose's solemnity vanished. A suspicion of a smile appeared at the corner of her mouth. "No doubt you made him furious, but he's a man, and men are flattered by the attention of an attractive woman."

"I'm not attractive," Fern said. No matter how kind Rose's intentions, it made her angry that Rose would try to make her feel better by telling her she was pretty.

"Who told you that?"

"Everybody I've ever known. My cows usually come out on top in a direct comparison."

"Then you've got to get some new friends."

"I know what I look like," Fern said, tears rising in the back of her eyes. "It doesn't help to have you tell me otherwise."

"Okay, I won't, but Mrs. Abbott said she never would have guessed you could look so fetching once you were out of that hat and vest. George has remarked on it, too. He thinks you're rather statuesque. From a man like him, a single word is a tribute. If you ever get a whole sentence, you'll know you're beautiful."

Fern picked at the sheet clutched in her hand. If Rose had any idea how much she longed to feel just the tiniest bit attractive, she wouldn't torture her this way. "It's nice of you to say those things, but it doesn't matter. Madison doesn't think so."

"You'll never know if you don't give him a chance to tell you. And he won't tell you if you're at each other's throats all day."

Madison would never tell her she was pretty. He probably didn't even think of her as a female, just one of the peculiar species of fauna found on the Kansas prairie.

"I'll try to be nice to him, but I don't expect him to tell me I'm pretty. I give him credit for honesty."

"So do I. Now I think I hear Mrs. Abbott coming

with your milk. It'll probably taste awful, but drink it up. It'll help you sleep. We'll talk some more in the morning."

But it was a long time before Fern could get to sleep.

Rose's comments had cracked the seal on a part of her soul she hadn't dared look into for a long time. It was almost as though she had lifted the lid to Pandora's box. A whole flock of demons swirled about her. Hopes and longings she had thought abandoned long ago, open wounds she had thought long healed, slights and hurts she had thought long forgotten, filled her head until she felt dizzy with confusion.

Struggle as she might, she couldn't get the lid on again. She was going to have to confront everything she had tried to avoid all these years.

And all because of Madison Randolph.

She wished Hen had shot someone in Ellsworth or Newton instead of Abilene. Then Madison wouldn't have come here. She wouldn't care whether he was unhappy, and she wouldn't have to be nice to him.

It would be a lot better if she could just go back to the farm and forget she had ever met him. Then she wouldn't have to wonder whether he really might like her, whether that moment when he held her in his arms, that thrill of excitement before he kissed her, was real or just her imagination.

It was important that she know. She hated herself for being so weak—she had a terrible premonition it would lead to all kinds of trouble—but she had to know. And as long as Rose thought there was the slightest possibility he could like her more than a one-eyed saloon girl with a squint, she would hang around.

Besides, she had two things to prove to him: that

she wanted justice as much as he did and that Hen *had* killed Troy.

Light spilled from more than a dozen Abilene saloons, gambling establishments, and hotels. Cowhands trying in just two or three wild, uninhibited nights to forget the loneliness of two months on the trail, laughed, drank, and played with desperate haste. The noise of dancing, singing, occasional shouts, and the clang of the ubiquitous piano poured into the street.

During the day, merchants tried to empty the cowboys' pockets by hawking hot baths, haircuts, and a shave, the finest in new clothes and custom-made boots, as well as the chance to sleep in a warm, dry bed. By night the saloons, gambling halls, and an assortment of soiled doves tried to relieve them of any money they might have left.

As long as their sixty or ninety dollars lasted, they lived like princes. When it was gone, they quietly left for Texas, tired and broke, but determined to do it all over again next summer.

Madison didn't enter the first saloon he reached. He kept walking until he reached the loudest and noisiest, the Bull's Head. It pleased his sense of the ironic that he should have had to pass the schoolhouse and the Baptist church to get there. It was rather symbolic of leaving civilization behind and entering an area of Texas Street where the savage passions of men were freed from their chains.

He felt a lot like a wild beast straining against the manacles of expectation. Expectation based on who he was, who he had been, and who he intended to become. All three decreed that he should return to his hotel, have a quiet drink in his room, and go to bed in the hope that tomorrow would be a better day.

But Madison had a strong streak of his father in him.

He didn't feel like a quiet evening. He wanted to do something loud and physical; he wanted to do anything that would strike at the heart of the anger and resentment that choked him. He wanted to hurl firebrands at his brothers' cold-hearted refusal to extend to him the same forgiveness they allowed everyone else.

No, he wanted to say to hell with all of it. He wanted to show them that their approval or disapproval didn't mean a thing to him.

"Give me a bottle of your best brandy," Madison said to the seamy-looking character behind the bar.

The Bull's Head Saloon was not a pretty building. It had been built of raw lumber, likely shipped in from wooded hills farther east. George said it had been put up in less than a week, clearly with more attention to haste than detail. The only attempts at decoration consisted of several posters tacked to the walls and a mirror behind the bar.

A few women sashayed among the customers, encouraging them to drink and accepting invitations to visit the rooms upstairs. Other customers sat around tables engaged in various games of chance. One man stood at the bar. He looked up when Madison ordered his drink.

The bartender placed a bottle and a glass on the counter. Madison eyed the glass with distaste. He held it up to the light. "Is there a certain number of fly specks required before people are allowed to use your glasses?" he asked, handing the glass back.

"Nobody else complains."

"Maybe Abilene should advertise for an eye doctor."

The bartender chose a new glass and wiped it

carefully before he snapped it down before Madison. The force shattered the glass.

"Probably the only clean one in the place," Madison murmured.

The now surly bartender produced another glass, which he set down with more care. Madison poured out a finger of brandy. He didn't like the color of the liquid. He didn't care for the bouquet. He hated the taste.

"Do you have any *real* brandy," he asked, "the kind you keep for the owner?"

"This is real brandy," the bartender insisted.

"Only in Kansas. Bring me something decent or find someone who can."

The bartender stepped through a door at the back and returned a moment later with a second bottle.

"See if this pleases your highness," he said.

Madison recognized the brand. "It will if you haven't tampered with the contents."

The bartender moved away to tend to another customer and Madison tasted the brandy. It was good. Some of the tension left his body. He could stay here as long as he wanted, knowing that the brandy at least would fulfill his expectations.

"You must be George Randolph's brother." His neighbor at the bar had moved closer.

"So?"

"You here to see about getting Hen out of jail?"

"So?"

"You won't get no help in this town." He took a taste of his whiskey and shuddered as the liquid burned its way down his throat. "The merchants are all for the Texans, but the farmers and land speculators are against them."

Madison took a deep swallow from his glass. He didn't know what was worse, teasing himself about Fern or listening to this hayseed ramble on about the close-held sentiments of the citizens of Abilene.

"'Course, you can't blame the farmers, not when your herds trample their fields."

"More crops are destroyed by your own people wintering over longhorns than by Texas herds," Madison told the man. "Besides, the drovers pay for the damage their herds do." He knew because he had asked. He hadn't spent all his time in Abilene running afoul of his family and Fern Sproull.

"Sure you do, but it don't make the farmers like you 'cause of it."

Obstinate people. You'd think they wouldn't care what happened to their crops as long as they got paid for them. But that was the attitude he'd seen everywhere since he got here. All temper and emotion. Nobody seemed capable of rational thinking.

That described himself as well when he was around Fern. He couldn't understand how she could get to him so easily. Usually he was an even-tempered man not prone to senseless outbursts.

"You think your brother did it?"

"Would I be here if I did?"

"Sure. Blood's thicker than water."

"Not always," Madison said, remembering George's chilly greeting and Hen's open animosity.

"Who do you think done it?"

Madison looked deep into his glass. He had no idea who had killed Troy, and he wasn't likely to find out as long as the killer thought he was safe. Even if he could prove that Hen had been elsewhere the night of the murder, the killer only had to remain quiet and no one would ever discover his identity. Something had to be done to cause him to make a mistake, and maybe this talkative hayseed was just the person to make the murderer believe that his secret was no longer safe.

"Can you keep this close to your vest?" Madison asked in a conspiratorial tone.

"Won't utter a peep," the man assured him, his eyes alive with curiosity.

Chapter Eight

"I've been looking around the Connor farm, and things don't add up the way they're supposed to," Madison confided. "I think somebody killed Troy Sproull somewhere else, took his body to the Connor place, and then tried to blame it on Hen."

The man's eyes grew wide with surprise. "Who?"

"That's what I've got to find out. Do you know anybody who wanted Troy Sproull dead?"

The man's sharp bark of laughter caused several heads to turn. "Just about everybody in Dickinson County," he said, dropping his voice into a whisper. "Troy was real mean, and he'd cheat his mother. Nobody liked him. Not even his uncle."

Great. I've got a murder victim the whole state of Kansas wanted to see dead.

"Baker Sproull fired him sometime back in the spring. Troy swore he'd kill him for it, but nobody took him serious. He was always swearing to kill somebody. Can't think of anybody who liked him."

"Fern Sproull thinks he was some kind of saint."

"He weren't too nice to her either, but she always did take his part. Never could figure it."

Neither could Madison. He tried to pay attention as the man rambled on, relating one disreputable incident from Troy's past after another, adding name after name to the list of people who had a grievance against him, but he found nothing more than petty irritations. And no one seemed to have a reason to try to blame the murder on Hen.

Instead of listening, Madison found himself wondering why anyone as rigidly moral as Fern Sproull would champion a man who apparently had no morals at all.

" . . . hated Buzz Carleton. They bristled at the sight of each other . . ."

Why did Fern like her cousin so much? Or maybe more accurately, why did she dislike Hen, or the Randolphs, or Texans, so much she wanted to see Hen hang whether he was guilty or not?

" . . . surprised when he went to work for Sam Belton. Never figured Troy to be a draw for farmers looking to buy land. More likely to shoot them for trying to fence in the range . . ."

Two men came up to the bar, a cross between farmers and cowhands, if Madison was to judge by the look of them. He moved over to give them room.

"If you need to know anything about anybody else, you just ask me," Madison's companion continued. "I was here when the buffalo still crowded the plains. Ain't nobody I don't know something about."

"Who're you talking to, Amos?" one of the newcomers asked.

"This here's George Randolph's brother," Amos said rather proudly.

"You're drunk," the man replied. "Hen Randolph is in jail."

"This ain't Hen. It's another brother."

"I know them Randolphs breed like rabbits, but the rest of them is still in Texas."

"I'm Madison Randolph," Madison said, "and any resemblance I may have to a rabbit is probably due to the quality of whiskey in this establishment."

"This is Reed Landusky," Amos informed Madison. "He owns a place next to Baker Sproull. He and Pike sometimes work for Fern."

Madison turned back to Reed only to find him in whispered conversation with Pike.

"That's got to be him, I tell you," the medium-sized dirty blond was saying to Reed. "It couldn't be nobody else."

"Fern wouldn't go off with nobody who looks like a squirrel."

"You seem to be on terms with an unusual number of rodents," Madison observed.

"Are you the dude who brung Fern back so banged and bruised she can't ride?"

"I'm the *dude* who brought her back to town after she fell off her horse," Madison said.

"Fern never fell off no horse," Pike stated emphatically. "She rides like she was born on one."

"Perhaps she was reborn since you saw her," Madison said.

"A smart one, are you?"

"I have it on good authority that that has been one of my failings since childhood."

He ought to leave before he said something that would cause trouble. The more he drank, the sharper his tongue became.

He got that from his father.

But a stubborn streak wouldn't let Madison stir from the spot. It was unthinkable he should run from anybody. If Reed and Pike wanted trouble, they could have it.

He got that from his father, too, and neither Harvard nor Boston had been able to take it out of him. He sometimes wondered if it ever could.

"Maybe you thought there was nothing wrong with having a little fun with the local females while you were here," Reed said.

Madison was stunned that any stranger would presume to pass public judgment on his morals, but he was infuriated they would so thoughtlessly include Fern in their loose talk.

"I'm not familiar with local customs, but it's not my habit to abduct innocent females to satisfy my carnal appetites. Nor, I'm certain, is Miss Sproull in the habit of allowing herself to be abducted."

Reed pushed up against Madison, jostling his hand, causing him to spill his brandy.

"You're about to find out one custom we got hereabouts."

"What's that?" Madison inquired. "Rudeness or clumsiness?"

"We don't take kindly to fancy swells hitting on our women," Reed said, crowding Madison a little more. Pike positioned himself on the other side.

Madison was hemmed in.

He felt an upsurge of energy, a feeling almost of euphoria rising in him. In Boston he would have had to control his anger and work it out in the boxing ring. Here there was no such restraint. He felt his muscles gather, his grip tighten on his glass. He was ready to fight.

"Miss Sproull suffered no harm at my hands. She fell when her horse stumbled. I brought her to town because her father was away from home."

"The last dude who tried something like that was carried out of here on his back," Reed said.

"I have every intention of walking," Madison said. He could feel anticipation in every limb. He wanted the fight. He wanted it now.

Reed grabbed a handful of Madison's shirt. "I'm going to wipe the floor with you. When I get through there won't be enough for your brother to sweep up."

Madison felt the dead calm he always felt before a boxing match. His concentration narrowed until nothing existed for him except Reed. "Remove your hand, or I shall remove it for you."

"You remove it for me," Reed said, laughing. "Did you hear that, Pike? He's going to remove it for me. And how do you propose to do that?"

"Like this."

Reed looked mystified when Madison merely grasped the wrist of the hand holding Madison's shirt. But the moment Madison found the exact pressure point he was seeking and his fingers closed in a viselike grip, Reed turned dead white. The veins stood out on his neck as he struggled to keep his hold, but it was useless. His hand popped open like a lock when the key is turned. The men in the saloon stared at him in disbelief.

"Now I would appreciate it if you would drink your whiskey and leave," Madison said, smoothing his shirt.

"I'm going to kill you," Reed exploded.

"Allow me to remove my coat first," Madison said.

"It don't matter what you're wearing. You're going to be dead."

"He's the best fighter in town," Amos warned as Madison took off his coat, folded it with great care, and placed it on the bar. "He'll murder you."

"You ain't doing it in here," the bartender objected.

"Aw, let him, Ben," one of the customers asked. "He won't last long, and we ain't had no fun in days."

"You'll pay for anything you break."

"We'll take it out of his pockets before we throw him into the street."

Madison could feel exhilaration in every part of his body. This must have been the way his father felt when he was about to fight. No fear, no worry, just barely-contained anticipation.

"Who wants to go first?" Madison asked.

"Don't make no difference," Amos predicted gloomily. "Either one of 'em will kill you."

"He's mine," Reed said, coming at Madison with a rush.

"I want every man in this room to understand that Miss Sproull received no harm at my hands," Madison announced to the spectators as he easily danced away from Reed. "And that I intend to batter this man's face in for impugning her reputation."

"Stand still and fight," Reed shouted. He charged Madison again.

The series of blows that landed on Reed's chin came with blinding rapidity. Reed tried to overpower Madison with his greater size and strength, but he couldn't pin him down. Pike started to enter the fray when it became clear that Reed was getting the worst of it, but the bartender held him back with a shotgun pointed at his belly.

"He asked for it. Now you let him get all he can stand."

He didn't stand long. Less than two minutes later Reed was on the floor.

"What did you do to him?" Pike demanded. "You musta done something. You couldn't never beat Reed in a fair fight."

"I didn't do anything except apply some scientific

knowledge of boxing," Madison told him. "I went through three years at Harvard without defeat."

"You won't go much longer," Pike said, and reached for his gun.

Faster than the eye could follow, Madison charged Pike and they both went down in a heap. The sound of the gun discharging in the close confines of the saloon reverberated in everyone's ears, and Pike slumped to the floor. Madison got to his feet. The gun slid from Pike's slackened grip.

"You killed him," the bartender said, swinging his shotgun toward Madison. "You jumped him and killed him."

"It has apparently escaped your notice that I'm not armed."

"You killed him with his own gun," one of the onlookers shouted.

"Let's lynch him!"

The chorus of assent was deafening.

"Anybody got a rope?"

"I got one outside on my saddle."

"Get it. We'll hang him from the rafter."

Moving more quickly than anyone expected, Madison struck down the bartender's shotgun and leaped over the bar. Before the man could collect himself, Madison rendered him helpless with a powerful blow to the throat. About the time several men in the saloon produced guns they shouldn't have had, they found themselves facing an irate Madison Randolph with a loaded shotgun pointed into their midst.

The hands relaxed.

"Now let's get a few things straight," Madison said, panting slightly from his exertion. "I didn't start this fight. I don't even know these men. I didn't kill anybody. I don't even own a gun."

"For an unarmed man, you sure can cause a

mortal lot of trouble." The unexpected voice came from the doorway of the saloon. It was Marshal "Wild Bill" Hickok. Hickok walked forward until he came to the two men on the floor. Reed was stirring. Pike wasn't. "You expect me to believe you outfought Reed and wrestled Pike to the ground, overpowered Ben, and held a lynch mob at bay, all without a weapon?"

"He did, Marshal. I saw it," Amos insisted. "It was just like he said. Reed started the trouble."

"Can any of you say different?" the marshal asked.

"We didn't pay no attention until they started fighting," one man said, "but we sure saw him jump Pike and shoot him dead."

"Pike shot himself with his own gun," Madison said. "I only took this shotgun to keep from dancing at the end of a rope."

"I guess you'll have to come with me until I sort this out," Hickok said.

"Certainly," Madison said. He laid down the shotgun, making sure to place it beyond the bartender's reach. Rather than force his way though the crowd at either end of the bar, he vaulted it once again, landing practically at Hickok's side.

"A nimble sort, aren't you?"

Madison picked up his coat, dusted it off, and put it on. "I'll be old and stiff soon enough," he said.

"True. Well, come along. I got a card game to finish. I can't be standing here jawing all night."

"You just going to let him go?" someone asked.

"Seems to me like these Randolphs can do anything they want," said another.

Hickok turned back to the mob. "I'm putting him in jail. But he ain't going to stay there long unless you can show me cause." He turned his back on the angry men and walked out into the street. "All

I need now is for Monty to come galloping into town," he complained to Madison as they crossed the street, "shouting at the top of his lungs like the crazy fool he is."

"He won't come on my account."

"It won't matter why he comes. He'll be trouble when he gets here."

But it did matter to Madison. It mattered a lot.

Madison sat up in his cell when he heard the jail door open and someone come in. He looked at his watch. Twenty-eight minutes had passed. He didn't know how rapidly news traveled in Kansas, but he figured that was pretty quick considering it was the middle of the night. They would have had to wake George, get him out of bed, and give him time to dress.

And he knew it would be George who had come. At least he cared. Hen had turned his back when Hickok brought Madison in. He hadn't looked at him or spoken to him since.

He wondered if Fern would come.

Merciful God! He wanted to see Fern, that fire-breathing, pants-wearing, Randolph-hating rebel against everything soft and alluring in the female sex. He had to be out of his mind. Wanting to see Fern was like sticking his head into a lion's mouth. People might admire his courage, but they wouldn't think much of his intelligence.

There must be something attractive about her, something you like. You can't get her out of your mind.

There was, and it wasn't merely her body, though he couldn't get that out of his mind either. Both of them were fighting battles neither could win, battles they didn't even want to win. Yet they had to fight, or they would lose everything.

Fern

He hadn't known how important that bond was—he'd barely just recognized it—until she'd destroyed it by getting Reed and Pike to attack him. There could be no other reason for him to be set upon by strangers. She wanted him out of town and they worked for her father—the connection seemed obvious to him. He wondered if she'd paid them. The thought was enough to set his blood boiling.

How could he have been so mistaken in her character?

There was nothing to do now but put her out of his mind. It wouldn't be too difficult to overcome the physical attraction, he'd done that before, but the feeling of having found a kindred spirit wasn't going to be so easy to banish.

Even if she hadn't pulled such a despicable trick, he wouldn't have wanted her to see him now, not looking as he did. He needed a bath and a change of clothes. He looked like somebody from Kansas. Oddly enough, his being in jail didn't bother him in the least, though it was bound to upset George.

"You got here faster than I expected," Madison said when George came to a halt outside the cell. The tone of his voice was slightly caustic.

"You got yourself thrown in jail just to see how fast I could get out of bed?"

"No, but I knew you would come."

"You've upset Rose."

"I'm sorry about Rose."

"But you're not sorry about me?"

"Should I be?"

"Why did you come back, Madison?"

Madison gripped the bars in his hands. "Don't you mean to ask *Why did you leave?*" he growled. "That's the question you want answered."

"I know why you left."

"No, you don't," Madison answered, savagely

121

angry. "I thought you would. I thought you of all people would understand, but you don't have the vaguest idea."

"Then tell me."

"Why?" Madison said, stepping back from the bars. "I left. That's all that matters."

"I'd like to think that your coming back is all that matters."

Good old George. Just when you thought you could get really mad at him, he cut the ground out from under you. He was too damned stiff and full of prickles to like, but he loved you so much you ended up forgiving him no matter what he said.

"I was dying just as surely as Ma was dying, but nobody could see it. Nobody understood. Nobody cared."

"The twins needed you."

The twins needed him! That was a laugh. The twins never needed anybody, especially him. But how could George understand that? All he could see was two fourteen-year-olds left to run a ranch on their own. He would never understand that they were better suited to the job at twelve than he had been at twenty. Or was now at twenty-six.

"You ask Hen if he wanted me there," Madison said. "I know I'm not easy to like, but I tried to do my part. I got to know every miserable inch of that ranch. If you dropped me anywhere within ten miles of the house, I could be home inside an hour. But no matter what I did, it wasn't good enough for them. Monty even told me to stay home with the babies and leave the real work to them."

"Monty doesn't mean half of what he says."

"He sounded just like Pa," Madison continued, recollection strong in him now. *"Why can't you be like George or Frank or Joe's boys?* Pa used to say. *Why do you have to embarrass me by spending all your time with your nose in a book or trying to show everybody how smart you are?* Do you know Pa told me he had the money to pay for my schooling? He thought I was getting too big for my britches, so he decided to let the school send me home. He figured the disgrace of being kicked out would bring me down a peg."

It had been the most searing experience of his life. He could still feel the humiliation, the rage that clouded his brain for weeks after he returned home. His mother never blamed or chided him. Worse, she pleaded with him to try to understand his father, to strive to be the kind of son he wanted.

George was the only reason he hadn't run away right then. But now he realized that for George no selfish consideration came before duty.

"I had to get away to find out who I was. Pa was suffocating me. The ranch was suffocating me."

"Going home did that for me. Showed me who I was."

"We're not all the same, George. Maybe I could come back now without losing myself, but I won't if you don't want me."

"You never told me where you went, what you did."

It seemed like such old news now. Hardly worth telling. "A few months before Ma died, I got a letter from Freddy. His father offered to send me to Harvard and give me a place in his firm. It was everything I'd always wanted. I thought of writing you, but I knew there was no point."

"But how could you leave the boys in the middle of a war?"

"Damn the war! Do you have any idea how sick I am of hearing about it?"

"Didn't you understand what we were fighting for?"

"Of course, I understood. I'm the bookish one, remember. You wanted the right to secede so every time somebody got mad at somebody else they could go off and start their own country. That's a stupid way to run a government, and I didn't believe in it. Certainly not enough to die for it."

"Don't ever say that to Jeff."

"I don't expect I'll have anything to say to any of you again."

"Are you leaving?"

"No!" It was almost a shout. "I came here to prove that Hen didn't kill that man, and I mean to do it. Not you, not Hen, and certainly not that Delilah in sheepskin is going to stop me. When I've done that I'll go back to Boston."

"Then why did you come? You could have hired a lawyer in St. Louis and saved yourself a lot of trouble."

"Dammit to hell, George. Can't you give me any credit? Do you think I could know that Hen was about to hang and send somebody else?"

"But you left them in Texas."

"Because I knew they didn't need me!" Madison shouted. "They didn't want me. Because if I didn't get out of there, I would have gone crazy."

"I can't understand that."

"You used to," Madison said, sitting down. Some of his passion ebbed from him. "You used to be the only person who did."

"You were different then."

"No, only unsure of myself."

"You, unsure!"

"Don't sneer. Not everybody had your self-confidence. Tom Bland wasn't forever telling me how wonderful I was. I only had my brain and a sharp tongue, something nobody appreciated except Freddy and a few teachers. And you, I thought. I can remember you telling me to wait, not to be discouraged. But we moved to Texas and then the war came. When Ma died, I had to leave. I knew if Pa came back before I left, I'd be there for the rest of my life."

"And what's so damned bad about the ranch?" It was Hen who spoke. Finally.

"I don't know if I can explain it. I just knew that everything I needed to survive was somewhere else."

"George came back," Hen said.

"So did I," Madison said. "But apparently he used up all the welcome."

"That's not it," Hen said. "George left to fight the war."

"I left to fight for my life," Madison said. "I don't know why I thought you might understand that, but I did."

"I might have if I hadn't come so close to dying," Hen said.

"Before I left," Madison said through gritted teeth. "Admit I didn't leave until I'd helped drive out that nest of rustlers. I was the one who got shot that day, or have you forgotten the bullet Ma dug out of me? A bullet that could have killed you if I had stayed at home like you and Monty wanted."

"I don't suppose it'll do us any good to keep dredging up the past," George said. "What we need to do now is try to start over again."

Start over. Was that why he had come to Kansas? Had he been waiting all these years for a chance to go back on his own terms? Maybe. He wasn't sure, but he was tired of looking for answers. They didn't seem to make any difference.

"There's nothing to start over," Madison said. "I could never fit in here. And you don't want me. Deep down inside, you still don't trust me."

George stared hard at his brother. "Getting away from Texas wasn't the only reason you left, was it?"

"No. I was running away from having the only people I loved hurt me. I was strong enough to take all the distrust and anger that strangers could dish out, but I wasn't strong enough to take it from my family. Looks like I'm still not."

Fern hurried along the street, a basket of food on her arm. Every step brought on shooting pains, but that didn't matter. Along with her breakfast, Mrs. Abbott had brought the news that Madison Randolph was in jail for killing Pike Carroll.

Something was wrong. Madison wouldn't kill Pike. They didn't even know each other. They shouldn't have been in the same place. Where was Reed Landusky? If anybody was going to cause trouble, it was Reed.

"Miss Sproull."

No one called her Miss Sproull, not even Amos Rutter, whose voice she recognized coming from a narrow alley between the Bull's Head and Old Fruit Saloons.

"What is it, Amos?"

"You going to the jail 'cause of that new Randolph killing Pike?"

"Yes."

"There's a few things you'd better know before you do."

"I'm listening."

"I'd appreciate it if you'd step over here. There's some people who might not want me telling you."

Fern felt a shiver of apprehension, but she stepped into the alley without hesitation.

When a little while later she emerged from the shadows between the buildings and headed toward the jail, her steps had lost their former urgency. Her emotions were in a terrible tangle. It didn't surprise her to know that Madison had neither started the fight nor killed Pike—she hadn't believed it when Mrs. Abbott told her—but it stunned her to learn that Madison had fought the two men to save her reputation.

Some people might argue that Madison had been trying to protect his own character, but Fern knew better. No man that arrogant would care what a few farmhands and cowboys thought about him.

He had fought for her.

No one had ever done that. She'd had no way of knowing it would make her feel so wonderful. If she hadn't been in such pain, she would have run the rest of the way.

But along with the euphoria came disgust that she could be so easily flattered, that her objections to the way Madison had treated her, and what he was trying to do, could be so easily swayed by a little attention. Okay, so fighting Reed and Pike was more than a little thing, but she was still a foolish, fickle female to think that Madison would feel any different about her, or the things that really mattered.

It was fine to be upset about his being in jail. It was okay not to want him to hang when he was trying to defend her honor. But he had been fighting for a principle. Madison was big on principle. It was just people he had trouble with.

By the time she reached the jail, she didn't feel quite so jaunty. Deputy Tom Carson was sitting outside.

"I hear you have Madison Randolph locked up for killing Pike," she said.

"He's not dead yet," Tom said. "We're keeping him till we find out if he's going to make it."

127

"But Mr. Randolph wasn't wearing a gun. Pike was shot with his own gun."

"Folks don't agree on what happened," Tom said. "Some say Randolph took Pike's gun and shot him in cold blood."

"But why would he do that? He doesn't even know Pike."

"Beats me, but then I don't try to understand these Texans."

Fern started to tell him Madison came from Boston, not Texas, but decided she was wasting her time. "Where is he?"

"Inside, but you can't see him."

"Try and stop me," Fern said as she strode past.

Chapter Nine

"Now see here, Fern, it ain't fair you being a man most of the time and a girl when it suits you," Tom said, following her.

"I'd be a man all the time if I had the choice." She shoved him back outside and closed the door.

She felt a little nervous about facing Madison, but being back in her pants and vest gave her more confidence. She had felt terribly vulnerable in Rose's nightgown, especially knowing that Madison had undressed her. She wondered how much of her he had touched. Better she didn't know. Just thinking about it made her hot all over. No man had touched her since that terrible night eight years ago.

He was in the first cell she came to. He jumped to his feet when he saw her, stopping her in her tracks with his coldly furious gaze.

"Have you come to gloat, or are you here to make sure I hang next to Hen?"

The vehemence of his words shocked Fern. It didn't surprise her that he was embarrassed for her to see him in jail, but it never occurred to her that he would think she wanted to see him hang. That hurt almost as much as the pain in her chest.

After what you've said about his brother, how would he know that?

Didn't he know she only felt that way because she wanted to see Troy's killer punished? She didn't dislike the Randolphs, and she didn't dislike him, at least not any more. It was his reason for being in Abilene that she hated.

"I was worried. I knew you couldn't kill Pike." She held up the basket. "I brought you some breakfast."

"You ought to be a happy woman today," Madison said, ignoring the proffered food. "Two Randolph brothers in jail and not likely to get out soon. Now if you can just get George to do something foolish— but that won't be easy because George is not a foolish man—you can have all three of us locked away. But if you plan to hang us, you're going to need a lot of ropes. There are more Randolphs where we came from."

"They're not going to hang you," Fern said. "Amos said it wasn't your fault."

Madison paced his cell like a caged animal, his anger curbed and dangerous. "This is a Randolph you're talking about, a dude, a fancy Eastern lawyer trying to circumvent justice, a Boston snob who looks down his nose at anybody not born and bred in the original thirteen. You know it's my fault."

"Madison, do you think it's fair to—" Hen interrupted.

"I'm just repeating the things she said to me," Madison said, "with an occasional contribution from you and George. I don't want her to think

I'm in very good standing with anybody."

"Amos told me everything that happened," Fern said.

"And you believed him? I'm disappointed."

"I know I haven't been very nice to you, but I never thought anybody would blame you for what happened to me. I certainly never expected Reed to imply that . . . to say . . . I . . ."

Fern was so upset she could hardly keep her voice under control.

"You expect me to believe that fight wasn't your idea, that two people who'd never seen me before just walked up and picked a fight?"

"You can't really believe I'd set somebody on you."

"Why not? It would have been a convenient way to get rid of me, settle Hen's hash, and make sure George never brought any more cows to Abilene. A Randolph-free town. I thought that's what you wanted."

He wasn't listening to a word she said. He was convinced she had paid Reed and Pike to attack him, and nothing she said seemed able to punch through his anger.

"You're twisting what I said."

"Tell me what you said."

What had she said? A lot of things she regretted now.

"I said a lot of things I shouldn't have," Fern shot back, "but I'd never sink low enough to ask somebody else to drive you out of town. I'd do that myself."

Madison hooked her with his fiery gaze. "After what has happened to me in the last two days, there is nothing on God's green earth that's going to get me out of this town until I've finished what I came to do. I don't know what you did or didn't do.

I don't care what you meant or didn't mean. I didn't shoot Pike Carroll, and Hen didn't kill your cousin. And before I'm done, every person in this town is going to know it."

"I didn't—"

"Now you'd better get back to Mrs. Abbott's. I've got some sleep to catch up on. After your fall yesterday, you've got no business being out of bed. You must be hurting like hell."

She looked at the food she had brought and felt like an idiot. He wouldn't eat it. He'd probably think she had poisoned it.

She was glad that anger helped numb the pain. She didn't want him to know what it cost her to come see him; she wouldn't give him the pleasure of feeling sorry for her. She wanted to be able to hate him with a clear conscience.

"I don't know why I bothered to come," Fern said. "You are incapable of understanding human kindness."

"I don't think I'm incapable," Madison said, appearing to give the idea serious thought, "but after being met at the train with verbal pitchforks, it's a little difficult to believe you've developed a kindly interest in my welfare."

"You haven't changed a bit," Fern replied.

"Of course I haven't. I'm the same person who left Boston to defend his brother, who took you to Rose when you refused to see a doctor, and who tried to keep himself from being murdered by your henchmen. It's your perception of me that keeps changing."

"That was my mistake," Fern declared, throwing the food down on a table outside his cell. "You're everything I thought from the very beginning." She spun on her heel and headed toward the door.

"I'm so glad to hear that," Madison called after

her. "I hate to disappoint people."

The slamming door shook the frame building.

"If that's a sample of how you behave in Boston, I bet you have all the dowagers clamoring to invite you to tea," Hen said sarcastically.

"Actually they do. As strange as it may seem, I'm thought to be a very charming fellow—friendly, cheerful, amusing, always to be depended upon to do the right thing. Something must have happened when I crossed the Mississippi."

He had scored a clear victory, he had foiled Fern's every attempt to feel sorry for him, but it was a sour triumph. He had no trouble controlling his temper in Boston. Why couldn't he do it here? He had a reputation for being able to talk anybody into anything, but here he couldn't open his mouth without making everybody furious with him.

The basket of food leveled its silent condemnation.

Last night he had been hoping Fern would come to see him. Today she'd come, and he had done everything in his power to drive her away. What was it about Fern, this town, his family that caused him to act completely unlike himself? His teachers had always told him he could solve any problem with his mind. Well, it wasn't working.

"Nobody told me the fight was over Fern Sproull," Hen said. "I hope you get me out of jail soon. This is one courtship I don't want to miss."

"Go to hell!" Madison growled.

"You had no business out of bed," Rose scolded as she settled the nightgown over Fern's head and tucked her in. "I wouldn't be surprised if you have to stay in an extra day."

"I hate him," Fern fumed. "He's the most stubborn, hateful, sarcastic, narrow-minded man I've ever met. He has no concept of human kindness, not in himself or in anyone else."

"He has no proper manners, either," Mrs. Abbott put in, unwilling to forget Madison's strong-arming his way past her.

"I don't see how he can be your husband's brother," Fern said to Rose. "George never says a cross word to me, even though he knows I think Hen killed Troy. But Madison . . ."

Words failed her, but they didn't fail Mrs. Abbott.

"Mr. Randolph is a true gentleman," she said. "And he's ever so kind to my Ed, the poor fatherless boy."

"Madison has been under considerable strain since he got here," Rose said. "Perhaps this is not his typical behavior."

"I should think not," Mrs. Abbott stated. "It would give me a very strange notion of Boston society."

"I don't know how he usually behaves, and I don't want to know," Fern fumed, ignoring Mrs. Abbott's pretensions. "I just want him to go back to Boston as soon as they let him out of jail. He despises everything here, and I'm sure we don't think any more of him."

"I don't," Mrs. Abbott said, casting her lot firmly against Madison. "You should exercise great care to keep him away from your little boy," she said to Rose. "It would be a terrible shame if he was to corrupt that darling, precious child."

"If William Henry can survive the influence of his other uncles, not to mention about a dozen very rough cowhands, he'll have nothing to fear from Madison," Rose answered rather sharply. "Now Miss Sproull could use some more breakfast. She didn't eat anything earlier. She'll never get well that way."

"I should say not," Mrs. Abbott echoed. "I'll be right in with it."

"Take your time," Rose said. "I want her to be more calm before she puts anything in her stomach."

"Very wise," Mrs. Abbott agreed. "You can never be too careful of a delicate stomach."

"I don't have a delicate stomach," Fern stated the moment the door closed behind Mrs. Abbott. "In fact, my father says I have no delicacy at all."

"I thought you needed to be free of Mrs. Abbott for a while. I know I do."

Fern smiled. "She is a bit overpowering."

"She's convinced that everyone she likes is kind and generous. If she doesn't like you . . . well, you know what she said about Madison."

"In his case it's deserved."

Rose sat down on the end of the bed. She spent so long studying her, Fern started to feel uncomfortable.

"Do you really want to understand Madison?" Rose asked. Her gaze was particularly penetrating. "Answer me truthfully. Not for my sake, but for his. And possibly yours."

"I g-guess so," Fern admitted reluctantly, unsure of what Rose was getting at. "I had started to think he might be different from the other men I've known. But after this morning," she said, her anger flowering again as she remembered his words, "I'm sure I was wrong."

"I've seen less of Madison than you have," Rose began, "but I know a little of his history. However, it's quite painful. I would hate to think you might use it against him."

"I'd never do that," Fern said, unable to understand why Rose seemed to have the same reservations about her as Madison did. "Contrary to his beliefs, not everyone in Kansas is insensitive."

"Madison had a very difficult time growing up,"

Rose began, apparently deciding to ignore Fern's last charge. "None of the boys learned how to love or trust anyone."

"Why?"

"As best as I can determine, they had a brutal, abusive drunk for a father and an ineffectual, weak-willed mother. During the war, Madison disappeared, leaving the twins to run the ranch by themselves. His brothers never forgave him."

"But he came back to help Hen. Doesn't that make a difference?"

"Apparently not. Even George, and he's as fair a man as I know, can't quite forget."

"Didn't he tell them why he left?"

"He told them last night when George went to the jail."

"What did he say?"

"You'll have to ask him."

"I can't ask him a question like that."

"Maybe he'll tell you. He seems to like you."

"You wouldn't think that if you'd heard him a few minutes ago."

"For God's sake, Fern, you drove the man out of here last night in a temper after he'd ridden miles holding you in the saddle. Then he goes to a saloon and your hired hands pick a fight and try to kill him. When he tries to defend himself, and your reputation I might add, they throw him in jail. What do you expect of him? He's not a saint, but he'd need the faith of one to believe you weren't behind it."

"But I wouldn't do anything like that."

"How's he to know that? By your own admission, you met him at the train with threats to run him out of town. I can't speak for Madison, but it would look to me like those men were trying to help you keep your promise."

Fern

Fern was horrified. She hadn't meant for Madison to take her anger personally. She was fighting to see justice done. It had nothing to do with Madison himself. She would have been furious at any lawyer the Randolphs hired.

But hadn't she taken his words as a personal attack on her? Maybe those words had no more to do with her than hers had to do with him. Maybe he was just reacting as he would to anyone who treated him as she had.

"Not that his brothers have been much better," Rose added. "I had a good deal to say to Hen and George last night. I hope it has some effect, but I don't know. Some of this family's wounds go so deep, nothing can heal them."

"Do you really think he believes I hate him?" Fern asked.

"I don't see how he can think anything else. I was very doubtful myself."

"But I don't," Fern protested. "I don't even hate Hen, and he killed Troy."

The friendliness left Rose's expression and her voice turned hard. "As long as there is no eyewitness to Troy's murder, I think you should at least give Hen the benefit of the doubt. Madison, George, and I all agree that Hen couldn't have killed Tory. That ought to count for something."

It was easy to see that however much Rose might sympathize with Fern, her loyalties were unquestionably with her husband's family.

"But somebody killed him, and the only evidence points to Hen."

"What did Madison find yesterday?"

In the aftermath of her fall, Fern had forgotten that Madison had raised some doubts in her mind.

"Madison thinks someone else killed Troy, carried

his body to the Connor place, and tried to blame it on Hen."

"Did he tell you why?"

"He said the body shouldn't have been stiff only an hour after the murder, and he thinks it was too dark inside the soddy for the murder to have been done there."

"That seems reasonable."

"But why would anybody here want to kill Troy? Everybody has known him for years."

"I know nothing about your cousin," Rose said. "Just don't dismiss Madison's ideas because you're mad at him. You may not be able to believe in the integrity of the family as I do, but you ought to be able to respect his intelligence."

The door opened to admit Mrs. Abbott carrying a tray loaded with pots, plates, and cups.

"Your breakfast," she chirped. "And you're to eat every bite while it's hot. It'll make you feel better."

But Fern hardly tasted any of the food she put in her mouth, or heard any of Mrs. Abbott's endless chatter as she tidied the room for the second time that morning. Her head was filled with Rose's words.

Suppose Troy had been killed by somebody else. The thought sent chills down her spine. It could be almost anybody. She could have talked to his killer a half dozen times since his death.

Even her own father.

Of course, her father wouldn't kill anybody, but Madison felt the same way about his brother. If she was going to accept her father's innocence on faith, she had to at least consider the possibility of Hen's innocence. But the more she thought, the more possibilities she found to consider. The only easy thing was to hold to her conviction that Hen was guilty.

Fern

But she couldn't. Madison had shaken her confidence in Hen's guilt.

And just about everything else.

Madison remained in jail for two days before Pike recovered sufficiently to tell the marshal what really happened.

"You're fortunate," Marshal Hickok said when he released Madison.

"Fortunate has nothing to do with it," Madison said, not the least impressed by Hickok's reputation. "You never had a case against me."

"Shame you can't say the same for your brother," Hickok replied, nettled by Madison's reply. He was used to everyone being a little afraid of him. This brash Eastern lawyer's self-assurance didn't sit well with Hickok. Come to think of it, he didn't like any of the Randolphs very much. George treated him with courtesy, but Hickok suspected it had more to do with his position than his personal merit. As for Hen Randolph, Hickok couldn't find much of anything that boy did respect. He just plain didn't care.

"If you'll take some advice—" Hickok began.

"People have been giving me advice from the moment I stepped off the train," Madison said, not bothering to look up as he prepared to leave the jail. "But it was all concerned with their own comfort, not mine." Madison put on his coat, smoothed a few wrinkles out of his pants, and emerged from the cell. "So I've decided not to listen to any more advice."

"That might not be a good idea," Hickok said.

"Leaving Boston wasn't a good idea," Madison said, "but now that I'm here, I intend to finish what I came to do."

"And what's that?" Hickok knew. Everybody in Abilene knew, but he wanted to hear Madison say it.

"I mean to find out who killed Troy Sproull. And I mean to be standing right here when my brother walks out of that cell a free man."

"Not everybody gets what he wants," Hickok said.

"I do," Madison declared, and he walked out without a backward glance.

"Your brother always been that modest?" Hickok asked Hen after Madison had gone, irritation causing him to glare angrily at the retreating figure.

Hen chuckled softly. "Don't tangle with him, Marshal. He'll tie you in knots."

"Ain't nobody done it yet," Hickok said, not without some pride.

"Maybe not, but you haven't run up against Madison before."

Madison checked his appearance to make certain that no signs remained of his stay in prison. He was about to leave for Mrs. Abbott's, and he had been cursing out loud for the last several minutes. He was going to see George and Rose. But he was also going to see Fern.

That was why he was cursing.

He knew he had to apologize for his behavior. No matter what she had said to him when he arrived in Abilene, no matter what she'd done to irritate him since, once he'd calmed down enough to think rationally, he didn't believe she had had anything to do with the attack on him. As usual, he couldn't think straight where she was involved.

Maybe it would help if they stopped fighting every time they met. She had every right to want her cousin's murderer punished, just as he had every right to want Hen cleared of the charges. She had no reason to dislike him, at least not if he stopped behaving like an arrogant hothead. If he couldn't convince *her* of Hen's innocence, how could he hope to convince a judge and a jury?

Besides, he had a job to do, and their running battle was distracting him. Every time she got him angry, he struck back. Then he'd start to feel guilty and think he needed to apologize. And that would make him angry. By then all he could think of was Fern, not Hen.

He was developing a grudging respect for her. She treated him rotten, but she took her medicine without whining and complaining. He couldn't understand why he wanted her to like him. How could he like anything about this savage land?

It seemed as if every occupant of the hotel was in the narrow passageway when he left his room. Some greeted him with a congratulatory pat on the back, some with curiosity, others with anger. It pleased him to greet them all with a beaming smile.

Maybe because he was thinking of Fern the whole time.

Why couldn't he get her out of his mind? It wasn't as if she were beautiful, rich, or had any accomplishments. She was a nobody from a squalid little town perched on the edge of nowhere.

He had to hand it to her. Nobody else could wear pants like she could.

"Good morning, Mr. Randolph," the desk clerk greeted him when he reached the lobby. "I hope the bath was to your liking."

"It'll take several more before I feel clean, but I imagine the lingering effects of incarceration are all in my mind."

"It can't be nothing like what a man of your position is used to," the clerk said.

Unctuous devil, Madison said to himself. Wonder what he's up to.

"I heard Reed and Pike forced the fight on you. Probably thought you was an easy mark."

"Apparently everyone else did, too. They seemed willing enough to enjoy the fun."

"From what I hear, you handled yourself real good. It came as a surprise to some."

"I have one sport at which I'm considered rather good," Madison said, not without a touch of pride. "Boxing."

The streets were quiet despite the number of people about. Early morning was the time of day when the solid citizens of Abilene conducted their business. Even the cowhands ambling about looked sober.

Women shopped and gossiped while their children darted from one spot to another in search of entertainment. Madison had come to understand that these women probably had to be as tough as Fern just to survive being married and raising a family in the West. It was a quality he was learning to appreciate.

Not that he would consider marrying a Western woman. She would never fit into Boston society. Besides, there were dozens of young women in Boston who would make him an excellent wife. Freddy's sister, Samantha, was exactly the kind of girl he admired. Lovely, cultured, always properly behaved and dressed. Unfortunately, he'd never found anyone of decorous behavior lively enough to interest him.

It was odd he should be thinking of marriage. Maybe seeing George and his growing family had touched off the mating instinct in him. He guessed he'd have to give it some serious thought when he got back home.

Leaving behind the business district of Abilene, Madison walked past several residences. They were small frame dwellings of mean appearance completely unlike the spacious stone or clapboard homes of New England, but at least they were better than the sod and log homes he had seen at the edge of town and scattered over the prairie.

He wondered how old Fern was. He also wondered if she'd ever wanted to be married. Even in Kansas, he imagined she'd have to wear a dress before a man would ask her to be his wife.

He wondered what she would look like properly clothed. He couldn't picture her in anything but pants and a sheepskin vest with the brim of her hat pulled down over her eyes. Not a picture, one would have supposed, to keep him awake at night.

Yet she had done exactly that.

It's nothing more than irritation, he thought. She's an irritation to look at, an annoyance to think about, and an aggravation to deal with. At that thought, he made up his mind to see her in a dress at least once before he left Abilene.

"Morning, Mr. Randolph."

"Do I know you?" Madison said, turning to face a man who spoke to him from the doorway of one of the houses.

"No, but I heard about you."

"After the other night, I imagine everybody has."

"I don't mean that. I mean about why you're here."

"I guess everybody knows that, too."

"They don't like it, neither. Lots of people like Texans as long as they're spending money, but nobody likes fancy lawyers from back East."

"So I've learned."

"They won't tell you nothing."

Madison's gaze intensified. "Do you mean you will?"

"I don't know nothing for sure, but I got a couple

of questions out looking for answers."

"I've got more than enough questions myself."

"I know somebody who might be able to answer one or two of them. You want to come inside? Some people might not be too happy to see me talking to you."

Madison was fully alert to the possibility of danger. He was unarmed. He knew he could very well step into this stranger's house and disappear into an unmarked grave somewhere on the vast prairie. Or he might find a way to prove that Hen hadn't killed Troy Sproull. To achieve one, he must chance the other.

Madison turned toward the house.

Chapter Ten

The room was plainly furnished but scrupulously clean. It seemed like such an honest room, Madison felt he could trust the man who lived in it.

"Have a seat," the man said, motioning Madison to the most comfortable chair in the room.

"I'll stand if you don't mind. I've spent too much time lying down or sitting the last two days."

That seemed to make the man uneasy, but Madison wanted information, not comfort. He was also anxious to see Fern.

"My name's Tom White," the man said, extending his hand. "I run a small freight business."

Madison took Tom's hand. "I imagine you get around."

"A bit."

"And meet a lot of different people."

"A few."

Madison curbed his impatience while Tom rolled

and lighted a cigarette. He obviously wasn't going to talk until he was ready.

"Amos tells me you got a different idea about how Troy died," Tom said. His empty eyes showed nothing. "How'd you come by it?"

"The body was stiff, so Troy had to have been killed at least eight hours earlier. And no one could have put a bullet through a man's heart in that pitch black soddy."

"Do you have any idea who the killer might be?"

"No. Do you?"

Tom shook his head.

"Then why did you bring me here?"

"A friend of mine says he saw Hen the night Troy was killed."

Madison's body tensed. "Who is your friend? How can I get in touch with him?"

"I'm not sure he'll talk to you. He may want some money first."

Madison stiffened. Maybe this man was going to try to blackmail him, to threaten to say he saw Hen at the Connor place if the Randolphs didn't pay up.

"What does he know?"

"He says your brother wasn't anywhere near that soddy when Troy was killed."

Madison's well-schooled features didn't betray his mounting excitement.

"Where did he see Hen?"

"He wouldn't say."

"Will he tell it to a judge and jury?"

"I don't know."

"I've got to talk to him."

"He may not agree to meet you. He's not a trusting man."

"Tell him I'll meet him anywhere, any time," Madison said.

Fern

"I'll do what I can. I'll let you know."

Madison turned to go. "What do you get out of this?" he asked, turning back.

"I want to know who killed Troy."

"Why?"

"I want to shake his hand. I hated the son-of-a-bitch."

"You shouldn't leave yet," Rose said. "You're still so stiff you can hardly move."

"I have to go home," Fern said. "There's nobody to do my work. Besides, there's nobody to take care of Papa."

"There's not a man alive who can't get along by himself if he has to," Rose stated. "I can't describe the condition of the house we live in when I arrived at the Circle Seven. It was enough to kill rats, but the Randolph men were thriving."

"I don't imagine they'd want to live like that again," Fern said, thinking of the meticulous care that Rose took of her family.

"Wait until you meet Monty. As long as he has a full stomach, he could live in a creek bottom and be happy."

"I don't imagine I'll meet any more Randolphs," Fern replied, thinking of the things Madison had said to her in the jail. She had tried to put the entire exchange out of her mind, without success.

"You'd like Monty. He's not like Madison."

Fern was surprised at how much Rose's comparison irritated her. She'd accused Madison of nearly every shady practice she could think of, yet now she found herself wanting to defend him. Her brain must be getting soggy.

"Take this nightgown with you," Rose said.

"I can't," Fern answered.

"Of course you can. I've got lots more. They're

about all a woman in my condition can wear."

Fern had to admit she had liked wearing the gown. It made her feel feminine even if she knew she didn't look it. It was a small vanity, like her hair and her lace chemise, but harmless as long as she remembered it was just an illusion.

"Okay, I'll take it, but I don't know when I'll wear it. If Papa sees it, he'll swear I've taken sick."

She wondered what Madison would think. A stupid question. If he wanted to see a woman in bedclothes, he would look for someone much prettier, much more feminine, much more fetching in pink.

She wondered if he had a mistress.

He was much too straightlaced to seduce a lady. If he was to satisfy his physical needs, it would have to be with a soiled dove, much as the Texas cowhands did when they reached Abilene after being on the trail for two or three months. She wondered what soiled doves in Boston were like. Probably a lot more ladylike than anybody in Abilene.

"You ought to have more than one nightgown," Rose said. "Pretty dresses, too. A woman owes it to herself to look her best as often as possible. It does wonders for the way men treat us."

It wouldn't do wonders for the way they treated her. No one in Abilene could remember seeing her in a dress, and they never would.

"There's not much call out here for women to look pretty," Fern said. "Men are more pleased if we're strong and hard workers."

"They like strong, hardworking women in Texas, too," Rose said, "but there's no reason we can't be both. Besides, I expect George to look attractive. Just because he keeps company with horses and cows is no reason to smell like one."

Fern laughed. "I'll have to tell Papa that next time

he comes in smelling like the barnyard."

"You can't use reason on them," Rose warned. "They don't understand it, for all they consider themselves rational creatures."

"Don't make me laugh. It still hurts."

"Which proves you have no business leaving. How do you plan to get home? You can't mean to ride your horse."

"I've ridden a horse more than I've walked," Fern said, trying to think where to pack the pink nightgown. She had nowhere but her saddle bags, but she didn't want it to smell like her horse by the time she got it home. Not that she planned to let anybody know she had it. It would just be nice to know that it was tucked away in the bottom of her drawer.

"That may be true, but you're in no condition to ride just yet."

"I'm much stronger than you think."

"Maybe, but I can see you wince every time you bend over."

"I'll probably keep on wincing for another week, but it won't kill me."

"Are you always this stubborn?" Rose asked, her exasperation showing.

"I'm usually worse," Fern said, trying to smile. "I'm being very polite."

"Damn your politeness. I'm more concerned about your well-being."

"I'll be just fine. I've taken much worse falls and had no one to look after me. My mother died trying to have the son Papa always wanted."

"Mine died when I was twelve, but I think my father was well satisfied with his daughter."

"So is mine, as long as I do my share of the work."

"You mean as long as you act like a son."

"It's not his fault," Fern said, not meeting Rose's gaze. "It's my choice."

"Why?" Rose asked, baffled. "You're pretty enough to have half the young men in Abilene wearing out the trail to your farm."

"Don't!" Fern said, so desperate to block out the words she almost put her hands over her ears. It had taken her years to accept the fact she wasn't pretty, that she never would be, and she didn't want anybody trying to tell her differently now. It would just set her up for someone like Madison to tear her down again.

"You may have gone through an awkward age," Rose said, "I did myself, but you aren't in one now. I don't know any woman with a more stunning figure. I've been envying it ever since you arrived. Even Mrs. Abbott noticed."

Fern could see that Rose wasn't going to give up until she discovered why she preferred to dress like a man. It was almost with relief that she saw Madison enter the room, though she wondered why her heart started to beat so fast.

"What's this Mrs. Abbott tells me about you going back home?" he asked. "You're not well enough."

Mrs. Abbott trailed in on Madison's heels. "That's what Mrs. Randolph has been telling her for the last hour, but she won't listen."

"Maybe you'll have better luck," Rose said to Madison. "She's still in a lot of pain."

The symptoms Fern was experiencing just now—light-headedness, shallow breath, and a decidedly uneasy feeling in the pit of her stomach—had nothing to do with pain.

"Judging from our last conversation," Fern said, "he's more likely to chase me from the house with a shotgun than try to keep me here."

She tried to calm her reaction to his presence, but

she couldn't act as if he were just another man when merely looking at him made her feel faint. He was freshly washed and shaved; his hair still glistened with moisture. He looked like a newly minted penny, all bright and shiny. She couldn't understand why he was still single. If she were a Boston heiress, she'd pay someone to kidnap him for her.

"This has nothing to do with my ill-chosen remarks," Madison said. "You took a terrible fall. You shouldn't even have gotten out of bed to come to the jail."

Fern wondered why men were always thinking they could put the parts of their lives into separate little boxes and deal with one box without even peeking into the others. Even cows didn't do that. If they were depressed, they'd stop giving milk. Didn't people have the same right to be all tied together in a single bundle?

"I figured that out about a minute after I entered the jail."

Madison looked chastened. In fact, if she hadn't known it was impossible, she'd have said he looked repentant.

"That's part of the reason I'm here," he said, "to apologize. I shouldn't have said those things. I didn't mean them."

Fern was stunned. She could see that the apology cost him a great effort, but she was even more surprised at the effect on her. It wasn't just that her anger dissolved; she felt weak and weepy. It was disgusting that a few kind words, a tiny vein of decency in the man, should make her feel like crying.

She wanted to be able to be in the same room with him without arguing, but she didn't want to stand here gaping at him, wondering how he could breathe with such a stiff collar, why a man who didn't care what anyone thought of him should be so meticulous in his appearance. In a town where scruffy beards, threadbare clothes, and the smell of sweat and cow dung was the norm, he took her breath away. Even though she couldn't quite accustom herself to a man smelling of scent, she found the faint aroma of shaving cream appealing.

Jerking her mind out of its rumination, Fern said, "I have to go home. I'm behind in my work."

"If you have any intention of picking up a knife and going after those poor young bulls—"

A tremulous smile appeared on Fern's lips. "I wish Reed and Pike had taken out their anger on those bulls instead of you."

"Maybe your father has taken care of it already," Rose suggested.

"Not him. The only person who ever helped me was Troy. Until Papa fired him. There's no need to look like a cat that's just been handed a bowl of cream," she said to Madison. "Papa didn't kill Troy. They just never got along. Everybody knows that."

"Then you're better off without him," Madison said. "But as for this going home today—"

"I must," Fern said. "I've trespassed on Rose's kindness too long."

"It's no bother," Rose assured her. "We'd already hired the house."

But Fern knew that Rose would offer Mrs. Abbott extra compensation. She also knew that Mrs. Abbott would ask for it if it weren't offered.

Fern bent over to pick up her saddlebags. Only through a heroic effort did she prevent her face from reflecting the agonizing pain that tore through her chest when she tried to lift it. Instinctively, her gaze cut to Madison. He saw. He knew.

She left the saddlebags in the corner.

"You're not going to ride," Madison stated. It

wasn't a question. It was a flat denial, and denials always got her back up.

"And how do you propose to stop me?"

"I'll take you out of the saddle myself if I have to."

Fern didn't know why she got so angry. Maybe it was the way he said it, as though she were a mere female and he could do anything he wanted because he was a man.

"Nobody has been able to do that yet."

"I don't imagine there are too many men with the courage to try," Madison said, his look just as formidable as she thought hers was. "You've got a right terrible snarl when you want."

"Then why isn't it working on you?"

"Because I've got an even better one." A miracle. He smiled at her. "Now if you insist upon going home, I'll drive you in a buggy."

"You don't have a buggy."

"I can rent one."

"I don't want you spending money because of me."

"I'll rent the buggy," Rose said, intervening. "But you've got to let Madison drive you."

"I'd rather not."

Madison's expression didn't change, but something between them did. It was nearly tangible. Audible. Like a door swinging shut.

"If it's that difficult for you to be around me, I'll ask Tom Everett to drive you."

"It's not that," Fern protested, upset he would think she couldn't stand to be with him. Never before had her words had the power to hurt anyone. She didn't understand why it should be happening now.

"Then what is it?" he asked.

"I don't like a fuss being made over me."

"Then stop arguing, and I'll stop making a fuss."

Fern could see that Rose had aligned herself with Madison. There was no way she could ride home alone without giving grave offense.

"Okay, hire the buggy, but if you're not back in ten minutes, I'll leave without you."

"No, you won't," Madison said. "I'm taking your horse with me."

"Madison Randolph, don't you dare take my horse," Fern said, but she was wasting her breath. Madison had already left, Mrs. Abbott following close on his heels. "He's the most infuriating man I ever met," Fern said to Rose. "I don't know how anybody can stand to be around him for as much as five minutes without being ready to scream."

"I used to feel that way about Monty," Rose said, "but he grew on me. I expect it's the same with Madison."

"The only way that man will grow on me is if you tie me down and set him on top of me," Fern said. "I wouldn't be surprised if they move Boston while he's away. If this is the way he acts all the time, they can't want him to find it again."

"You going to let that man take you home?" Mrs. Abbott asked, reentering the bedroom as soon as she had made certain that Madison was safely outside her house.

"I don't seem to have much choice," Fern said. "It would take an army to stop him."

She glanced at her saddlebags and decided to leave them on the floor. If Madison insisted upon driving her home, he could carry them.

And he would. He was such a strange combination of brusque bully and protective male.

Much to Fern's surprise, she was glad he was taking her home. She was a fool, an idiot, but she didn't care. Being with Madison made her feel completely unlike herself. None of her usual worries mattered. His opinionated, high-handed ways made her furious, but for the first time in her life somebody was showing an interest in her.

She was certain she'd live to regret going with him, but she was equally certain she'd regret it if she didn't. It was like being drunk. She knew she'd awake with a terrible headache, but she wanted to enjoy every moment of the intoxication.

"Well, if I was you, I wouldn't let him take me home," Mrs. Abbott said. "You'll be miles away if he starts to get ideas."

"He won't bother me, at least not that way," Fern said, carefully adjusting her hat over her hair. She wanted to comb her hair again, but just putting on her hat caused pain.

"You can never be sure."

"Yes, I can," Fern said. She picked up her vest and slipped into it, being careful to move her upper body as little as possible. "I don't look enough like a woman to tempt him. I'm sure he's used to the most beautiful women wearing the most beautiful gowns and living in the most beautiful houses. What could there be about me to tempt him?"

"Why don't you ask him?" Rose suggested.

"We're halfway to your house, and you haven't said more than a dozen sentences," Madison said.

"I've said enough already," Fern replied. "More than I meant to."

"You mean you've changed your mind about me?"

"Not about why you came," Fern told him. "I mean to see Troy's killer hang."

"I notice you said *Troy's killer*, not *Hen*."

"I decided it would be better if I didn't name names. There'll be plenty of time for that later."

She couldn't tell him she no longer felt a burning need to do everything she could to thwart him. Neither could she tell him she looked upon him as a temporary diversion, or that she intended to enjoy the game as long as it lasted.

"I didn't set Reed and Pike on you the other night," she said, getting to the subject she had been avoiding.

"I realize that now," Madison said. He was quiet a few moments. "I guess I said some pretty rough things."

"No worse than I said."

"According to George, I should have been incarcerated for that alone."

"George is a gentleman. I doubt he would understand a person of your temperament."

Madison practically shouted with laughter. "I have to keep reminding myself you don't know my family very well."

His unexpected reaction surprised her. "You can't deny that George *is* a gentleman," Fern said.

"And I'm not," Madison answered, still laughing. "Something even my fancy education and expensive clothes can't disguise."

"I didn't say that."

"But you meant it."

"I didn't say it."

"Point taken. Since you're likely to be seeing more of the Randolph men over the coming weeks, at least three of them, let me offer you a piece of advice. We may all look different on the outside, we may act different, but inside we're very much like. No one alive, not even Hen, would be more ruthless than George if anything threatened his family. No one, including George, can be more truly understanding than Hen. But all of us are the sons of our father, and there was more evil in that man than in the entire state of Kansas."

Fern stared at him.

"When you look at George and Hen and me, you're looking at three faces of the same man."

"But you're nothing alike."

"It just seems that way. You'll never really understand us if you try to separate us."

That frightened Fern. If what he said was true, she didn't know anything about him at all. It made her uneasy, as if there might be someone different sitting beside her the very next minute.

She remembered the gentleness of his kiss. He might have kissed her against her will, but it hadn't felt like it.

She'd like it if he acted like George, but it made her uneasy to think he could be like Hen. She'd only met Hen once, but she found him totally lacking in emotion, a killer who felt nothing, who regretted nothing, who probably didn't give his victims a second thought.

It gave her cold shivers to think that Madison could be the same way.

"Tell me what you do back East," she said.

"You wouldn't be interested."

"Maybe not, but I won't know until you tell me." At least he hadn't said she wouldn't understand.

"I'm a lawyer. I help businesses find ways to use the law to make money."

"But that's nothing at all like trying to find out who killed Troy."

"It's close enough. Besides, I'm the only lawyer in the family."

"Doesn't your brother have the money to hire a lawyer?"

"So far George has done me the courtesy to think I don't need any help."

"Tell me more about your work," Fern said, reminding herself that she wanted to steer away from anything to do with his family or Troy's death.

But while Madison explained what he did, Fern found herself wondering about the kind of women he met, the kind of women he liked, and how he behaved when he was with them. Troy had been to Chicago and New Orleans. He had told her about the fabulous mansions, the wild parties, the women that rich men sought out when they wanted to have a little fun.

She couldn't help but wonder what it would be like to live in that world, even for a short time. She couldn't imagine being able to sleep as long as she liked, having a maid bring her a breakfast of exotic foods she could only imagine, another maid to dress her in gowns worth more than her father's whole farm, having dozens of handsome men begging to talk to her, walk with her, dance with her, sit next to her, or being ready to lay down their lives for a flower from her hair, a handkerchief, or a stolen kiss.

It seemed a fairy-tale world, one much too enchanted to exist, even for the beautiful, rich, and overindulged women who occupied Madison's universe. Even the richest and most spoiled beauties must have to do some work.

But she had the uneasy suspicion that they didn't, that the world Madison had inhabited before he came to Abilene was so far removed from her experience, she would be totally lost if she suddenly found herself transported there.

Which would serve you right if you were to do anything so stupid as go to Boston.

Fern pulled herself out of her daydream. She would never go to Boston or any place like that. She had been born in Kansas, and she expected to spend the rest of her life here.

"That's pretty much it," Madison concluded. "Not very much to get excited about."

Especially when you haven't heard a tithe of what he's said. You'll look like a fool if he asks you anything about it.

They turned from the dim track across the prairie to the more deeply worn ruts leading to the house. "Looks like your father's home," Madison said.

Chapter Eleven

Her father's mongrel dog, Wink, jumped up from his spot under the house and raced to meet them, barking the whole time.

"I wonder what Papa found to eat," Fern said. "He hates cooking." Wink didn't stop barking when he recognized Fern.

"Maybe he went into town."

"He hates that even more."

"He ought to have hired someone to help you the day he fired Troy. With all you do, you don't have time to cook too."

Fern felt a shiver of pleasure skitter through her limbs. No man had ever concerned himself with the amount of work she did. She didn't understand why Madison should be the first. She wouldn't have thought he'd have even been aware that women worked. Maybe there was more of George in him than she had guessed.

Fern

Madison brought the buggy to a halt in front of the house. The dog still put up a deafening roar.

"Shut up, Wink," Fern ordered. "It's just me."

The dog subsided.

"You stay here while I make sure it's your father," Madison said, getting down from the buggy. The dog seemed disposed to take up his barking again, but a sharp command from Fern caused him to whimper and wag his tail in welcome.

Baker Sproull came through the doorway just as Madison alighted from the buggy. He ignored Madison.

"It's about time you got home," he said to his daughter. "Things have been going to hell in a hurry since you been gone. Whatever possessed you to lay up so long?"

Madison's anger flared like lightning. "She was badly hurt in a fall," he informed Sproull, his voice and look as cold as a winter gale. "I only brought her back after she promised to take the greatest care of herself for at least a week."

"Fern never needed to stay in bed a day in her life," her father said, his scorn for such an idea evident in the way he looked at Madison, "much less a whole week. Besides, she's got too much work to do. There's nothing in the house fit to eat."

"I'll have something ready in less than an hour, Papa," Fern said, climbing down from the buggy. She gritted her teeth to keep from grimacing in pain.

"You don't have time to worry with the cooking now," her father said. "There's hell to pay with that herd. Your steers have been all over. I even had to chase a couple out of my fields. If they get into old man Claxton's corn, he's liable to start shooting. Then you'll have to answer to him and me."

161

"Rose will have a fit if she finds you've been on a horse," Madison told her.

"Set my things inside the house," Fern said, not meeting his gaze. "I'll see to them when I get back."

"And you'd better get started castrating those bulls," her father added. "You wait much longer, and they'll be jumping fences to get at cows."

"I'll take care of it," Fern said. Quickly untying her horse, she intended to swing into the saddle and be gone before Madison could stop her.

She expected it to hurt when she took hold of the saddle horn. She was ready for the arrows of pain when she raised her foot to the stirrup, but she wasn't prepared for the wall of agony that knocked her almost senseless when she tried to swing into the saddle. She felt herself grow dizzy. The world spun around, and she lost her hold on the saddle.

She was falling.

Fern couldn't believe it. She was so weak and helpless she couldn't mount a horse.

"I said you weren't fit to ride," Madison said as he caught her in his arms. "I want you to go straight to bed and not get up again until tomorrow. I'll check on you first thing in the morning."

"She'll do nothing of the sort," Sproull said. "Who's going to do her work?"

Even through the layers of pain that wrapped themselves around her like ever-tightening coils of a giant constrictor, Fern could feel Madison tense. He seemed to pause, as though some decision hung in the balance.

"I don't care who does it," Madison said, moving again with his usual decisiveness. He carried Fern to the buggy and eased her into the seat she had left just minutes earlier. "I don't care if the steers trample your fields or devour every stalk of Claxton's corn."

He tied her horse's reins to the buggy, then turned toward her father. "And I hope those bulls terrorize every cow within a hundred miles of Abilene. It's your herd, Sproull. It's your problem."

Madison retrieved Fern's bags from the stoop and placed them in the buggy.

"What the hell are you doing?" Sproull demanded.

"I'm taking Fern back to Rose where she'll get proper care."

"She's my daughter," Sproull shouted, "and I say she stays here and does her work."

"Say anything you please," Madison said, his calm unruffled, "but I'm taking her back."

"She stays," Sproull roared, approaching Madison menacingly.

Fern's heart caught in her throat. Madison was a big man, but he was very slim. Her father was a bear of a man, and years of hard work had made him strong as an ox. She couldn't remember him actually getting in a fight. Even Troy had backed down rather than fight him.

When Madison started to climb into the buggy, Sproull charged without warning.

Fern closed her eyes, unwilling to see Madison knocked to the ground, but when she heard a thump and opened her eyes, it was her father who lay on the ground. Before Baker could get up, Madison jumped into the buggy, cracked the whip over the horse's head, and drove out of the yard at a trot. They departed to a chorus of barks from Wink and curses from her father.

"Don't think I'm running away because I'm a coward," Madison said as he turned onto the track leading to town. "I just don't feel right hitting your father."

Fern was too stunned to reply. In less than fifteen minutes, Madison had turned her world upside down. The herd would continue to be a problem, but she didn't care. Her father would come to town sooner or later, but she didn't care about that either. Until a few days ago, Troy, the cattle, and her father had been the only things on her mind. This afternoon she had trouble remembering them at all. All she could think about was Madison.

And those damned bulls.

She started to laugh. And once she started, she couldn't stop, even though it caused her ribs to hurt something awful.

"What's so funny?" Madison asked.

"What you said about the bulls," she said between giggles. "I can just picture them chasing terrified cows all over the county with Papa following behind brandishing a knife, the bulls looking over their shoulders calculating how many cows they can mount before he catches them." She broke down in an outburst of laughter. "I'm certain it's something no lady would think about, or admit if she did."

"Do you think your father would chase them?" Madison asked, grinning.

"Not if he was smart. He'd wait until they came back from their revels too exhausted to run away."

She laughed again, but it hurt so much she stopped.

"You shouldn't have to take care of the herd by yourself."

"We haven't been able to get steady hands since Papa fired Troy. I warned him, but he wouldn't listen."

"Why did your father fire him?"

"They couldn't see eye to eye on anything. Troy was cattle. Papa is a farmer."

"I'm sure George could find you someone."

"Why are you so certain your brother can fix anything?"

"Because he can. George is a born fixer."

"Then why didn't you leave Hen's defense to him?"

"That's something else altogether."

Madison lapsed into silence, and Fern tried once again to understand the contradictions of this man. One minute he was ready to say George had the answer to everything, the next he implied there were no answers. One minute he couldn't wait to get her off his hands, the next he was taking her back to Abilene so he could take care of her. One moment he was furious with her, and the next he was willing to fight her father so she didn't have to go back to work before she was well.

He was just as incomprehensible as the change in herself.

She should have been worried about her father, but she wasn't. She ought to have been furious at Madison for knocking him down, but she wasn't. She ought to have been worried about her cattle and the neighbors' crops, but she wasn't. She ought to have been anxious to get back to her old life, but she thought only of going back to Mrs. Abbott's and getting to know more about Madison Randolph.

Most of all, she should have been worried that continual contact with Madison would break down her resistance, would make her vulnerable to everything she had spent years trying to resist.

It scared her to death, and she had no idea what would happen tomorrow, but if this was a ride into the jaws of hell, so be it. She couldn't do anything else.

"Do they have many parties in Abilene?" Madison asked.

The question was so unexpected, it took Fern a moment to answer. "I don't know. I never go to parties."

"Why not?"

"I never wanted to."

"I'd have thought you'd jump at the chance."

"Some might, but not me."

"Not ever?"

"No."

"Would you go if I invited you?"

No man had ever invited her to a party. No one had ever dared.

"You couldn't take me to a party in this town," Fern said. "Nobody approves of me."

"I don't approve of all the things you do either, but that doesn't answer my question."

"If you don't approve of me, why should you want me to go with you?"

"I didn't say I didn't approve of you, just of some of the things you do."

"It comes down to the same thing."

"If that's what you think, you don't know much about men."

She didn't, but she wasn't about to admit it to him.

"You're avoiding my question," Fern said. "Why would you ask me to a party?"

"I don't know any other women."

She meant for her laugh to sound skeptical, but it came out more like a snort of disgust.

"You don't have to. They'll fall over themselves to talk to you."

"You sound like you don't approve. Don't you think young women should talk to me?"

"I didn't mean that and you know it. I'm sure Mrs. . . . whoever is giving the party, will invite plenty of unattached young women."

"Maybe I don't want to take the chance of being frozen out by the local swells."

Fern nearly hooted. "With your looks, there'll be

a gaggle of females panting after you inside ten minutes."

"Then you do approve of the way I look? That's a relief. I had gotten the definite impression you thought a chunk of river mud had more charm."

"You know you're a nice-looking man," Fern said, hardly able to believe the words that fell from her tongue. "And you know you can turn on the charm when you want. It's just when you're around me you behave like a beast."

"Your reflections on my character are fascinating," Madison said, "but we've wandered far from the original question. Would you go to a party with me?"

"Whose party is it?"

"Mrs. McCoy."

"The mayor's wife!" Fern exclaimed. "She'd never let me in the front door. She gets heartburn every time she sets eyes on me."

"You'd have to wear a dress, but I don't see anything about you to cause heartburn."

"So I'm not good enough to go as I am?" Fern said, her temper rising like a water spout.

"I didn't say a word about being good enough," Madison replied. "I'm sure Mrs. McCoy's only objection is to your mode of dress."

"Would you take me to the party dressed like I am now?"

"It's an evening party. I wouldn't take *myself* dressed like I am now."

"Why not?"

"Do you always wheedle out of answering questions?"

"What are you talking about?"

"Fifteen minutes ago I asked you if you'd go to a party with me. Not only have you managed to avoid answering the question, you've put me through the third degree. I'll ask you again. Will you go to Mrs. McCoy's party with me?"

Fern felt something crumple up inside her, as if she were being offered something she wanted so desperately she could taste it but knew she couldn't have it.

It was the party, she told herself. She wanted to go to the party. She didn't understand why. She'd never wanted to go to parties before. Some of the kids used to tease her because she was never invited, but they stopped when they found out she wouldn't have gone anyway.

But this had nothing to do with the party. She wanted to be with Madison. That shocked her even more. She had never wanted to go anywhere with a man.

"Thank you for the invitation, but I can't accept it." She hoped she sounded disinterested. If he guessed how much she wanted to go, he would never give up.

"Surely you're not afraid of wearing a dress? Or are you afraid you don't have anything to wear?"

"Neither."

She didn't own a dress. She had burned every one she had eight years ago.

"Why then?"

"There's nobody there I want to see or who wants to see me."

"I'll be there."

She knew he was only teasing, trying to get her to say yes, but she hoped he had no idea how much remarks like that hurt. Her foolish heart wanted to believe him.

"You just said I needed to stay in bed."

"The party's a couple of weeks off. In fact, you ought to be able to go back to your young bulls by then. Hopefully, they will have sown their wild oats."

"Why are you so concerned with a bunch of yearling bulls?" she asked, hoping he would forget all about the party. "I bet you never saw one."

"Not only saw them. I castrated them. It made me feel positively queasy." Madison gave her a measured glance. "I don't like the way you're looking at me."

Fern had to laugh. "Don't worry. You're quite safe. I wouldn't want to disappoint all your lady friends."

"What kind of lothario do you think I am?"

"I'll bet there are hundreds of women counting the hours until you return."

"I'd like to think at least one or two have noticed my absence, but I doubt they're counting the hours. There's an old saying about a bird in the hand being worth two in the bush. It counts for swains as well. The absent suitor might make the sweetheart sigh, but it's the lover in arms, so to speak, that makes her heart beat faster."

"I'm sure you speak from experience."

"Limitless. My conquests litter the Eastern seaboard."

Fern smiled again. "I hope not quite literally. It would be a great hindrance to the bathers."

"All this sympathy for swains, lovers, and bathers, and none for me."

Fern felt her chest tighten as her heart beat faster. He was flirting, just having fun. It would be best if she flirted back, but she didn't have the courage. Each meaningless word penetrated her heart like an arrow.

"You'll do quite well without my sympathy."

"Then accept my invitation just to spite me. You could always refuse to dance with me."

"I wouldn't do that."

"Isn't there anything I can say to convince you to go with me?"

"I might go if you'd tell me quite honestly why you asked me."

"It's a deal."

"I said *might*. I wouldn't put it past you to tell me some great whopper, then take enormous pleasure in debunking it later."

"You think I'd do that?"

His reaction had rattled her. He actually looked upset, as though he really cared what she thought of him. She had seen him angry, furious, livid, determined, even apologetic, but never upset. She had decided he didn't care deeply for anything.

It shocked her to discover she had the power to unsettle him. It also excited her. She had felt so helpless around him, she couldn't help but feel a tiny twinge of pleasure. Maybe she shouldn't, but she did.

"Maybe I shouldn't have said that," she said. "It's just that we've done nothing but see how much trouble we can cause each other. I don't know if you're really like that. I never thought I was, but I can see why you'd think so."

"Then let's start over again. Today can mark a new beginning."

Fern was beginning to think this journey back to town would never end. She realized now she wanted a new beginning. That was really why she had gone to the jail. But she'd had time to think since then, time in which to realize that a new beginning might only bring more hurt. Madison fascinated her, she admitted that, but fascination was a poor reason to continue a relationship that might only go sour in the end.

And no matter what the outcome of Hen's trial,

the relationship would end. Madison would go back to Boston and his wealthy, beautiful, captivating women. He would probably even make jokes about Kansas and the females he'd met there. He would certainly make jokes about her.

No, it had to end, so it might as well end now.

"I don't think it would be a good idea."

"The party or the new beginning?"

"Either of them."

How could she tell him he had awakened a part of her she had tried to forget ever existed? He had made her remember she was a woman. How could she tell him she had run from her femininity for so long, had fought against being a woman for so many years, that she was afraid she didn't know how anymore?

"Will you think about it?"

"No."

"That would be a great pity."

Fern could practically see the pit yawning at her feet. She knew she ought to turn the conversation to another subject. She should get down and walk back to town if necessary. But she didn't.

"Why?" she asked.

"Abilene might never discover that a swan has been masquerading as an ugly duckling. More importantly, *you* might never discover it."

Fern looked away. She didn't want Madison to see the pain in her eyes.

"Don't," she pleaded. "I know what I look like."

Madison took her chin in his hand and gently, so as not to cause her any pain, turned her face until she was forced to look straight at him.

"You don't know what I think you look like."

"Please." She tried to turn away, but he wouldn't let her.

"I see a young woman who's hiding from herself,

from what she is and what she wants to be, because she's afraid, afraid to admit she's pretty because it'll force her to confront something that frightens her."

"Stop!" Fern cried out, wrenching her chin from Madison's grasp.

Madison pulled the buggy to a stop. He took Fern by the shoulders and turned her to face him.

"It would be cruel to let you go on believing you're ugly and unwomanly."

"Just because I choose to wear pants—"

"If I thought you believed in yourself, I wouldn't say another word about your pants," Madison said. "But I don't want you to wear them out of fear."

"I don't. I—"

"You're afraid a man might want to kiss you, so afraid you try to pretend you're unattractive."

"Don't be absurd. I—"

"But I know better, and I intend to make you believe it."

"How?" she asked fearfully.

Gently drawing her to him, Madison lifted her chin until she had to look at him. "By making you believe I want to do this."

Then, ever so gently, he feathered a kiss across her lips.

Fern's breath stilled in her lungs; her heart beat erratically. The universe stood still, stranding her somewhere between heaven and hell.

She nearly dissolved under his touch. No man had ever shaken her determination, yet Madison nearly destroyed it. Never had she wanted so much to give in.

His lips felt warm and soft as they brushed her own like two pieces of silk. She could feel the warmth of his breath on her skin. The chill of excitement caused her to welcome the sun's heat.

The next instant she felt so hot she thought she might faint.

Madison's lips enticed her to join him in a tentative kiss. Her breath caught in a gasp when the tip of his tongue left a velvety trail of moisture on her lower lip. She felt paralyzed, unaware of anything in this vast open space except Madison.

Just as she started to pull back, Madison's hold tightened and he drew her into a kiss that was much more than the brushing of lips. Fern felt passion, need, desire, a sudden urgency that made the day seem suddenly too hot and dangerous. This was no longer a languorous kiss of two people exploring each other. Nor was it a kiss of idle curiosity, a kiss motivated by the desire to make her feel good about herself. It was a kiss filled with the promise of a passion that would last more than a day.

Frightened, Fern drew back, her breath uneven, her eyes wide and uncertain.

"You deserve to be kissed often," Madison murmured. "You deserve to know you're a very desirable woman. Is that what Troy did? Is that why you're the only person in Abilene who has anything good to say about him?"

The bubble burst, and Fern felt herself floating toward hell. She removed Madison's hands from her arms.

"No," she said, drawing away from Madison. She fought down the fear that always enveloped her when a man touched her, even by accident. She only had to remain calm until she could tell him to stop, tell him to never touch her again.

"Will you tell me why?"

"No."

"You will someday."

She shivered. Her will seemed to shake. She fought to regain control. She had to tell him to leave her alone, and she had to do it now. "I can't accept your invitation," she told him.

"Why?"

"I don't want to go. But it's not just that." She didn't look at him. She couldn't. "I don't want you to touch me or kiss me. I don't want any man to do that. Not ever."

Madison didn't know whether he was more shocked by his own actions or by Fern's words. He had invited her to the party on a sudden impulse. Her refusal piqued him. He might have kissed her to tease her, but it had turned into much more than that. He might have wanted to shock her into seeing something about herself, but he was as shocked as she.

He had been swept away by a strong yearning that had nothing to do with shocking or teasing. It had to do with a feeling that there was more to her than a sheepskin vest and Spanish spurs. Somewhere buried inside was a woman no one knew, not even Fern.

Her refusal upset him quite a lot. He had suspected she was trying to keep her distance from him, but he never imagined she might mean it to become a permanent barrier. It never occurred to him until now that he would care.

But he did.

Fern had been awake for some time. But rather than get up, she lay in bed, listening to the sounds of the house, letting her thoughts wander at random.

She tried to keep them from wandering to Madison, but he seemed to fill every corner of her mind. He had become an obsession that had taken over her life and would not be banished.

She didn't dislike him anymore, but that didn't make it easier. In fact, it made things worse. She could have hated him with a flaming passion and it would have died a natural death when he left town. She might have thought of him from time to time, much as she occasionally thought of accidents or natural disasters, but that would have been all.

Now she liked him. It shocked her to admit it, but she couldn't help it. She did.

It was an odd kind of liking. It wasn't easy or comfortable. It was like something that had invaded her life. She had no control over it. She could shout at him, argue with him, call him every name she could think of, and know all the while she didn't mean it. She could urge him to go back to Boston and never come back, but she didn't mean that either.

Just the thought of never seeing him again caused a kind of panic. What was there about this man that made him different from all others? What had he done to become unforgettable?

The only answer that made any sense was completely unacceptable. She wouldn't allow any man to be that important to her. These feelings would go away if she could just put him out of her mind.

But how could she put him out of mind when the feel of his kiss still lay on her lips like something tangible?

All her life she'd thought of men as competitors. She had had nothing but contempt for women who swooned over their touch, who could think of no greater purpose in life than to attract their attention.

Now she understood, at least enough to know it wasn't just his kiss, magical as it was. Madison's willingness to fight for her, his determination to protect her, had staggered her almost as much.

But he believed she was attractive; he was determined to make her feel pretty. And that went beyond the realm of the credible. No man, not even one as quixotic as Madison, would do all that for nothing. He must have some ulterior motive.

Maybe he was setting up a flirtation. Maybe after being surrounded by countless fawning females, he was bored. Maybe he thought of her as a charity case. Much like Prince Charming, he would enliven her dull life for a few weeks. A little flattery, some attention, a few stolen kisses, and he could go back to Boston patting himself on the back for having given her a few precious moments in the sun.

It had to be something like that. A man like Madison Randolph couldn't be seriously interested in a woman like her.

Could he?

She experienced his kiss all over again, felt the wonder, the excitement, the wonderfully healing sincerity. No matter what Madison might have felt when they first met, or what he would do in the future, that kiss had been real. She could feel it.

But what did it mean?

She didn't know now, but Madison wasn't one to keep secrets. She would know soon enough.

In the meantime she needed to get out of bed. Rose was already up. So was Mrs. Abbott. She couldn't tell what they were saying, but it was easy to tell who was speaking. Mrs. Abbott's voice was stern and sharp. She always seemed to be complaining, even when she was just talking. Rose's voice was soft but firm. She didn't speak as often or as long as Mrs. Abbott, but her words were heeded.

Fern wondered what it was like to be Rose and command so much respect and admiration. She knew it didn't just happen, but it seemed so effortless.

It wouldn't have happened if Rose had gone about wearing pants and doing her best to act like a man.

Fern

She's a strong, determined woman, but she's totally feminine.

But even as Fern thought somewhat regretfully of the years she had spent learning to disassociate herself from anything feminine, the thought of men wanting her, lusting after her body, of a faceless man ripping open her dress, touching her breasts, covering her neck and shoulders with his hot mouth, holding her body down with his weight, petrified her. She didn't want that. Never. She might have to give up all thought of marriage, but she couldn't face that.

Her good mood completely destroyed, she decided to get up. Just as she started to throw back the covers, she heard someone ride up to the house. A furious knocking a few moments later brought an immediate response from Mrs. Abbott.

"Mr. Sproull, you know better than to be banging on a lady's door this hour of the morning. We're not even dressed yet."

Her father! Fern's body stiffened. He had come to get her. Madison and George were away. There was no one to stop him this time.

Chapter Twelve

"I don't care," Baker Sproull replied. "You got my daughter in there, and I want her."

"She's sound asleep," Mrs. Abbott told him.

He wouldn't care about that. It rubbed at Fern's pride to know that strangers showed more concern for her than her own father did.

"Nonsense," Sproull said. "There's nothing wrong with that girl. You're just coddling her."

"I must remind you that I have guests staying in my house," Mrs. Abbott said, the full weight of her disapproval in her voice. "You must remain outside."

Fern imagined that her father must be attempting to force his way past Mrs. Abbott. She wondered how long the woman could keep him out.

"Get out of my way, woman. My daughter's inside, and I mean to have her outside."

Fern

"You'll do nothing of the kind until she's recovered," Mrs. Abbott replied. "She was so weak when she returned yesterday she had to be helped into bed."

Fern knew that her father expected no more than token resistance from Mrs. Abbott, but he had underestimated her if he thought he could wave her aside. After the way she'd objected to Madison visiting Fern in her bedroom, Fern imagined she would vigorously oppose any man's entering her house before she and Rose were properly dressed. Her form was lean and her height only moderate, but Fern imagined that Mrs. Abbott would be a difficult person to dislodge from any position she decided to occupy.

"You've ruined her already. She won't be good for anything unless I beat her."

"Mr. Sproull," Mrs. Abbott expostulated, "you can't mean to strike that girl. I don't approve of the way she dresses—no decent woman could approve such attire—but to speak of beating her . . ."

"Used to work wonders."

Fern thought of the numerous times her father had taken a strap to her. It hadn't knocked the nonsense out of her. It had only caused her to erect more barriers between herself and the rest of the world. Unfortunately, her father couldn't see that.

"You won't do any such thing in my house," Mrs. Abbott declared. "You try it, and I'll have the marshal on you faster than you can—"

"If you can wake him up after staying up half the night gambling," Sproull said. "Now let me pass. I mean to have my girl, and I mean to have her now."

Fern started to get out of bed. Mrs. Abbott couldn't stand against her father for long. Fern wasn't terribly fond of the woman, but she had taken good care of her. Most of her scolding was no more than motherly concern.

"Mrs. Abbott, what is the meaning of this uproar?"

Fern froze. It was Rose. Fern couldn't let her father bully Rose, not after all she had done for her. And especially not in her condition. If anything were to happen . . .

"This is Mr. Sproull. He's come to—"

"So you're Fern's father," Rose said, her voice heavy with censure. "It's about time you showed some concern for your daughter. I had expected you before nightfall the day she arrived."

"A little fall is no call to go chasing after Fern," Sproull said. "I expected her home in time to fix my dinner."

Fern could hardly believe her ears. Her father's voice had lost so much of its bluster he sounded almost apologetic.

"If you had bothered to inquire, you would have found she was in no condition to fix your dinner, or perform any other chores."

"I never spent a day in bed in my life."

"Not all of us are as fortunate as you."

"People like to cosset themselves. Makes them feel important."

"I'm sure you're right, but Fern was quite badly injured."

Fern began to worry about her father's temper. He wasn't used to opposition, especially from women. He used to get livid when Troy argued with him.

"Well, she's had time to get over it."

"Not at all. I should have thought you would have realized that when she couldn't mount her horse."

"That came from lying about in bed for so long. Let her stir about for an hour or two and she'll be good as new."

"I'm afraid I disagree with you. She needs several

more days before she will be able to resume even a *limited* number of her former duties."

He didn't like being contradicted, either. Nothing made him madder. That was what had caused the last fight between him and Troy.

"I mean to see she's in the saddle before the sun goes down. You can't think I'm going to do her work as well as mine."

"I don't care who does her work. Fern stays here until I say she's ready to leave."

"Look, lady, I don't know who you are—"

"My name is Rose Randolph. My husband is George Randolph."

"—but you got nothing to say about what I do with my daughter. Now get out of my way before I have to lay hands on you."

Fern slipped out of the nightgown and reached for her shirt. He couldn't touch Rose. Fern would never be able to face Madison if he did.

"If you so much as touch me, my husband will kill you," Rose stated. She said it quite naturally, with no more fanfare than if she were announcing they were in for another hot day. "That is if Hen doesn't do it first."

That statement, not unnaturally, produced a silence. Fern's fingers froze on her shirt buttons. Visions of George in jail for the murder of her father rose before her eyes like demons escaping from hell. It would be a nightmare past all imagining.

"No man would kill me for something like that," Sproull sputtered.

"I can't speak for other men," Rose answered, "but I can speak for the Randolphs."

"I don't believe you."

Fern's fingers flew over the last two buttons, and she reached for her pants. Her father never believed anybody. He was firmly convinced he was the only authority in the world.

"Mr. Sproull, you earn your living selling to the drovers, don't you?"

"Mostly."

"I have only to say a word to my husband, and no one from Texas will ever buy from you again."

Silence.

Fern had never thought of the influence George Randolph might wield with the other Texans, but she had no doubt he would be more than willing to ruin anybody for the sake of his family.

She couldn't be the cause of her father's ruin. She hadn't meant for any of this to happen, and she certainly hadn't meant for him to threaten Rose, but she should have foreseen it.

She searched for her socks, but Rose's next words stayed her hand.

"I understand you have cattle, the herd you're so anxious to have Fern attend," Rose said. "If you don't get back to them right away, something might frighten them so badly they wouldn't stop running until they were several hundred miles from here. The Indians would probably get them before you could find them."

Fern could almost hear her father making gulping noises. He might pretend the herd wasn't important, but she knew he liked the money she brought in.

"It's sometimes very difficult to keep a trail herd from overrunning fields, especially if those fields are filled with succulent green vegetables."

"Are you threatening me?" Sproull asked. He still sounded rather fierce, but Fern could tell that much of the steam had gone out of his bluster. She sank down on the bed, her bare feet forgotten.

"I'm simply telling you what could happen if you continue to leave your farm unsupervised. We'll keep

Fern here. That way you won't have to wait on her and do your work as well."

"I ain't never waited on a woman in my life," Sproull shouted, "not even her mother."

"It was probably very wise of Mrs. Sproull to die at her earliest convenience. It must have seemed preferable to a life spent as your wife. Now if you will excuse me, I have things I must do. Good day, Mr. Sproull."

"Good day," Mrs. Abbott repeated, closing the door in his face with considerable vehemence.

"I never thought Baker Sproull could be so unfeeling," Mrs. Abbott said. "He's downright cruel."

"He's probably never had anyone to tell him when to stop. A good, strong-minded wife might have made a fairly decent man out of him."

"I shouldn't want to try."

"I imagine it's too late now."

Fern felt the tension gradually leave her body until she collapsed on the bed. She wouldn't have guessed until now just how much she had dreaded her father's appearance. She had known she would have to go with him, had been prepared to get out of bed and leave immediately, but Rose had sent him away with a good deal to think about. Fern doubted he would come back. He loved money more than he loved her.

That hurt. She had thought she was used to his coldness. She never really looked for anything else. But Rose and Madison had shown her that people didn't have to be related to her to care.

Still more amazing, they had extended this circle of protection to her after she had done everything she could to alienate them. She didn't understand that. It wasn't as if they were missionaries bent on saving her soul.

Even more profoundly shocking, she didn't want

to go home. She wanted to stay with these strangers. It had nothing to do with her injury. For the first time in her life, somebody cared for her enough to be concerned about what was happening to her, *about how she felt*.

She was drawn to Madison because he saw something in her that no one else had seen, something that made him want to kiss her, want to invite her to Mrs. McCoy's party. It made him want to make her believe in her own attractiveness. It made him care that she still hurt. It made him care how others treated her. Enough to fight for her.

She wouldn't forget that. Not ever.

She undressed and slipped back into bed.

"You're very quiet," Rose said to Fern. "Do you still have a lot of pain?"

"No. I've really felt much better today. I probably ought to go home."

"You can't leave until Madison gets back. He gave me the most explicit instructions on that score."

Fern smiled, but almost immediately her expression turned serious. "Why did you take me in? I've been nothing but trouble."

Rose smiled comfortingly. "Because you were hurt and needed attention. You refused to let a doctor examine you, remember."

Fern nodded. "But why did you keep me?"

"Because you needed someone to take care of you. Besides, we like you. As for your cows, they'll get along without you. I sometimes think cows are the only other creatures in God's creation to have eternal life."

"You don't like cows?"

"Good Lord, no. How can anybody actually *like* a cow, especially a longhorn? George doesn't care much for them either, but it's the way we make our living."

Fern could hardly believe her ears. She'd never heard a Texan say he disliked longhorns. From the way they defended the beasts, you'd have thought they loved them as much as their children.

Quick on the heels of that discovery came another. Fern hated cows. She had hated them for years without even suspecting. She had depended on them to give her independence. She had identified with them because it was necessary, but deep down she loathed the huge, stinking, stubborn, noisy, stupid beasts. She'd be perfectly happy if she never saw another one.

The discovery turned everything upside down— again. Her place in the community, her reason for getting up each day, had been tied to that herd. Now it was gone. None of the old equations worked anymore. The whole fabric of her life was unraveling.

And all because of Madison Randolph.

If he had stayed in Boston, none of this would have happened. If she hadn't taken him out to the Connor place, this wouldn't have happened. If he had taken her home and left her there, this wouldn't have happened.

Now it was too late.

But what made it too late? She had been able to forget every other man who had crossed her path.

But from the moment he stepped from the train, she hadn't been able to forget Madison. The way he treated her made his name tremble on her lips. His attention and genuine interest caused his image to dance before her eyes, made her memorize his every word, deed, and expression. She had drunk him in like life-giving water.

Now she was addicted.

She couldn't go back to things as they had been. He had ruined that for her. But what was she going to do now? Her father wouldn't accept the change.

She didn't even know if she could.

She felt frightened and helpless. And she'd never felt that way before. There'd always been something she could do. There must be something now, but she couldn't think of it.

"What's wrong?" Rose asked. "You don't look ready to go home."

"I don't feel like it. I don't have any energy."

"That doesn't sound like you."

"It doesn't feel like me either. I've always been active, in the saddle, sure of everything. Now I'm lying around in bed in a pink nightgown."

Rose laughed softly. "I imagine half the women in town are jealous of you. It isn't every woman who gets carried off by a handsome young man."

"And that's something else."

"I thought it might be."

"None of this would have happened if it hadn't been for Madison."

"Maybe not now, but it would have happened sooner or later."

"Are you sure?"

"No one can make you feel what you don't want to feel, be what you aren't, or want what you dislike. We all have reasons for hiding from ourselves, but sooner or later something happens to tear down the walls we've built up. Then we find out who we really are."

"I haven't found anything. There's nothing behind that wall. There never was."

Madison poured himself a cup of coffee, then settled the pot over the tiny campfire.

"I have to admit I've enjoyed the last few days," he

said to George. "But after riding a hundred miles, I would much prefer a hot bath and a decent dinner instead of warm beans and my saddle for a pillow."

There were too many farmers around Abilene for the town to continue as a cattle shipping center, so George had been scouting the new cattle trail the town of Ellworth had laid out to attract the Texas herds. Madison had ridden along with him, spending his time retracing Hen's route the night Troy died, looking for anyone who might have seen Hen, spoken to him, or recognized his horse. He hadn't heard from Tom White's friend, and he was desperate for a witness.

"You don't have a hankering to go back to Texas?" George asked.

"Not for one minute. What would I do there?"

"You could become part of the family again."

Madison supposed he should have expected George to get around to that sooner or later. His family was vitally important to him. Not that Madison thought that was all bad, but George seemed to think that nothing else mattered.

"There's no place for me in this family. That's one of the reasons I left Texas. I know you think we all ought to make up our differences and live happily ever after, but that won't happen. Hen and Monty will never understand me any more than I understand them. There's no feeling of love between us. There never was.

"I hated the noisy way they attacked life and everybody in it, especially me. They didn't trust anything found in a book. There's no use trying to create something where there's nothing."

"You left your comfortable niche to make sure Hen didn't hang," George said. "That must mean you have some feeling of family."

Madison felt nettled. "I may not be the most loving of brothers, but I'm not without feeling."

"You had to know I would have gotten the best lawyer available. I'd have broken him out of jail if necessary."

"I had to see for myself."

"Didn't you worry about what we would say?"

"I didn't expect Hen to understand, but I thought you would."

"I would never have left."

"Don't judge everybody by yourself."

"That's what Rose said, but it's not easy."

Madison decided the family owed more to Rose than he had reckoned. He hadn't thought anybody could change a Randolph, but apparently she could. He wondered if it was just Rose, or whether any woman who could love her husband that much could have the same effect.

He cursed himself when Fern popped into his mind. She was the last person this family needed. Someone like Samantha would be a more logical choice. Or Sarah Cabot. Or Phoebe Watkins. Or any one of a dozen women he knew—all charming, graceful, beautiful, and with a strong desire to be married and make a home for their husband and children.

So why did he keep thinking of Fern?

Probably out of perverseness. All his life he'd done things the hard way. He'd insisted upon going to boarding school when everybody else studied at home. He'd left the ranch to try to make a place for himself in the North during a bitter, bloody war. He had made up his mind to move into the tightly knit, very exclusive upper echelon of Boston society. He had set his course to ultimately compete with the financial barons who were revolutionizing American industry. It was entirely of a piece that he would be interested in the most irreclaimable female he had ever set eyes on.

Yes, he was interested in her. God only knew why. Madison didn't understand it any more than he understood why he had enjoyed these few days of being in the saddle from dawn to dusk, riding over hot and dusty trails, or becoming acquainted with a breed of people he was gradually learning to respect.

"Did Rose say anything else?"

"Yes. She said you wanted to become part of the family again or you'd never have left Boston after eight years."

"Do you believe everything she says?"

"She hasn't been wrong so far."

Madison knew he couldn't spend a few weeks deeply involved with George and Hen and then go back to Boston and forget about them. He couldn't know that George had named his firstborn after a father they both hated, and not ask why.

He couldn't get on a train and forget he'd ever met Fern.

"I guess she's right this time, too. I spent a lot of years trying to forget just about my whole life," he said. "I especially wanted to forget all the failures, the waste, the anger and bitterness, the times I wanted to kill Pa, or myself, and didn't have the guts. But the minute I heard about Hen, I knew I had to come."

"Did you ever try to find out what happened to us after the war?"

Leave it to George to find the one spot he didn't want exposed. There were some things that Madison didn't want to admit, even to himself. Just like Fern. She had constructed walls all around herself to keep out things she didn't want to see, to support the narrow world she had created for herself, to blind her to the things about herself she didn't want to know.

His walls might be less formidable, but they were walls just the same.

"Freddy's father has friends in Washington. It wasn't too difficult to have the army locate you."

"Then you were responsible for General Sheridan."

"No, but when your application for a pardon turned up—"

"How did you know about that?"

"Freddy's father."

"Then Grant didn't send the pardons."

"Yes, he did, but they might not have come so quickly."

"And Sheridan?"

"He was chasing bandits. It was easy for him stop by the ranch."

Madison remembered how anxiously he had waited for news. Freddy's family had been kinder and more generous than his own, but during those dark years he'd learned that no one could replace your own family. Just knowing they were alive made everything easier.

"And Hen?"

"The Kansas Pacific is one of our clients. They don't like anything that might disturb the flow of longhorns from Texas. Their trains go west loaded with goods, but they come back mostly empty. Your cattle are sometimes their margin of profit. A war between the Texas drovers and the citizens of Abilene, a war which could easily be set off by the hanging of a member of one of Texas's most prominent families—"

"Good God, whoever called us that?"

"—is bad for the railroad. They notified us immediately."

"So you knew about Hen's arrest almost as soon as I did."

Madison nodded.

"Will you continue to keep up with us through the company reports after you go back to Boston?"

"I hope that won't be necessary."

"It won't, not if you really want to know."

"I do."

Surprising how difficult it was to say those two words. He felt as if he were admitting to a weakness. It seemed to imply he'd been wrong when he left eight years ago.

"I'd do it over again," Madison said. "I couldn't have done anything else."

"I don't guess I'll ever understand, but I'll try."

"The twins never will."

"We're all learning to accept things we can't understand. Jeff has his arm. I have Pa."

"We all have Pa."

"But it's not so bad if we have each other."

Madison hoped it was true. The need for his father's love and approval was something he'd never admitted. There was no point in it. It was easier to admit he needed George's approval.

"Why did you name your son after him? I could have fallen over when I found out."

"I'll tell you some day."

"Why not now?"

"You're not ready."

That angered Madison. "What do you mean? Is there some special understanding that only people who live in Texas can appreciate?"

"No. It's something no man can appreciate unless he's laid down his weapons, called off all quarrels, and turned his attention to the things he never thought he'd be able to have. You're not there yet. There's too much anger inside. You're fighting too hard to understand."

Madison didn't like that answer, but he had enough innate honesty to know that George was right. He was still fighting to prove he was right when he left the ranch.

"Do you mind if I ask what's in that box?" George asked.

Madison's mood changed abruptly. "Curiosity about to kill the cat?"

"It's not quite that bad," George said, smiling without embarrassment. "One of the drawbacks of being interested in everybody's welfare is being curious about their business as well."

"That shouldn't cause any problem with all of you living in the same house."

"You don't live with us."

A momentary shadow crossed Madison's face. "I don't think I want to tell you. It's a gamble, one that might not work out. I'm not too fond of advertising my failures."

"Want some advice?"

"No."

"Good. I'm not good with women."

"Who said it had anything to do with a woman?"

"No man can be married for five years and not learn to recognize a dress box," George said, amusement dancing in his eyes. "Either there's a woman involved, or you've taken up some very strange habits since you went to Boston."

Madison laughed aloud.

"I'd forgotten how you always seemed to know what was going on in my mind, even when I was most determined to keep it from you."

"Some things never change."

"But so much has."

"Things that matter don't. We just to learn to look at them differently."

Madison wasn't sure he understood that statement, but he didn't want to explore it at the moment. He had all he could do to explain to himself why he was taking that box back to Abilene.

Chapter Thirteen

"Have you thought about a dress for the party?" Rose asked Fern.

"No. I—"

"Madison did invite you, didn't he? He said he was going to, but men don't always remember things like parties. Not when they can inspect cattle yards or check out dusty trails."

"Yes, but—"

"For a terrible moment I thought I had put my foot in it." Rose gave Fern a searching look. "We could go shopping if you don't have anything at home you want to wear. Do they sell party dresses in Abilene?"

"I don't know. I've never bought a dress."

"Never?" Rose said, her eyes widening in surprise.

"Not one," Fern said, a little defiantly. "I don't wear dresses."

Fern

"Did you tell Madison?"

"I told him I wouldn't go with him."

Rose's expression was inscrutable. "He told me he thought you would."

"Madison never listens to what he doesn't want to hear, especially if I'm the one saying it."

Silence.

"Will you go?"

Fern had made up her mind to refuse, several times in fact, but she heard herself say, "I might."

"But you can't without a dress."

So Rose wasn't any different from anyone else. Fern didn't know why she had expected she would be. She supposed it was because Rose was usually so understanding. Somehow she'd expected her to understand this as well.

"Why can't I? If it's okay for a man to wear pants, why not for a woman?"

"I know you and Madison have fallen into the habit of doing exactly the opposite of what the other wants," Rose said, rather impatiently, "but Mrs. McCoy's party is no place for personal squabbles, especially if it'll get everybody's back up. People go to a party to relax and enjoy themselves. If you can't enter into the spirit of things, you shouldn't go. Besides, you've already had the benefit of Madison's opinion on your attire."

"I've had his opinion on lots of things."

"Apparently you haven't been listening. Randolph men have many admirable qualities, but pliability isn't one of them."

"I'm not interested in bending him," Fern insisted.

"Good. I should dislike it if you were to engage his affections only to reject him in the end."

"Engage his affections! Me?"

Fern could hardly manage a coherent thought.

How was it possible for anyone, but most particularly Rose, to think she was trying to make Madison fall in love with her? Even if she could, she wouldn't have tried. She didn't want to attract men. Not after that night.

"I've never attempted to engage Madison's affections. Besides, if he insists I wear a dress, he can't really care about me."

"His wanting you to wear a dress could mean he cares a great deal."

"How?"

"Maybe he thinks a dress would bring out a part of you that's been locked away since you started wearing pants."

"Like what?"

"You'll have to ask him."

Fern felt a warm ball of excitement spinning in her abdomen. Madison must like her a little. He had kissed her. And he told her she was pretty. He said he'd keep telling her until she believed it. She hadn't dared let herself believe him. But if Rose said he liked her, it might be true.

But Fern had spent so many years telling herself she was homely she'd come to believe it. Now she was stunned by the intensity of her need to be admired. It gnawed at her gut like a physical hunger.

Piss and vinegar! You're just like Betty and all the others. In spite of your cussing and pants and sunburn and callused hands and Spanish spurs and fancy cutting horse, you're nothing but a vain female.

She didn't care. She wanted Madison's eyes to light up when he looked at her. She wanted it so much she could feel the muscles knot in her stomach. But she didn't have the courage to accept his invitation to the party and find out. Rose might be wrong.

Fern

Dammit! She couldn't believe that after all these years she wanted to go to a party.

What could she hope to gain?

She hoped to gain Madison.

God help her, she must be crazy. She couldn't have fallen in love with him. She didn't want to be in love with anyone.

Oh my God, she did love him! She had been so busy arguing and threatening to hang Hen that she hadn't noticed what was happening in her own heart.

A feeling of panic took hold of her. She got to her feet. She had to be alone.

"Are you all right?" Rose asked. "You look rather pale."

"I guess I'm not as well as I thought," Fern said.

"Why don't you lie down until lunch. I'll see that no one disturbs you."

You're too late, Fern thought to her self. Much too late.

"But I don't know how to dance," Fern protested.

"It's not necessary," Madison said. He still wouldn't accept her refusal to go to the party.

"I can't dance, either," Rose said, patting her stomach. "Too clumsy."

"You're as graceful as ever," George said.

"It's sweet of you to say so, dear, but I think I'll find a quiet corner and sit down."

"Why don't you let Madison teach you to dance?" George suggested to Fern.

"We can start now," Madison said, getting to his feet.

"I can play," Mrs. Abbott offered. Everyone looked at her in surprise. "But not very well," she quickly added.

"Nobody's going to teach me to dance," Fern said,

heat rising in her face. "I keep trying to tell you I'm not going. But even if I were, I wouldn't let you drag me around the room with everybody watching. I'd feel like an idiot."

They had fallen into the habit of lingering around the table after dinner to talk over the day's events. The dark, flowered wallpaper and the painted wood failed to provide much cheer, but it was better than the stiff formality of the parlor.

"Well, you two can argue it out between you while we're gone," Rose said, getting to her feet. "If I don't get started on my walk, I'll never get William Henry to bed on time."

"You can move to the parlor," Mrs. Abbott said. "I've got to clear away the dishes."

They ended up on the porch watching Rose and George walk down the street arm in arm. William Henry ran ahead pointing at one thing after another and talking excitedly. But his parents were nearly oblivious to anyone except each other.

Fern had never known that two people could be so much in love. It made her feel terribly alone. She wondered if Madison could feel that way about her. He was spending time with her, taking an interest in her, but there were times when she felt like a reclamation project.

She doubted it ever occurred to him she might have good reasons for behaving as she did. No more than he realized he was the only reason she would consider changing. And she wouldn't tell him. What a stupid thing it was to be in love, especially when there was no hope her love would be returned.

"We can start now," Madison was saying.

"Now?" she practically squeaked, jerked abruptly out of her thoughts.

"Sure. It's almost dark. No one will see us."

"If we were having a total eclipse, it wouldn't be

Fern

dark enough for me to let you teach me to dance on Mrs. Abbott's front porch," Fern declared. "I grew up here. I know these people. They'd never let me hear the end of it."

"Then come sit down." Madison took her hand and pulled her toward a bench just big enough for two people.

"I'd rather stand. I've been sitting or lying down for days."

He pulled her down next to him. She thought of standing up again, but decided he'd only sit her down a second time. Better to let him have his way this once.

"I forget you're the active sort. You probably can't wait to get back on your horse."

Oddly enough, Fern hadn't missed her horse.

"If Rose says it's okay, I'll take you for a ride tomorrow."

It made her sick the way her heart beat faster just because she was sitting next to him. She was even more dismayed by the excitement that coursed through her body. She knew what that meant, and she hated it, but she couldn't stop it. It had been getting worse each day. The only cure was never to see Madison again.

But she couldn't do that.

"I can't go riding. What if Papa should see me?"

"I won't let him force you back to work, if that's what you're worried about," Madison said.

Fern felt something inside herself relax. He was still ready to stand between her and the rest of the world. He still cared.

She wasn't worried about going back to work. She didn't even mind the work. But she was worried he wouldn't want to see her enough to come to the farm. She wanted to see him enough to stay here no matter how angry her father got.

"Why are you afraid of what people say about you?" Madison asked. "I get the feeling you won't feel comfortable until you've hidden yourself from view. You've developed a perfect camouflage."

"I'm nothing but a farmer's daughter."

She was finding it hard to concentrate. His arm was behind her along the back of the bench. Their bodies were only a few inches apart. They seemed like the smallest inches in the world.

"Trying to look, act, and be treated like a farmer's son."

"What's so great about being a woman?" she demanded. "Men are always telling you where to go, what to do, what to say. They don't think you can do anything by yourself except cook, clean, and have babies. You don't even think I can pick out my own clothes."

"Is that all?"

"No, it's not," Fern said, trying to put a little distance between them as she turned to face him. "If you don't want to be the perfect young woman waiting patiently to become the perfect young wife, they try to turn you into a soiled dove, or something just as bad."

Her whole body shivered as if the temperature had dropped fifty degrees. Memories of that night eight years ago flooded her mind. With fierce determination, she shoved them back into the dark corner where she kept them locked away.

"That's not it," Madison said. "You're no more afraid of the people in this town than I am. It's your father."

"No." Fern wanted to defend her father—Madison blamed him unfairly—but she couldn't tell him about that night.

"Rose told me what he said. If he ever lays a hand on you, I'll break both his arms," Madison swore.

Fern

"He wouldn't hurt me. He loves me," Fern insisted.

Madison moved closer. Not much, but it seemed like a lot.

"I doubt your father is capable of loving anything except his bank account. What would he do if you put on a dress and refused to do anything except the housework?"

"I can't afford to stay in the house, not with just two of us," Fern insisted, unwilling to admit, even to herself, the doubts in her heart.

"He could hire a couple of hands. Your herd brings in more than enough to pay the wages of two men like Reed and Pike."

Fern didn't know whether to be angry that Madison had been prying into her father's financial affairs or pleased that he was so concerned about her. She decided to be pleased. That made everything different.

It allowed her to react to him purely as a woman.

That meant he was no longer her adversary but instead an object of limitless curiosity. She wanted to look at him, to absorb him through her eyes and ears. Though she didn't dare, she wanted to touch him. She wondered how it would feel to place her hand on the strong arm that had supported her on the long ride from the Connor homestead.

She looked at his face as if for the first time. She wondered how eyes that black could seem so alive, so full of fire. She wondered what he would look like when he wasn't so perfectly groomed, if his hair fell in his eyes, if he ever went unshaven.

She wondered if he ever got tired of being so independent, if he didn't occasionally long for someone to lean on. She wondered if Boston women expected their men to have the answers to everything. She wouldn't stop caring for a man just because he'd made a mistake.

Of course, people like Madison never admitted to a mistake. That must be a terrible burden. He ought to have somebody with whom he could be himself, somebody who could love him for himself.

She wondered how just being around him could make her feel like somebody else. She didn't understand why everything she had tried to accomplish for so many years should suddenly prove to be the opposite of what she wanted. Most confusing of all, part of her wanted these changes so badly she didn't know if she could deny herself.

Whenever she was around Madison she could feel her resistance eroding. And she didn't seem to have the energy or the inclination to build it up again. Slowly but surely he was tearing down her defenses, stripping away her camouflage, exposing the soft inside she neither wanted to admit existed nor wanted anyone to see.

Fern snatched up the loose reins on her wandering thoughts. They embarrassed her. They even frightened her a little. She averted her gaze for fear that Madison could see her thoughts in her eyes.

She felt his arm brush against her, and her whole being reacted as if she had been stung by a thousand pinpoints of ice. Every atom in her body was aware of his presence.

"I think I'll have a talk with him tomorrow," Madison continued.

"I can talk to my own father," Fern said, gratified that Madison would go to so much trouble, worried about her father's reaction, and a little irritated that Madison would decide to talk to her father without asking her first.

"But you won't."

"How do you know?"

"Because you've got it into your head that the

only way to be treated the way you want is to do more work than a man. You'll never be more than a poor imitation of a man. But I suspect that if you gave yourself a chance, you could be a very special woman. Good-looking, too."

Fern was speechless.

Madison's scorn for her accomplishments made her furious. Did he know how really well she could ride, rope, or use a gun? No. Did he have any idea how hard she had worked to achieve the position he was blithely dismissing in a single sentence? Absolutely not.

He just made an assumption as he always did, based upon his experience in hoity-toity Boston, and took it for granted he was right.

But it was impossible for her to be angry at him. No one had ever called her a very special woman, or said she could be nice-looking. And he had never seen her in anything except pants. It wasn't until today that she had stopped wearing her hat inside the house.

"What makes you say that?" Fern asked. She knew she shouldn't be so curious—knowing Madison, he was bound to say something she wouldn't like—but she couldn't resist.

"What?"

"That I might make a good-looking woman." It was difficult to confess her curiosity. He would know she cared.

"You'd have to stay out of the sun and wind long enough for your skin to stop looking like old parchment." A slow smile curved Madison's lips. "You look more like an Indian maiden than a Boston miss."

His finger touched her shoulder through her shirt, and her body burst into flame like dry tinder.

"I'd much rather be an Indian maid than a

Boston miss," Fern snapped. "At least there'd be some gumption in me."

"You've got plenty of gumption. It's one of the things I like about you."

"You didn't used to like anything about me."

"I've changed my mind."

"About what?"

"Just about everything. I still wish you wouldn't dress the way you do, but you've got a very nice shape. It wouldn't be so easy to see all covered up in yards and yards of skirts."

Fern turned crimson. Until this minute, she'd have ridden her cutting pony over anybody who had dared comment on her body. But Madison's fingertips were rubbing ever so gently against the fine hairs at the back of her neck. It drove her crazy. She couldn't concentrate enough to find the words to answer him.

"I like you without the hat, though. You've got nice eyes. They used to be bloodshot from the sun, but they look pretty now. Most of the time they're hazel, but they turn pure green when you get angry."

He took a lock of her hair between his fingers.

"I'm surprised you didn't cut your hair. I'd like to see it falling down your back, billowing in the wind."

Fern wasn't about to tell him that her hair was the one feminine attribute she had been unable to part with. She considered it a weakness, and she already had enough weaknesses where he was concerned.

"It would catch in the first tree I passed."

"I was thinking of you riding with me, not chasing those poor bull yearlings. Can't you think of anything else?"

"I wasn't thinking of—"

"I like it when you smile. It changes your face entirely. You're not meant to frown."

Boldly his fingers caressed her neck. Fern wondered how his touch would feel on her bare shoulders.

"You should take your own advice," Fern managed to slip in before he plunged on.

"You've got dimples. I didn't notice them at first."

Fern had despised them for years.

"They're cute. They make you look less like a trail boss chewing out a green hand for stampeding the herd."

If he kept on like this, she was going to be sorry she'd asked him anything. She'd never known anyone who could make the things he liked sound so unattractive. At this rate she wouldn't be surprised to hear him say he was glad she looked like a bulldog calf, that he'd been looking for a girl like that for years and couldn't find a single one in Boston to fit his requirements.

"I'm relieved to hear that," she answered, "since all my sympathies would be with the green hand. My experience with Texas drovers has been something less than wonderful."

"You haven't met my brother Monty."

"Rose keeps saying that. She seems to think I would prefer him to you."

She hadn't meant anything by that remark—she was just repeating what Rose had said—but it had an electric effect on Madison.

He jerked his hand back as he sat up and pulled away. She felt shock at his withdrawal.

Madison could hardly believe that Fern's idle words would irritate him so much. He had never gotten along with Monty, but until now he'd never felt like strangling him. He didn't care if Rose liked Monty ten times as much as she liked him, but it hurt to think that Fern might prefer his roistering sibling. He had come to think of Fern as belonging to him alone, and he'd tolerate no poaching, not even by long distance.

Do you know how ridiculous that sounds? If you heard anybody else talk like this, you'd take him for a fool.

Maybe so, but he couldn't help the way he felt. Neither could he help the desire that uncurled in him like slow-rising heat.

He'd been intrigued by Fern from the very beginning, but now he felt an overwhelming desire to touch and hold her. For some time he'd been aware of a strong desire to protect her, to help her find some of the happiness she deserved, but now he felt much more.

It hadn't taken many days before the allure of her body had seduced him into forgetting his disapproval of her pants. She had a trim waist, rounded hips, and long slim legs, the image of which had taken up permanent residence in his thoughts and dreams. There was just enough sway in her walk to tantalize any red-blooded male.

He liked the feel of her in his arms, the taste of her lips, the warmth of her body. He found himself dreaming of holding her close, of making love to her, slowly, thoroughly, with satisfying attention to every part of her body.

He no longer saw her as a female who defied custom. Neither did he see her only as a person with whom he felt a strong bond of sympathy. He saw her as a woman who excited his desire, a woman longing to be loved.

But even as he felt tension pull his muscles taut, he held back. Something about the way Fern always kept her distance warned him to proceed with caution. Instinctively he knew that some experience had hurt her badly. In his ignorance, he could hurt her just as badly again.

Fern

And Madison didn't want to do that. Her life had already given her too much pain and too little pleasure. As much as he would like to make love to her this very minute, he would condemn himself to celibacy before he would hurt her.

Her expression of guilty concern almost caused him to smile. It also made him feel better. He didn't mind her feeling a little ashamed of what she'd said. It showed she had come to care about his feelings as much as he cared about hers.

Neither did he mind that she seemed concerned she had upset him. She had been keeping him at a distance ever since they met. This just might be the wedge he needed to break through the wall she had built around herself.

And he did intend to break through. Like a fragile sea creature, Fern had encased herself in a shell so tough no one had been able to crack it.

But Madison had set his heart on claiming that treasure. And he meant to do so tonight.

Chapter Fourteen

Fern wished she could unsay her words. Madison looked crushed.

No, he never looked crushed. Disappointed or upset, but nothing could crush this man. If he didn't accept what you told him, he would try to change it.

But he did look hurt, and she was as mystified at his reaction as she was shocked. It didn't make sense unless he liked her a lot. But the way he talked, that seem unlikely.

Yet he must. Otherwise he wouldn't be telling her all the things he liked about her. His idea of sweet-talk wouldn't sweep a woman off her feet, but then Fern didn't want to be swept away. She just wanted to feel pretty, desirable, to be liked.

Fern's attention was caught by a man walking slowly down the street. He didn't stop, but he kept glancing in their direction. She was glad she had refused to let Madison teach her to dance. She didn't recognize the man, but she was certain he'd have spread the news over half the town before midnight.

"Rose says Monty's cow crazy," Fern said. "I could never like a man who preferred cows to women."

Madison relaxed, but his hand stayed away from her neck.

"What was I saying?" he asked.

"That my dimples kept me from looking like a crazed drover, though how that's supposed to be an improvement on being compared to a heifer I don't know."

Madison chuckled easily.

"I threw that in just for fun. I thought you might be getting too satisfied with yourself."

Fern squared up to Madison. "You tell me my face looks like old parchment, that no self-respecting woman would parade about in these clothes, that everything I've said, thought, or done in my whole life is wrong, and you have the gall to say I might be becoming too set up in my own conceit. That gives me a very strange notion of the women you consort with."

Madison laughed again and pulled her back against the bench.

She loved his touch. His magical touch. This time he was more adventurous. His arm moved around her shoulder, his fingers gently teasing the flesh beneath her shirt.

Fern had never suspected that skin could be so sensitive to the slightest touch, the barest pressure, the smallest change in warmth. It seemed as though every part of her mind had focused on her shoulder.

"You are the most peculiar man," Fern said, trying to decide if this was a lover-like declaration or if she was crazy to think she had heard a caress in his voice. She had no experience with men, nothing but instinct to guide her. George didn't behave this way with Rose, and no one could doubt that he worshiped his wife.

Madison's body remained unbending, but the distance between them seemed to be shrinking. She could almost feel the softening in his eyes. All the while his fingers were saying things to her his lips never had.

Then she realized that it was just as hard for him to admit to feeling any deep emotion as it was for her to admit she was a woman subject to all a woman's wants and needs. He might not even know he felt something out of the ordinary for her, but she did. She could see it in his eyes.

His arm closed around her, pulling her gradually to him. "I also said I liked your gumption. I think I like you best when you're a little angry and can't decide whether you want to hit me or ride me down."

"What kind of man would prefer a woman like that?" she asked. Clearly his wits were addled. She hoped they would stay that way for a little while longer.

"I don't know," he replied, apparently as mystified as she. "Certainly not the kind of man I thought I was. It seems that Kansas is bringing out my protective instincts."

"Didn't anybody in Boston need protecting?"

"Not like you."

"Me! From what?"

"Yourself, your father, this town. And something else you won't tell me about. What is it? Your father may overwork you, but he would protect you."

Fern noticed that man again. He was coming back up the street. He seemed to be walking slower this time. He was definitely watching them. A tiny shiver ran down her spine. She was glad Madison was here. She found his presence comforting.

"I can't tell you," she said.

"Why not?"

"Some things are too hard to explain."

For a moment, Madison looked as though he wasn't going to honor her wish for privacy. But unexpectedly his gaze softened, and Fern felt he was suddenly offering her a bottomless wellhead of understanding.

"It's time you started being a woman and being proud of it. Your father probably won't like it at first, but he'll get used to it. He might even grow to be proud of having a daughter like you."

Fern felt a nearly overwhelming urge to throw her arms around his neck and cry, but she resisted the impulse. Men never cried, and they hated crying women.

"What about you?" she said, hoping to focus attention on him until she could bring herself under control.

Instead of answering, he took her by the shoulders and turned her so her face was out of the deepest shadows.

"Why are you crying?"

"I'm not crying."

"Okay, why are you not crying like that?"

"You're not making any sense," she said, a choke of laughter forcing its way through her tight throat.

"Neither are you."

"Females don't have to make sense. Didn't you know that?"

"I didn't mean to say anything to hurt you."

"You didn't. It was already there."

Instead of asking more questions or assuring her

that everything would be all right, he pulled her close and put his arms around her. With gentle strength, he drew her resisting body forward until her shoulder rested against his chest.

"That's the worst kind of hurt, when it's there all the time," he said, and kissed the top of her head.

It was the understanding in his voice that made her relax against him. He knew how she felt because he felt the same way. Madison understood that her resistance had nothing to do with being strong. It simply had to do with being. Her doubt wasn't something that would go away. It would always be there, and it would always hurt.

But if she could find a shield that would never leave her, would never wear out, would be so strong and tough that nothing could penetrate it, maybe it wouldn't always hurt so much.

She didn't know what that shield might be, but if she ever found it, she hoped it had something to do with being in Madison's arms. Never in her life had she felt so safe and protected.

All her life, people had wanted her to change to suit them. But now, resting against Madison, his arms around her, she knew he wasn't wishing she were different. He knew where his arms were and was content for them to be there.

She knew he was being gentle with her because of her ribs, but even as she felt a twinge of pain, she wished he would hold her closer, harder. She longed to feel so tightly bound that nothing could ever tear her loose.

She felt her arms slowly encircle Madison's waist. She didn't direct them to do so. They just did it on their own.

It was a strange feeling.

Fern had never been held by a man. Uneasiness and expectation heightened the wondrous feeling of contentment until she felt she had found the answer to her every question.

But putting her arms around Madison was even more wonderful. He felt strong and sturdy, as though nothing could shake him. After a life of compromise built upon the shifting sands of human emotion, it was like finding herself come to rest on a monolith.

She was in safe harbor. She was home.

Madison's kiss was soft, his touch tender, but his embrace had all the reassurance of solid rock. There was a sweet persuasiveness about his kisses that Fern found irresistible. She liked being coaxed to do exactly what she wanted.

Madison placed cool kisses on her waiting lips, but her willing compliance soon turned his coolness to heat. He covered her face with passionate kisses. Fern had never heard of a man kissing eyelids and ears, but she found she liked it very much.

She found it hard to believe that Madison, who could be so abrasive, abrupt, and dispassionately critical, could throw aside all his reluctance to show emotion and act so lover-like. He had changed as much as she had.

Sometime, somehow she had worked her woman's magic on him until he forgot he disapproved of her, forgot so completely he wanted to kiss her instead. It gave her a much more wonderful feeling of power than roping and throwing a steer ever had.

But his power over her was just as revolutionary.

She had never wanted to be pretty for some man. She had never wanted to be held close or to feel protected. She'd never thought she would like being kissed, not even casually, certainly not in the energetic way Madison was now employing.

She gasped with surprise when he forced her

teeth apart and his tongue invaded her mouth. She was certain that nobody in Kansas did that. She had a deliciously exciting feeling that it was highly improper, that even the soiled doves would disapprove. But after a moment's hesitation, she found she liked that, too. Her tentative parry to his thrust caused his tongue to plunge deep into her mouth.

The pain in her ribs told her that Madison was holding her too tightly, but she didn't care. It was a small price to pay to nestle in the comforting circle of his arms.

But everything changed when he pulled her into a closer embrace, when their bodies came together, chest against chest, thigh against thigh. It acted as a signal, an alarm, a tocsin.

From somewhere deep inside her, the fear that had lurked there for eight years awakened. Even as she leaned into Madison's embrace, even as she longed to lose herself in his arms, she felt her muscles begin to stiffen. Panic reared like an angry monster roused from a deep sleep. It routed the budding excitement that skittered along her nerve endings when she felt her breasts press against his chest. It evaporated the slightly nervous fluttering in the pit of her stomach when their bodies touched from hip to knee. It robbed her of the comfort she found in the circle of his arms.

In its stead came an imperative need to break away from the prison of his arms. She felt her body stiffen, her muscles bunch for a supreme effort.

She tried to tell herself she trusted Madison, that he would never harm her, but her trust was too new, too untried to survive the onslaught of her fears. She must be free.

Even as she raised her hands to push him away, she searched her mind for an excuse. Madison would demand a reason. She couldn't tell him. She could never tell anyone.

Then she saw the man coming back down the street.

"There's a man across the street staring at us," Fern said as she pulled out of Madison's arms. "This is the third time he's come by."

For a moment Madison seemed unable to focus on anything beyond her, but when he at last looked across the street, his body immediately became taut with suppressed energy. He pulled his watch from his pocket.

"He's come," he said excitedly, almost jumping to his feet.

"Who's come?"

"The man who can prove that Hen didn't kill your cousin."

Madison had already forgotten her. All he could think about was Hen. She looked across at the man. "Are you sure it's safe?" If the man was willing to give evidence, she didn't understand why he wouldn't come out of the shadows.

"No, but I can't throw this chance away because of something that might happen. Will you be all right until George and Rose return?"

The last of the magic moment vanished. Madison was his old efficient, energetic self once more, and she was just someone he was talking to.

"If I need help, I'll call Mrs. Abbott."

Madison smiled absently, clearly anxious to be gone. "A formidable weapon."

"Go before he changes his mind," Fern urged. "You'd never forgive me if I caused you to miss gathering a piece of evidence."

Madison turned back, a bemused look on his face. "You have no idea how much I might be persuaded to forgive you," he said. For a moment, Fern thought he would linger, would say something else, but he turned and went down the steps and along the walk. The moment he left her side, the man across the street disappeared between two houses. Fern's apprehension grew. If this man feared for his safety so much he wasn't willing to meet Madison even on a dark street, what kind of danger might Madison be in?

He had become very precious to her, very necessary. He had given new meaning to her life. Under the influence of his attention, his prodding, she had been reborn, had begun to feel like the woman she should have been. He was her champion, her talisman. He was her life.

She loved Madison.

A cold chill knifed through her, leaving her feeling sick and miserable. What good would it do to love him if she couldn't stand for him to touch her? She couldn't keep him at arm's length forever. He wouldn't accept it. She didn't want him to.

She could never be his wife.

But that was what she wanted to be. She saw it as clearly as if she were standing by his side, exchanging their vows.

Piss and vinegar! What was she going to do now?

As Madison followed the man into the darkness between the houses, his mind was more on where he had been than where he was going.

He hadn't intended to put his arms around Fern; neither had he planned to kiss her as if he were starved for the feel of a woman. He tried to tell himself it was something he would have done with any of several women, but he knew it wasn't true. He tried to tell himself that Fern was upset, that she needed comforting, that there was nothing unusual in his wanting to give comfort, but he knew that wasn't true either.

He had wanted to do much more than comfort her, more than sit with his arms around her. A simple kiss wasn't nearly enough.

It ought to have been too much.

He emerged from between the houses and started up Spruce Street.

He really shouldn't find her so irresistible. He would love to take her back to Boston and turn her into a respectable young woman. He could hear her screams of protest now. Just thinking about it made him smile.

But he hadn't been drawn to that part of Fern, no matter how beautiful or fascinating she might prove to be. He knew only the Fern who wore pants, swore like a Texan, and was as tough as a piece of Spanish rawhide.

He turned on Second Street and headed west.

What in hell did he like about her? Aside from her rounded hips, her long, slim legs, and the pleasant pressure of her breasts against his chest.

For one thing, they were very much alike. Each had been badly hurt and was trying to deny it. Both of them were afraid to allow themselves to care for anyone; they tried to deny they wanted to.

He liked her spunkiness. Both of them felt alone in the world, she more than he even though she lived with her father. But she hadn't let that defeat her. She had forced the world to accept her on her own terms, terms which should have been impossible for a woman.

Yet even that didn't account for everything. He was forced to acknowledge he was attracted to her for herself alone. With her delightful body evident even beneath her scruffy clothes, he couldn't imagine why the local farms boys weren't standing in line at her door. She must have done a wonderful job of scaring them off.

Odd that she had never tried to drive him off. She had tried to drive him out of town, but not away from her. Only now did he realize that the two were really quite different.

He saw the man waiting for him in the shadows of the schoolhouse, and his thoughts snapped like a thread. He slipped his hand into his pocket and his fingers closed over the butt of his gun. He didn't expect trouble, but he meant to be ready in case it came.

"I near 'bout left," the man said. "I wasn't supposed to have to show myself."

"I had some unexpected business."

"I saw your *business*."

"Never mind," Madison said, irritated at this invasion of his privacy. "What do you have to tell me?"

The man looked about nervously. "I don't like being in town. I don't trust people who live all in a heap like this. It ain't natural."

"Maybe not," Madison agreed impatiently, "but that's something neither you nor I can change. What can you tell me about Hen's whereabouts that night?"

"I can tell you he weren't nowhere near the Connor place."

"Where was he?"

"About ten miles south, over in the direction of Newton. Don't know if he went there, but he was coming from thataway."

"When?"

"I can't be sure."

"You've got to be as specific as possible. The time is important."

"Couldn't have been no earlier than ten o'clock and no later than eleven. Probably somewhere in the middle. I'm right good at reading stars. They're the only timepiece I've ever had."

Madison could hardly contain his excitement. Dave Bunch had said he'd seen Hen's horse leaving the Connor place about ten fifteen. If this man could put Hen ten miles away fifteen minutes later, there was no way anyone could believe he'd killed Troy Sproull.

"Will you state that in court?"

"I ain't going to no court!" The man seemed on the verge of leaving. "Somebody killed Troy and tried to blame it on your brother. They ain't going to like it much if I come along and punch a hole in what looks like an open-and-shut case. What's to stop them from killing me?"

"I'll guarantee your protection."

The man laughed scornfully. "What the hell would a fancy city fella like you know about protecting me from the likes of a man who could kill Troy and then watch somebody else hang for it?"

Madison had to fight to control his spurting anger. This man was just like the twins. When would people learn that neat, clean clothes and a sophisticated manner didn't make a man a weakling?

"George will add his guarantee to mine."

"He's not much better," the man scoffed. "Now if Hen was out of jail, you'd have a guarantee worth something. He'd sooner shoot you for asking a question then answer it."

"Maybe you have more confidence in Marshal Hickok."

The man spat out a curse. "He can't never get his nose out of a card game. I could be murdered and my body carried all the way to Mexico before he'd know what happened."

"Will you talk to a judge?" Madison asked.

"If you give me enough money."

"Look, I'll pay for your protection. I'll even pay to have you resettled somewhere after the trial, but if it ever came to light that I paid you to give evidence, your testimony won't be worth a hill of beans."

"Why not? It's the truth."

"Nobody would believe you. They'll think you were saying what I paid you to say."

"You mean you're not going to give me any money?"

"I just told you what I can do," Madison said.

"But that ain't enough. I want gold. I heard your old man stole plenty of it during the war. Shouldn't be no trouble to give me a pocketful. Nobody has to know about it."

"That's a false rumor that got started in Texas," Madison said, exasperated. "But it makes no difference. I couldn't give you the gold if I had it."

"I ain't sticking my neck out for nothing," the man said, turning to go. "When you get serious, you go tell Tom. He'll know where to find me," he called over his shoulder as he headed off into the night.

"Would twenty dollars a day be enough?"

The man stopped. He didn't reply, but he was listening.

"It's legal to pay a man for his time if giving testimony keeps him away from his work."

"How many days would it take?"

"It could run to several hundred dollars if you agree to stay in town until the trial."

"I ain't staying at no hotel."

"It's the best I can do."

The man remained standing for a full minute. "I'll let you know," he said, then turned to go.

"Wait! What's your name? How can I find you?"

"You can't," the man answered without turning around.

Madison knew that if this man disappeared, Hen's

best chance of getting out of jail went with him. Without pausing to consider the consequences, he sprinted forward on cat feet. Before the man could sense anything was wrong, Madison had his hands around his throat. Pressing his windpipe closed to stifle any cry, Madison searched for and found a pressure point. The man slumped to the ground like a dead weight.

"I can't afford to let you disappear," Madison said. "Hen's life may depend on it." He lifted the man over his shoulder and headed toward the Drovers Cottage.

"You need a hand?" the clerk asked when Madison entered the lobby staggering under the weight of his witness.

"It would help if you could open the door to my room," Madison said, breathless from the long walk.

The clerk hurried ahead. "A friend of yours?"

Madison nodded.

"He sick?" he asked.

"No. Drunk. From the looks of him, you'd think he could hold his whiskey better."

"Sure looks like he ought to."

"Thanks," Madison said when the clerk held the door for him to enter his room. He fished in his pocket for a coin. "I'd appreciate it if you wouldn't mention this. My friend would be terribly embarrassed to think everybody knew he passed out cold."

"I wouldn't think of it," the clerk said, his eyes growing large at the sight of the coin in his palm.

"And tell them not to clean the room tomorrow. I imagine he'll be sleeping late." A wink sealed the bargain, and the clerk left grinning.

"Unless I can find somewhere else for you to stay, they won't be cleaning this room for many days to come," Madison said to the unconscious man. "You're going to stay where I can find you until Hen's hearing."

"Is he a credible witness?" George asked.

"As credible as Dave Bunch," Madison replied. "Besides, their evidence isn't in conflict. Bunch never said he saw Hen, only his horse. I think the killer painted a horse to look like Hen's so anyone seeing the horse would naturally assume Hen was riding it."

"It would have to be that," Hen said. "Brimstone won't let anybody ride him except me."

Much to everyone's surprise, Marshal Hickok had let Hen out of jail the moment Madison told him he had a witness who could place Hen ten miles from the Connor place at the supposed time of the killing.

"I never really figured Hen for a sneak killer," Hickok had said.

Now they were sitting around the table after dinner. Fern still hadn't recovered from the shock of finding herself seated across from the man she had hated for so long. It made her uneasy.

He could kill. She could see it in his eyes.

Not because of simple hatred or anger. He would never lose control enough to do that. Fern didn't believe he had any emotions. His eyes were as blue as the sky on a perfect summer day, but they held none of the warmth, the heat, or the passion of his brothers' eyes.

It was like looking at two beautiful pieces of glass, perfectly made, perfectly colored, but totally devoid of humanity. He might only kill if he must, but there would be no hesitation. And no regrets.

She turned to Madison and George. With a twinge of horror, she realized that if what Madison had said was true, if the brothers were three faces of the same man, Madison and George were just as dangerous. Maybe they would try harder to avoid it, but they would kill.

It made her shiver.

"Do you think he'll testify?" Fern asked. She had thought of Hen as the murderer for so long, it was hard to believe it was someone else.

"Yes," Madison answered. "He's angry now because I've got him tied up, but that's not what concerns me. So far the killer has had everything his own way. He could sit back and watch. But if he finds out we can prove Hen is innocent, if he thinks we have a clue to his identity, he'll have to do something."

"Do you have any idea who he is?" Fern asked.

"No," Madison admitted. "I just know the killer had something to gain by killing Troy and causing Hen to hang for it."

"What?" Rose asked.

Madison shrugged. "I don't know. Nobody much liked Troy. Even Fern's father fired him, yet somehow he seems to have had money."

"Troy never spent much," Fern said.

"That's what I heard at first, but I found out he liked to gamble. Nothing big, but more than a man could afford on the wages Sam Belton paid him. He was getting money from somewhere."

"Are you thinking blackmail?" George asked.

"It's got to be considered."

"But who?" Fern asked.

"That's what I was hoping you could tell me," Madison said. "You knew your cousin better than anybody. You also know the people in this town. Go back over everything you can remember for as long as you've been here. See if you can think of anything Troy could possibly hold over someone's head."

A scene immediately took shape in Fern's mind, the vivid detail causing her to cringe inwardly. Surely that couldn't be the reason. That man had left Kansas years ago.

Or had he? Blackmail was exactly the kind of thing Troy would do. Fern felt a shiver of fear. If the man had come back, she could have walked by him on the street.

"But why Hen?" Rose asked. "He hadn't been in town more than a few days. He never stays long when he brings up a herd."

"Do you think it has anything to do with that rumor about the gold?" George asked.

"No. I don't see how getting Hen hanged would get the killer the gold. No, he's trying to hurt you and the family, or he's trying to get at Texans in general."

"Texans? Why would anybody do that?" Rose asked. "They make a fortune off us."

"Not everybody wants a cattle market here," Madison pointed out. "According to Fern, many of the farmers and ranchers hate us."

Fern's own words rang in her ears with a humiliatingly loud clang. No Kansan had stated his dislike of Texans any louder than she.

"Not to mention anyone trying to sell homesteads to immigrants. Then there are the owners of the stockyards at Ellsworth and Newton," Madison said. "It would be to their advantage to drive the Texans out of Abilene. It could mean a couple of hundred thousand dollars in business."

"In other words, it might be just about anybody in the state of Kansas," George said.

"It's not quite that bad," Madison said, "but yes, it could be."

"What are you going to do?"

"Spread information. Some true, some not quite

so accurate. We've got to make the killer uncomfortable. We've got to force him to make a wrong move."

"We can't do anything until tomorrow, so I'm going to bed," Rose said, getting to her feet. "You must be tired too," she said to Fern.

Fern didn't feel the least bit tired. She doubted she would be able to sleep for hours, but she wanted to be alone to think.

Who could have killed Troy and why? The notion that Troy had been blackmailing anyone was fantastic. She wouldn't have paid any attention to it if anybody other than Madison had mentioned it. But everything he mentioned had a disconcerting way of proving to be true. She had to know if he was right this time as well.

And she meant to find out tonight.

Chapter Fifteen

Fern waited impatiently in her room. Rose had sent the brothers to the Drovers Cottage so their discussion wouldn't keep everybody awake. Rose had gone to bed, but Mrs. Abbott still moved about the house.

Fern peered out the window into the dark and windy night. Now was a perfect time to slip out of town unobserved.

She intended to go to the Connor place, and she didn't want anyone to know. She needed to know about the soddy. She had to convince herself that Madison had been right when he said no one could have seen to shoot Troy. Maybe the witness was lying in hopes of getting money. Everybody knew the Randolphs were rich.

Finally, she heard a door close at the back of the house and knew that Mrs. Abbott had gone to her room. Without wasting a second, Fern slipped out of her room, tiptoed along the hall and out the front door Mrs. Abbott had left unlocked for George.

Madison had stabled her horse at Tom and Richard Everett's Twin Livery Stable. That was practically across town. She would have to pass the Drovers Cottage. She could only hope that no one would recognize her.

Fern walked quickly along Second Street, careful to avoid shafts of light coming from several windows, until she came to Buckeye Street. She paused only a minute before she turned left and started north toward the railroad tracks at a brisk pace. She pulled her hat further down over her eyes. She wore her darkest, baggiest clothes.

At least the saloons were down on Texas Street, far enough away so she probably wouldn't pass any cowboys. She could never pass them without being recognized.

She slowed her steps as she approached Texas Street and the Drovers Cottage, but she saw no one on the porch. Ducking her head, she hurried past.

There was no cover now until she reached the livery stable a hundred yards away. The huge open area on either side of the railroad tracks offered not the slightest cover.

Tom Everett was at the stable.

"I wouldn't be going out if I was you," he said when she told him she wanted him to saddle her horse. "It's working itself up to a real blow out there."

"I know, but I've got to check on the farm. Papa's away for a couple of days."

"Shouldn't be riding off into the night, either," Tom said. "What if something was to happen to you?"

"I've been riding over this country any time of

the day or night since I was six. Why should I stop now?"

"If you was to fall off your horse, there wouldn't be nobody to find you until morning."

Fern opened her mouth to say she never fell off her horse, but by now everybody in Abilene knew why she was staying at Mrs. Abbott's house.

"I could get myself back. My ribs are almost healed."

Minutes later she was in the saddle and headed out of town. She had to pass the Drovers Cottage once more, but she felt relaxed this time. In the saddle, she looked like any other farmhand.

She felt for her rifle to make certain it was in place. She never used it, but since that night eight years ago, she hadn't gone out at night without it.

"Until we find out who killed Troy Sproull, no one's going to believe Hen's innocent," Madison said. "They're more likely to believe we paid Eddie Finch to lie for us."

George had found a soddy out on the prairie where they could keep Eddie until the hearing. It was far enough from town that no one could hear a shout for help. But so far George's cowhands had managed to convince Eddie he'd be happier not shouting at all.

"Especially since money's exactly what the witness wants," George said.

"Hen could always go back to Texas," Madison suggested.

"I don't run away," Hen said, looking straight at Madison.

"That's no way to show your appreciation," George chided.

"Don't stop him," Madison said. "Let him get it out of his system."

"I'll never forget waking up and finding you gone," Hen said, the familiar anger blazing in his eyes.

"There are things I won't forget either," Madison shot back. "If I didn't like hunting cows, or riding in the boiling sun until I was too tired to see straight, or tearing my body apart wrestling with wild steers, you couldn't wait to tell me what a poor figure of a man I was. Whenever I mentioned wanting to go back to school, or you caught me reading a book or trying to clean up that pigpen we lived in, you used to say it was a shame I hadn't been born a girl."

"I don't remember plaguing you so much."

"It was such a habit I doubt you even heard yourself. It was like having two of Pa around all the time."

Hen rose to his feet, coldly furious. "I'll kill you if you ever say I'm like him again."

"You can shoot me where I stand, but the truth isn't going to disappear just because you don't want to hear it," Madison said.

"You were always cutting at Monty," Hen accused. "You knew he couldn't retaliate except by getting mad or getting into a fight. You knew he couldn't do that without hurting Ma. That was a coward's way."

"Was it any better than your doing everything you could to prove I couldn't measure up to your standards? The more I tried, the more you despised me."

"We didn't despise you," Hen said.

Just like Pa, Madison thought. God, how he hated that man, but it seemed he ran into him no matter where he turned. "Pa did his best to make me hate myself. Why do you think I begged to go away to school? Why do you think I was nearly crazy when I had to come home? Living with you and Monty was just like living with him."

"You left because of Monty and me?" Hen asked.

Madison wanted to answer with a shout. For years he had tried to force Monty and Hen to admit to their brutality. Being able to ride and shoot and rope had never given Madison any sense of accomplishment. The twins could do all of it better. But the things he could do didn't give him a sense of self-worth because his father had scorned them.

Now he had a chance to pay off an old score, maybe heal an old wound, and he couldn't. He couldn't remember ever seeing Hen vulnerable. He had thought that both Hen's and Monty's souls, if they had any, were encased in leather. Now he could see that the leather had cracks in it. If he could make Hen believe he had driven him away, Hen would never forgive himself.

Madison admitted he had never had much understanding for anyone but himself, much sympathy for anyone except George. Maybe trying to understand Fern had made the difference, but for the first time in his life he could sense some of his brother Hen's torment. He didn't know the cause, but he could see the pain.

No matter what Hen and Monty had done, nothing he said now could change it. If they were to have any chance of being a family again, they had to forget the past.

He didn't have to look at George to know how he felt. Dear George, he cared so much and tried so hard to keep them together. Would he ever see the day when they would be a real family again?

Madison doubted it, but he didn't want to be the one to destroy George's dream.

"No. I left because I had to."

Madison saw the crack close. The precious soul inside was safe for a while yet. He was glad he hadn't hurt Hen. He couldn't hurt him without hurting himself just as much.

"About the only time I felt human was when I sat with Ma," Madison said. "Sometimes I would read to her. Other times I would just listen to her talk, mostly about when she was young. Can you understand any of that?"

Hen didn't answer. In fact, he didn't seem to be listening at all. Madison knew there was no way his brothers were going to understand him. And until they did, they would never be able to forgive him. He didn't know why he bothered. Living so far away, it shouldn't be important.

But it was. He finally knew why he had left Boston. He had been looking for a way to ask their forgiveness.

He walked over to the window and looked out, reluctant to face Hen, yet anxious for his answer.

"I used to wonder why Ma couldn't try harder to be happy," Hen said, his voice softened by memories. "Even while we were at Ashburn, she seemed to give in to everything. When we got to Texas, she wouldn't even try. She wanted to die. I tried to get her interested in things, but I couldn't."

Madison never had understood why Hen, the toughest and least emotional member of their family, should have been the one most closely attached to their mother.

"I didn't like Rose at first," Hen went on. "She could do everything Ma couldn't. That made Ma look bad. Then when I started to like Rose, I found myself getting angry with Ma. Finally I figured out Ma had left everything she loved in Virginia. Her family, beauty, a way of living that gave her life meaning. Coming to Texas was like taking her food away. It was only a matter of time before she would starve to death. Was it like that with you?"

"Yes."

Hen looked as though he finally understood. "You like it in Boston?"

"Most of the time."

"George can fit anywhere," Hen said.

"I can't," said Madison.

"Neither can I," Hen admitted. "But it was so soon—"

"That's Fern!" Madison exclaimed when a figure on horseback rode by the window.

"You've got to be mistaken," George said. "She was going to bed as soon as we left."

"I thought I saw her go by on foot earlier, but I know she just rode by."

"What would she be doing?" George asked.

"I don't know," Madison replied as he grabbed his hat, "but I'm going to find out."

"Why should he care what happens to Fern Sproull?" Hen asked after the door closed behind Madison. "You think he's gone sweet on her?"

"He's been extremely attentive to her ever since the accident."

Hen whistled long and low. "Jeff will have a fit. Her father was a Jayhawk. Some people even say he rode with John Brown. That's worse than being a Yankee."

"She said she was going to check on the house 'cause her father was away," Tom Everett told Madison. "I told her she ought not be going about at night, but she wouldn't listen. Fern never did listen to nobody."

"I'm well aware of that," Madison said. "Saddle Buster. I'm going after her."

"I ain't saddling Buster for you to kill in the dark," Tom argued.

"I don't plan to kill him, but I can't ride your other nags. I might be the one killed."

"Not you," Tom declared. "Anybody who takes up with Fern Sproull has got to have more lives than a barnyard cat. Riding about in a rainstorm ain't going to use up more than two or three."

"I haven't *taken up* with her," Madison said. "I just can't allow her to go out there alone. She's not well yet. Anything could happen to her. Besides, she's a woman."

"Maybe, but no man around here is going to remind her o' that fact. Last time anyone tried, she practically rode her horse over him."

Madison chuckled in spite of his irritation. "She does get a little touchy, doesn't she?"

"You might call it touchy. There's others that call it loco."

"They'd better not within my hearing."

But a short while later Madison began to think he was the one who was loco. He would probably find Fern sitting quietly at home, dry as toast and safe as a lamb in a fold. From the looks of the sky and the sound of the wind, he was more likely to arrive soaking wet and be faced with the return ride to town through the worst part of the storm.

He didn't expect an invitation to stay the night.

But the farther he rode, the more uneasy he became. It didn't make sense for Fern to be going home. How did she know her father was away? Madison hadn't heard anything about it. Not that he expected Fern to tell him everything, but he did expect to know something like that. And even if her father was away, and even if she knew about it, why would she want to check on the house? She hadn't been home for days, and it hadn't worried her.

But if she wasn't going home, where was she going? Madison didn't have an answer to that question either. But the farther he rode, the more certain he was that he was going on a wild goose chase.

*   *   *

The trip to the Connor place was long and tiring. Fern hadn't recovered as much of her strength as she'd thought. Long before she reached the homestead, her chest ached painfully. So did her muscles. All those days in bed had left her weak.

She kept looking over her shoulder. She couldn't decide whether she was afraid that someone was following her or if she was hoping Madison was. She kept telling herself it was foolish. Madison didn't know she had left town, and nobody else would care.

A storm was coming up. A bad one from the feel of it. Thick clouds raced across the sky, obscuring the moon. A sharp wind plowed through the grass in undulating waves. She had brought a rain slick, but it wouldn't be much use against a wind blowing so hard the rain came straight at her. She just hoped she would reach the soddy before it started.

The deserted buildings of the homestead presented an eerie appearance in the dark. The soddy looked slate gray in the dim light, and the shadows were impenetrable. According to Dave Bunch, it had been much like this the night Troy was killed.

The rain started just before she reached the soddy. It came with a rush out of the opaque night, like a huge angry beast pummeling the earth. In just a few moments the dry, powdery soil turned into mud.

Fern dismounted and tied her horse securely to a tree. If a crash of thunder should cause it to run away, she would be forced to spend the night in the soddy. The certainty that the roof leaked badly didn't bother her as much as the feeling that something was not right about this night.

But she was no longer a frightened girl of fourteen. And she carried a rifle. A sudden flash of lightning illuminated the empty landscape, making

Fern feel even more alone. Banishing a senseless shudder, she stepped inside the doorway.

The interior lay in utter darkness. She walked to the back of the one-room house and took out a white shirt she had brought, draped it over the end of the bed, and retreated to the doorway.

She couldn't see anything. Moving around inside didn't help. Moving outside made vision into the house worse. Madison was correct. The killer couldn't have seen Troy crouched in the inky shadows. He could only have killed him with a lucky shot. But Troy had been shot once, in the heart. And there were no stray bullets buried in the walls. It had been no lucky shot.

She moved to the back of the room and faced the doorway. Anyone entering the house would have been silhouetted against the light. It would have been very easy for Troy to kill his assailant with a single shot.

Fern leaned against the back wall, surprised she felt such tremendous relief. Hen couldn't have killed Troy the way they'd thought.

Madison really was trying to discover the truth.

This was of vital importance to her. Over the last few days her feelings about Madison had changed. She would have been devastated if her original evaluation had been true. She felt her body shiver and relax, as with an internal sigh.

It was safe to love Madison.

It didn't matter. She loved him anyway.

The storm broke over Madison with savage intensity. He pulled the rain slick around him, thankful that Tom Everett had insisted he take it. He wished he had accepted the offer of the wide-brimmed hat as well, but it was too late now. He could dry off when he reached the Sproull farm.

Yet he wasn't surprised when he reached the house to find Baker Sproull by himself. He had felt certain for some time that he was on the wrong track. Fern's father had no more idea than he where she might be going.

"She ought to be looking after her steers," Sproull muttered sullenly, not moving from his chair or inviting Madison to sit down. "I don't suppose she is, though, not with your crowd doing everything you can to ruin her."

"Where is the herd?" Madison asked.

"About three miles south of here," Baker said. "There's as pretty a piece of prairie as you've ever seen. Several miles of bottom land with plenty of water and grass, out past the Connor place. Fern's kept her herd on it for years. Won't let nobody touch it. And I can tell you a bunch of men have tried."

"How do I find it?"

"You don't. Not on a night like this."

"Then you'll have to go after her."

"Are you crazy? That's one helluva storm. If she wants to get herself blown from here to Missouri, it's her business."

"You lazy bastard!" Madison exploded. "If you had half as much interest in your daughter as you had in your chickens, she wouldn't be out there right now."

"How do you figure that?" Baker asked.

"You'd never understand even if I had time to explain."

As Madison headed back into the night, he felt certain that once again he had failed to guess Fern's destination. He was no more sure of his own. The only landmark Baker Sproull had given him was the Connor place. Once he passed that, he was on his own.

Fern

* * *

The howling wind whipped the rain into a froth and flung it at Fern's face like thousands of tiny arrows. She would be soaked to the skin before she reached town. Her horse probably looked forward to reaching the livery stable as much as she looked forward to slipping into her warm, dry bed at Mrs. Abbott's.

She was tempted to turn around and wait out the storm at the soddy. She thought momentarily of stopping at home, but she doubted that her father would let her go back to Mrs. Abbott's. It was just as unlikely that Madison would let her remain without a confrontation. She wanted to avoid that.

Besides, she didn't want to see her father just yet. Tonight's ride had forced her to admit she wasn't ready to get back into the saddle. She might not want to admit that to Madison, but she had no trouble acknowledging it herself.

She also had some thinking to do about her own future. Madison had forced her to confront some truths about her relationship with her father. If she went back now, she would be stepping back into the same role for the rest of her life. She knew her father would never change. This was her one chance to be treated differently. She had to be certain of what she wanted. Once she made her decision, her father would never allow her to change it. He wouldn't want her to leave. But if she did, he wouldn't let her come back.

It hurt her to admit that, but she had known he had no warm feelings for her. If he felt anything, it was resentment that she was alive rather than her brother. All her life she had tried to fill the place of that dead infant. All along she had known she never could.

But what would she do if she left home?

All of a sudden she knew what she wanted. And just as immediately she knew it was impossible. Madison would never ask her to marry him. She was crazy to think he might. She would be even crazier to say yes if he did.

There couldn't be two more mismatched people in the whole country. It didn't matter that she thought he was the most handsome man in the world or that he haunted her dreams. It didn't matter that his kisses had planted hopes in her heart which even the most ruthless logic couldn't eradicate. It didn't matter that she kept telling herself she wanted nothing to do with being a woman and a wife.

She wanted to be with Madison for the rest of her life, but she didn't have the slightest idea how to bring it about. Not that the prospect of success didn't frighten her almost as much as the thought of failure. She couldn't work out the answers just now, not with the storm doing its best to sweep her away. She had to concentrate on getting back to town without being washed down some creek.

The presentiment that someone had followed her bothered her more than the rain. It grew stronger and stronger as it became more difficult to see the trail. A flash of lightning showed her an empty landscape, but she couldn't shake the feeling she wasn't alone.

Fern slipped her hand inside her slick and let her fingers close around the stock of her rifle. Just knowing she could protect herself made her feel better.

She peered into the night, straining to see and hear, but she couldn't have heard a stampede above the roar of the wind. Her body remained tense, her muscles taut. She fingered the rifle stock nervously.

She tried to think of what she could do to help

Madison find Troy's killer. She tried to decide what to do when she went back to the farm. She even tried to think about going to the party with Madison, but she couldn't think of anything except that someone was out here with her.

The feeling was so strong she drew her rifle halfway out of the scabbard.

As the empty minutes rolled by, nothing happened. The lightning became less frequent, the rain eased off, but the wind whipped about her with such ferocity that she was conscious of little more than a nearly deafening roar in her ears. Even her horse wanted to find shelter in one of many dips in the prairie. Tomorrow morning Fern expected to see that virtually every tree had been torn up by the roots and blown away.

A bolt of lightning came to earth so close she could feel the searing heat; a deafening crash of thunder frightened a scream out of her; a rider appeared in silhouette less than thirty yards ahead.

Chapter Sixteen

Instinctively Fern pulled her horse to a halt and drew her rifle. A second bolt of lightning threw the figure into silhouette once more, and she fired. Then turning her horse, she started back across the prairie at a gallop.

Common sense reasserted itself almost immediately. No one in his right mind raced through a storm like this. She couldn't see. Her horse would almost certainly fall. Even if she didn't kill herself, the animal would probably have to be destroyed.

But as soon as her horse slowed to a trot, Fern's thoughts reverted to the man behind her.

That could have been her father or any one of a dozen men who had a perfect right to be on this trail. Whoever it was, she had shot him. She must have. She never missed. She couldn't just leave him.

She turned back but left the trail for a path on lower ground. The run-off from the storm would soon make it a dangerous route, but she should have time to reach the rider unseen.

The roar of the wind was so loud, Fern couldn't hear if the man had fired his rifle to call for help. A flash of lightning illuminated the landscape.

Nothing.

The water rushing along the streambed was rapidly becoming a torrent. Even now it swirled around her horse's legs. Soon it would become treacherous. Trees, branches, and other debris would make it lethal.

Another flash of lightning revealed a horse nearly a hundred yards away, the rider slumped in the saddle.

The man she had shot!

Feeling terribly guilty, Fern drove her horse up the sloping ground until she reached the trail. As she drew near the man, her fear returned. He could be anyone. She wasn't safe just because he was wounded.

Fern shook off her misgivings. She had shot him without provocation. He could be dying. She must help him. If there was danger, she had to risk it. She had never before let herself be ruled by fear. She didn't know what had happened to her tonight.

She approached warily. Between the dark and her horse's skittishness, she couldn't make out the rider's features.

"Are you hurt?" she called out as she drew close.

"Of course I'm hurt, dammit," the man answered. "You put a bullet in my arm."

It was Madison, and he was furious.

Fern's heart beat wildly. The full impact of what she could have done made her so weak she feared she might faint. She gripped the pommel to steady herself, but it was several moments before the blurred scene stopped swimming before her eyes.

She could have killed the man she loved. And she probably would have if she hadn't fired so quickly. And all because of blind, stupid fear.

"You did say you were going to have my blood."

"Are you bleeding a lot?" she asked.

"I don't know. How much did you want, a cup? A pint?"

"I'll take you to the house." They had to shout to be heard even though their faces were only inches apart.

"I'm certain your father will be delighted to give me a matching bullet hole in my heart."

She'd worry about her father later. Madison was hurt, and right now that was all that mattered.

"I'll lead your horse."

"No, you won't," Madison yelled back. "If I can't make it on my own, I'll stay here until I can."

His anger and sarcasm made her feel better. Maybe she had hurt his pride more than his arm.

The roar of the wind hurt her ears. Both the horses were becoming difficult to control. She almost reached out for Buster's bridle when he tried to veer from the trail. Only the knowledge that Madison would never forgive her enabled her to draw her hand back.

"Is the wind always this loud?" Madison asked. "It sounds like a train coming up behind us."

Fern hadn't been paying much attention to the wind. But now that she did, she heard the ominous timbre. Normal storms didn't sound like that. She had heard that sound before.

"It's a tornado," Fern exclaimed.

"What?" Madison shouted.

"A tornado," Fern screamed into the wind. "We've got to find a place to hide."

They were too far away to reach the Connor place before the tornado would strike.

She wished she could see. The horses plunged almost out of control. She took hold of Buster's bridle and pulled as hard as she could to get him to follow her off the trail onto the lower ground that led to the stream.

"We've got to find shelter," she shouted. The wind tore her words from her mouth, taking them past Madison and into the black void of the night.

She could see nothing, but she could tell from the horses' skittishness that what her ears were telling her was correct. The tornado was coming toward them. She just hoped they weren't in its path.

If they were, nothing could save them.

The rain was to her back. She peered into the night, trying to find a small gully she remembered playing in as a child. It lay between two trees near the stream, but she didn't know if she could find them in the dark.

The barely perceptible shadows of the trees loomed against the black sky. Digging her heels into her mount's side, Fern drove the frightened horses forward.

When they reached the trees, Fern dismounted and tugged and pulled the horses into the lee of the first tree. "Can you get down by yourself?" she shouted at Madison, but he slid from the saddle before the words left her mouth.

She struggled against the wind and the horses to tie them securely to the tree.

"Follow me," Fern shouted as she took Madison's hand and started to lead him toward a gully which appeared as a dark shadow on the ground.

Without warning, the roar approached a shriek and she heard a tree limb overhead crack. Before she could react, Madison threw his good arm around her, lifted her off her feet, and started running.

They stumbled in the gully and fell, with Madison on top.

Immediately Fern forgot the tornado, the splintering tree, the torrents of rain, the screaming horses. She couldn't think of anything except that night eight years ago when a man lay atop her, ripping off her clothes, clawing at her body.

She fought Madison with all her strength. He was much bigger than she was; his weight nearly crushed her, but she fought to bunch her knees and push him away. All the while she screamed and clawed at him, hitting him with all her might. She was only dimly aware of the gut-wrenching cracking sound, the tree limb that fell over the gully and pinned them in place.

"What's wrong with you!" Madison shouted. "You trying to tear my arm off?"

"Get off me!" she screamed.

"I can't!" he shouted back, his mouth close to her ear. "My arm's caught under you."

He couldn't get off her until he could get his arm free. He couldn't get his arm free until he moved the limb. He couldn't move the limb until he could move off Fern. They were trapped.

Fighting against the suffocating wall of terror, Fern tried to tell herself she was with Madison, that he wasn't going to rape her. But nothing could loosen the grip of the unreasoning panic that held her in its grasp.

They heard the horses scream, then the world seemed to be obliterated by a whirling, twisting, screaming wind storm which all but sucked the breath out of her lungs.

Seconds later it was gone. Even the rain seemed to be slacking off.

"Are you all right?" Madison shouted.

The weight of the limb had pushed his face into

her left shoulder. She could hardly understand his words.

"Can you get off me?" she shouted back. She felt dangerously close to the edge of panic. Anything could cause her to slip over. She clutched her hands at her side, trying to keep from screaming, trying to drive away the memory of another man.

"You're going to have to lift up so I can free my arm," Madison said.

Exerting all her strength, Fern managed to lift her body enough for Madison to pull his good arm from under her. He rolled off to one side, and some semblance of sanity returned. Taking several deep breaths, she tried to calm her racing heart.

Madison tried to lift the limb, but failed.

"I can't lift it with just one arm," he said.

They moved the limb together. The effort left her weak and panting, but the desperate need to be free of the gully, free of being so closely confined with Madison, drove her to her feet. The rush of air as she stood up helped restore her sense of reality.

She was stunned to see that a twisted stump was all that remained of one tree. Everything else had been torn away and hurled though the sky. Turning to look behind her, Fern could hardly believe her eyes. The second tree stood as it always had, its limbs intact, their horses still tethered to its trunk.

"Good God!" Madison exclaimed, gaping at the mangled stump. "I'd heard about tornados, but I didn't believe half of it until now." He climbed from the gully and walked over to inspect the torn and twisted stump. "Do you get these often?"

"No." She looked at him standing there, so big, so strong, so protective even with his injured arm. How could she possibly think he would hurt her? He had ridden into the teeth of a storm to find her.

But when she remembered the weight of his body

on top of her, the panic threatened to overwhelm her once again. She would never be free of it.

"Let's get you to the house and see about your arm," she called to Madison and started toward her horse.

The rain slacked off and the sky started to clear, but they didn't talk much. She didn't have the energy. The events of the evening had left her weak and drained.

A sense of foreboding filled Fern before she noticed anything wrong. They should be approaching the house, but the prairie lay still and empty. Only when they came closer did she realize that the posts she saw were not fence posts. They were all that remained of the barn. With a strangled cry she dug her heels into her horse's flanks.

Madison galloped after her.

The house had vanished, too. Even the floorboards. It was almost as though the farm had never existed. The pig pen, the chicken coop, everything. One chicken staggered about, dazed. The tornado had chewed a clean path through the sparse growth of trees and bushes. Pieces of dismembered vegetation lay everywhere.

Madison could only guess at the desolation she must feel at seeing everything she and her father had worked for, everything she associated with her home, simply vanish as if it had never existed. He could understand the feeling of being cast adrift in a world that suddenly seemed cruel, strange, and very frightening.

He could understand because it had happened to him.

He put his arm around her. Her body remained stiff, immobile. He didn't know what to say. There was nothing he could say that would make any difference. He wondered where her father had taken shelter. As far as he could see, the ground was flat, without dips or folds.

There was no place to hide.

"I've got to find Papa."

"I'm sure he left long before the tornado reached here," Madison said. "Maybe he's with the animals."

But he didn't believe it. He remembered how hard it had been to control their horses. He didn't see how Sproull could have driven his livestock to safety alone. He'd have had enough trouble taking care of himself.

"Let's go back to town," Madison said. "There's nothing you can do here."

"I've got to find Papa," Fern repeated

"He must be miles away by now," Madison said. "We'll never find him in the dark."

When he tried to pull her away, she shrugged his arm off her shoulder.

"He's not here," Madison said fifteen minutes later when they still had found no sign of Baker Sproull.

"He wouldn't leave," Fern insisted, looking at Madison for the first time since they had reached what was left of the farm. "This farm was the most important thing in his life."

Madison realized Fern was in shock. She had lost her hat, and her hair hung down in a wet tangle over her shoulders. She hardly knew what she was doing. But it was her eyes that unnerved him. They were wide open, staring, as though she had lost touch with the world.

"Your arm," she said, some semblance of life returning to her eyes. "I'd forgotten about it."

"I hadn't," Madison said with a trace of a smile.

"I promised to bandage it when . . ." Her voice trailed off.

"It can wait," Madison said. "We ought to be going. You're drenched to the skin. You'll be lucky if you haven't cracked some more ribs."

"It's gone. Everything. Just like that."

Madison wanted to say something, but what do you say to a woman who has lost her home, who may have lost her father? He had lost both, but Fern hadn't hated her father or longed to escape her home. For him, relief had blunted the pain.

She only had the pain.

"Your father can rebuild."

"It makes everything seem so temporary," Fern said, "so futile."

"Let's go. You need to get into bed."

Fern made a brave effort to smile. Her failure tore at his heart.

"Here you are trying to get me to take care of myself, and you're the one who's wounded. You must think I'm an awful fool. I didn't mean to shoot you, but you frightened me coming out of the dark like that."

"You've got to get some streetlights out here," Madison said. "A couple of good gas lanterns would work wonders. You could use a couple of street signs as well. I'm surprised people ever manage to find their way around this prairie."

He was talking nonsense, but it made him feel better to see a weak smile. When he brought her horse, she mounted up. They rode out of the yard without looking back.

"I've got to find somewhere to stay," she said, half to herself.

"I'm sure Mrs. Abbott will let you stay on until your father decides what to do."

"But your family has hired the house. I feel as if I'm intruding."

"Rose enjoys your company. George has been

gone an awful lot. I know she'll be glad when Jeff gets back from Denver."

"I really think I ought to stay somewhere else."

Madison listened as she cataloged the houses where she might board and then enumerated the reasons why each would be unsatisfactory. Certain she would soon talk herself into remaining with Mrs. Abbott, he turned his thoughts to her dilemma.

He had no idea what they would do about the farm—her father would make that decision—but he wasn't going to wait for Baker Sproull. The man had never concerned himself with Fern, and Madison didn't expect him to start now.

But Madison couldn't interfere without a good reason.

And he wasn't sure he had one, at least not a sufficient one. Interfering in people's lives implied a willingness, no, a desire, to assume responsibility for them. He felt quite strongly about Fern now. He liked her, a lot, but he didn't know exactly what he wanted to do about it.

He was definitely angry at the way everybody treated her. She deserved more, and he was going to see that—

A gasp and a strangled cry brought him plummeting back into the present.

Fern slid from her horse and ran a short way into a cornfield flattened by the winds. When Madison reached her side, he found her kneeling over her father's body. He could see no wounds, but Sproull's body lay at such odd angles with itself that Madison was certain most of his bones were broken. He must have been sucked up by the wind and flung a long distance.

"I knew he wouldn't leave the farm. It was all he ever cared about."

Fern touched him in little ways, brushing wet hair

out of his eyes, buttoning his shirt, wiping mud off his cheek, but she didn't straighten his limbs. It was as though she couldn't face the final proof he was dead.

"He made Mama leave her family to come out here. He made her have another baby so he would have a son to leave this place to. Everything had to be sacrificed for this place. Even me."

Madison couldn't think of anything that would ease the hurt she must be feeling, the pain of losing her father, the feeling of being lost, homeless, and alone. He had endured the same things, so why didn't he know what to say?

Because his own wounds weren't healed.

George was right. Madison wasn't ready to live life, to build, to sow and reap.

Madison took Fern by the shoulders and tried to lift her, but she wouldn't stand, just continued bending over her father's body. He would have felt better if she'd broken into hysterical weeping, but she remained dry-eyed.

Taking her hand with his good arm, Madison pulled her to her feet. Ignoring the pain of his wound, he drew her closer. She came to him, her back to him, her eyes never leaving her father's body, letting him put his arms around her, accepting his warmth and comfort.

Then the tears came. She cried softly, her body shaking as he held her, tears rolling down her cheeks and dropping onto his arms.

"He did love me," she said. "He just wanted a son so much he sometimes forgot."

Madison didn't tell Fern what he thought about Baker Sproull, but if he could have gotten his hands on him, Baker Sproull would have died a second time that night.

"We have to get him to town," he said.

Fern

Madison brought up her horse. Fern, her gaze never leaving her father, gripped the horse's bridle while Madison draped the body across the saddle. Madison shivered with loathing. Everything felt loose inside Sproull's skin, like beans in a bag. Securing the body was almost more than he could endure.

He was glad that Fern hadn't been alone when she discovered her father. He doubted she would have ever gotten over it.

"We can take him to the livery stable until you can make arrangements," he said.

She stared at him out of sightless eyes. She had no strength left, no more resources to absorb shock. He led her to Buster and lifted her into the saddle. She made no comment when he mounted behind her. Leading her horse, they started toward Abilene.

Eddie Finch glared at Madison out of wrathful eyes. "I ain't eating a bite."

"You might as well," Madison answered, unmoved by Eddie's anger. "It's not easy to get food to you without anybody wondering where it's going."

"I don't care. I ain't eating it," Eddie repeated.

"Suit yourself, but you're staying here until Hen's hearing in Topeka. You'll get awfully hungry before then."

"I won't testify. I won't say a word."

"After staying here so long, that would be a waste. Besides, then you wouldn't get your twenty dollars a day."

"This is kidnapping. I can have you put in jail."

"It sure is," Madison agreed. "But you're withholding evidence. That's illegal, too. You'd probably find yourself in the cell next to mine."

Madison heard the sound of hoofbeats and looked out the window to see one of George's men ride up. "Here's Spencer. Maybe you'll feel like eating for him."

"Maybe I will testify after all," Eddie said angrily. "Maybe I'll tell the judge you tried to bribe me. Maybe I'll tell him I saw Hen riding straight for the soddy."

Madison smiled at Finch, an overtly friendly smile, but one that made Finch suddenly very nervous.

"I sympathize with your irritation," Madison said, his voice cold and threatening, "but you will testify, and you will tell the truth. If you don't, you won't live one day past that hearing."

Despite the limitations caused by his wound, Madison spent most of his time at Fern's side. She made all the decisions about her father's funeral, but she wouldn't discuss the farm.

"There's nothing to discuss," she said, and apparently dismissed it from her mind.

But Madison's experience with longhorns gave him more faith in the ability of the irascible animals to survive, even a tornado, so he hired Reed and Pike to see what they could find. He also saw to it that every piece of the house and farm buildings which could be found was gathered up and burned. He didn't want Fern coming across something she recognized months later and having to relive the pain of her father's death.

Justifying Madison's faith in their hardiness, the herd had escaped without much loss, but not even that news could rouse Fern from her lethargy. Rose and Mrs. Abbott tried to lift her spirits by keeping up a steady flow of talk and quiet activity. Fern would join when invited, but only did as she was told.

"How long is she going to be like this?" Madison asked Rose. It had been a week since her father's funeral, and he didn't see any change.

"It's hard to say," Rose replied. "Not everybody recovers at the same rate. It must be even worse for Fern because she doesn't have anybody else. She has so many decisions to make, especially about the farm, she must feel overwhelmed."

"I'd be happy to take all the work off her shoulders, but she won't let me."

Rose regarded her brother-in-law with a narrowed gaze. "Are you in love with her?"

Madison had avoided putting that question into words, even in his thoughts. In his own mind, he had kept his life in Boston very neatly separated from Fern and his family.

But these last few weeks had breathed new life into a part of him he had left behind years ago. He *liked* the physical activity of riding miles across the trackless prairie. He liked the challenge of the inhospitable environment, the taciturn natives. He even enjoyed some aspects of the rough-and-ready frontier society, the adventure, the feeling of living on the edge. He had even learned to accept Fern's pants without wanting to throw them away.

Now that he'd found this part of himself, he wasn't sure what to do with it. But whatever he did, it would involve Fern.

"I'm not sure," Madison answered Rose. "Sometimes I'm sure I couldn't possibly be. I must be crazy. I've never been so addle-brained in my life."

"Have you said anything to her?"

"No."

"Then don't until you're sure. Right now the last thing she needs is to have that thrown in her lap as well."

"You make it sound like a burden," Madison said, feeling a little crestfallen. He hadn't expected his feelings for Fern to be looked on as a hardship.

"Who you marry is none of my business," Rose said, "but I would hate to see her hurt. And don't get in a huff," Rose scolded. "I know you'd try very hard to make her happy, but think carefully before you decide. You two have been at each other's throats since you got here. There's not much you approve of about each other. Then there's the question of where to live. You can't stand it here, but would Fern do any better in Boston?"

"I'm sure we could reach a rational decision." He hoped he didn't sound miffed, but he was sure he did.

Rose laughed easily. "If there's one thing missing in this relationship, it's rationality," she said.

Madison withdrew, his feelings abraded. He still hadn't recovered when Fern unexpectedly came out of her room dressed for riding.

Chapter Seventeen

"I'm going to the farm," she announced. "I've asked Reed and Pike to meet me there."

"I'll go with you," Madison offered, getting up from the table.

He thought for a moment that she was going to argue, but instead she smiled and said, "I'd like that."

"Would you like Mrs. Abbott to pack you a lunch?" Rose asked.

"Of course she would," Mrs. Abbott said. "And if she doesn't, I'll warrant Mr. Madison does."

At first Mrs. Abbott had called Madison "Young Mr. Randolph," but with Hen now a constant visitor to the house, she was driven to using first names. And Mrs. Abbott didn't like using a man's first name. It was familiar, and anything of the familiar concerning men made Mrs. Abbott fidgety.

"You go see about your horses," Rose said. "We'll have everything ready by the time you get back."

"Why did you fight me so hard when we were in the gully?" Madison asked. They had passed the outskirts of town and their first topic of conversation had fizzled out.

He hadn't thought much about her actions right after the tornado, but for the last two days he hadn't been able to ignore the feeling that she had tried to throw him off because she was frightened, not because he was crushing her. That didn't make any sense, but the more he thought about it, the more convinced he became that he was right.

"I don't know what you're talking about," Fern said. She kept her eyes on the trail.

"You kicked and screamed like you were in a frenzy."

"You hurt me. You're a big man."

"Maybe, but you acted like I was about to tear your throat out."

"The storm made me nervous."

She wasn't telling him the truth. He knew that. She wouldn't meet his eyes. She even urged her horse ahead of his. Madison caught up.

"It's something else. Why won't you tell me?"

"It's nothing," Fern said. She looked at him this time, her expression blank. Too blank.

They rode in silence for a while.

"I used to have a nightmare," Madison said. "Always the same one."

"I never have nightmares," Fern declared.

"I was locked in a closet and nobody knew where I was. The more I shouted to let someone know where I was, the more the walls closed in on me."

"I don't even dream."

"Sometimes, if my father caught me reading when

I was supposed to be riding or cleaning leathers, he would lock me in the stable feed room. There weren't any windows. The mice made tiny squeaking noises as they looked for kernels of dropped grain to eat. If I was locked up for very long, they would run across my legs."

"What's the object of this story?"

"To assure you we all have nightmares. It helps to share them. I still hate small rooms, but I haven't had that nightmare in years."

He thought of the many hours he had spent talking to Freddy. Fern had never had anyone to talk to.

"Is it so bad you can't tell me?"

She didn't answer.

"Maybe you don't trust me not to repeat it."

He really couldn't expect her to trust him with a secret she had refused to share with her own father. But in the last few weeks he'd developed a very strong interest in her well-being, and it hurt that she might not trust him.

"That's not it," Fern hastened to assure him. Her expression showed that she realized she had virtually admitted there was something to hide.

"Does it have something to do with the reason you wear men's clothes?"

"Why are you so persistent? You know I don't want to tell you. It should be obvious, even to someone from Boston."

For a change he wanted to help someone else. Ever since he had come to Abilene, since he had met Fern, he hadn't been running from anything. He wasn't asking for help. He wanted to give it.

"You've been alone too long. You've buried everything inside you, denied it existed, until it has become a part of the way you think, the way you act, the way you face the world."

"There's nothing wrong with that."

"There is when it keeps you from doing what you want to do and being what you want to be."

Just as his own fears had made him hide from his family for eight years. He had lost too much by that. Fern had lost, too. Now it was time for both of them to stop.

"How do you know I'm not doing what I want?"

"Because I see the difference between you and Rose. Rose is doing what she wants, being what she wants. I've never seen a more contented, happy, out-going, honest, giving, sharing person in my life."

"So now I'm selfish and mean."

"No, but you hide from people. You're not shy about attacking me when you think I'm wrong, but let me ask you about yourself and you run for cover."

"I'm none of your business."

"You weren't when I stepped off that train, but you are now."

Their lives would be entwined forever. He could no more forget her than he could forget his family.

"I don't want to be."

"Then why have you stayed?"

Silence.

"Fern, I'm not prying out of idle curiosity. I know something has hurt you, and I'd like to help."

"It's over and done with," Fern said. "Nothing can be changed."

"But your feelings about it can be."

He could see her stiffen, as if she were closing her ears, blocking out his voice. He could almost see the walls going up between them, high and topped with broken glass. Then, without warning, her resistance collapsed.

"Eight years ago a man tried to rape me," she shouted, emptying her bottled-up anger and pain over him. "Can you change that?" With a sob, she kicked her horse into a gallop.

Madison spurred his horse to catch up with Fern.

He had been prepared for many things but not this. What could he possibly say or do that would make any difference?

He couldn't begin to imagine the horrible memories she must have lived with all these years, the feeling of being defiled, the fear that another man might do the same. He thought of the years she had spent hiding behind her clothes, laboring to become something she wasn't, slowly squeezing the life out of the girl she should have become.

The thought kindled in him a murderous rage at her unknown assailant. If he could have met the man at that moment, he wouldn't have hesitated. He would have killed him.

The sight of Fern's tear-stained face as he drew alongside only made him angrier. Madison pulled both their horses to a halt. He vaulted from the saddle, and Fern slid into his waiting arms.

And they stood there in the middle of the empty Kansas prairie, under a clear summer sky, while Fern cried out the hurt and grief and anger that had been buried inside her for eight long years. She clung to him with all the tenacity of a woman who has finally shared her most closely held secrets with the man she loves.

Madison almost smiled at himself. He had always prided himself on his rigidly correct conduct, yet here he stood wrapped in the arms of a weeping female with no chaperon but their two horses. He had no idea what his friends would say, but he didn't care. He intended to stay here as long as Fern needed him.

You want to stay because you're in love with her.

The realization so stunned Madison that for a moment he felt that Fern was holding him up rather than the other way around. He must be mistaken. He couldn't be in love with Fern. Not that he didn't like her a great deal. He did. He had come to have a great deal of admiration for her courage and her integrity, but that had nothing to do with love. He didn't even like her kind of woman.

Wouldn't Freddy laugh. Madison had spent years avoiding the clutches of some of Boston's and New York's most practiced and enticing *femmes fatales* only to be snared by a farmer's daughter in pants.

Fern's sobs had stopped. Giving a determined sniff, she slipped her arms from around Madison and pulled out of his embrace.

"I didn't mean to start blubbering," she said. "That's what you get for trying to make me act like a woman."

"I'll risk it," Madison said, still feeling shaky but rallying. "I like it better than your trying to run me out of town."

"I'm sorry for that. Troy saved me that night. I owed it to him to see his killer hang. We'd better get going," she said, and remounted her horse. She pulled out a handkerchief and attempted to remove all traces of her tears. "Reed and Pike will be waiting. I don't want them starting another fight."

Her moment of weakness past, she slipped back into her shell. She didn't even wait for him to climb back into the saddle before she clucked to her horse and rode away. But Madison wasn't willing to let her close the door on him now, or ever again. He meant to share her burdens. Now and always.

Fern couldn't go it alone. The damage had gone so deep, had been so profound, it had changed her whole life. This, combined with her father's coldness, had distorted her view of everything. She thought no one loved her, that men could only lust after her. He must help her learn to believe in herself, to believe that a man could love her for herself, not for the work she could do or the pleasure she could give to his body.

At the same time, it was crucial that he control his own growing desire for her. If she even guessed how much he wanted to make love to her, she might never let him come near her again. He would certainly lose her confidence.

And at the moment, that was the most important thing in the world to him.

"Tell me about it," he asked as he came alongside.

"Why?" she demanded, whipping around to face him. "So you can relish the gory details?"

"Do you believe that?"

She turned away, fighting to control the anger and the tears. "No, but it happened a long time ago. It's over."

"Not yet. You're still afraid. That's why you wear men's clothes."

"That's absurd. I wear pants because it makes it easier to work."

"You're afraid if you dress as a woman, you'll attract attention and some man will force himself on you again."

"That's not true."

"Then why did you fight me as if I were trying to rape you?"

"You were crushing me."

"You're lying, Fern, to me and yourself."

"Did they teach you to read people's minds at Harvard?"

"No, but when you start to care for someone, you can sense things you never saw or even suspected in the beginning."

He'd never believed that before. He had thought

that cool, impersonal observation could tell you more about a person than clouded emotion. But now that he loved Fern, he not only sensed her mood, he could guess the reason behind it. When she hurt, he hurt. When she tried to hide from the truth, he understood.

"You don't care about me," Fern said, "not really. You probably decided it would be fun to teach this peculiar female to walk and talk and dress like a proper woman. Then you could go back to Boston feeling you had brought a little refinement to at least one person in the wilderness. It probably stems from a highly developed social sense. I'm told Bostonians are like that. Probably a leftover from the Puritan days."

"That's not how I feel. I—"

"I hope you're not going to say you love me, because I won't believe it. I'll bet you've got half the females in Boston chasing after you."

He couldn't miss the hard, cynical edge in her voice. Her defenses were all in place. She had told him what happened, but she didn't intend to let him any closer. She didn't believe he cared. She wouldn't let herself. She was too afraid.

"What did your father do when you told him?" Madison asked.

"I never told him."

Her answer shocked him. "Why not?"

"There was no point. Troy chased the man out of Kansas."

"You should have told him."

"No. Papa would have gone after him, and everybody would have found out. I'd always be the woman some man tried to rape. Some of them would even start saying it must have been my fault. I already suffered for it once. I didn't see any sense in paying for it twice."

Madison knew Fern was right. Even basically kind people would think she must have done something to encourage the man.

"Did you know him?"

For eight years Fern had kept the memory of that night locked in the dim recesses of her mind. Every time it tried to creep out, she had built the wall a little higher. She had felt safe until Madison showed up with his beguiling smile, tender kisses, and electrifying touch.

Now his demands had caused the wall to come down with a resounding crash, freeing all the ugliness she had tried so desperately to hide.

"It was too dark to see his face," she said, gradually allowing herself to remember. "I was coming in from the herd. I wasn't paying attention. I knew Papa would be furious I was late, so I was trying to figure out what I could fix for supper in a hurry."

"What happened?"

She could see it now just as if it were happening all over again. She shivered. She wished she had the courage to ask Madison to put his arm around her.

"He jumped out of a buffalo wallow before I knew what was happening. He pulled me off my horse and threw me down on the ground. I couldn't see anything very well in the dark, but I wasn't trying to. I was just trying to get away."

She could see him rising out of the night, a dark ominous shadow. She couldn't remember anything but that voice, that soft, breathless sound that reminded her of a hissing snake.

"He was cruel. He liked hurting me. He tore my shirt open. He kissed me all over and grabbed at me."

"How did Troy find you?"

"He was coming back from playing cards. If he

hadn't been so drunk, he might have caught him. But I didn't care about that. I only cared that he stopped him."

"And you've kept all this inside you all these years."

"What else was I supposed to do?" she demanded, rounding on him.

"Nothing, I guess, but you can let me help now."

"And what can you do?"

Madison had always prided himself on being able to think a problem through to its resolution, but this one had no solution. Something had happened which couldn't be undone. Fern would have to live with it for the rest of her life. Nothing he could do would change that.

But he could let her know he cared, that his feelings hadn't changed.

"I don't know," he admitted, "but I'll think of something. In the meantime you've got one question you need to answer."

"What?" she asked. She seemed edgy, wary.

"Have you decided on a dress for the party? It ought to be something really special. I want everybody to be stunned at the beauty who's been parading around under their noses without them knowing."

Fern laughed, probably at the incongruity of such a question after what they'd just talked about.

"I've got a few more questions to ask before I can worry about that," she replied, but he could see her relax. Now if she just didn't kill him when she reached the farm and found out what he'd done, maybe he could work up the courage to tell her he loved her.

"He bought the Pruitt house," Pike explained. "He had it sawed into quarters and loaded on a wagon.

It didn't take more than a couple of hours to put together."

"But the barn," Fern said, staring at the building of fresh-cut lumber.

"I ordered that from Kansas City," Madison explained. "They shipped it out on the railroad. It only took a day to put it up."

Neither building was very large, but the house had a floor, an iron stove, and furniture. The barn was more than adequate for the few chickens, pigs, and the single cow that occupied it.

"Why did you do this?" she demanded.

"I didn't want you to feel you had no place to stay."

"But you've been trying to get me to stay with Mrs. Abbott."

"I didn't want you to feel you had to."

Fern blushed faintly as she glanced at Pike and Reed. "You'll have them thinking you did compromise me. I wish you'd go back to town and let me get on with my work." She looked around. "At least the work you've left me to do."

"I want to talk with you first."

She looked ready to refuse.

"Just a few minutes. Alone."

"Find something to do," she said to Pike and Reed, clearly irritated with Madison. "I won't be more than five minutes."

"I guess I'd better talk fast. I'd hate to keep the pigs waiting. And your chickens might have a nervous breakdown. Do chickens have nervous breakdowns?" he asked.

"I'm sorry if I sounded abrupt," Fern apologized, smiling at his foolishness in spite of herself, "but making me remember about that night has stretched my nerves badly. I've got Lord-only-knows-what kind of mess facing me, and you want to talk.

We've done nothing else for days. What can you possibly have to say?"

"That I love you."

Fern froze. She knew she loved Madison, she had known it for some time, but she'd never thought he could love her. She had attributed his constant attention to boredom, certainly no more than a mild liking.

In fact, during the last few days she had been thinking of what to do with her life after he returned to Boston. Part of her hesitation in telling him about the attempted rape had stemmed from not wanting to forge any more ties in a relationship that had no future.

Now Madison said he loved her, and the bottom fell out of her life.

"I thought you might be surprised," Madison said—he sounded hurt—"maybe even speechless, but I never thought you'd look so dismayed."

"I-I'm not d-dismayed," Fern stammered. "I'm just shocked."

Stunned. Incredulous. Disbelieving. None of those words could describe how she felt. Heartsick came a lot closer. Madison didn't love her, not really. He had confused sympathy—over her father's death, the loss of her farm, the attack on her—with love. But it wouldn't have mattered if he had loved her. She couldn't marry him. She knew that. She'd already accepted it.

"Aren't you going to say anything?" Madison asked.

"I don't know what to say."

"The usual response is *I love you, too*, but I gather from your expression that isn't the right one this time."

"No . . . I mean I don't . . . You see . . . It's just such a shock."

Fern

She couldn't tell him she knew he didn't love her any more than she could tell him she loved him with her whole heart but couldn't marry him. "You never said anything before."

"I wasn't sure until today."

"I haven't had time to think about it."

That was a lie. She hadn't thought about much else.

"Do you think you could think about it now?"

Fern had never felt so utterly miserable in her life. The one thing she wanted above everything else was for Madison to love her. Now he had said he did, and she couldn't tell him she loved him in return, had loved him for weeks.

She knew she couldn't marry Madison. Not when anything beyond the most casual embrace conjured up unbearable memories of that night. Not when she could never be his wife in the fullest sense.

"I can't think with you here," she said. "I never can when you're around."

"That's the way it's supposed to be when two people are in love."

"Maybe, but I'd prefer it if you went back to town. We can talk again tonight."

She hated the hurt in his eyes. It hurt her, but she couldn't do anything else. She needed time to think of something to tell him.

"Can't we talk now?"

"Madison, I never thought you'd like me more than a little. Honestly, I didn't. We're very different people. We don't really have anything in common."

"But—"

"There are a lot of things we've never talked about. Your family, the kind of wife you want, my clothes—"

"They don't matter."

"Yes, they do. And if they don't now, they will

later. Give me some time to think and—"

"Do you love me?" Madison asked. "If you do, nothing else matters. If you don't, well, I guess it doesn't matter then either."

Fern couldn't look at him. She didn't trust her eyes not to give her away.

She stood poised on the threshold of everything she wanted in life, knowing she couldn't have it. After being alone for so many years, after finding no one who could understand her or wanted to try, it was cruel to have to give up Madison. But she must, for his sake as much as her own.

"I need time to think," she managed to say. "I'll tell you tonight."

Madison lifted her chin until she had to look him in the eye. "There's something you're not telling me."

"It's not that," Fern said, removing his hand and dropping her gaze. "Please, Madison, I can't think now, not with you standing over me demanding an answer."

"I'm not demanding—"

"Yes, you are," she contradicted, looking up. "You're the most impatient man I've ever known. You want everything your way and you want it immediately. I can't give you a quick answer, not about something like this."

"Okay, I'll go back to town, but I'll be back this afternoon."

"Reed or Pike can see me into town."

"I'll be back," Madison repeated.

Fern realized it was useless to protest. He would be back.

And she was glad.

Madison allowed Buster to drop into a walk. He had never imagined the scene when he finally told a woman he loved her, but now he realized he had expected Fern to fall into his arms. He certainly thought she'd be able to answer yes or no, not *I've got to think about it*.

He hoped it wasn't mere male vanity, but her reaction had stunned him, had left him feeling betrayed.

No, you just never thought a woman would refuse you.

Not exactly. He couldn't imagine falling in love with a woman who didn't care for him. Fern did care. Maybe that was what threw him off, but it couldn't be very much if she had to think about it. After all, what was there to think about?

Well, quite a few things. *Most* things, actually, but he had thought they could do that afterwards, basking in the glow of their mutual adoration. Too, he had changed, and most things didn't bother him anymore.

But had he *really* changed?

He had gotten over his initial shock at Fern's mode of dress. But even if it hadn't been completely out of the question for a woman to wear pants in Boston, he wasn't sure he could live with it for the rest of his life.

Then there was the question of Fern's ability to fit into Boston society. It wasn't that she couldn't learn. She simply hadn't been raised to that kind of life. He wondered if it was fair to ask her to try. You probably had to be born in Boston to really fit in. There were so many rules, so many conventions, so many ties that held the established social order together and kept others out.

But even as part of his mind brought up one objection after another, another part just as quickly found reasons why they didn't matter. Her courage and spirit were enough to counter any difficulty she might have. She could do anything she wanted.

But only if she loved him enough to want to try.

Another assumption. Because he felt something, he had been sure she must as well. She had accused him of being arrogant and self-centered, and he had just convicted himself.

There was no reason for her to fall in love with him. No reason for her to marry him. He had nothing to offer her except Boston and a life of wearing dresses and riding sidesaddle.

She didn't need him to take care of her. She had her own farm and her own money. Maybe she didn't want anything to do with a man. Not even a husband. After what had happened, he couldn't blame her.

Try as he might, Madison couldn't regret Baker Sproull's death. Sproull should have been proud to have a daughter with only half Fern's courage, spirit, intelligence, and good looks. He should have been equally proud to protect her.

Madison wanted to make up to Fern for these injustices. Not with things like houses and servants and clothes and trips to Europe. He wanted her to feel safe, to know he cared for her happiness, that he wanted to share her burdens as well as her moments of happiness.

He wanted her to know she was loved.

He wanted her to believe she was worthy of love.

He wanted her to know she would never have to be alone again.

He spent the remainder of his ride back to town thinking of ways to restore her ability to trust men, her desire to reach out to other people, her ability to share the love he knew was inside her just waiting for a chance to get out.

He tried not to think of what he would do if she said she didn't love him.

That made the shock all the greater when he stepped into the Drovers Cottage and came face to face with the life he thought he had left safely behind in Boston.

Chapter Eighteen

At least two dozen times during the day Fern told herself she didn't want Madison to come back for her. But as the afternoon wore on, her gaze strayed toward town more often. Now as she prepared to head back, she shaded her eyes and looked down the trail.

Empty. Madison was nowhere in sight.

"Not enough time to start anything else today," Pike said. He and Reed had finished work earlier, but they had found a few small tasks to keep themselves busy while Fern waited.

"You'd better start for home," Rose advised. "Otherwise you won't get your own work done before dark."

"We'll see you to town," Pike offered.

"There's no need," Fern insisted. "I can find the way myself. I've been doing it for years."

"I know but—"

Fern

"But nothing," Fern said. She took a deep breath and put into words what they all knew. "Mr. Randolph must have forgotten, but I'm well enough now to take care of myself."

She didn't know if they believed her injury was the reason Madison had offered to be her escort, but she hoped they didn't think she had fallen in love with him and he had forgotten her. She could just imagine the fun everybody would have with the notion that snooty Fern Sproull had fallen for a fancy dude who threw her over.

"I'll meet you here tomorrow an hour after sunup," she said. "I can't start living here again until I buy a few things, but I mean to move in before the end of the week."

It was time she left Mrs. Abbott's. Being around Madison so much had given her foolish ideas. She had started to think she might actually fit into his family. From there it would be just a small step to thinking she might be able to ignore her fear of physical intimacy.

This was impossible, and she knew it. She also knew the only way to put an end to the stubborn hope that something would work out was to stop seeing Madison altogether. She couldn't possibly wean herself from him when he was constantly at her side doing everything he could to win his way into her heart.

"You can't mean to stay here by yourself," Pike protested.

"Of course I do. I won't be the only woman in Kansas living alone. Besides, I can't run the farm from town."

"You could hire us to help you," Pike offered.

"I might, but I've got to make sure I've got the money to pay you."

"Mr. Randolph's already paid us for a month."

Fern felt the heat of embarrassment flush her cheeks. "Then I guess I'll have to pay Mr. Randolph." She didn't want to be beholden to him. Maybe she'd give him those young bulls he was so worried about. "Now both of you be on your way."

"I'm not leaving until you do," Pike said.

"Me either," echoed Reed.

This would never have happened before Madison came to Abilene. Pike and Reed would have been in the saloon by now with no thought for her whereabouts. It was amazing what leaving off her vest and wearing her hair down could do.

"Mount up," she called. "The last man out of the yard gets to clean out the well."

Pike beat Reed to the road, but Fern beat both of them. She waved gaily to the men as she headed toward town, but the smile faded the minute she turned around.

She was worried. Something must have happened to Madison.

Two weeks ago she would have figured his profession of love had been a mistake, that he had confused the role of Prince Charming with Fairy Godmother. But she had come to a better understanding of him since then. He really did care. Despite his own injury, he had hardly left her since her father's death. Not even Rose had spent so much time with her.

Besides, if Madison didn't want to do something, he was only too willing to tell her. No, he had meant to come back. Something had happened to prevent it.

She didn't think it was anything really terrible—surely Rose would have sent someone out to the farm to tell her—but she couldn't shake her uneasiness. Madison was such a determined man. Nothing stopped him from doing what he wanted. She'd certainly had enough experience on that score.

But what could have happened? That worried her so much it almost drove a more important question from her mind. How was she going to tell him she couldn't marry him?

She wondered if the words would pass her throat. She wanted to marry Madison more than she wanted to go on living. She would have been willing to accept separate beds, separate rooms, to forgo his kisses for the rest of her life, anything just to have him nearby.

But she couldn't do that to him. It had to be all or nothing.

It shouldn't be so hard. She had had nothing her whole life. She ought to be used to it. But after a month of being the focal point of Madison's day, of believing he cared for her, the gall of that emptiness tasted more bitter than ever. It was only because she loved him so much she could even think of giving him up.

"I haven't seen Madison," Rose told Fern.

Fern tried to appear casual when she asked about Madison, but she knew Rose could hear the anxiety in her voice, see the worry in her face.

"I thought he intended to spend the day with you," Rose said.

"I sent him back. There was nothing for him to do, but he said he would come to get me this afternoon."

"He didn't come here for lunch," Mrs. Abbott said. "And a man who misses his lunch is a man with a lot on his mind."

"He probably went off with George," Rose suggested. "He's been looking for a farm to winter cattle."

"Couldn't have," Mrs. Abbott said. "Lottie Murphy

told me she saw Mr. Randolph heading out of town not fifteen minutes after Fern and Mr. Madison left here."

"Maybe some business came in by the mail," Rose said. "His firm has him looking into various projects while he's out here. He probably got so involved he forgot. You know how men are about business." Rose led Fern into the parlor away from Mrs. Abbott's doomsday announcements. "Wherever he is, I'm sure he'll be irritated with himself when he realizes he failed to meet you. Why don't you go to the Drovers Cottage? Maybe it'll give him such a nasty shock, he won't forget again. He sounds more like Monty every day."

Fern bit her tongue. She found it increasingly difficult to tolerate Rose's unfavorable comparisons without making a rebuttal.

As she hurried along the street to the Drovers Cottage, she wondered what kind of business Madison had been doing. She had been so caught up in her own troubles she hadn't even noticed. It worried her. She had nothing to offer him that could compare to Boston. She could almost see his former life reaching out to draw him back. She pushed the thought aside. It didn't matter. She was going to refuse him. She just wanted to know he was okay.

She couldn't miss the looks that followed her down the street. They seemed more numerous than normal. She didn't imagine it was sympathy over her father's death. They weren't sympathetic glances. They were openly curious, even speculative. Then she remembered. She had started wearing her hair down and leaving off the sheepskin vest, because of Madison. She might be wearing pants, but there was no doubt she was a woman. It was that fact that turned the glances into stares.

That made her uneasy. She wondered if she would

ever be comfortable having men stare at her. She made a mental note to put her hair up and take out the vest once more. Madison would soon be going home. After that it wouldn't matter what she looked like.

She was relieved to reach the Drovers Cottage. She hurried into the relative privacy of the lobby only to be brought up by a shock as devastating as an earthquake. Madison was seated on a couch in one of the small alcoves. Next to him sat the most beautiful woman Fern had ever seen.

She didn't need anyone to tell her this woman and the man seated on her other side had come from Boston. It leaped out at her. Everything about them spoke of a world of wealth and sophistication completely beyond Fern's experience.

Just looking at this woman made Fern feel ugly. She wished she were any other place else on earth.

Fern tried to back out of the hotel, to run away before Madison noticed her, but it was too late. Even as she gasped in dismay, he saw her and came to his feet.

"Fern, come here. There's somebody I want you to meet."

Fern couldn't remember when she had seen Madison so cheerful. He smiled at her, but he smiled because of this woman.

Fern wanted to hate her. She would have if the woman had showed even the tiniest trace of shock, surprise, or disapproval at Fern's appearance. But she didn't. She rose to her feet, a welcoming smile nearly as broad as Madison's on her lips.

She was breathtakingly beautiful. Not even Rose could match this woman for loveliness. If Boston was full of women like this, Fern couldn't understand why Madison had ever left.

In contrast to the cream color of her plain skirt,

the woman wore a Spanish jacket decorated with deep red scroll braid, pleated fabric ruffles, and innumerable tiny buttons. Her hat was decorated with ribbons, puffs, and feathers. But Fern's eyes were drawn first to her dark brown hair, blue eyes, pink bow mouth, and flawlessly white skin.

It was stupid to think Madison would be interested in Fern when he was obviously on the friendliest of terms with this stunning creature.

She had thought all along that Madison had mistaken his feelings, but she had let herself hope he might love her. Even though she dreaded it, she had been looking forward to his coming out to the farm. Even though she knew it must end, she prized every moment of her time with him.

It hurt more than she could say that this woman only had to appear in Abilene to make Madison forget her. She was angry and jealous, and the fact that she was being totally irrational made no difference at all.

But as she stood there gaping, her entire world crumbling around her, her pride wouldn't let her allow Madison or this beautiful woman to suspect she was dying inside. She forced a smile and allowed Madison to drag her forward.

"This is Fern Sproull," Madison said, introducing her. "She's been out on her farm—"

He broke off; the smile slid from his face.

"I was supposed to ride back with you," he said.

"That's all right. I didn't get lost," Fern said, striving for a light tone. She didn't want anybody to suspect she had spent the last hour agonizing over why Madison hadn't come to meet her, that she had spent the entire day agonizing over her love for him.

"I got so busy talking to Samantha and Freddy I forgot all about the time."

Fern

"Since Madison can't seem to keep his mind on anything for more than a minute, I guess I'd better introduce myself," the woman said. "I'm Samantha Bruce and this is my brother, Frederick. We've known Madison ever since I can remember."

Fern didn't know how fancy ladies greeted one another, so she gave the gloved hand extended to her a hearty shake and hoped there was no dirt on her buckskin gloves to soil Miss Bruce's cream-colored mittens.

"Sorry I'm such a mess, but as Madison said, I've been on the farm all day."

"Madison has been telling us of your misfortunes. You are a very brave woman."

The worst part was that Fern could tell Miss Bruce meant what she said. Fern couldn't hate anyone who was so genuinely sympathetic, no matter how beautiful she was.

"It's not very brave when you're doing the only thing you can," Fern said.

"It is when you do it with courage," Samantha said, "and from what Madison has been telling us, you've got plenty of that."

"I'm sure he exaggerated," Fern said, embarrassed. She was unused to compliments. She kept thinking Miss Bruce must be making fun of her.

"Madison exaggerate?" Freddy quizzed with a lazy laugh. "I've never known a more matter-of-fact person in my life.

Yes, Madison did exaggerate. He couldn't have loved her very much. Samantha Bruce was exceedingly beautiful, but if a man loved you, wouldn't he remember you even in the presence of a more beautiful woman?

Maybe, but if the woman he loved was as unattractive as Fern, maybe not.

"Madison has been trying to cheer me up," Fern

said. "I don't believe half the things he's said."
Madison looked sharply at her. "Did he tell you
he bought me a house so I'd have some place to
live? He didn't warn me or anything, just bought
it, had it carted out to the farm, and set it up
with furniture and everything. A man who'd do that
would say practically anything."

Fern was doing everything she could to hold
back the tears, but she could feel them pooling in
her eyes.

"I didn't do anything I didn't want to do," Madison
said.

"You're a fine gentleman," Fern said. "I didn't
think so at first, but you are."

"I didn't do it because I'm a gentleman," Madison
protested.

"That makes it even better." She turned to Miss
Bruce. "Well, I'm real glad I got to meet you, ma'am,
but I've got to go. If I don't get cleaned up, Mrs.
Abbott won't let me come to the table." She started
to leave.

"I'm coming with you," Madison said.

"No, you stay with your friends. You can't leave
them on their first night in town. I'll tell Rose so
she won't worry."

"Fern, wait! I'll be right back," Madison said to
Freddy and Samantha and hurried after Fern.

"A most extraordinary young woman," Freddy
said. "I could hardly believe my eyes when she
walked through the door."

"I shouldn't have expected her to be anything else,"
Samantha replied. "I would never have expected
Madison to fall in love with any but the most
exceptional female."

"Madison, in love with her! You can't be serious."

"I could see it the moment he mentioned her
name."

Fern

"Oh, my dear sister, I'm so sorry."

"Dammit, wait up," Madison called as he hurried after Fern. If she had been wearing skirts like a sensible woman, she wouldn't be able to walk so fast. Then he wouldn't have to mortify himself chasing after her in front of half the town. He could see the amused smiles, imagine people telling their friends over a drink how Fern Sproull had the Yankee tenderfoot wriggling on a spit like a stuck pig. Knowing he was likely to be the butt of jokes in a half dozen saloons didn't improve his temper.

"If you don't slow down, Fern, I'll—"

"Go back to your friends, Madison. Go back to Boston where you belong."

"Boston and my friends have nothing to do with this," Madison said, catching her by the hand and forcing her to turn to face him. "Do you really believe I've said things I didn't mean just to make you feel better?"

"Well—"

"Dammit, Fern. You can't toss an accusation like that at a man and then walk off."

"Why not? You said you were coming out to the ranch but you didn't."

She knew she was being unfair, but she couldn't help it. The pain of one more rejection made her lash out. It helped her protect herself, keep herself under control until she could be alone.

"I never expected to see Samantha out here. It surprised me so much I forgot."

"She was accompanied by her brother, or haven't you noticed him yet?"

"Of course I noticed Freddy, but his coming didn't surprise me. It was Samantha."

"Oh, she's too good for Kansas, is she? Afraid some of our dirt might rub off on her?"

"Don't be stupid."

"So now I'm stupid again. I should have expected it. People from Kansas can't stay intelligent very long. Apparently I used up my whole supply in just a few weeks."

"Now you're being absurd. You know I didn't mean anything like that. Are you jealous of Samantha or are you just angry I forgot?"

"Neither," Fern snapped. "I'd never waste my time being jealous because of some man. As for your not coming out to the ranch, I admit I did expect you. You've fallen into the habit of doing just about everything I don't want you to do. I was also foolish enough to be worried something might have happened to you."

"I said I was sorry," Madison repeated. "We got to talking and it was later than I thought."

"Well, I'm sure you've got lots more to talk about. Don't let me keep you. Will you bring them by the house later, or would you prefer that Rose and George meet you at the hotel?"

"When you get your teeth into a man, you rip and tear for all you're worth, don't you?"

"I don't know what you're talking about."

"I thought you were different from other women, but apparently it makes no difference whether you wear pants or skirts, you all fall into jealous fits if a man even speaks to another woman."

"I've got better things to do with my time than be jealous over a conceited greenhorn from Boston," Fern shouted, oblivious to the eager ears listening from all sides. "I wouldn't care if you talked to a hundred women."

"I'm not sure if I have the strength for that many," Madison shot back, "especially if they're like you."

"You don't have to waste any of your precious strength on me. Or your false promises," she flung at him, remembering his words of love.

"I meant them, but I thought I was talking to a different person."

"Then it's good you found out in time."

"It certainly is."

Fern turned and all but ran from Madison. The sobs in her chest choked her. She refused to cry on the street, but she didn't think she could hold them for a minute longer.

She hadn't realized until now how much she depended on being the sole object of his attention. She would never have believed she could have acted like a jealous shrew, but she had. There were at least a dozen witnesses to confirm the fact in case she had any doubts.

But what could he expect her to do? Not eight hours earlier he had insisted he loved her. She had spent the whole day agonizing over how to tell him she didn't love him when she loved him desperately. She had opened up the old wounds to see if they might be healed. She had subjected herself to pain and hideous memories that had haunted her for years, and for what? For him to forget her when this "childhood friend" came into town?

She probably shouldn't blame Madison. No doubt he believed every word he'd said that morning. It was just that after he saw Samantha he couldn't remember Fern anymore.

Fern turned up the short walk to Mrs. Abbott's house. To her horror, Rose and George were sitting on the porch. Using every ounce of her willpower, she tried to look as though nothing had happened.

"Madison won't be coming to dinner," she announced. "Some friends have come into town, and he's going to eat with them."

"Will he bring them by later?" Rose asked.

"He didn't say," Fern said. And all of a sudden she

couldn't hold back the tears any longer. With a sob, she wrenched open the door and ran to her room.

"What was that all about?" George asked.

"I have no idea," Rose answered, her brow creased, "but I would bet every cow you own that at least one of Madison's friends is a very attractive young woman."

Fern didn't know how long she cried. She had so many things to cry over—her innocent enjoyment of life which had been lost that terrible night, the love her father never gave her, the years of loneliness when she tried to carve out an existence for herself against the laws of nature.

But most of all she cried over the lost hopes she had hung around Madison's neck. She knew she couldn't marry him, but she had counted on the knowledge of his love to give her the strength to refuse him, to support her through the lonely years ahead. Now she didn't have even that.

She managed to stop crying long enough to take her bath and change for dinner, but she couldn't eat. She declined Rose's invitation to linger at the table with her and George, but her room soon became an unbearable prison. Sitting on the porch wasn't much better. She tried to concentrate on the farm and what she wanted to do with it, but she couldn't keep her mind on pigs and chickens when every thought in her head had Madison at its core.

She could talk about her pride all she wanted. She could say she was hurt, that she would never believe him again, but when she was through saying all those things, she realized that only one thing remained. Only one thing was important. She loved Madison. She couldn't say she didn't care about all the rest. She did, but loving Madison was all that really mattered.

No, the only thing that really mattered was that

Madison be happy. And if she couldn't love him as he ought to be loved, as any man needed to be loved, then she ought to make sure she didn't do anything to stand in the way of his being happy with someone else.

Samantha Bruce loved Madison. Fern had seen that at a glance. Probably the only person who didn't know it was Madison himself. But he would soon figure it out, probably as soon as he returned to Boston. She was exactly the kind of wife he ought to have—beautiful, cultured, rich, and totally in love with him. She wouldn't mind his dictatorial habits. She wouldn't remind him of the times he had been wrong. She wouldn't argue with him, and she would see that everything in his household went exactly the way he wanted.

More important, she would love him just as much as Fern loved him. Most important, she would love him the way Fern wanted to love him but couldn't, with her mind *and* her body.

It wasn't the same as having him herself. Nothing would ever be as wonderful as that, but she knew his heart would be in good hands. She had only met Samantha for a few minutes, but that was enough to see the sweetness in her character, the genuine warmth in her heart. He would be getting a better wife than she could ever be. Even though it hurt more than anything in her whole life, she would be doing him a favor.

No sooner had she made that resolution than she looked up to see Madison coming down the street.

Chapter Nineteen

Fern wanted to run inside and lock herself in her room, but she made herself sit still. She had to see Madison. She had to tell him she didn't love him. Even before he climbed the steps, she asked, "Why didn't you bring your friends?" She wanted to control the conversation. She sat in a chair a little way from the others. She didn't want him to get too close. She wasn't sure she could stick to her resolution if he did.

"They were tired."

"Rose and George want to meet them." She pointed to the light coming from inside the house. "They're still up."

"There'll be plenty of time later. Freddy came on business. He'll be here for several days."

He came toward her, and she felt the panic sweep over her. "Sit down," she said, pointing to the other chair. Madison remained on his feet. "Why did his sister come?"

"To keep him company. Their parents died last year, and they don't have any family but each other."

"They have you."

"I'm just a friend."

"You're more than just a friend."

"Maybe, but that isn't what I came to talk about. I came to apologize for losing my temper. I shouldn't have said those things. You know I didn't mean them."

"Neither did I," Fern said, struggling to control her voice. "Don't," she said, when Madison tried to take her hand. "Please sit down. I can't think with you towering over me."

"Then stand up."

"I can't think when you're close, either."

"I love you, Fern. What is there to think about? We had a foolish argument, but it's over now."

"That's not true."

"You just said you didn't mean what you said."

"Sit down, Madison. This is very hard for me to say, and I can't do it with you crowding me."

"What's hard to say?"

"I'll tell you if you'll sit down."

Madison looked mulish, but he finally sat.

"I want to apologize again," Fern began. "Not for this evening, but for this morning, for not telling you the truth sooner."

Madison stiffened. She opened her mouth to say the words, but her throat closed up. Her tongue refused to utter the words that would destroy her chance at the kind of love she had seen between Rose and George, the kind of love she felt for Madison.

But she must speak. He could have no future with her. She had to send him away, quickly, before her courage failed entirely.

"I don't love you."

She was surprised that a crack hadn't appeared in the sky when she uttered those words. No mortal had ever uttered a greater lie.

She was equally surprised that Madison didn't know at once that she was lying. Surely the lie had disfigured her features. Ice filled her veins. Her heart had turned to stone.

"I should have realized it before now, but I guess I was bowled over by having a handsome Yankee lawyer—"

"I'm a Southerner," Madison stated, his pride as stiff as his backbone.

"—say he loved me. I wish I could love you. You're the kind of man every woman dreams of."

"But not you, is that it?"

"I like you an awful lot. Maybe after feeling so alone all my life, I wanted to be in love so badly I didn't want to admit the truth."

"And when did you discover the *truth?*"

"When I met Miss Bruce and realized she loves you much more than I ever could."

"Samantha? She thinks of me like a brother."

At least she had startled some life back into him. He didn't look so stiff and lifeless.

"She loves you, Madison. You may not be able to see it, but I can. She's crazy about you."

"But that has nothing to do with us. I'm not in love with Samantha."

He looked like his old self now. There was nothing like opposition to revitalize a man like Madison.

"Maybe not now, but you will be."

"That's crazy," Madison objected. "I've known Samantha for years. I've had more than enough time to fall in love with her if I were going to. I didn't. I fell in love with you. I don't know what you're trying to do, but I don't believe you."

Fern

Madison jumped up. Taking Fern by the arms, he pulled her from her seat. "You love me. I can see it in your eyes. I know you do."

"Let me go," Fern said. The old panic rose so fast her body shook involuntarily. Madison was so stunned by her reaction that he dropped his hands to his sides and stepped back.

"I only touched your arms."

It made her sick to see him recoil. He thought she loathed his touch, that she couldn't stand to be near him. She hated the agony in his eyes. She knew what it was like to be rejected. She couldn't do that to Madison. He deserved the truth. It couldn't hurt him any more than a lie.

"Sit back down," Fern said. "There's more."

Madison remained standing, his expression of stoic resolve a more bitter reproach than anger.

Fern remained standing as well.

"I'm not going to lie to you anymore," she said, trying to hold her gaze steady. "I do love you. More than I ever thought I could love anybody"—she dashed behind her chair when Madison tried to take her in his arms—"but it's no good. I can't stand for you to touch me. I've tried, oh God, how I've tried, but I can't help it."

"Don't be absurd. You can't mean—"

"You saw it just now. You touched me and I cringed." He didn't believe her. He didn't understand. "You felt it. I know you did. I saw it in your eyes. It would be worse if we were married. You'd want to touch me all the time. I would soon dread seeing you. I tried to like it, I tried to want your arms around me, but just thinking about it scares me to death."

Madison forced himself to stand still, to keep his hands at his side. He cursed himself for a fool. If he loved her half as much as he thought he did, he should have known. He should have understood.

"It's because that man tried to rape you, isn't it?"

"Yes."

He could only imagine her torment in watching her friends fall in love, of knowing it could never happen to her, of being afraid it might.

And now it had.

"You can get over that. I'll help. It may take a little while but—"

"Are you prepared to marry a woman you can never touch for the rest of your life? Are you ready to give up all thought of having a family of your own?"

"It won't be like that," Madison assured her. "You think so now, but you won't after you have a chance to get used to being with me."

"I won't sleep in your bed," Fern said. "I won't even sleep in the same room."

Madison could hear the determination in her voice, see the rigid set of her jaw, the desperation in her eyes. She was scared, much too scared to be able to control her reaction to him.

"I've thought about little else since the first time you kissed me," Fern said. "I've wanted it to be different. I've tried, but I can't."

Madison felt his own happiness slipping through his grasp as easily as the Kansas wind blew through his hair. His entire body tensed to fight back. He had given up too much when he left Texas. He wasn't willing to give up any more. Certainly not Fern.

"I'll wait as long as it takes," he said. "I'll take you to see any doctor in the world."

"You don't understand," Fern said. "I used to think when I was wearing pants and swearing and riding horses, I was just trying to hide being afraid, that someday everything would be all right again. Now I know it won't be."

"That's not true."

"You want a wife who can love you the way all men want to be loved. I can't do that."

"Fern, you're giving up too quickly. You have no idea how patient I can be."

"Yes, I do," she said with a bittersweet smile. "Ever since I've known you, you've wanted everything yesterday. But this is not a matter of patience. I can't do it. I've tried."

Madison could feel her moving farther away, out of his reach, and his control snapped. He gripped Fern by her arms. "You can't mean this. You're still upset about my forgetting to come by the farm. You'll feel different when you have a little time."

"Madison, please—"

Fern felt the panic start to rise. The same old black fear, taking all the joy out of being with him.

"You know I wouldn't hurt you."

"You're hurting me now." Nothing seemed to stop it. Not anger, not frustration. She could feel her muscles getting tighter.

"I love you, Fern. I want to marry you. I'll do what I have to do, wait as long as necessary, but I want you to be my wife. I won't let you sell yourself short."

"Please—" The pounding of her heart was so loud she could hardly hear him. Couldn't he feel it? Couldn't he tell?

Madison slipped his arms around her waist. "See, this isn't so bad. You aren't shaking. In a short while you'll start to feel better. You'll even want me to touch you." He drew her close. "I love you, Fern. I won't let you go."

The feel of his chest pressed tight against her breast caused Fern's body to go rigid. She pushed against him with all her might. "If you don't let me go, I'll scream."

"You don't mean that," Madison said. "You just have to wait long enough to realize nothing's going to happen."

Fern couldn't breathe. She saw black spots before her eyes. She was afraid that if she didn't escape Madison, she would go mad.

So she kicked him. Very hard.

"Son-of-a-bitch!" Madison exclaimed as he released Fern. "What are you trying to do, break my leg?"

"I asked you to let me go, but you wouldn't."

"You really mean this, don't you?"

"Yes."

She could see his face set hard with anger.

"Let me tell you something, Fern Sproull, you've just talked yourself into being afraid of me. Don't get all mad and puffed up. I know that what you went through was terrible, but I love you. I wouldn't do anything in the world to hurt you."

"I know. I tried, but I can't."

"Well I don't believe it. I don't know the answer, but there is one, and I don't mean to give up until I find it."

"Madison, go home and marry Samantha. She loves you. She'd be the perfect wife."

"I love you," Madison growled, "though God only knows why. After the hell I've been put through with my family, you'd think I'd get a break when I fell in love."

"You did. You got Samantha. What more could any man want?"

"I don't know about any man, but I want you, Fern Sproull, and I mean to have you."

"But—"

"No more buts. I'll leave you alone tonight. I don't want to, but I will, but you'll be ready to go to that dance."

Fern

"Madison, be sensible. I can't—"

"I can't be sensible. I fell in love with you, so I must be crazy. But if so, I'm going to be crazy all the time. I'm going to take you to the dance. We'll only touch fingertips if necessary, but you're going to dance with me. And you're going to walk with me, and you're going to hold hands with me, and you're going to kiss me. And we're going to keep doing it over and over again until you can do it without turning green. Then if you can look me in the eye and tell me you don't love me, you don't want to marry me, *then* I'll leave you alone. But not until then. Do you understand? Not until then."

Madison grabbed Fern, pressed her hard against his body, and kissed her ruthlessly on the mouth.

"There," he said as he released her. "You can scream all you like. But I'll still be here tomorrow. Tell Rose I'll bring Samantha and Freddy by for lunch."

With that, Madison vaulted over the porch rail, barely missing one of Mrs. Abbott's prized flowers, and stalked off toward the hotel.

When Fern reached her room, she found she still had a lot more tears to shed.

Madison traced the outline of Fern's pursed lips with the tip of his tongue. Her moist warmth caused his limbs to tense with anticipation. Groaning with unsated desire, he took her mouth in a greedy kiss. She impatiently returned his embrace, her tongue darting in and out of his mouth like a hungry hummingbird, her body pressed tightly against him, her firming nipples rubbing against his bare chest through the thin material of her white lace gown. A shudder of delicious anticipation shook his body. Fern trembled in response.

His hand cupped her breast, gently massaging the

293

inviting mound until the nipples stood up firm, full, and rosy. Forsaking her hungry mouth, Madison tongued her pulsating nipple through the thin cotton material. Fern's groan of erotic pleasure, her body writhing against his own, only increased his need of her. Even as he continued to suckle her breast, his hand slipped down her side, along her hip and down her thigh. Her purr of pleasure as his hand slipped under her gown and between her legs drew forth a sympathetic moan from him. His own body grew uncomfortably hard.

Slipping her gown off her shoulders, Madison let his tongue trace warm, wet circles on her breast. The feel of her nearness, the heat of her desire, caused the blood in his veins to reach the boiling point. Throwing caution to the winds, he pulled the gown down her body, slipped it under her hips, and cast it from him.

He gazed in wonder at the perfection of her beauty. Reaching out with eager fingertips, he touched her skin, trailed his fingers over her abdomen, reveling in the softness of her body, the warmth of her skin. Fern's hands explored his body, nipping, pinching, caressing, teasing until his control evaporated.

Madison wrapped her in a crushing embrace. She wrapped herself around him, drawing him closer and closer until they seemed to merge into one body, become one soul. It was as though their corporeal bodies dissolved and they coalesced into a single spiritual whole.

But even as they achieved this perfect union, Madison felt himself drift away, borne aloft, floating alone, watching Fern wrapped in the embrace of someone else.

Her face no longer mirrored ecstasy. Anger and fear distorted the features he held so dear. Instead of clinging to his embrace, she fought against it. The man wasn't Madison, and he wasn't making love to her.

A stranger was raping Fern.

Madison tried to reach out, to tear them apart, but he floated away, helpless, as Fern silently screamed his name.

With a gulping breath and a convulsive shudder, Madison came awake. His whole body shook. The single sheet clung to his damp body. The dream had been terrifyingly real. He threw the sheet aside and got out of bed.

He couldn't get this man out of his mind!

Somewhere out there was the man who had attacked Fern. He might be a killer, he might be a model citizen, but he had paid no penalty for the life he'd nearly ruined. Madison could no longer be satisfied with just proving Hen's innocence. He had to find this man and make certain he never attacked a woman again.

Madison also vowed he would never give up Fern. Some day he would make her his wife. She would come to him in her own time, when she wanted to, when she could no longer resist the need that drew her to him, or she wouldn't come at all.

Fern didn't see Madison the next day since she left early for the farm. But that evening he brought Samantha and Freddy to meet Rose and George. If he'd been trying to convince Fern she was wrong about Samantha, he made a big mistake. Miss Bruce was too much of a lady to wear her heart on her sleeve, but Fern saw that Rose knew Samantha was in love with Madison inside of fifteen minutes. Even Mrs. Abbott could see it.

"I never thought I'd be saying such a thing about Mr. Madison," Mrs. Abbott said after Madison and George had left to escort the young Bruces back to the hotel, "but he and that Miss Bruce do make the prettiest couple. Do you think they're going to get married? It's for certain she's just waiting for him to ask her."

"I can't say," Rose responded with a covert glance at Fern. "I haven't known Madison any longer than you have."

"I know, but you being his sister-in-law and all—"

"He doesn't confide in me. According to George, he doesn't confide in anyone."

"It's a pity she's not going to the dance," Mrs. Abbott said. "Nobody in Abilene has ever seen the likes of her."

"Mrs. McCoy has sent a special invitation to Miss Bruce and her brother," Rose informed her.

"I didn't think Mr. Madison would let her sit home, not when he could be dancing with the prettiest woman I've ever seen."

"I'm certain Madison will dance with Miss Bruce, but she's going with her brother. Madison will be escorting Fern."

"Fern!" Mrs. Abbott exclaimed, spinning to face the blushing Fern. "I'm sure she doesn't even own a dress, much less a party gown."

"Nevertheless, Madison assures me he will be escorting Fern to the dance."

"I never said I'd go," Fern told the two women. "Madison just assumed I'd do what he wanted."

"That may be, but surely you don't mean to tell him no at this point?" Mrs. Abbott exclaimed.

Fern wondered what Madison had done to graduate from a man suspected of trying to sneak into her bedroom to a gentleman even a female like Fern couldn't refuse. She wished she could enjoy the same elevation in people's eyes.

She couldn't see how going to the party would

help. If she had been concerned before about how she would look compared to the local belles, she would have been foolhardy to even dream of appearing at the same party as Samantha Bruce.

Yet she did dream of going. She dreamed of it every night. Dreamed of appearing in a gown more beautiful than anything Samantha could buy in Boston or New York. Dreamed of being more beautiful than any woman Madison had ever seen. Dreamed of dancing the night through, of being held in his arms, of seeing his eyes so filled with love he wasn't aware there were other women in the room. Dreamed of him whispering words of love and eternal devotion in her ear. Dreamed of the kisses that would set her soul on fire, the desire she would ignite in his body.

But each morning, the light of day, and cold reason, scattered her dreams with ruthless regularity.

She had no dress. And she felt certain Samantha Bruce had dozens that were prettier than anything she could buy in Kansas City or St. Louis. Even Chicago.

And there was no way she could dazzle anyone with her beauty. Her hair was a mess, and her skin was unfashionably brown. Besides, she wasn't pretty.

And as much as she longed to be held and kissed, she knew that the old panic would make her drive Madison away. It always did, even though she sometimes ached so much for Madison that she cried.

But she couldn't give up. No matter what argument she offered, no matter what happened, a part of her continued to believe she would find a way. That part of her was never more insistent than right now.

"I'd probably go if I had a dress," Fern told Mrs. Abbott. "But there's no place to buy one in Abilene, at least not one suitable for Mrs. McCoy's party."

"That's for sure," Mrs. Abbott agreed. "I've been telling Sarah Wells for years she ought to get her husband to stock some decent fancy clothes. There's lots of people in Abilene that's tired of calico."

Fern had expected Rose to pepper her with suggestions, but she said nothing. Instead she studied Fern in a manner that made her uncomfortable. Fern didn't understand it, and she didn't trust it. She had grown very fond of Rose—she was the closest friend Fern had ever had—but Fern reminded herself that Rose's first loyalty was to her husband and his family.

"I had thought about going to Kansas City, but with Papa's death I just forgot about it."

"I'm sure Madison will understand that," Mrs. Abbott assured her, "but I don't expect he'll be too understanding about the party. Men never do understand when things go contrary to what they want."

Still Rose made no comment.

"He'll expect it of me," Fern said. "I've done little more than make him mad since he got here."

She wondered how long he would keep thinking he loved her, how long he would want to hold her in his arms, how many more weeks before her image began to fade from his memory. How long before he forgot what it was that made him fall in love with her in the first place, forgot all the little things that made her much more than just a woman in pants.

She would never forget him, not a single detail. No one else walked into a room the way he did— as if he owned it. His mere presence made her temperature climb ten degrees. It made colors brighter. It made the words in every sentence ring with more meaning. She felt a sense of expectation, as though something wonderful were about to happen.

Fern

Seeing Samantha Bruce, and realizing that he would inevitably return to Boston, drained the life out of her. She felt deflated and spiritless. Expectation and anticipation were gone. In their place was a certainty that Madison would marry Samantha. She wanted to be with him as much as she could before he left, but it hurt more each time.

She longed to go to the dance. Deep down inside she wanted to know if she could compete with Samantha. It was a stupid thought—there was no comparison between them—but Fern couldn't banish the hope that if she could just get to the party, somehow Madison would see she loved him as much as Samantha ever would.

"I just may have a dress that will fit you," Rose said finally.

Fern felt her body tense. She had made her statement in the certain knowledge there wasn't a suitable dress in all of Abilene. She had never *really* considered facing all those scowling, censorious people. She didn't know what would make her more uncomfortable, their looks or the dress itself. She couldn't remember what it felt like to wear a dress. How to walk, how to sit. She had no idea what to do with her callused, chapped hands. Not even gloves had been able to protect them from the rough work of roping cows.

Then there was Samantha. No woman in her right mind would wish to be compared to her. Fern would be stepping out of her element and right into the world in which Samantha was at home, the world she had been born to rule.

If they were having a rodeo, it would be different.

But Fern couldn't give up the chance to be with Madison. Hen's hearing in Topeka was coming up in three days. Hen would be released and all charges dropped. He would be free. There would be no reason for Madison to stay in Abilene any longer.

It hurt to think of his leaving. She couldn't turn down a chance to spend a few more hours with him.

"You're much smaller than I am," Fern said. "I couldn't fit into one of your dresses if you split every seam."

"You could fit in this one." Rose laughed, a little self-consciously Fern thought. "I got so depressed at looking like a buffalo cow I ordered two dresses in St. Louis. I ordered another in Kansas City. The shop in St. Louis sent me the wrong ones. If they fit you, it'll save me having to send them back."

Fern relaxed. There was no way that anyone could misjudge a dress for Rose so badly it would be large enough for her. But even as she felt relief that she wouldn't be going to the party, she felt regret as well.

For once in her life she'd like to have some fun, a chance to be herself, not to have to worry about convincing everyone she was as much of a man as anyone else. And to be honest with herself, she'd like to have a man want to dance with her. She didn't know how to dance, but she'd sure love to try.

But most of all, she'd like to have someone think she was pretty. She knew she wasn't. She had known that since she was ten and a boy had told her she was uglier than a bulldog calf. She'd knocked him down and bloodied his nose. She'd done it more to keep from crying than to hurt him. But it had hurt so much she'd never forgotten it.

She'd never thought about being pretty until Madison started spending all his time with her, telling her she was pretty, telling her he loved her. It was all Madison's fault. Everything was his fault.

"We've done enough talking for one night," Rose

said when she heard George's footsteps on the front porch. "Tomorrow we'll have to see if we can turn our thoughts into substance. Meanwhile, you'll have to stay away from the farm," she told Fern. "Working with pigs is no way to get ready for a party."

Madison couldn't find Rose. After working up his courage to talk to her about Fern, it irritated him that she shouldn't be at the house. He decided to wait but quickly grew tired of his own company. He moved from the parlor to the front porch, then to the back yard where he found William Henry playing in the shade of a cottonwood tree. Ed was nowhere to be seen.

William Henry had put together a log cabin of real logs. He had also put up a corral made of tiny posts notched to hold the rails. The corral contained about a dozen carved horses and cows. Three cowboys on horseback patrolled the perimeter, presumably to ward off rustlers.

"That's a handsome set," Madison commented as William Henry galloped one of the riders about the corral. "Did your father order it for you?"

"Nope," William Henry answered, not looking up from his play. "Uncle Salty made it for me. And he's going to make me some more while I'm gone."

The first rider completed the circle of the corral. William Henry chose a second rider and began a second circuit.

"Does the rider have a name?" Madison asked.

"This is Uncle Monty." He held the figure up so Madison could get a good look.

"See, he's making a face."

"Why? Did someone rustle one of his cows?"

"No. That girl has been bothering him again. Uncle Monty doesn't like girls. He says they cause too much trouble."

Madison thought he and his brother might agree on something after all. Fern had certainly turned his life upside down.

"Who's your other rider?" Madison asked.

"This one's Daddy," William Henry said, showing him the largest figure. "And this one is Uncle Hen. He doesn't like girls either."

"It's a good thing your daddy likes girls."

"Daddy doesn't like girls," William Henry declared emphatically. "He likes Mommy."

"I like your mommy, too," Madison said, trying to hide his smile.

"Everybody likes Mommy," William Henry declared. "She never causes trouble. She fixes things."

There, in a nutshell, was a description of the girl Madison had hoped to marry. It was a description of Samantha. But he had fallen in love with Fern, the greatest natural disaster west of the Mississippi.

"I guess not every girl can be like your mommy."

"Uncle Monty says tangling with Iris is worse than going after a mossy back steer in a thicket of cat's claw. Uncle Monty says Iris ought to be de-ported."

Madison laughed. "Where does she come from?"

William Henry looked around. Then coming over to Madison, he whispered in his ear. "Uncle Monty says she comes from hell." William Henry giggled delightedly. "Mommy says I ought not say hell, but Uncle Monty says it all the time. Mommy says lightning will strike Uncle Monty, but Daddy says lightning wouldn't waste its time."

Madison knew he shouldn't encourage the child, but for the first time he had a feeling of fondness for his nephew. He'd never had any interest in children, but William Henry was different. Maybe because he was George's son, part of his own flesh and blood. Maybe because he saw in him the child he had been before his father's brutality destroyed his innocent faith in the world.

Maybe he saw in him the son he might have with Fern.

Whatever touched him, he no longer needed to talk to Rose. He knew what he wanted, and he knew how to get it. But he had added a new item to his list. He wanted a son just like William Henry. He wanted to help bring a generation of Randolphs into the world for whom being part of a family was at once the most important and the most rewarding part of their lives.

Chapter Twenty

A knock on the door broke Madison's concentration. Muttering a curse, he pushed the papers aside. He opened the door to find the Pinkerton investigator he had hired standing in the hall.

"Come in," he said.

The invitation didn't sound genuine, but the man entered as readily as if it were.

"How's Eddie's family?" Madison asked.

"Doing fine. Better with the money you sent them. The wife's a good manager."

"And their ranch?"

"Your brother's men have done more work in one week than her husband has done since he bought the place. I don't think his wife would mind if you kept him."

"She's welcome to him the minute the hearing's over. Have you gotten any response to your inquiries?"

"A little. There's only one man who fits the description you've worked out, but so far I can't turn up anything to connect him to the killing."

"Do you have any ideas?"

"No. Do you?"

"One."

"Tell me," the man said, and sat down.

The day of the party Rose got up from the breakfast table, announcing briskly, "It's time to try on that dress. Let's go to my room."

Fern had thought all night long of the moment she would put on the dress, but she was unprepared for her reaction to the two dresses that lay across Rose's bed. One was a day dress with a solid blue skirt and a white top decorated with alternating thin blue stripes and tiny blue flowers. A very handsome dress, but insignificant next to the other, a party dress of brilliant sunflower yellow. Fern had denied the desire to wear a dress for so long she had forgotten she ever felt it, but she knew in a flash that she wanted to wear this golden dress more than anything else in the world.

"What do you think of them?"

She thought the yellow dress was absolutely beautiful. She would have traded her favorite cutting pony just to be able to wear it for Madison, but she knew it wouldn't fit.

"I don't know anything about dresses," Fern replied. She felt embarrassed, as though she were confessing a guilty secret. "What do you think?"

"I think they're lovely," Rose said, "especially the yellow. It would be just perfect with my coloring. The blue would probably be more to your liking. It's a little more plain, less frilly."

Fern looked at the blue, but her gaze turned back to the yellow dress.

"Which one would you wear to a party?" Fern asked.

"The yellow. The blue dress is meant to be worn at home or when visiting friends."

"Then I guess I'd better try on the yellow dress first."

Fern knew wearing that dress wouldn't be the answer to anything. It would probably cause more problems than it would solve, but she didn't care. She wanted to go to the party, and she wanted to go in that dress.

But it wasn't that simple. If she went to the party, she doubted she could ever go back to the life she had led before Madison got off that train. Fern resolutely closed her mind to the consequences. If she didn't, she wouldn't have the courage to go through with it.

All her life she had lived with fear, letting it dictate everything she did. Today she would cast caution to the winds. She would wear this dress, she would look as beautiful as she could, she would go to the party, she would dance all night even though she had no idea how to dance.

Very soon Madison would go away and there would be nothing left of her dreams. She had no choice but to accept that, but she would have this moment, this one last chance to unfurl her wings and fly toward the sun with all the other butterflies. Just once in her life she would pretend she was just like any other woman, that she had the same chance for love. Just this once she would ignore reality, defy reason, thumb her nose at the sensible.

She would fly as high and as long as she could. It didn't matter if she singed her wings and plunged to earth. After tomorrow, nobody would see her again. Tomorrow she would move out to the ranch.

Fern

Tomorrow she would put Madison Randolph out of her mind forever.

Only he would remain in her heart until she died.

"Strip down to your skin," Rose ordered. "I'll see if I can find a shift that will fit you."

"What for?" Fern asked. "I can put the dress on over my own underclothes."

"You can't try on a dress like you would a pair of shoes," Rose said. "You have to prepare yourself."

"What do you mean?"

"You'll see."

For the next half hour Fern allowed herself to be pushed and pulled, prodded and poked, discussed and argued over. Rose and Mrs. Abbott discussed styles and lengths of hair, lamenting that Fern had allowed her luxurious locks to become so dry and brittle. Mrs. Abbott virtually went into mourning over Fern's skin.

"I've seen better on a man," she wailed. "Don't you ever put cream on at night?"

"Papa would have taken a stick to me if he'd ever caught me putting grease on my face."

"Cream," Mrs. Abbott corrected. "Grease is for boots. And look at her shoulders—not that they aren't much better than I thought, but her shoulders and arms are white as a sheet while her neck and hands are brown as an Indian. Where will you ever find a dress to cover her from the top of her head to the tips of her toes?"

Fern's self-confidence hadn't been very high, but Mrs. Abbott's strictures caused it to take a nosedive.

"It's not that bad," Rose said, "but we will have to improvise a high collar and long sleeves. Let's hope it's a cool night."

"It's never cool in July, not even at night," Mrs. Abbott told her.

307

"Well, there's nothing I can do about the weather, but I can do something about this skin," Rose said. She took a jar from the table, touched her fingertips to the white contents, and gently massaged it into Fern's skin.

"It's disappeared already," Mrs. Abbott exclaimed. "Her skin's as dry as paper."

"I've got a big pot of cream," Rose said, dipping into the jar once more.

Fern let them rub and massage. She knew it wouldn't make any difference. Even the paint the girls down at the Pearl Saloon wore couldn't make her beautiful.

"Now we've got to do something with her hair."

"What?" Mrs. Abbott demanded. "It's like trying to comb a bristle brush."

"We've got to wash it first," Rose said. "Probably half the Kansas prairie is hidden in there."

"I wash my hair regularly," Fern protested.

"I was just kidding," Rose said. "One day in the Texas brush and everything needs washing."

Fern wasn't mollified by the tacit apology, but she meekly submitted to having her hair washed. Somewhere during the oil treatment she lost herself in a daydream. She was dressed in the yellow dress and surrounded by men clamoring for a chance to talk to her, telling her she was beautiful, wanting to dance with her, to bring her something to eat or drink, to escort her home, to take her for a ride.

Before she could decide how to distribute her favors, Madison appeared on the scene. Sweeping everyone aside, he took her into his arms and engulfed her in his embrace. Deaf to the shocked exclamations around him, he pressed his body against hers until she thought she would burst into flame from the heat.

Fern

"I don't think we ought to do any more than trim the ends," Rose was saying.

"I think we ought to cut it short and curl it."

"No!" Fern said, horrified at the thought of appearing anywhere in curls. "My hair has never been cut."

"What do you think about wearing it in an elegant chignon on the nape of your neck?" Rose asked. "Or you could wear it on top of your head."

"She'd be the tallest person at the party," Mrs. Abbott objected.

Fern didn't care what they did as long as they left her hair untouched. She'd kept her hair long despite all the trouble it caused her. Her mother's hair had been long, and Fern had always wanted to be like her mother.

"It's a shame we can't show your shoulders," Rose said, "but your skin will improve if you stay out of the sun."

"Not by tonight," Mrs. Abbott said.

"No, not by tonight," Rose said with a sigh. "But I think I have a bolero jacket she can wear."

Fern had lunch in her room while her hair dried. Rose visited with George and William Henry.

Fern decided that if being turned into a beauty meant having her hair washed all the time, her skin rubbed with oil until she felt like a greased pig, and dresses, jackets, and shifts by the dozen pulled over her head, young ladies like Samantha Bruce were much to be pitied. The waiting was awful. And boring. She was used to being active, being outside, giving orders, yet all morning long she'd sat in the same chair, never leaving her room, and agreeing to everything Rose said.

"What's that thing?" Fern asked when Rose and Mrs. Abbott returned after lunch.

"It's a corset," Rose said of the garment in her

hands. "You put it on before you put on the dress."

"You're not putting that thing on me," Fern said, backing away from the stiff garment. She had heard about corsets. She had seen them on the girls at Pearl's. Sometimes a corset was about all they had on.

"It won't have to be tight," Rose said. "You're already very slim."

"I'm not putting it on," Rose said.

"You can't wear the dress without it."

"No." Fern eyed the corset as though it were some malevolent beast. She thought it was a barbaric contraption, the kind of thing Madison would have said had been thought up in Kansas.

"I'll hold her down while you slap it on her," Mrs. Abbott offered.

"No," Rose said. "She has to wear it because she wants to. It won't work any other way."

"Are you wearing one of these things?" Fern demanded of Rose.

"In her condition?" Mrs. Abbott exclaimed. "I should say not."

"I would if it would keep me from looking big enough to be two women," Rose said.

"But you will after the baby is born?"

"Every woman wears a corset," Rose told her with a sigh of resignation. "It's part of being properly dressed."

If you're going to this party, you can't do things by half measures. Samantha Bruce is bound to wear a corset. You've got to wear one too.

It wasn't as bad as Fern had feared. It wasn't the tightness that bothered her. It was feeling as if she couldn't bend in the middle. She doubted she could mount a horse in this rig. She knew she'd never be able to brand a cow. She wasn't even sure she could take a deep breath.

Fern

"I think it's time to do your hair," Rose said. "It's going to take quite a while to pin it all up."

"By the time we're done, she'll be ready to cut some of it off," Mrs. Abbott proclaimed.

Fern didn't think she could stand to sit still long enough for them to do her hair, but she knew she wasn't going to let anybody cut it.

"That's not half bad," Mrs. Abbott said when they had shoved what Fern was certain were at least a hundred pins into her hair.

"Actually it's quite good," Rose said. "Much better than I had hoped for."

"Let me see," Fern said.

"Not until we get you in the dress," Rose said. "I don't want you to see anything until you're completely done."

The last several hours had seemed long and tedious and, most of the time, boring and lacking any excitement. Fern had had to keep reminding herself the ordeal was necessary to getting dressed for a party, necessary because of Madison.

Putting on the dress was different. All the drama of the day was now distilled into a few minutes. Any moment now the transformation would be complete.

Nothing bored her any longer. She could feel the same excited expectation she imagined every woman feels when she dresses up, when she is about to see herself revealed as something more glorious than she had supposed.

She silently endured the fitting of the dress, the tugs and pulls to settle it into place. The fit was so perfect the dress might have been bought for her. She also endured the questions of whether to wear the jacket or a shawl to hide her shoulders. They settled on a jacket. She even managed to endure the discussion of jewelry and Rose and Mrs.

Abbott trying several combinations before they were satisfied.

But when they started to discuss whether she would wear flowers in her hair, and if so, what kind, she could stand it no longer.

"I've got to see what I look like," she said, fidgeting with impatience.

"I still say flowers would give just the right touch," Mrs. Abbott insisted. "Besides, her complexion might not look so rough."

"There's nothing any flower can do for my face," Fern stated. "It's always looked like old leather, and it's going to keep on looking like that. Now let me see what I look like."

"I guess we have kept you waiting long enough," Rose said. She took the mirror and held it up for Fern to see.

Fern could hardly believe she was looking at herself. She wasn't beautiful, she never would be, but there wasn't a bulldog calf in all of Kansas that looked as pretty as she did right now.

But the biggest shock was that she didn't look anything like herself. That wasn't Fern Sproull. She might as well be looking at a stranger, someone nobody in Abilene had seen before.

"You like it?" Mrs. Abbott asked, more impatient than Rose with Fern's silence.

"I don't look like me."

"I should think that would make you happy," Mrs. Abbott said, causing Rose to frown at her quite severely.

"I guess it does," Fern said, "but it's strange to look at yourself and see someone else. It's almost as if I don't exist anymore."

"It's another side of you," Rose said. "It's always been there. You've just been hiding it."

"It's just as well," Fern said, hardly knowing what

to say. "What would I do with her on the farm?" she said, pointing at the woman in the mirror. She was talking as if there were two of her. She *felt* like two people. Surely this other woman would be completely different, would feel and act unlike herself. That made Fern feel uneasy. Madison had already introduced too many uncertainties into her life. She wasn't sure she could handle any more.

"You'll learn," Rose said. "It's not always easy, but we all learn."

But Fern wasn't sure she wanted to. It had taken years to become comfortable with herself. Now she knew what was expected of her. Everyone knew what she expected of them. She had no idea what to do with the woman in the mirror. But worse than that, she was afraid of what other people might expect of her. She was most afraid of what she might expect of herself.

Fern felt sick with apprehension. Despite the evidence of her own eyes, as well as Rose's and Mrs. Abbott's assurances that she looked lovely, she was petrified of what Madison would think. He'd never seen her in a dress. If he was telling the truth and didn't love Samantha, he might not love her now that she neither looked like herself nor was half as pretty as Samantha.

"Stop chewing your nails," Rose said. "You look lovely."

"I'm not chewing my nails. I can't even find them." Fern wore mittens, something else that made her uncomfortable.

"Well, you are biting your lips. If you don't stop, they'll be swollen twice their size before Madison gets here."

"I thought men liked women to have generous lips."

"Maybe, but I doubt they like the taste of blood on them." George came into the room. "Tell her she looks nice," Rose directed her husband.

Fern made herself smile for George, but it didn't matter what George thought. It only mattered that Madison like her. She couldn't go to the party if he was ashamed of her. Neither could she stay home, not after all the work Rose and Mrs. Abbott had done.

"You look very lovely," George assured her. "I have to confess I didn't expect you to be so pretty. You've done yourself, and the men of Abilene, a grave injustice by dressing in pants all these years."

"See, I told you," Rose said, smiling, needing no one's approbation except her husband's to make her happy. "Now as soon as I can find William Henry to say good-bye, I'll be ready to go."

Mrs. Abbott came in with William Henry dressed for bed. He dutifully kissed his mother and father.

"Where is Fern?" the little boy asked when he emerged from his mother's embrace. "I want to kiss her good night, too."

"That's Fern," his mother said.

"You can't fool me," he said, laughing happily because he thought his parents were trying to trick him and had failed. "Fern wears pants like me and Daddy."

"You don't recognize her because she's wearing a dress," Rose said.

Fern knelt down until she was face to face with the child. "I'm just dressed up so I can go to a party. Do I look so very different?"

William Henry didn't look convinced. Fern felt panic. If the child didn't recognize her, what would Madison think? It would be like coming face to face with a stranger, and Madison wasn't a man to take quickly to strangers. What's more, he hated being surprised.

"You don't look like Fern," William Henry said.

"But I am," Fern assured him, tears starting to gather in her eyes. "I just got dressed up so I could go to the party with your Uncle Madison."

"It really is Fern," Rose said. "Now hurry up and give her a kiss. You have to go to bed."

William Henry seemed willing to take his mother's word. "You're as pretty as that other lady Uncle Madison brought here," he said. "You're almost as pretty as Mommy."

Fern gave the child a big kiss and a quick, fierce hug.

"You're a shameless flatterer. I hope your wife is as beautiful as a princess and all your children little angels. Now run away to bed. I promise to tell you everything about the party tomorrow."

"Boys don't like parties," William Henry announced very solemnly, "but I'll listen if you want me to."

"Scram," George said. "It's the Randolph in him," the proud father explained to Fern. "We can't seem to do anything about it."

"Don't change a thing," Fern said. "It may drive his wife crazy, but it'll make her love him all the more."

"Yes," Rose agreed softly, her luminous gaze on her husband and son as they left the room.

"It's hard to imagine Madison was ever that small," Fern said, almost to herself.

"George, too," Rose agreed. As if suddenly remembering something, she left the room and returned moments later with a photograph. "You might like to see this." She handed Fern the Randolph family photograph. "Can you find Madison?"

Almost as if guided by an unseen finger, Fern's

eyes went immediately to the tall, thin boy standing to the left of George.

"He was sixteen," Rose said.

"He looks so young." Fern said. "As if nothing unkind or cruel had been able to touch him yet."

"It had even then," Rose said. "His father made his life miserable. Madison won't tell you, but I will." She pointed to William Henry Randolph. "Look at him. He must have been the most handsome man in the world, the kind of man women only dream about."

"No wonder George and Madison are so good-looking," Fern said, "but even they're not as handsome as their father."

"I can't begin to tell you the things he did to those boys," Rose said. "He must have been the most cruel and vicious man who ever lived. Did you know Madison was born on Valentine's Day?"

Fern shook her head.

"According to George, their father taunted Madison with it, teased and badgered him until he refused to celebrate his birthday. When he asked to be sent away to school, their father made him come home because he knew Madison liked it."

"How could he have been so cruel?"

"It was no worse than what he did to the other boys. But I'm not telling you this to make you feel sorry for them or angry at their father. I just want you to know why Madison might have some difficulty expressing his love, even being able to believe in your love."

"I . . . we . . ."

"I'm not asking you to tell me anything," Rose assured her, "but I couldn't help but notice that things have been strained between you, especially since Miss Bruce and her brother arrived."

"It's not—"

"I'm sure it's not. But Madison still has some questions to answer, not the least of which is whether he wants to become part of the family again."

"But I thought . . . he and George . . ."

"George isn't all the family. Hen still hasn't forgiven him. And then there's Monty and Jeff."

"And the others?"

"Tyler and Zac were too young to remember much."

"What can I have to do with this?"

"You've been as hard on Madison as anyone else, maybe even harder. I'm not blaming you," Rose said when Fern colored with embarrassment. "Circumstances conspired to put you at odds with each other, but that's over now. Madison is at a crossroads. The decisions he makes now will determine how he lives the rest of his life. He very much needs someone who can accept him for what he is without any qualifications. I don't think he's ever had that before."

"I'm sure Miss Bruce accepts him without qualification." Fern was ashamed of herself for saying that. It sounded petty and small.

"Maybe, but it's not Miss Bruce's acceptance he's looking for. If it were, he probably wouldn't have left Boston."

Fern had never thought of it like that. She had always assumed he had left Boston against his will, that he couldn't wait to get back so he could forget that Kansas ever existed.

"I don't know if I should tell you this yet," Rose continued, "but Madison bought that dress for you. He bought the blue one, too. He thought you probably didn't have anything to wear to the party and might not go."

Fern felt a shiver of anger, a splinter of betrayal.

She had been duped again. This was just one more example of Madison's determination to get his own way.

"But he told me not to pressure to you wear either one. He said he'd take you in pants if that was the only way you'd go."

"But you said I couldn't go without a dress, that he wouldn't take me."

"I was wrong," Rose said. "He obviously cares more for your company than he cares for convention. In fact, he gave me the impression he didn't intend to go if you didn't."

Once more Fern's hopes flowered, but this time she couldn't feel that everything was hopeless. This time she felt sure that something would happen, somehow things would work out. If anybody could make things work out, it was Madison.

"But what about Miss Bruce and her brother?"

"Miss Bruce has been going to parties without Madison for years. I imagine she can manage one more."

Fern tried to tell herself to keep a tight rein on her hopes, but there was no holding them now. If Madison could accept her pants, if he could prefer her to Samantha, he really did love her.

Chapter Twenty-one

Madison kept his horse to a walk. He was on his way to pick up Fern in the buggy he had rented for the party, but for the last hour he'd been telling himself he was an idiot in refusing to recognize that Fern Sproull wasn't in love with him.

She couldn't be and give up so easily.

She might think she hadn't gotten over what happened years ago, but he was kidding himself if he believed it. The way her body froze every time he got near her was all the proof he needed. If she loved him half as much as he loved her, she'd be over it. As far as he could tell, she hadn't tried.

Then why haven't you gotten over the things your father and the twins did to you?

He could still remember being locked in that dark feed room. The memories no longer had the power to reawaken the fear and loathing he had experienced, but he remembered the time the

319

snake crawled across his body. He had kept from crying out by telling himself it wasn't a rattlesnake or a copperhead, only a black snake looking for the mice that came to eat the grain. But he could still remember the nearly mindless terror as the huge reptile slithered across his body. He could still feel it against his clothes. He could still hear the whisper of its rough scales against the dry corn shucks as it prowled among the feed bins for mice.

A cold shiver arced through his body. Maybe he hadn't completely erased the memory of that day any more than he had forgotten the humiliation of being sent home from school. But not even the mortification of that experience could compare to the sheer gut-churning fury he'd felt when he learned his father had intentionally refused to pay the tuition because he thought Madison was too happy away from home.

No, he supposed there were some things he would never forgive. Hurts that might take a lifetime to heal. If that was true for him, it must be so for Fern.

He turned the corner and saw Rose and George coming out of the house. So Fern had decided to stay home. He didn't know why he had thought she would leave. It would have taken great courage to face the townspeople wearing a dress. It also would have meant she was ready to make some changes in her life.

Her refusal meant she was comfortable with things as they were. Madison could understand it, but he couldn't accept it. Not anymore. When he came to Kansas, he turned his back on the status quo. And he didn't mean to allow Fern to hide behind a life built on fear and misunderstanding. There was more than her future at stake. There was his happiness as well. And he wasn't about to give it up so easily.

"You're late," Rose said as Madison alighted from his buggy.

"Doesn't seem to have been any reason for me to have come at all."

"Oh, I don't know," Rose said, smiling broadly. "I think you're in for a big surprise."

"At least William Henry thought so," George said. "He thinks your date is very pretty."

"William Henry?" Madison repeated, confused. "What are you talking about?"

"He wanted to kiss Fern good night, but he didn't recognize her. I hope you'll do a little better."

Madison's heart skipped a beat.

"Then she's going? When I saw you two alone—"

"She's waiting inside," George said. "We'll see you at the party." He took his wife's arm and helped her into a second buggy. Even though it was only a short distance to the McCoy home, it would have been impossible to walk through the dusty streets and arrive in a presentable condition.

Madison covered the distance on winged feet. Gone was the doubt, the reluctance to put Fern's courage and love to the test. He knew there were still questions to be answered, but she had come this far. Maybe, with his help, she could come the rest of the way.

She was seated when he entered the room. She rose to her feet, her heart in her eyes. Her fear that he wouldn't like what he saw was so clear that he would have said she was beautiful even if she looked like a mottled heifer.

But she *was* beautiful, more beautiful than he had ever dreamed. Unlike William Henry, he recognized her immediately. Not even the dress or the flowers in her hair or the fact that she wasn't wearing pants and a sheepskin vest could cause him to mistake Fern. Every detail of her face was burned into his memory.

"You *are* a swan," he said.

"What?" Fern asked, confused.

"It was a story mother used to tell us about a duckling that thought she was ugly until one day she grew up and saw her reflection in the water and realized she was the most beautiful and graceful of all birds."

He could see the tension flow from Fern's body as the wary expression turned to a timid smile.

"I don't look ridiculous? People aren't going to laugh at me? I couldn't stand that. I'll leave if one person even cracks a smile."

"No one is going to laugh," Madison assured her, "but they are going to be shocked. You're beautiful. Really beautiful."

"I'm glad I'm not ugly," Fern said, apparently still unable to believe him. "It would be a shame after all the trouble you went through to get this dress."

Now it was Madison's turn to feel uneasy.

"You don't have to look like you're about to turn and run," Fern went on. "I wasn't too happy when Rose told me, but I changed my mind when she said you told her not to pressure me to wear it, that you'd rather miss the party than make me uncomfortable."

"I see Rose talks as much as everybody else in this family."

"It was a really nice thing to do," Fern assured him. "I couldn't stay home after that, could I? And if I really am not ugly . . ."

"You won't have to take my word for it," Madison said. "Wait and see what happens."

"Did you see Miss Bruce and her brother before you left the hotel?"

"I escorted them to the McCoys' before I came here." He leaned a little closer. "I wouldn't say this to anyone else, but you look every bit as lovely as she does tonight."

Fern felt as if she were walking on air. Madison thought she was as pretty as Samantha. She didn't believe it, not for a minute, but it didn't matter that it wasn't true. It only mattered that Madison had said so. That made it as good as if it were true. No, it made it better.

The drive was much too short. Fern didn't care if they never arrived at the party. She was content to be with Madison, to bask in his admiration, to listen to him praise her, but she was petrified of everybody else.

"Every man at the party is going to want to dance with you," Madison said. "But remember, I'm very jealous."

"Don't worry. I'll refuse them all. Even you. I can't dance."

"I forgot. I was supposed to teach you."

But things got in the way, Fern thought. Something was always getting in the way.

"I'll think of something," Madison said.

Dozens of wagons and buggies surrounded the McCoy house. Light streamed from every window, and the lilting sounds of fiddle music competed with the more strident strains floating in from the saloons on Texas street.

"I'll drop you at the door," Madison said. "It shouldn't take long to find somewhere to park this buggy."

Fern thought of facing everyone alone and her heart froze. She wouldn't enter the McCoy house alone, not even if she had to turn around and walk home.

"I'll go with you," she told Madison.

"But you may get your dress dirty."

"I don't care. It took every bit of courage I had to let Rose and Mrs. Abbott put me in this dress. I'm not going into that house by myself."

"You don't have to go in. You can wait outside until I get back."

"No," Fern said, shivering at the thought of being stared at by men she didn't know, whispered about by women she did. She could stand it if she was with Madison—she could stand anything as long as he was with her—but not alone.

By asking the drivers of a wagon and a buggy to move closer together, Madison was able to make a place for his buggy near the wooden boardwalk that ran along the front of the McCoy house.

"I'll carry you to the walk," Madison said when Fern started to climb down.

"I can walk."

"After all the work you've gone to, I don't want you to get dirty."

"You can't be carrying me about like a saloon girl. People will never stop talking."

"Is that what they do with saloon girls?" Madison asked, a devilish grin on his face. "I should have spent less time at the hotel."

"You know what I mean."

"I do, and I also know you can't arrive at a party looking as if you've been trailing through the muck. They'll talk even more."

Before Fern could make any further objections, Madison scooped her up in his arms. Gasping for breath, and from fear of losing her balance and tumbling into the dust, Fern wrapped her arms around Madison's neck. But that increased the feeling of shock even more.

She had never been carried in a man's arms while conscious, not even that night when Troy had found her dirty, half naked, and crying from fear and shame. The near hysteria which overtook her every time a man touched her had caused her to steadfastly avoid any man's embrace. Yet all at once she was in Madison's arms with her arms around his neck, her body pressed tight against him.

Much to her surprise, she didn't feel panic. Another feeling, nearly as uncomfortable and totally unexpected, caused her nerves to grow taut and the pit of her stomach to tighten. Rather than fear and revulsion at his touch, she felt excited by the strength of his arms, the way he carried her as though she were a delicate, priceless treasure. She found that the necessity of leaning against him was neither a burden nor a terrifying experience. Confusing, yes, but also exhilarating. By the time Madison set her down on the walk, Fern was flushed, breathless, her senses in a turmoil.

So was her heart. Madison had done much more than touch her. He had held her in a tight embrace. She had been powerless to resist, to escape, and she hadn't panicked. True, the old fear had begun to rear its ugly head by the time her feet touched the ground again, but the feeling of excitement, of anticipation, was even stronger.

Suddenly the night seemed too warm. And too crowded. She needed time to explore these new feelings, but she didn't have it. Even as she felt her cheeks flush with heat and her heart beat with unusual rapidity, Madison took her arm firmly in his and directed her steps toward the house. And the light. And all those people.

"I don't want you to act as if there's anything unusual about tonight," Madison said. "If you behave as though everything's perfectly normal, everyone else will, too."

"But I don't *feel* normal," Fern said. "I feel like a freak in a sideshow."

"Well, I don't," Madison said, holding her hand even more firmly. "I feel like a man lucky enough to be escorting the prettiest girl in town to a party. I know everybody else will try to steal her from me, but I intend to defend my prize."

"You make it sound like dogs fighting over a bone," Fern said. She knew Madison was just saying these things to build up her confidence, but his praise warmed her heart. He must love her. If he could say she was beautiful after seeing Samantha, it was certain he was blind.

The sound of music growing louder, the sound of voices raised in laughter, the image of people moving against the light brought home the realization that very soon the shield of darkness would be removed. Fern moved closer to Madison and held his arm a little tighter.

The panic had faded. The feeling of excitement, of yearning to be close to him had banished her fear. For the first time, she could touch a man, could let a man touch her, and not tremble inside. Maybe, if Madison did truly love her . . .

"Evening, Madison," Doug McCoy called as Fern and Madison approached the steps. "Your Miss Bruce has brought the traffic to a standstill. There's no getting near her." He peered into the semidarkness. "Looks like you done turned up another beauty. Where did you find her?"

"Right under your nose," Madison said, urging a reluctant Fern into the stream of light coming through the open door. "Don't you recognize Fern Sproull?"

Fern knew Madison was enjoying himself, but she felt like crawling under a stone. She had been stared at and gawked at and gaped at all her life, but no one had ever gazed at her with the look of stupefaction that now settled firmly on Doug McCoy's face.

"That's not Fern," McCoy said. "Why, she . . ." He stared at her again. Then taking her by the arm, he pulled Fern closer to the light. "Holy cow!" he exclaimed. "Edna!" he bellowed. "Edna, come out here this minute. You're never going to believe your eyes."

Fern tried to pull away. But Doug McCoy had a viselike grip on her arm, Madison stood right next to her, and people were coming up the steps behind her. She was trapped. Instinctively she reached out for Madison. She felt some of the tension leave when his strong fingers closed around hers.

"Go on," he whispered. "This is your big moment. Enjoy it."

Fern tried to feel like a princess being escorted to her throne, but she felt a lot more like a prisoner being brought before a judge who was going to give her hell for even thinking she could be pretty. The guests were a jury waiting to condemn her.

She walked through the door and encountered a sea of eyes, all turned on her.

But even as she felt the urge to run from the room, she felt Madison's hand on the small of her back, urging her forward, letting her know he was there, that he stood at her side. She also caught sight of Rose beaming a smile of support in her direction. Drawing confidence from both of them, Fern stepped into the circle of light.

Several men stared at her, their jaws dropping in stunned surprise. A couple more stared in curiosity, obviously unaware of her identity. But in all of them, she saw a man's appreciation for a lovely woman.

She saw something else in the women's eyes. She caught sight of Betty Lewis, and memories of that childhood party were swept aside by the look of pure anger she saw now, anger she saw reflected in other women's eyes, all looking at her as though she had done something wrong.

Fern realized it was the anger of women who feared they would be eclipsed, who feared they might be forgotten. She understood, but she felt no sympathy. They had all made her feel that way too many times.

Fern could feel the resentment settle over her like a suffocating cloud. She could feel Madison's fingers tighten around her hand; she saw Rose look about her with disgust at the women's coolness. Then much to her amazement, Fern saw Samantha Bruce making her way through the crowd toward her.

Fern didn't know how anyone could think she was beautiful, not after seeing Samantha. She was breathtaking. Fern was surprised that anyone had even bothered to notice her own arrival. How could anybody think she was a threat with such a gorgeous creature in their midst?

"I'm so glad you're here," Samantha said, coming forward and slipping her arm around Fern's waist. "It's so nice to see another familiar face. Freddy and I are depending upon you to introduce us to your friends."

"I'm sure they can speak for themselves," Fern said, hard-pressed to recognize most of the men in their party finery. She wondered how many of the girls wanted to be introduced to Samantha. Most her age were married. She could see them holding on to their husbands as though they might fly away if they weren't tied down.

"I'm sure they can," Samantha said, "but it always helps to have the guidance of someone you trust."

Fern decided that if anyone deserved a place in heaven, it was Samantha Bruce. She swore she would never again be jealous of her, never think a harsh thought, never begrudge Samantha her beauty, wealth, or anything she had in this life.

Except Madison. Her gratitude didn't extend that far.

"That's a lovely dress, dear," Rose said, moving forward to add her support. "It goes so marvelously well with your coloring."

"It certainly does," Freddy said, coming forward. "I hope you will give Samantha the name of the shop. She doesn't have the advantage of your color. She has to be so careful not to slip into the insipid."

As they moved into the main room, Fern felt enveloped in a cocoon of protective warmth, a shield so thick nothing could harm her. With Rose and Samantha on either side and Madison, George, and Freddy following behind, she *did feel* like a princess entering her court.

The feeling grew stronger as the evening progressed. Everyone wanted to meet the Bruces. The wives wanted to meet Rose. To do so, they had to come to their acquaintance Fern. It was a situation that was just as frightening to Fern as it was annoying to them. And of course the women wanted to meet Madison. They had all seen him and heard about him. They knew he was a rich Boston lawyer who had all but proved that his brother didn't kill Troy Sproull.

But the final cachet came when Hen Randolph entered the room and went straight to Fern's side. She may have been the local tomboy, the butt of their jokes and whispers—they may have ignored her and reviled her—but any woman who could attach to herself a wealthy Boston socialite and her brother, his shatteringly handsome partner, a powerful Texas rancher and his wife, and a notorious gunfighter *all in the same evening* was someone to be reckoned with. The past was cast into limbo; all was forgotten. Fern had gone from an outcast to a lioness of society in one evening.

But Fern wasn't sure she liked being a lioness. She was sure she didn't if it meant she couldn't spend any time with Madison. It seemed that everyone else in the room saw more of him than she did. Every time she turned to him, someone would push forward wanting to talk to her, to retell some experience she had forgotten, or to be introduced to her friends.

She cast more than one entreating glance in Madison's direction. After one particularly despairing look, he broke off his conversation with a man Fern didn't know and came over to the knot of people surrounding her. Madison made his way through the press of bodies until he reached Fern's side. "You ladies are going to have to get along by yourselves," he said, taking Fern by the hand. "Fern came with me, and I haven't been able to exchange two words with her all evening."

Madison headed toward the door.

"Don't go too far, Mr. Randolph," Mrs. McCoy warned. "We're about to begin the dancing."

"We wouldn't miss it," Madison said without slowing down.

After the heat of the room, the coolness of the night air felt like a bath in a cold stream. Fern didn't object when Madison drew her close. His warmth comforted and excited her.

"Are you feeling better now?" he asked.

"No, I'm terrified. Everybody was furious when they saw me, but now they act like we've been best friends forever."

"I don't think they were mad, just surprised."

"I'll be forever grateful to Samantha. She and Rose really made the difference."

"Samantha is a wonderful girl," Madison said,

his eyes shining. "You'll learn to love her as much as I do."

Fern didn't think she could go that far, but she told herself she had to be resolute in expunging every trace of jealousy.

"How does it feel to be the prettiest woman in the room? Isn't it worth doing without your pants?"

"It's nice of you to keep saying it, but I know I'm not the prettiest woman in the room."

"What is it going to take to convince you that you're a very beautiful woman?"

"At least two bottles of whiskey." Fern laughed. "I'm not sure I'd be drunk enough even then."

Madison put his other arm around her. "That has been your trouble from the beginning. You never have been able to believe in yourself."

"That's not true," Fern said, settling a little more deeply into his arms. "I proved I could do anything I wanted."

"You made them accept the person you created, but you kept your real self hidden because you didn't believe in it. Just like now. You can't believe you're beautiful. You don't believe in yourself as a woman. You don't believe you can be a real wife, so you're determined to deny yourself the right to be happy."

"Madison—"

"I'm talking about my happiness, too, and I'm not going to let you quit so easily. I understand your fear, at least I think I do—"

"I—"

"—but you can overcome it. I've been talking to Samantha, and she knows a doctor who—"

Fern felt the heat in her veins turn to ice so fast it flash-froze the expression on her face. She broke from his embrace. "You told Samantha Bruce what happened to me?"

"No," Madison said. "I've never uttered a word to anyone."

Fern felt the tension inside her ease a little. "Then what were you talking about?"

"We know someone who's been going to a new kind of doctor, one who helps people get over their anxieties. She was telling me this friend has made spectacular progress. I was thinking that maybe you would consider . . ." His voice trailed off.

Fern moved close to Madison and he put his arms back around her. "Didn't you notice something just a minute ago?" she asked.

"Yes. You didn't push me away."

"I wasn't afraid to let you hold me because I knew you weren't going to hurt me. Maybe, if you can be patient—"

"I can be the most patient man in the world," Madison told her, his grip tightening about her with satisfying vigor. "I can wait for as long as it takes. We can be married as soon as Hen's trial is over. Then once we get home to Boston, I'll contact that doctor immediately."

Madison was going too fast. Fern felt the old familiar fear creeping over her. She didn't know whether it came from the idea of moving to Boston, of having to bare her soul to a strange doctor, or the fact that Madison had pressed her body against his. But she told herself that none of that mattered, not now. She trusted Madison. He would never hurt her. As long as she could remember that, as long as she could believe it, there was a chance they could have a future together.

And she wanted that. She had only realized how much since Samantha had come to Abilene and she thought she would lose him. But Madison loved her. He preferred her to a beautiful, rich, socially prominent woman who could help him achieve all he had set out to accomplish. She didn't understand it, but she would keep telling herself it was true. She had to believe it.

It was a lot easier to believe it in Madison's arms. It was even easier when he kissed her. At first she was afraid someone would see them. She was afraid the fear inside her would expand until it consumed all her pleasure, but gradually the anxiety subsided and her body relaxed.

For the first time she was able to experience Madison's embrace without fear.

But there was more than that. There was pleasure. There was comfort. There was happiness. She had known for a long time there must be more to the feelings between a man and a woman than she knew. She had often wondered why the girls she knew talked of nothing but boys, had no greater ambition than to get married. With her life dominated by fear of men and fear of dying in childbed like her mother, she had never been able to understand it.

But now she did. The way she felt about Madison right now, she would take just about any risk to be with him.

"Are you sure you're not afraid?" Madison asked between kisses.

"Absolutely," Fern said, yielding herself up to the pleasure of kissing him back.

The feel of his arms around her was a comfort, a barrier against anything that might try to destroy her happiness. The warmth of his body against hers was exciting. She had never known that mere contact could be exhilarating, but gradually her body was throwing off the shackles of years of fear and repression. Natural instincts were coming to life, sending signals, issuing invitations, dancing with the sheer exuberance of release from years of restraint.

Fern didn't understand what was happening to her, but she loved every bit of it.

"Tsk, tsk, Mr. Randolph," Mrs. McCoy said, interrupting them. "The dancing is about to start. We must have everybody inside."

Chapter Twenty-two

Fern sprang away from Madison. The mild rebuke in Mrs. McCoy's voice made her too self-conscious to remain in his embrace. But even as she felt her face flush with embarrassment, even as she dreaded the thought of facing that august lady in the light, she smiled with secret pleasure.

She had finally gotten over one barrier; she had experienced some of what it meant to be a woman in love. And she meant to experience even more as soon as possible. She was almost ready to proclaim to the world that she loved Madison Randolph. After that, maybe she wouldn't care who saw her in his arms.

"Why are you grinning?" Madison asked as they walked back inside.

"Because I'm happy," Fern replied.

Madison gave her hand a squeeze. "You'd better look a little less happy, or everybody's going to be certain we've been doing something highly improper on Mrs. McCoy's porch."

Fern suddenly had a picture in her mind of Mrs. McCoy's face if anything so untoward were to happen, and she felt a bubble of laughter growing in her chest. She fought to contain it but lost. It erupted in a silvery cascade that drew the attention of nearly everyone in the room.

"Whatever have you been doing out there?" Betty Lewis asked, her gaze on Madison rather than Fern.

"Nothing," Fern said.

"It doesn't sound like nothing."

"Oh, that," Fern said, trying to dismiss her laughter. "Madison was just telling me a funny story."

"You've got to tell us," Betty said.

"I can't," Fern said, giving Madison a mischievous look. "It wasn't very proper."

"I can't believe that Mr. Randolph would tell warm stories, and certainly not to a . . . lady."

"Then you don't know him very well," Fern said. "There's not much he wouldn't do."

Fern could hardly believe she had had the courage to talk back to Betty Lewis. Just the thought of drawing so much attention to herself made her feel weak. Instinctively she reached for Madison's arm.

"Would you like to lead us in the first dance?" Mrs. McCoy asked Madison.

"You'll have to find him another partner," Fern said. "I don't know how to dance."

There was only one woman in the room Fern would have wanted to dance with Madison, but it was out of the question for Rose to dance in her condition. That left the young women of Abilene or Samantha, not an easy choice for Fern until she remembered the warmth of that young woman's greeting.

"Why don't you ask Samantha?" she said. "You can show us the dances you do in Boston."

Madison tried to demur, but Samantha accepted without hesitation. Slipping into the crowd next to Freddy, Fern said, "If we can find a room where no one can see us, would you teach me to dance?"

"You really don't know how?" Freddy asked.

"No. I stupidly wouldn't let Madison teach me when he offered."

"Why don't you try the side porch," Rose suggested. "It might be better than a secluded room."

Fern started to say that no one would suspect a man of doing anything improper with her, but stopped. As Madison said, she was always underestimating herself. If a man like Madison with so many women to choose from could love her, she must be pretty. Maybe even pretty enough to tempt a worldly man like Freddy.

Fern found it wasn't too hard to learn to dance. That is, it wasn't when she could keep her mind on her steps and not on what Madison and Samantha might be doing inside.

"You have to know the steps so well you can do them without thinking," Freddy was saying. "That allows you to carry on a conversation with your partner."

"You must practice dancing all the time," Fern said, marveling that anybody could talk and dance. It was like asking her to carry on a conversation while she roped and tied a calf. She could shout commands, but you couldn't call that a conversation.

"We start learning early," Freddy explained. "It's a very important social skill."

"We don't have more than one or two dances a year unless you count the saloons, and nice people don't," Fern added.

"We have dances every week."

"What for? You must get tired of dancing with the same people."

"We have strict rules about dancing with anyone more than two times in one evening," Freddy said.

"If you like your partner, why not?"

"Because it could be taken as a sign of serious interest. A young man must speak to the young lady's father before he can show such attention to her."

"You mean you'd have to talk to my father before you could dance with me three times?"

"Yes."

"But he's dead."

"Then I'd speak to your guardian."

Fern decided it must be awfully difficult living in Boston if you had to ask permission to do something as simple as dancing. She didn't know how Madison got along. He never asked anyone's permission to do anything. He must cause quite a stir among the guardians whenever he showed up.

"I think you've got the hang of it now," Freddy said.

"As long as they don't change the music or go faster," Fern said as they returned to the party.

She almost wished she'd stayed outside. Madison and Samantha were dancing again, this time in the center of the room. Everybody had stopped to watch them. They were so graceful together. Fern knew she'd never be able to dance like that, not if she practiced on the porch for the rest of her life.

Even worse, they seemed to be having a wonderful time together. They were talking, laughing, apparently not missing her or Freddy at all.

She felt like sneaking away, but she couldn't. She wouldn't. Madison had said he loved her. She had to learn to believe it was true, even when he held another woman in his arms.

But it was hard.

Fern felt some of the tension leave her muscles. She had almost completed an entire dance, and while she had made mistakes, none of them had been serious.

"Can you talk now?" Madison asked.

"Only in short sentences," Fern replied, favoring him with a worried smile.

"I'd rather you watched me."

Fern looked up at him and immediately took a wrong step. "I'd better watch my feet. I can look at you tomorrow."

But she kept looking up anyway. Now she understood why she sometimes found Rose sitting quietly just looking at George. If she looked at Madison every day for the rest of her life, she would never get enough of him. And tonight, of all nights, she finally saw something beyond the handsome face and arrogant smile and supreme confidence.

She saw the man who cared enough to never give up even when she did her best to drive him away. She saw the man who had looked past her defenses to the woman inside and decided it was time for her to come out, who saw the person she could become and wouldn't let her be anything less.

Now, through his insistence that she attend this party, she had created a new identity for herself. She felt reborn. No, she felt born for the first time. She no longer had to hide behind men's clothes or confine herself to men's work. She had choices.

"Are you enjoying yourself?"

"Yes and no," she replied. "I'm a nervous wreck for fear I'll do something wrong. But I've never done anything half as exciting before. I can't believe I'm actually here, wearing this dress and dancing with you. I'll probably wake up in the morning and not believe a bit of it."

Madison glanced at the other people in the room. "I don't think they'll let you forget."

Gaining enough confidence to look around her, she was surprised to see looks of envy and admiration all around her.

She knew the female envy stemmed from her dancing with Madison. It didn't take much to see he was the most handsome man present. Some might vote for George, but Fern preferred Madison. The roguish smile, the devil-may-care attitude, the supreme confidence, the very things that used to annoy her, now seemed to make him most dear.

But she couldn't explain the admiration in the men's eyes. Surely they couldn't be admiring her! These were the very same men who only yesterday had passed her on the street without even noticing her. Yet Joe Tebbs stood looking at her with his tongue hanging out, just like he used to look at Nola Rae Simpson down at the Pearl Saloon.

"Close your mouth, Joe," she hissed. "You'll catch a gnat."

Joe flushed up to his hairline, grinned, and shifted his weight on feet crammed uncomfortably in new boots, but he didn't stop staring.

"Let the boy look," Madison said. "He probably can't get over the fact that he's been looking at you for years and never had any idea you were such a beauty."

"You've got to stop saying that before I start believing you," Fern said.

"Look around. Everybody's staring at you."

"They're staring at you."

"They hardly notice me. It's your transformation that has left them speechless."

"I think I deserve a chance to dance with Miss

Sproull," Freddy said, tapping his friend on the shoulder. "After all, I taught her how."

Madison acquiesced gracefully.

"See where their eyes go," he said.. "They won't be following me."

"What's he talking about?" Freddy asked.

"Oh, he's trying to make me believe everybody's staring at me instead of him."

"He's right," Freddy said. "Nobody's interested in Madison, not tonight. Everybody's talking about you. I know because I've been trying to answer their questions."

"But why?"

"You pulled a surprise on them. They can't get over how beautiful you are. Haven't you ever worn a dress before?"

"No."

"I guess that explains it. I hope you won't take offense, but when Madison introduced you that first day, I had no idea you could look this pretty."

"You mean I really am pretty?"

"Of course you are, but I'm sure you knew that all along. I've heard Madison tell you."

"I guess I was afraid to believe him," she said, half to herself.

"Well, you can believe me. You're one lovely woman. And unless I'm mistaken, that fella staring at you is trying to find the courage to cut in on me."

Joe didn't find it until moments later when the dance came to an end. Then he walked up to Fern, his Adam's apple bobbing from nervousness.

"Could you see your way clear to giving me the next dance?"

Fern glanced around for Madison and saw him talking to Sam Belton. At least she thought that's who it was. She'd only seen him the night he got off the train with Madison. She didn't want to interrupt Madison, but she wouldn't have refused Joe anyway. After he'd tried so hard to work up his nerve, it would have been terribly unkind. She remembered how it felt. She would dance with anybody who wanted as long as her feet held out, but she wasn't sure how long that would be. She was used to doing her work from a horse's back. She was also used to wearing boots. These slippers didn't give her feet any support. It was almost like walking barefoot.

Madison wanted to dance with Fern. Actually he wanted to take her back to the porch and kiss her again. She hadn't pushed him away tonight. He had always been certain he would find some way to convince her to marry him, but now he could almost believe they'd soon be making plans for their wedding. He'd even rather be talking to her about Boston than listening to Sam Belton prose on about the evils of Texans and Texas cattle.

"Have you ever seen a cow die of your Texas fever?" Sam Belton demanded of Madison.

"I've hardly been in town a month yet," Madison replied. "It's not likely I'd spend my time searching out dying cows."

"It starts to arch its back and droop its heads and ears," Belton said, ignoring Madison's caveat. His eyes glowed with a reformer's zeal as he warmed to his subject. "Its eyes become glassy and staring. It begins to stagger from weakness in its hind legs. Its temperature rises and its appetite fades. The pulse becomes quick and weak and the animal pants for air. The breath acquires a fetid odor and the urine becomes dark or bloody. Some slump into coma-like lethargy and refuse to move. Others become delirious and toss their heads about so violently they crack their horns."

"I don't own any cows, so it's no good trying to intimidate me. Why don't you talk to my brother George?"

"I've tried, but he keeps bringing his herds to Abilene."

"Then I assume your citizens keep welcoming him back each year."

"Well, he won't be bringing cattle here much longer. I'm organizing the citizens," Sam declared, his expression becoming impassioned. "We're petitioning the governor to enforce the quarantine line. We want to get rid of Texas cattle and all the transients who cater to your people's depraved appetites. We're going to make this town safe for farmers to raise their cattle and their families."

"I think that's a wonderful idea," Madison said.

"You agree?" Belton said, surprise derailing his burgeoning ardor.

"Certainly. There'll always be some town that wants the longhorn business. Besides, the land is getting too settled around Abilene. George has already decided to ship out of Ellsworth next season. Now if you'll excuse me, I have a partner to claim."

The light in Belton's eyes flickered and dimmed as he followed Madison's gaze to where Fern was dancing with another cowboy. "Is that really Baker Sproull's daughter?" he asked, the light only a dull glow now.

"That's Fern Sproull," Madison confirmed.

"She's sure been a surprise. Imagine all that hidden under a god-awful sheepskin vest."

"It wasn't hidden," Madison said. "People just don't see what they don't want to see."

"Well, the Texans had better see their days in Abilene are numbered."

"Find someone else to lecture," Madison said,

turning away. "You've told me enough already."

More than enough, Madison thought to himself.

While Madison was winding up his conversation with Sam Belton, another cowboy claimed Fern. By the time the dance was over, Madison had disappeared.

Fern tried hard not to show her disappointment. She had danced with everyone who asked her, but she was tired of being the belle of the ball. She wanted to be ignored. She wanted to be with Madison. She wanted to rest her aching feet. She was pleased with her success, but she had done all this for Madison, not for herself. If Madison wasn't going to be here to enjoy her success, she was going to sit down and give her feet a rest.

Two more men asked her to dance, but she refused both. "I'm worn out," she confessed. "This is harder work than calf roping."

"I'll get you something to drink," one offered.

"I'll get you something to eat," the other said, and both disappeared, leaving Fern to look for Madison. She saw Rose and George talking to Mrs. McCoy. She didn't see Samantha just then, but Freddy was dancing with Betty Lewis's younger sister, a fact which didn't seem to please Betty nearly as much as it pleased her sister.

Then she spied Sam Belton. Maybe he knew where Madison had gone. She worked her way over to him. "Excuse me," she said, "but did you happen to see where Madison Randolph went when he left you?"

Fern decided there were some definite drawbacks to being beautiful, and one of them was being stared at by strangers. It made her uncomfortable. She felt as if she were public property.

"I think he went through there," Belton said,

pointing to a hallway leading to the rest of the house.

The man's gaze never left Fern's face. It gave her the creeps. There was something about his voice that sounded familiar, but she'd never talked to him before. Pike said he lived in Topeka. He was only staying in Abilene until he could find someone to take over Troy's job.

"Thank you," Fern said, glad to escape. She supposed it wasn't fair to make a snap judgment, but she didn't like him, and that was all there was to it. She would have to find some way to refuse him if he asked her to dance. She started to wait for Madison to return from wherever he had gone, but Belton's stare unnerved her. She considered joining Rose and George, who were talking with Mrs. McCoy, but she decided against it. Mrs. McCoy intimidated her.

Fern had never been in a house as big as the McCoy home. Doug McCoy had built it with his enormous profits from the cattle trade, far more money than Belton would ever make selling farms. Until he understood that half the merchants in Abilene would go out of business if the cattle trade went elsewhere, Belton wouldn't understand that his real opponents were the businessmen of Abilene, not the Texans.

Fern wondered what the McCoys could want with so many rooms. There were three parlors, or rooms that looked like parlors, all flooded with light, available for people to relax from the dancing or have a little quiet talk.

Madison and Samantha were in the second room. Fern opened her mouth to speak, but Madison's words stopped the words in her throat.

"I've always loved you, Samantha," Madison was saying, "but never more than tonight. You're one in a million."

Then he kissed her. Right there in the light. He didn't even bother to close the door or glance around to see if anyone was looking. He just kissed her, brazenly, as if he weren't doing anything wrong.

"I love you too, Madison," Samantha said. "You know I'd do anything for you."

Fern couldn't listen to any more. She had to get away. Madison had lied to her. He did love Samantha. She had heard him say it with his own lips.

Fern turned back, but she couldn't face the thought of going through the crowd of people in the front of the house. Someone was sure to want to dance with her. Rose would want an explanation for her leaving the party so soon. Somebody would tell Madison and he might come after her.

Turning toward the back of the house, Fern stumbled past the last open door and into the kitchen. Several women were there putting food together for the guests, but Fern didn't stop long enough to see if she recognized anyone. She rushed through the kitchen, out the back door, and into the darkness of the night.

Nearly blinded by tears, Fern found her way to the street, only to be brought up short by the circle of waiting carriages, buggies, and wagons. She started to turn away, but recognized Madison's buggy. With a swift flash of decision, Fern attempted the unfamiliar task of gathering her skirts so she could climb into the buggy.

"Could I help you?"

Gasping in surprise, Fern turned to find herself staring at a stranger.

"You probably can't climb in with those skirts."

"It is something of a problem," Fern answered, thankful for the dark which hid her tear-streaked face. "I would appreciate some help."

Fern

"It's a shame you have to leave the party so soon," the young man said as he took Fern's hand and steadied her while she put her foot on the first step. "It seems to be going real good."

"I have a headache," Fern said. "It doesn't go very well with the music and loud talking." She managed to get into the buggy. She settled herself and untied the reins.

"I'd appreciate it if you'd untie my horse," Fern said.

"You'd better avoid Texas Street," the man advised. "Those drunks get one look at you, and they won't be satisfied with dance hall girls anymore."

"Thank you," Fern managed to say. As soon as she backed the buggy into the street and turned toward the house, her tears started to flow once again.

Fern was grateful there was no light burning when she reached Mrs. Abbott's. She didn't want to see anyone, to have to explain anything. She hurried to her room and lighted her lamp. She nearly tore the dress to pieces in her haste to rid herself of the symbol of her shattered dreams. If she hadn't put on that dress, she wouldn't have changed her mind about being able to marry Madison. If she hadn't put on that dress, she wouldn't have destroyed her image forever. If she hadn't put on that dress, she wouldn't have broken her heart.

Cursing her own stupidity, Fern quickly changed into her familiar pants and shirt. She wanted to blame Madison and Samantha. She wanted to blame Rose and George and Hen and Mrs. Abbott and everybody else who had come into her life since that fateful day when Madison stepped off the train.

But she knew she had no one to blame but herself. No one had made her forget her common sense and think that someone like Madison could love her more than Samantha. No one had made her think she could be anything but what she'd always been, a misfit. No one had made her cast aside the only life she had known to reach for something only a fool would think she could have. Madison might have held the carrot in front of her, but she was the one who had opened her mouth to take a bite.

Fern had just shoved her feet into her boots when Mrs. Abbott entered the room, a robe thrown around her shoulders, her hair up in papers.

"What are you doing home so . . . What have you done to this dress?" she practically shrieked. "It's ruined."

"Good," Fern said. "If I had time, I'd burn it."

"What happened? Where is Mr. Madison?"

"I don't know and I don't care," Fern said, grabbing as many of her belongings as she could carry in her arms. "But you can tell him for me, if he should remember me long enough to ask, that I'll have his buggy back first thing in the morning."

"But where are you going?"

"To the farm where I belong. I should never have left. It just goes to show what happens when you try to be something you aren't."

"I don't understand what you're talking about," Mrs. Abbott complained.

"It doesn't matter. For the first time in weeks, I do understand. Please thank Rose for everything she tried to do for me."

"You're bound to see her yourself."

"I doubt it." Fern put her hat on her head and turned for the door. "Thank you, too. You've been very kind."

"Well, I don't know about that," Mrs. Abbott demurred, "but I do know Mrs. Randolph is going to be very upset. She's extremely fond of you."

"I'm fond of her, too," Fern said, "but some things just aren't meant to be."

Tears almost choked Fern as she ran for the door. She refused to cry in front of Mrs. Abbott or anybody else. This was her own private folly. She would get over it in her own private way.

The ride to the farm was very lonely. She felt none of the friendliness she always felt when she was out on the prairie, none of the freedom of spirit she had always enjoyed so much. Whether she wanted to admit it or not, she had left her heart in Abilene, and she wasn't at all sure she would ever get it back again.

Madison couldn't find Fern anywhere. Outside of missing her, he had so many things he wanted to tell her. Samantha had offered to smooth Fern's path into Boston society. In fact, she had offered to let Fern live with her and Freddy until she felt comfortable enough to run a house of her own. For a woman of Fern's temperament, trying to enter Boston society was bound to be troublesome and upsetting. Madison wanted to do everything he could to make it as easy as possible for her.

"If you're looking for the young lady," Sam Belton said to him, "she was asking after you a short while ago. I told her I had seen you enter the hallway."

"When did she return?"

"I don't believe she has."

Madison couldn't imagine what Fern was doing sitting in one of the parlors all by herself. Maybe she wasn't by herself. Madison felt a pang of jealousy. He didn't like to think of her sitting alone with anyone, even Freddy. Especially Freddy. Madison's stride lengthened as he impatiently pushed his way through the crowd.

He didn't acknowledge several people who spoke

to him. He didn't even hear them. His entire concentration was on finding Fern.

She wasn't in any of the rooms. They were all empty. Where could she have gone? There was nowhere else. The noise of the women in the kitchen caught his ear. Maybe they would know of some room he didn't. He pushed through the door.

"I'm looking for one of the guests who came this way," he said, staring at the women who stared back just as forthrightly. "She's not in the sitting rooms. Is there anywhere else she might have gone?"

"A pretty girl wearing a bright yellow dress?"

"You know she had to be pretty," another woman said, giving her friend a nudge. "A man like him ain't going to be hanging around no ugly woman."

Madison tried not to smile.

"Very pretty, and in a very yellow dress," he replied.

"She came running through here about twenty minutes ago. She struck out across the yard. I couldn't see where she went after that."

Madison began to feel uneasy. Something was wrong. The last time he saw Fern she seemed to be having fun. He wouldn't have left her if he hadn't thought she was enjoying herself.

There was no sign of Fern outside, but he didn't expect there would be. She wouldn't leave the house to go wandering about the garden. Something had happened to upset her. Not finding him, she had run away. He didn't stop to wonder why she didn't go to Rose. He had become so used to being her comfort, to being at her side nearly all the time, he didn't consider she would go to anyone else.

Why should she? He was the man who loved her. He was the man she was going to marry. He was the man who wanted to take her back to Boston and give her everything money could buy. He was the man who was going to spend the rest of his life trying to make up for the awful things the last twenty years had done to her. It was only natural that she come to him.

Why hadn't she?

When he noticed his buggy was gone, he really started to worry.

"She didn't say why she left," Mrs. Abbott told him. "She didn't say anything at all. She just tore in here, grabbed as many of her things as she could carry, and headed out again. But not until after she had ruined that dress. Do what I will, she'll never be able to wear it again."

The minute Madison saw the dress, he knew that Fern was more than upset. She was mad.

He got mad as well. He didn't know who had upset her, he had no idea what had been said or done, but he would see that somebody thought twice before doing anything to Fern again. It was about time people learned she was no longer without a man willing to stand up for her. In fact, he was quite willing to tackle just about anybody on her behalf.

"She did tell me to tell you she would send the buggy back in the morning," Mrs. Abbott said.

"Don't worry. I'm going out to the farm now. I'll bring it back myself. And I'll bring Fern back as well."

The drive had done nothing to calm Fern. Quite the contrary. By the time she had rubbed down the horse and put him in a stall, she was even more agitated. Everything reminded her of Madison. His horse, his buggy, his barn, his house. She was surrounded by the man. She felt suffocated by him.

But she had nowhere else to go, at least not

tonight. Maybe she could sell the farm, maybe she could burn the house and barn. It sounded like a stupidly wasteful thing to do, but right now she was ready to do anything that would purge her life of his influence. She didn't think she could go on breathing when the very air was tainted by the things he had given her.

As she stalked across the yard to the house, she realized that the only things she had which hadn't come from Madison were the clothes on her back, eleven chickens, four pigs, and one cow. Even the herd, thanks to his jokes about the young bulls, was tainted by his touch.

She entered the house and slammed the door behind her. She could remember when she'd thought his buying this house was the most wonderful thing anybody had ever done for her. Now it felt like a prison.

She couldn't stay here. At least not tonight. She would spend the night at the Connor place. Madison might follow her, but he'd never think to look there.

Fern wanted to kick herself for the thrill of hope that surged through her at the thought of Madison following her. He wouldn't. She was certain of that, but it wouldn't do any good if he did. He might have thought he really loved her—people had done crazier things before—but Samantha's showing up had restored his common sense. He had been confused again when he saw her in the dress. Maybe it was the shock of finding she really was pretty.

Whatever, he had gotten over his shock in time to realize he loved Samantha. That was okay. Fern didn't want a man who didn't love her. She certainly wasn't going to be seen mooning over a man who loved somebody else.

Fern

Fern grabbed up a blanket and pillow and tossed them next to the door. She was looking for some sheets when she heard the sound of hoofbeats.

She froze. Piss and vinegar! Madison *had* followed her.

Chapter Twenty-three

Fern couldn't believe how her heart started to beat twice as fast, how her tired body suddenly seemed to have enough energy for two people.

"All he has to do is show his face, and you can't wait to fall all over him," she said aloud, disgusted with herself. "What do you want to do, go to Boston and be his mistress while he marries Samantha Bruce?"

That thought put an end to her vacillation. She could tolerate many things but not sharing Madison or playing second fiddle to another woman. She threw down the sheets she had just picked up, strode to the door, and flung it open.

Madison rode into the yard at a gallop, his mount lathered from the exertion of the five-mile trip. Fern felt a tug at her heart. He was still wearing the clothes he wore to the party. He looked gorgeous. Even after his perfidy, it caused her a severe wrench to have to tell herself she must send him back to town.

"Don't bother getting down," she called out as Madison rode into the yard. "There's nothing you have to say that I want to hear."

Madison flung himself from his horse. He didn't take time to tie it to the hitching post. He ran to Fern and took her in his arms. "Are you all right?" he asked. "What happened? Why did you leave? Why didn't you come to me?" Worry had etched deep lines in his forehead.

Don't let him fool you. You've fallen for his line too many times before. If you don't stop now, you'll go on doing it forever.

"No, I'm not all right," Fern declared, attempting to take a firm hold on her treacherous heart. "I've got a terrible headache, and I'm certain I'll have blisters on my feet tomorrow. I've got a few other parts that ache as well, but they're going to get better. I'm never going to let myself feel this bad again, not ever."

"Are you sick?" Madison asked. "You shouldn't have gone off by yourself. You should have told Rose or Mrs. Abbott."

"I'm through letting people take care of me," Fern said, wrenching herself from his embrace. "I should have known from the start it would only cause trouble."

"I thought you liked Rose."

Fern wished she had the courage to hit him. It was bad enough he should follow her. A man with decent feelings would just let things end. He certainly wouldn't stand here acting as if she were his only concern in the world. He ought to be back with Samantha and the McCoys. That was where he belonged, with the beautiful, rich, and sophisticated. If he had an ounce of kindness left, he would forget her and let her go back to her cows.

"Did somebody say something to upset you? When I saw your dress practically ripped to shreds, I was afraid something terrible had happened."

That was it. She couldn't stand it any longer. She hit him in the chest. Not as hard as she wanted to, but hard enough to make his eyes pop.

"How long are you going to keep up this pretense?" Fern demanded.

"What pretense?" Madison asked.

Fern snatched up her pillow and threw it at him. He batted it away effortlessly.

"Pretending you still care. Pretending you still love me."

She threw her blanket at him. It didn't hurt either, but it fell open and got twisted around his arms. Madison tossed the blanket aside angrily.

"What the hell are you talking about?"

"I'm talking about all the lies you've been telling me during the last week, all the lies I was fool enough to believe."

She threw a boot at him and missed, but she nicked him with the second one. That made her feel so much better she looked around for something else to throw. But there was virtually nothing in the house. She hadn't replaced anything destroyed by the tornado because she had been staying with Mrs. Abbott. In frustration, she reached for her pile of clothes.

"What happened to you? Less than an hour ago we were talking about getting married. Now you're throwing things at me."

"Don't you mention the word *marriage* to me, you deceiving snake," Fern said, throwing her sheepskin vest at him. "What were you doing, trying to keep yourself amused while you were exiled to Kansas?"

Madison fought his way through the flurry of shirts and pants that filled the air. He gripped her wrists. "What do you mean calling me a deceiver? I haven't so much as looked at another woman since I met you."

Terrible anger gave Fern the strength to break loose from Madison's grip. She reached for the cup she had used for coffee. It crashed against the wall behind Madison.

"I mean Samantha Bruce, you scalawag," she said, frantically looking for something else. She found her spurs. One missed, but the other hit him in the middle with a satisfying thud. "I can't believe you thought I'd be dumb enough, or desperate enough, to let you marry her and keep me on the side."

"Are you crazy?" Madison demanded, dodging the coffee pot. "I don't want to marry Samantha. I want to marry you."

"That's what you said to me, but what were you saying to her?" She threw a plate at him. It was a clean miss.

"What are you talking about? I spent practically the whole evening watching you dance with one cowboy after another."

"I mean when you were kissing Samantha in the back parlor, you mangy louse."

She threw another cup. This time she almost got him.

"I wasn't kissing anybody."

"Don't lie to me, Madison Randolph. I saw you with my own eyes. You were kissing her. You said you loved her. And she said she'd do anything for you."

"Oh, that," Madison said, as though she had just told him she was thinking about changing the kitchen curtains. "That was nothing."

"It may be nothing to you, you conscienceless lecher, but it sure as hell is something to me." She picked up the chair and raised it over her head to toss at him.

That was a mistake. Madison had taken her actions pretty much in stride up until now. Now he closed in on her before she could throw it and wrenched it from her grasp. Then before she could pick up a second chair, he caught her and pinned her in the corner.

"Before you break everything in this house, you're going to explain what you're talking about."

He held her close, her arms pinned to her sides, her body pressed against him. In her haste to leave Mrs. Abbott's house, Fern hadn't put on her chemise. She could feel her breasts pressed against him. It was almost as though she didn't have any clothes on. It frightened her, but it also excited her. The feel of her nipples brushing against the stiffness of his starched shirt sent unexpected tendrils of excitement arcing along her nerve endings. It almost took her mind off her quarrel.

Almost, but not quite.

"What's there to explain? Surely you understand what kissing a woman means."

"It depends on the woman."

Fern struggled to free herself, but Madison's grip was like steel. She tried to hit him, but he kept her arms clamped against her sides.

Gone was the anxiety caused by Madison's presence. She could only think of hurting him as much as he had hurt her.

"I don't know what Miss Bruce thinks on the subject, and I don't care what they do in Boston, but here in Kansas we don't expect a man swearing love to one woman and asking her to be his wife to be caught kissing his former sweetheart in the parlor minutes later. No doubt that makes us practically savages, but it's the way things are."

"You're really upset about that, aren't you? You really think I love Samantha."

"I saw you kissing her!" Fern shouted. "I heard you say you loved her. Why shouldn't I believe it?"

"Because I told you I love you. I asked you to be my wife."

"And I believed you, fool that I was."

"Samantha is my friend. We've known each other most of our lives."

"But that doesn't mean you have to kiss her!" Fern shouted. "Pike and Reed are my friends, but I don't go around kissing them. I sure don't tell them I love them. They'd think I was crazy."

"Do you want to know what we were doing in that room?"

"I already know."

"No, you don't. You only think you do."

"I suppose you weren't kissing her."

"Yes, I was."

"I suppose you didn't say you loved her."

"I don't remember, but I probably did."

"You don't remember!" Fern squeaked. "I don't suppose you remember you said you loved me either."

"I think I remember every word I've ever said to you."

There he was trying to sweet-talk her again, to make her think she was important to him. The part that made her so mad was that she wanted to believe him. She didn't, but she wanted to mighty bad. When she couldn't break away, she looked away. She might not be able to leave his arms, but she didn't have to look into his eyes and see the look of sincerity. She didn't know how he could lie with such conviction. She never could. She supposed it came from being a lawyer.

"Samantha and I were talking about you."

"And you got so carried away with your love for me, you had to kiss somebody. So you kissed the first female handy which just happened to be the beautiful Miss Bruce."

"I told her I had asked you to marry me, but I was concerned about taking you back to Boston."

"You probably thought I'd wear my pants and sheepskin vest to your fancy parties. That would embarrass you, wouldn't it? I can just imagine what your old friends would say. *I can't imagine what's come over Madison to fall for that female. Surely he can see she belongs in a saloon rather than a salon.*"

"I said I thought it would be very lonely for you, not having any friends."

"You can't expect virtual savages to have friends, particularly not in Boston. Maybe you should bring along a buffalo or a prairie dog to keep me company. But don't choose a rattlesnake. It would remind me too much of you."

"She said she'd be happy to introduce you to her friends and to be sure you didn't feel neglected when I had to be away on business."

Fern's anger faltered.

"Why should she do that? She's in love with you herself."

"Don't be ridiculous. Samantha's like a sister. I can still remember the first time I visited Freddy. She couldn't have been more than six or seven."

"It doesn't matter how old she was then. She's in love with you now."

"But I've never done anything to make her fall in love with me."

Fern could feel her anger deflate like a punctured balloon.

"You don't have to. Women fall in love by themselves all the time. I fell in love with you when I still thought you were the most miserable, conceited wretch on the face of the earth."

"Then you do still love me," Madison said, squeezing her so tightly she doubted she could take a deep breath.

Hope, the stubborn little bastard, just wouldn't go away. He popped up again like an apple in a tub.

"I said I fell in love with you," Fern corrected. "I didn't say I stayed in love."

"You're too stubborn to change your mind once you've made it up."

Damn, she was letting him sweet-talk her again. "You are undoubtedly the most conceited, obnoxious—"

Madison kissed her firmly on the mouth. "I think I fell in love with you that day you jumped on your horse and took out across the plains. And I haven't changed my mind, either."

She could feel herself giving in, believing him. "Then why were you kissing Samantha?" Fern demanded. "Why did you say you loved her?"

"I *do* love her," Madison said. "I love her whole family. They had the courage to take a penniless Southern boy into their home during a bitterly fought war. They paid for my education, made a place for me in their circle of friends, and made me feel like one of the family. I'll always love them, but that doesn't mean I want to marry Samantha. She's like my sister."

"That's not the way she feels."

"How do you know? Did she tell you?"

"No, but I can tell. Rose knew that first evening."

Madison looked stunned. "I never knew. Why didn't she say something?"

"She would never tell you, especially if she thought you loved someone else."

She could see the uncertainty in his eyes. He

clearly didn't want to hurt Samantha. It was impossible to disbelieve the sincerity in his voice, and Fern felt ashamed of herself for doubting him.

She should have realized long ago that Madison wouldn't lie. He didn't care what other people thought of him. If she hadn't been so uncertain of herself, so sure he couldn't love her for herself, she would have seen it.

Madison had never lied to her. She had lied to herself. For years. All the time.

Fern felt her resolution begin to crumble. Then it washed away like sand before an incoming wave. She loved him, hopelessly, irrevocably. She must trust him, and she must trust herself.

"I'm sorry if I've hurt Samantha," Madison said. "I never meant to, but I still love you. I still want to marry you."

"Are you sure?" Fern asked, her voice softer.

"I've never been more sure of anything in my life. You've made me so crazy I've even found myself going to William Henry for advice."

"What?" Fern asked, a bubble of happiness about to burst within her.

"I went looking for Rose, to ask how I could help you get over your aversion to me, but she wasn't there."

Fern sobered quickly. "I'm still not sure, but I think I can learn to let you make love to me. There's something else. I'm not sure I want any babies."

"Because of what happened to your mother?"

She nodded.

Madison held her more tightly. "I'll take you to the best doctors in New York. We'll even go to Europe if you like. Even then you don't have to have a baby unless you're absolutely sure. I never wanted any until I made the acquaintance of my charming little nephew, but I've got five more brothers. I doubt there'll ever be a shortage of Randolphs in the world."

"Are you certain you wouldn't miss having your own children?"

"I don't know, but I'm positive I'd miss you more." He kissed her on the end of her nose. "I've become very used to looking after you. I find I like it very much."

"But there's still the other problem," Fern pointed out.

There was a silence.

"What do you think we ought to do about it?" Madison asked.

"You don't think you could be married without . . . without . . ."

"I want you to be my wife, Fern, no matter what."

But Fern could tell he didn't feel the same way about celibacy as he felt about children. He would try, he would probably succeed, but it would take the heart out of their marriage. She wasn't sure she could endure it herself. Even now, as she felt her body trembling from the prolonged contact with his, she could feel some force within her urging her to cling to Madison, to press against him, to get as close as humanly possible.

She felt as if she were being pulled apart by two forces, her mind telling her that intimacy brought pain and fear and her body telling her that something new and wonderful waited for her in Madison's arms.

"I think we ought to find out."

Madison stared at her. "When?"

Fern swallowed. "Now."

"Are you sure?"

"Yes. I won't marry you until I know I can be the kind of wife you want and need." She put her fingers to his lips when he tried to speak. "I'd rather see you marry Samantha and have a normal marriage than marry me knowing you might be forever consigned to the other side of the bed."

"I won't let you—"

"This is not your decision," Fern said. "If I can't make love to you, I won't marry you. That's final."

"You know I love you, but I couldn't live with myself if I caused you any more pain."

"I'm asking you to," Fern said. "I'm scared, but I want you to." She pulled her arms from his grip and slipped them around him. "I still feel the queasy edge of panic when you hold me, but I feel something more. It's like I know that something wonderfully exciting is coming and my entire body tingles with anticipation. It's like there's something I want, something I need so badly I ache for it. I feel it more strongly every time you hold me, every time you kiss me. I want to touch you, Madison. I want you to touch me."

Madison gently smoothed the hair back from her forehead. After she'd ripped off her dress, ridden five miles in an open buggy, and thrown practically everything in the house at him, there wasn't much left of Rose's elegant coiffure, or of the pins that held it together.

"I want to make love to you so much my body aches," he said. "But more important than that, I want us to spend the rest of our lives together. I don't want to do anything now that might hurt you or endanger that future. Stop me the minute you become scared or uncomfortable or you just don't want to go on. Understand?"

Fern nodded.

"I mean it."

"I know. Now stop talking and kiss me."

The uneasiness, the now-tangible fear, wouldn't

go away, but Fern forced herself to concentrate on the pleasure of Madison's kiss. She loved him. She wanted to be his wife. She would overcome her fear of letting him make love to her. She had to. Her whole future depended on it.

But she didn't hate everything. She loved feeling Madison's arms around her. Even standing quietly in the middle of a room, his lips brushing hers in a gentle caress. She couldn't ever remember being held. Even as a little girl, her father wouldn't let her climb up in his lap. He didn't put her to bed. He didn't comfort her when she was hurt or frightened. All her life she had done everything for herself, tried to convince herself she didn't need anyone. That she didn't want anything more.

It was a lie.

She wanted it so desperately she had lied to herself because she thought she would never have it. Now in Madison's arms she knew she could have more of life's riches than any one woman deserved.

If she could only overcome her fears.

Fern focused her mind on Madison's lips. They were so soft and yet so firm and gentle. He nibbled at the corner of her mouth, brushed her lips with his, or moistened her lips with the tip of his tongue. He was still gentle when he pressed down with a more demanding kiss, even when he forced her lips apart and teased her with the tip of his tongue.

His hands held her easily in the strong circle of his embrace. She felt his fingers moving along her back, gently massaging the tense muscles, slowly pulling her closer, gradually pressing their bodies together until she could no longer ignore the heat building between them.

She erected a shield in her mind against the familiar terror that crept out of its dark cave to destroy her pleasure, to destroy her future.

And Madison's as well. Holding him tighter, Fern focused her entire mind on Madison's lips and the warm pleasure his kisses caused to flow into other parts of her body.

"Kiss me," Madison said.

"I am."

"No, I'm kissing you. There's a difference."

Madison's lips relaxed. Fern felt abandoned. Instinctively she withdrew her arms from around Madison, took his face in her hands, and drew him down to her. His lips were warm and moist but unresponsive. She brushed them with her own. They felt so smooth and soft. She pressed a little harder and still his lips didn't move. Relaxing her lips, she kissed him, tentatively at first, then with greater confidence.

Still he didn't move.

Letting her arms slide around his neck, Fern kissed Madison full on the mouth, her mouth opening, her lips covering his with all the hunger she remembered from his kisses. She could feel a tremor shake him, but he seemed determined that she make her own discoveries.

With mounting excitement, she accepted the challenge.

Hesitantly she traced the line of his lower lip with her tongue. Another tremor caused him to shiver, she hoped with pleasure. Growing more bold, and more impatient, Fern thrust her tongue between his parting lips to brush the smooth surface of his teeth. Fern let out a long sigh of satisfaction and tightened her hold around Madison's neck.

That broke his restraint.

Chapter Twenty-four

Madison's hold on Fern tightened until she felt she would be crushed in his arms. His mouth covered hers with a desperation born of long restraint. His tongue plunged into her mouth determined to devour every drop of her sweetness.

But even as his unleashed yearning ignited a similar need in Fern, she felt the muscles in her abdomen constrict. It spread throughout her body until it reached the muscles along her back, neck, and jaw.

Madison felt her tightness. "Do you want me to stop?" he asked, his voice husky with desire.

"Just hold me," Fern said, slipping her arms around him and holding him tight.

Odd that the very closeness, the embrace that caused her fears to escalate so quickly, should also give her the most comfort. But being in Madison's arms made her feel safe, secure, loved. And no fear could entirely overcome that wonderful feeling.

As they stood there, their bodies entwined, Madison's hands roamed restlessly over her back, shoulders, and sides, touching, soothing, warming. She held him close. Gradually the tension in her jaw eased and her back lost its rigid arch; gradually she felt tingling sensations in her breasts rather than the tightening in her diaphragm; slowly she became aware that her nipples were no longer soft.

She was also aware of Madison's arousal.

But the man who attacked her had gotten no farther than baring her body to the waist. Her fears centered on Madison's hands as they moved along her ribs, gently brushing the sides of her breasts.

He had handled her breasts. *He* had hurt her with his hands and his teeth. *He* had kissed her with his hot, feverish lips until she was almost sick. *He* had held her to the ground with the weight of his body. *He* had scared her almost out of her mind.

This is different. Madison is different

She loved his kisses and being in his arms. He wasn't holding her down and he wasn't keeping her here. She wanted to be there.

Still, when Madison's hands finally moved between them and covered her breasts, she found it difficult to remember anything except that night.

"Tell me if you want me to stop," Madison said.

Part of her wanted to stop, but part of her didn't. She said nothing.

Madison's hands moved to the back of her neck and gently rubbed away some of the tension. He traced the column of her throat, molded his hands around her shoulders, and pulled her to him.

"I want this to be good for you," Madison said softly. "It's no good if it's not."

"I'll like it soon," Fern said. She would. She wanted to.

Fern

Madison's hands slipped under the back of her shirt. The feel of his hands on her bare skin surprised a gasp out of her, but it was a gasp of pleasure. If his hands had felt wonderful on her back before, they felt absolutely marvelous on her skin. They were warm and soft. There were no rough calluses. Just warm, comforting smoothness.

But before she had become accustomed to Madison caressing her bare skin, his hands moved to her sides. She stiffened in alarm. She wore nothing under her shirt. There was nothing between her breasts and Madison's hands.

"I'm barely going to touch you," Madison whispered. "There's no need to be frightened."

I'm already afraid.

Madison's hands slid forward to lightly cup Fern's breasts, and she thought she would explode. The sensations that ricocheted throughout her body were so powerful and so contradictory she hardly knew what she felt. She clung to him, her fingers digging into the soft flesh of his back.

"Is this where he hurt you?" Madison asked.

She nodded. She couldn't speak.

"I'm not going to hurt you. I'll stop if you want, but soon you'll begin to know the pleasure I feel."

Fern doubted that. It was all she could do to keep from flinging herself away from him. Every nerve in her body screamed in rebellion.

When she thought she could stand it no longer, she told herself she had to hold on to Madison or let him go forever. Though she felt as if she were going through hell just now, she couldn't do that.

Despite the curtain of fear and the pain of remembering, Fern became aware of a new sensation, a feeling of liquid fire that started in her breasts and spread to the rest of her body. Her muscles remained tense; her loins still ached, but she was no longer prey to pure fear. A seductive warmth had permeated her body, focusing her concentration into ever smaller circles until she discovered the source of this miraculous sensation.

Madison was gently massaging the firm peaks of her breasts with his fingertips.

"He never did that," Fern managed to say.

"He wasn't in love with you," Madison whispered back.

That was the difference. No matter what happened, Madison loved her. He would never hurt or frighten her. All she had to do was learn to come to him without fear.

Somehow, without completely unbuttoning her shirt, Madison managed to slip the shirt over Fern's shoulders. Before she had time to be afraid of what he might do, he dropped his lips to the softness of her shoulder, laying a trail of kisses from the curve of her neck to a deliciously sensitive spot just below her ear.

Fern practically melted against him. It seemed that her body was under assault from virtually every angle. Pleasurable sensation overwhelmed her fear. She tilted her head to one side as Madison followed the outline of her collarbone, settled kisses in the hollow of her throat, and continued across her other shoulder. All the while, his hands continued to tease the firming peaks of her breasts until Fern was conscious of little else.

Shock stiffened her limbs when Madison let his lips sink to caress the tops of her breasts. Her gasp of surprise turned into a blissful moan as the warmth of his lips sent additional whirls of pleasure spiraling through her body.

"I'm going to finish unbuttoning your shirt," Madison murmured.

Fern fought the tension, but she could feel it

return. She could remember the feel of *his* rough hands as they'd grabbed at her tender breasts. She could remember the pain as *his* teeth had raked her soft skin.

But Madison's hands continued to gently caress and knead her breasts, cupping them, lifting them higher until she felt his tongue trace a circle of moist heat around her throbbing nipples.

No pain. No roughness. Only the delicious feeling that continued to flow through her body, fighting the tension, defeating it, washing it away on an ever-building wave of physical hunger, a hunger so pervasive Fern wondered why she had never suspected its existence before.

Madison took one throbbing nipple into his mouth. Her body jerked in anticipation of the pain she remembered, but the waves of enervating pleasure that washed over her body vanquished any remaining fear. With a sigh, she gave herself up to Madison and the sweet agony of his touch.

Without ceasing to worship her body, Madison helped her to sit on the bed, then lie down. Fern felt another moment of uneasiness when he leaned over her, but her body continued to send her signals that all was well.

"I want to touch you."

Fern said the words before she was conscious of the desire. But the moment they passed her lips, she knew that was exactly what she wanted to do. She had never touched a man, and the desire to know what it was like was suddenly overwhelming.

Fern felt the shock of withdrawal when Madison deserted her breasts, but as he removed first his coat, then his tie and shirt, eager anticipation took its place. Madison's body was lean and trim with only a fine sprinkling of midnight-colored hair at the center of his chest. A faint line trailed down the center of his abdomen and disappeared beneath the top of his pants.

Fern reached out to him.

Her first touch was tentative, almost as though she were touching a hot stove to gauge its warmth. Madison's chest hair was stiff and springy under her fingertips. Marshaling her courage, Fern ran her hands laterally across his chest, her joy in savoring the feel of his ribbed leanness almost as great as her astonishment that her touch left him relaxed and smiling. She ran her hands along his arms. How could they be so lean and yet lift her so effortlessly? His shoulders were the same.

Her fingertips encountered a scar.

"Rustlers," Madison explained. "They had Hen cornered. Monty and I surprised them."

She traced the curves and lines of his neck, felt the slight abrasion of his close-shaved beard, and feathered her fingers across the fullness of his lips. His forehead was cool, his eyebrows thick and bushy; a vein pounded softly in his temples. Taking her courage in hand, Fern allowed her touch to stray to Madison's nipples.

He twitched. Thinking she had hurt him, she snatched her hand away. Madison took her hand and replaced it on his chest.

"It tickles," he murmured.

"That's not what it does to me."

Still not entirely certain that Madison was telling her the truth, Fern tentatively traced the edge of his nipple with her fingertip. She was stunned to feel it gradually harden. She was even more surprised to feel her own nipples grow firm in response. She wondered if he felt the shivers of pleasure that darted back and forth along her limbs. Whatever he felt, he wasn't the least bit frightened.

Feeling more courageous, Fern leaned forward

and dropped a tiny kiss on his nipple. When he didn't move away from her, she kissed the other one. Again, when he didn't withdraw, she traced its outline with the tip of her tongue. Madison's shiver of delight sent a thrill running through her body. She could give him pleasure.

Taking his face in her hands, she pulled his lips down to her for an impassioned kiss. She didn't even flinch when his body pressed down against hers. She only felt the abrasions of his skin and hair against her ultrasensitive nipples. Her body tension increased tenfold in response.

"Did I hurt you?" Madison asked, quickly pulling away.

"No," Fern said, pulling him back. "I just didn't know my breasts would be so sensitive."

"You have beautiful breasts," Madison murmured, laying a trail of kisses along her jaw, down her neck, and across the tops of her breasts.

"I'm glad you like me," Fern said, smiling in love at him.

"I like all of you," Madison said.

"And I like you," Fern said, running her hands over his chest. "I never knew it could feel so nice just to touch a man."

Fern pulled Madison down for another kiss.

"And the best is yet to come," Madison promised.

"The best is having you here, being held in your arms. The rest is good, even wonderful, but that's the best of all."

"You're not afraid anymore?"

"No."

"You don't want to stop?"

Fern shook her head.

"Thank God," Madison moaned. "I don't know if I could have stood it."

"Can we just lie here?"

But Fern was acutely aware of the bulge in Madison's pants. It pressed against her thigh when he made love to her breasts. It pressed against her abdomen when he kissed her. It nestled between her thighs when she turned on her side to hold him. The tension in Madison's body, the heat, the fact it was *there* told her they couldn't just lie still.

"Do we have to?" he asked.

"No."

She could feel him relax.

"Let me know if anything frightens you."

But she wasn't scared anymore, only filled with wonder. She could hardly admit it even to herself, but even as his hand moved along her thigh, she realized she wanted to explore his body, too. Not just the fascinating bulge. She wanted to experience the feel of his powerful thighs, to know every part of him.

But it was hard to think of Madison's body when he was doing such wondrous things to her own. Her whole being seemed to be reduced to the spot under his fingertips. Even as he began once again to suckle her breast, his hand glided along the inside of her leg, lingering briefly between her thighs before crossing over and gliding across her abdomen. Her muscles bunched when she felt him start to undo the buttons of her pants, but it was only in anticipation. She no longer feared what he might do.

"I never made love to a woman in pants before," Madison murmured. "It feels strange."

"Everything we've done seems strange to me," Fern replied, squirming nervously as Madison slipped her heavy pants from her body.

"It won't for very long. When a man and woman are in love, it's the most natural thing in the world."

Fern didn't know about natural, but it was the

most deliciously exciting thing that had happened to her in her entire life. She was determined she would not be the only one to undress. She fumbled with the buttons on Madison's pants.

"If you don't want me to lose control, you'll go easy," he whispered.

"What do you mean?" she asked, a momentary finger of fear clawing its way back from oblivion.

"Nothing that would hurt you," Madison was quick to assure her. "It's just that a man can't control his body as well as a woman."

Fern couldn't understand that. She had absolutely no control over her body.

Then Madison's hand moved to the triangle between her legs, and Fern doubted she would ever take a normal breath again. Using the palm of his hand, he gently massaged her, helping her relax the rigid muscles that kept her knees pressed together, helping her release the iron band of tension that seemed to radiate from her stomach to all parts of her body.

"Open for me," Madison said.

"What are you going to do?" Fern asked.

"Nothing yet."

But it didn't seem like nothing when his fingers parted the lips of her sex and he rubbed the sensitive nub with his fingertip. Fern gasped, her body stiffened, her fingernails dug into the mattress. She felt as if her body would lift right off the bed.

"I won't hurt you."

But it wasn't fear of being hurt that sent her senses reeling. It was the most wonderful, agonizingly beautiful feeling she had ever experienced. It made her toes curl, her scalp tingle; it made every muscle in her body ache with delicious longing. Through the swirling mists that threatened to swallow her mind, Fern wondered if she could make Madison feel the same way. Without warning, she slid her hand deep into his pants.

Madison jumped as if he'd been jabbed with a cattle prod.

"I'm sorry," she said, snatching her hand away.

He placed her hand on his abdomen. "It's all right. You just surprised me."

"Are you sure?"

"Help me undress."

Being careful to put as little pressure as possible on the erection that now strained hard against its confinement, Fern unbuttoned Madison's pants and helped slip them to the floor. His drawers followed. Fern stared, fascinated. She longed to touch him, to squeeze him, to handle him as thoroughly as he was handling her, but she now knew she had to be as gentle with him as he had been with her. Her touch affected him just as profoundly as his touch affected her.

Fern rolled on her side in order to reach a hand around Madison's back. She let her fingers explore the ridges of muscle, drift down to the narrowness of the small of his back, scamper over his rounded, powerful buttocks, down along his thigh. She smiled to herself when his muscles quivered in response to her touch. Feeling more confident, she brought her hand forward, barely brushing his manhood in passing.

A delightfully satisfying shiver shook his body.

The thickness of the tangle of hair at his loins surprised her. It seemed almost like a fortress placed there to protect him from invasion.

It pleased Fern to think of herself as the invader. It pleased her even more to imagine Madison as the helpless object of her quest. Emboldened by this image, Fern reached out and allowed her hand to gently encircle his manhood.

Fern

A moan unlike anything she'd ever heard escaped Madison's lips. It was a moan of satisfaction, of happiness, but it was also a moan of surrender.

Madison was surrendering to her!

Fern's entire being sprang into an awareness so acutely sensitive she felt as though the slightest touch, the softest word, might cause her to explode.

Ever so carefully she explored him. His reaction wasn't anything like hers. While her body grew moist with desire, Madison had grown large and rigid, his length pulsating with heat. When her hand slipped lower and Madison opened his legs in acceptance, Fern felt so vigorously alive, so light she thought she might fly away like the feathery seeds of the thistle that would soon fill the late summer skies.

Abandoning his passive role, Madison rolled forward and placed his hand on Fern's abdomen.

She tried to continue her exploration of Madison, but his touch instantly demanded her attention. When his finger slipped inside her, her body flinched in response.

Her entire being focused on his invasion.

It seemed that he possessed her entire body all at once. Even as his hand ignited spirals that exploded in her loins, his other hand continued to tease her breasts. His lips scattered trails of fire from her forehead to her navel.

Unable to control her body, able only to writhe beneath the forces that tossed her like a feather in a whirlwind, Fern strained against Madison, begging for a consummation she knew must come soon.

"This may hurt a little at first," Madison warned, but Fern was beyond worrying about a little pain. Her entire body seemed to be twisting and convulsing in sweet agony. Dimly she felt Madison move between her thighs; when he entered her moist heat, she began to lose contact with reality. She seemed to be filled with him. Consumed by him. Overwhelmed by him.

A needle-like stab of pain. . . . Her body stretching as he entered her fully. . . . Her body exploding with the need to pull him deeper into her until he could reach the hidden core that fueled her need. . . . The more she tried to douse the flames lapping at her senses, the higher the blaze grew until she opened and surrendered completely to him.

Fern was acutely conscious of everything Madison did. Every movement, every breath, seemed to raise the pitch of her own excitement. She heard her groans as from a distance, her pleading cries that Madison somehow release her from this pinwheel of desire, her frantic efforts to force Madison to reach the core of her need before it drove her mad.

She dug her nails into his back. As the forces gripped her more fully, she sank her teeth into his shoulder. His answering moan seemed to be the trigger that released them both.

She felt a tremendous wrenching which seemed to start in her toes and explode through every muscle and nerve. Even as her body stiffened and rose to meet Madison, she heard him groan, felt his body shudder, and felt an explosion of moist heat inside her.

Fern felt that she had been flooded, filled to bursting with his vitality. Sensations rose in waves, each one more powerful than the other. She clung to Madison, pulling him deeper and deeper into the vortex of her spiraling need. Her own body grew taut. Like the coiling spring of a catapult, it wound tighter and tighter until she felt as though she would shatter into a million tiny shards.

Then as the agony grew too sweet to bear, it exploded within her in a shower of brilliant lights.

Fern

For the first time in her life, Fern didn't feel alone. She felt a part of Madison, so inextricably bound to him that she could never be alone again. She was his; he was hers. The bargain had been struck and would not be canceled.

She clung to him with all her strength, her body seeking to emulate the fusion of their souls. She felt elated, triumphant, not only at her discovery of the wonders of love, but in her new relationship with Madison.

After tonight, everything seemed possible.

Fern's muscles began to relax, and her body started to loosen its hold on Madison. Then quite suddenly she felt absurdly weak. With a shuddering moan, she sank exhausted to the bed.

Many minutes passed before either of them spoke.

"Are you going to marry me?" Madison asked, breaking the silence at last.

"Yes."

"You're not afraid anymore?"

"Only afraid you won't love me as much as I love you."

"That's something you'll never have to worry about."

Silence.

"Do you have to go back to the hotel?"

"No."

"Are you sleepy?"

"No."

"Neither am I."

Chapter Twenty-five

Fern woke to find herself naked and sharing a bed with an equally naked Madison. But that shock was nothing compared to the exhilaration she felt when she remembered they had made love together. She had conquered her fear of intimacy, her fear of letting a man have power over her body.

She relaxed, letting her mind concentrate on the exotic sensations of being unclothed. Never before had she been naked if she could help it. Even when she took a bath she remained covered as much as possible. As far back as she could remember, her father had encouraged her modesty. He left the house when she bathed. She did the same for him. Without realizing it, she had come to believe nakedness was wrong, even unpleasant.

She knew better now.

She luxuriated in the cool morning air on her skin, in the total freedom from the restriction of clothes, in the sheer joy of having exploded another fear. There was nothing wrong or hurtful or unpleasant about being naked. She felt perfectly natural. In fact, she felt better than she'd ever felt in her whole life.

Most important of all, there was no longer any reason not to marry Madison. She didn't have to be afraid of him, or herself, or the mysterious unknowns she used to feel must be lurking out there ready to pounce on her if she lowered her defenses, if she allowed herself to care. She cared, and it was the most glorious experience of her life.

She looked at Madison lying next to her and shivered with happiness. Never in her wildest dreams had she imagined that anything like this would happen to her. She loved this beautiful, wonderful man, and he loved her. And she could love him without fear, without reservation.

She couldn't stand being awake by herself any longer. She couldn't stand being quiet and letting him sleep. She couldn't stand bottling up her excitement.

She shook Madison awake.

"Wha—!" he said, coming awake with a start.

"Wake up, sleepyhead," she teased. "It's morning."

"No, it's not," Madison said, looking at the first streaks of dawn coming over the horizon. "It can't be any later than six o'clock." He turned over and pulled the pillow over his head.

"Wake up," Fern said, prodding him vigorously in the side. "I forgot you Easterners expect the sun to be halfway across the sky before you get up."

Madison groaned.

"Listen. Can't you hear the rooster? How can you sleep after that?"

"You wring his neck, and I'll show you fast enough," Madison said, grasping her hands to keep her from attacking him again.

"You can't mean to lie in bed all morning."

"I could try," Madison said, cocking one eye in her direction. "As I remember, we didn't get much sleep last night."

Fern blushed rosily. "That's no excuse. It's a new day. It's time to be up and around."

Madison leaned over and kissed her. "I liked the old one. Can't we try that one over again?"

Fern giggled. "Of course not, silly. If people could do that, we'd still be back somewhere with those awful Greeks you were telling me about."

"I like the Greeks. They knew how to have fun."

"If they did half the things in bed that you said, it's a wonder we didn't have a second flood. You do that here in Abilene, and they'd ride you out of town on a rail."

"Shall we try?" Madison asked, nuzzling her.

She giggled again. "We can't even do that," she said when his hands covered her breasts. "Pike and Reed will be here before long."

"Damn," Madison said, sitting up. "Here we are in the middle of a vast, uninhabited prairie and we don't have a bit of privacy. I wonder how the buffalo managed it."

"You're crazy," Fern said, laughing.

"It's all your fault," he said, pouncing on Fern and tickling her until she was helpless with laughter. "I was a perfectly sane, well-adjusted adult before I met you. Now I consort with women in pants and think nothing of riding into the teeth of a tornado. We'll have to change all that. The good people of Boston would never understand."

"Boston?"

"Yes, Boston. My home. Where I work. Where we're going to live as soon as I can marry you."

"Marry?"

Fern

"Yes, marry," Madison said, nuzzling her again. "I'm going to make an honest woman out of you. How would this morning do?"

"Don't be silly. I couldn't get married this morning. I haven't even fed the animals."

"Turn them out to fend for themselves. The antelope and prairie chickens have been doing it for millions of years. Surely your pigs could manage for one morning."

"You know I can't do that."

"Okay, but the only thing I'm going to let you have in Boston is a cat. And me, of course, and children if you decide you want some."

"When are you going back to Boston?" she asked. She almost wished she hadn't waked him. Everything seemed so much easier a minute ago.

"As soon as I get back from Hen's hearing. Do you think you can be ready then?"

"Ready for what?"

"To be married. To move to Boston."

"Do you have to go?"

"Of course I do. That's where I work."

"And you expect me to go with you?"

Madison sat up, his expression suddenly serious. "A man usually expects his wife to live with him."

"I know, but . . ."

"But what?"

"I'm not sure. Everything seems to be happening so fast. I hadn't thought . . . I don't think . . ."

"You're not still afraid of me, are you?"

"It isn't that."

"You do still love me?"

"Of course."

"Then what is it?"

Fern wondered how she could have been so simpleminded as to think falling in love with a man like Madison would be easy. She guessed she

383

had spent so long assuming that nothing would ever come of it, she hadn't really looked at what becoming his wife would mean. But now she did, and what she saw frightened her.

"I guess I haven't made up my mind about some things."

"Like what?"

"Well, there's the farm and—"

"Sell it."

"I can't just sell it."

"Why not?"

Why couldn't she? She could break it up into homesteads. She had some of the best land in Kansas.

"I don't want to sell it," she answered. "It's my home."

"Then keep it. We can hire Reed and Pike to run it for you."

"But—"

"But what?"

"I'm scared."

"Of what?"

"Everything. I don't want to go to Boston. Those people won't like me. I know you said Samantha would help me, but she really doesn't want to. She loves you herself. And don't say a word about feeling like she's your sister. Only a lawyer could look at Samantha Bruce and feel anything sisterlike."

"Is that all?"

"No. I'm afraid of having to wear a dress all the time. I won't mind once in a while—like dressing up special for a party—but I don't like dresses. They make me feel stupid. And I don't much like women. And from the way you talk, Boston is full of them."

"Fern—"

"Can't you see I'm afraid of what will happen

to me? I'll be lost in your world. There won't be anything left of Fern Sproull. There'll only be a scared, lost Mrs. Madison Randolph who everybody pities because she doesn't know what to do." Now that the barriers were down, the words came out in a rush. Fern wanted to tell him everything before she became too afraid to say anything at all. "She has no graces. She curses, she's awkward and tongue-tied, and she doesn't know how to ride sidesaddle. She doesn't like parties, she's uneducated, and she doesn't know anything about proper clothes or proper behavior."

"You don't have to worry. I told you, Samantha—"

"Piss and vinegar! I don't want to have to depend on Samantha Bruce to tell me what to do. I don't even want you to have to tell me. I want to *know*. How would you feel if you couldn't make a move, do or say anything until you cleared it with somebody else?"

A look of understanding came into Madison's eyes. He put his arms around her and drew her close. "What do you want me to do?"

"I don't know."

"Think of something. We have to start somewhere."

"Let's not decide anything just yet."

"We have to decide something. We can't just lie here with our clothes off waiting for Pike and Reed to find us."

"Then let me talk to Rose."

"What do you expect to learn from Rose?"

"I don't know, but she left home to marry your brother. She must know more than I do."

"When are we going to have the wedding?"

"I don't know."

Madison became deathly still. The quiet was ominous. He held her away from him and forced her head up until she looked straight into his eyes. "Fern, tell me the truth. Do you want to marry me?"

"More than anything else in the world."

"Then what's bothering you?"

"I told you. I'm scared. I used to think I was only afraid of being with a man or dying in childbed. I thought if I could not be afraid of those things, everything would be perfect. I know better now. I'm not like Samantha and I never will be. I can't speak French and talk about clothes and the places I've been and the people I'm related to. I don't think like she does; I don't act like she does. And I never will. I'd want to for you. I would try my hardest, but I'd fail. And the worst thing in the world would be for me to see your love for me dying a little bit every day."

"I never—"

"Let me finish," Fern said. "You wouldn't want to stop loving me, but it would happen. You wouldn't be able to help it. Even my own children would be ashamed of their mother. I'm not saying I won't marry you. I think I would die before I would say that, but I've got to believe I can be what you want. Not just a wife you're not ashamed of. A wife you could be proud of."

"I am proud of you."

"You're proud of me here, in Kansas, surrounded by chickens and pigs and bulls. That's not the same thing as being proud of me in Boston."

"I'll be proud of you no matter where we live. And if you can't live in Boston, then we'll live here. If George can learn to run a ranch, I can learn to run a farm. As long as I don't have to chase cows, I might not mind Kansas all that much."

Fern wanted to melt into his arms, but just because he had lost his mind didn't mean she had to lose hers as well. One of them had to be sensible.

"Didn't you tell me you left Texas because you thought you would go crazy?"

"Yes, but—"

"Kansas has got to be just like Texas, maybe worse. I remember how you acted when you first came here."

"But I hated everything then."

"And you don't like it any better now," Fern insisted. "Admit it. We both have to do some thinking. I love you more than anything else in the world, but we can't just get married and hope everything will work out for the best."

"What do you want to do?"

"I want to marry you right now and forget everything else," Fern said, "but I think we'd better wait."

"How long? I have to go to Topeka for Hen's hearing. I'd like a definite yes by the time I get back."

"I'll try."

"Now, before your barnyard bursts into frantic activity, and Reed and Pike show their unwanted faces, I have some unfinished business."

"I thought we finished that last night."

"We only started. We won't ever be finished."

Fern decided she didn't have to think about that.

Fern stared at Jeff with a fascination that had nothing to do with his missing arm. When Madison had told her Jeff was coming in from Denver on his way to Chicago, she'd expected another aggressive, confident, frequently abrasive, but basically cheerful person like Madison, George, and Hen.

Jeff wasn't at all like that.

He was shorter, thinner, and quieter than his brothers. But he made up for it in intensity. His eyes seemed to burn with an inner rage that made Fern uncomfortable. Worst of all, he glared at her as though he hoped the heat from his gaze would cause her to burst into flame. She knew he disapproved of her pants, but she stubbornly refused to change her clothes to please him. Madison, George, Rose, and Hen had come to accept her in pants. Jeff would have to do the same.

"You really don't need to go to Topeka with us," George was saying as they prepared to leave the house. "Madison and I can handle it by ourselves."

"I'm sure you can," Jeff replied, "but I'm going anyway."

Fern hated the way Jeff looked at Madison. He never said anything, but he stared at his brother as if he wanted to hit him. Fern wondered if the Randolph brothers would ever learn to love each other. Madison had finally worked things out with George and Hen. Now Jeff had shown up, and the tension that always simmered just beneath the surface had gotten worse. Would it get worse still when he encountered the other three brothers? Maybe it wouldn't be such a bad idea to go to Boston.

As much as Fern hated to be separated from Madison, she was anxious for him to get the trip over. Samantha and Freddy were traveling with him as far as Topeka. Fern had to admit she would feel better as soon as Samantha was back in Boston. She told herself she was being petty, mean, and totally unfair. But, try as she might, she couldn't be happy about Samantha's friendship with Madison.

"What did you think of Jeff?" Rose asked as soon as the men were gone.

"I expected him to look like George," Fern said, trying to avoid the truth.

"You weren't what he expected, either," Rose said,

a smile of understanding on her lips. "I take it Madison told him he'd asked you to marry him."

"Yes."

"And you still decided to wear pants."

"People are going to have to accept me as I am," Fern said, her defenses up. She liked Rose very much, but she didn't understand why Rose continued to disapprove of her wearing pants.

"I have no doubt they'll try," Rose said, inviting Fern to sit back down at the breakfast table, "but not everybody is going to succeed. Not everybody will even try."

"Will Jeff?"

"I think the more important question is, will the ladies of Boston try?"

Fern's shoulders sagged. "I know. I've already talked to Madison about it, but he thinks everything will work out. Even worse, he's depending on Samantha to work it out for me."

"And you?"

"How would you feel about depending on a woman who was in love with your husband to take you under her wing, teach you how to behave, and see that everybody important accepted you?"

"I'd feel just like you," Rose said, making a face. "Horrified."

"Then why can't Madison understand?"

"Men never do. They don't seem to care whether other men like them. I sometimes think they don't even want them to. They certainly can't understand why a woman doesn't look upon moving into a new community as akin to a Viking campaign."

"And that's something else. I don't know what a Viking is. I know everybody in Boston knows all about Vikings and Romans and those awful Turks Madison told me about."

"George has a much better education than I do,"

Rose said, "but I have to confess that living on a ranch is not the same as trying to become part of Boston society."

"I know. If I listened to Madison, I'd sell the farm, marry him this morning, and start for Boston this afternoon."

"There aren't many women who find a man who loves them that much."

"I know," Fern said. "I'm so worried something will go wrong I've started having nightmares again."

"About what?"

"The attack."

"Have you remembered anything about the man?"

"No."

"Then I imagine it's just nerves. They'll go away as soon as you make up your mind what you want to do."

"Do you have any advice?"

"Nothing that's going to answer your questions. Just don't let fear cheat you out of one minute of happiness. Marry Madison as soon as you can get him inside a church. Things won't be easy, but between the two of you, you'll work everything out."

"You make it sound so simple."

"It is. When you love someone as much as you love Madison, everything else becomes secondary."

"I can spread the rumor while you're in Topeka," the Pinkerton man said to Madison.

"No, wait until I get back," Madison said. "I can't get it out of my mind that Troy's murder had something to do with the attack on Fern."

"I can't see how. Sam Belton was never in Abilene until he inherited that land two years back. If Troy was blackmailing him, it must have been over something else."

"I know, but it fits so well the other way."

"You can't force the facts, sir. And they're just not there."

"I know," Madison said.

After weeks of investigation, they had no evidence to connect Belton with Fern. Madison could find no proof that Belton had murdered Troy or that Troy had been blackmailing him. Fern's failure to recognize Belton at the party further undermined his position.

But despite the evidence piling up against his theory, Madison couldn't shake the notion that Sam Belton had attacked Fern and murdered Troy.

Fern sat up in the bed with a shriek. She was breathing so hard, her heart was beating so fast, she felt dizzy. She had had the dream again, worse than ever. It was so real it was just as if it were happening all over again.

She heard footsteps in the hall moments before Rose entered the room, her swollen body barely covered by her nightgown.

"Are you all right?" Rose asked. "I heard you scream."

"I'm okay. It was just that dream again. It seemed so real."

"You sure there's nothing more?"

"No. It happens so often, I'm getting used to it." Pushing the nightmare aside, Fern threw off her sheet and got up. "You get back to bed or you'll be having that baby any minute. George would never forgive me if I caused you to have it early."

"I'm not due for another three weeks," Rose said, allowing Fern to lead her back to her room. "But

I wish I could have it tomorrow. I've never felt so big."

"Well, you just think about how slim you're going to be afterwards. I've told Madison we can't get married until your baby arrives. I want you to be my matron of honor, but I don't want to run the risk of you having the baby in the middle of the ceremony."

"That would be awful," Rose said, laughing. "You would certainly be upstaged."

They talked of trivial things until Fern had Rose settled under the covers. But Fern didn't go back to sleep. The dream tonight had been different from all the others. She still couldn't see the man's face, but she remembered his voice. She knew who had tried to rape her, and the man was in Abilene.

Chapter Twenty-six

The four brothers sat around the table in the hotel lobby, two gleaming blond heads alternating with two jet black ones. Madison could feel the tension. It had been there for his entire stay. It hadn't been as apparent while Samantha and Freddy were with them, nor did it seem to intrude while they still had Hen's hearing before them. But now, when everything had been resolved and the brothers were alone, it stood out, naked and undeniable.

As sorry as he was that his family couldn't get along any better than this, Madison was relieved he wasn't the only focal point of discord. For the last several days Hen had treated Madison with a kind of benign acceptance, but there seemed to be an active antagonism between Hen and Jeff.

"I suppose you'll be going back home now," Jeff said to Madison. "I hope Hen appreciates what you did for him."

"If you mean did I thank him for saving my worthless neck, yeah, I did," Hen growled. "But I didn't lick his boots."

George glared at Hen, who hunched his shoulders and turned away.

"I thought you'd leave with your friends," Jeff said to Madison. "It can't be much fun traveling that far by yourself."

"I won't be alone. I'll be traveling with my wife," Madison said.

The glow in Jeff's intense blue eyes turned to flame. It cooled slightly under George's stern gaze, but the intense heat warned Madison the fire was only banked, not extinguished.

"So you really are going to marry that Sproull woman."

Madison ignored his own anger. He was going to have to spend a lot of time explaining and defending Fern. It wouldn't do either of them any good if he got angry every time someone said something he didn't like.

"If she'll have me."

Fury smoldered in Jeff's eyes and caused his jaw to clench. "I don't suppose it makes any difference that her father was a Jayhawk, not after you spent half the war in the bosom of the Yankees."

"Jeff still likes to fight the war," Hen said, the acid of dislike in his voice. "It gives him something to do when he gets tired of feeling sorry for himself."

"Hen." It was George, and his frown of disapproval couldn't be ignored.

"Well, I get tired of hearing the same thing over and over again," Hen said. "You'd think Rose's being the best thing that ever happened to this family would be enough to shut him up."

Hen got up and stalked away.

"Jeff . . ." George began.

"I know. I know," Jeff said, some of his bristling hostility easing now that Hen was gone. "I should let the war die. We should try to heal our wounds. But how the hell am I supposed to do that with everybody marrying Yankees? Why can't one of you fall in love with a Southern woman?"

"Why don't you?" Madison asked.

"What woman would want a man with only one arm?" Jeff asked. "I'd rather remain single than have a wife who feels sorry for me."

George changed the subject. "Where do you and Fern plan to live?" he asked Madison.

"Boston."

"What's she going to do with her farm? You know she owns half the county, don't you? And the best half at that."

"I want her to sell it."

"How does Fern feel about moving to Boston?"

"Exactly how you'd expect. She's petrified."

"Are you going to make her go?"

"Not if she doesn't want to."

"What will you do?"

Madison would have preferred that George hadn't asked him that, at least not in front of Jeff. He certainly wasn't comfortable discussing his most personal concerns in front of his brother, especially since Jeff disapproved of his bride even more than he disapproved of Madison.

"I'm not sure yet, but I've been talking to Freddy about opening a branch of the firm out here."

"Where?"

"Chicago. New Orleans. Maybe St. Louis or Kansas City."

"Could you be happy living so far away from Boston and New York?"

"I'd be a hell of a lot unhappier living in Boston

without Fern," Madison said, his temper short. "There are trains, George. I can be in New York in a matter of hours."

"Have you ever considered helping her run her farm?"

"Yes," Madison answered, stunning both his brothers. "But though the idea of working out here has a strong appeal, I don't see myself as a farmer. Besides, I still like Boston. Maybe I ought to look for a place that's half city, half wilderness." He grinned. "What about Chicago?"

Madison didn't tell his brothers that he'd been thinking about this for some time now. His career wasn't tied to Boston. He didn't owe Freddy and Samantha the rest of his life.

Neither did he say he'd been wondering if the tightly knit, well-ordered Virginia society hadn't strangled their father. He might have lived an ordinary, possibly even a praiseworthy, life if he'd been born in the West.

"Would you consider working for us?" George asked.

Madison's eyes narrowed. "What are you proposing?" He was aware that Jeff had tensed alarmingly.

"Jeff doesn't like all this traveling. He'd like to settle in Denver. I thought you might be willing to take over part of his job."

Madison was relieved to see Jeff relax. If he hadn't, Madison wouldn't have considered George's offer, not for a minute.

"Are you saying you want me to be part of the family?"

"Isn't that why you came back?"

"In part. Mostly," Madison admitted reluctantly, "but I don't want to take away Jeff's job."

"I don't like meeting people any more than I have

to," Jeff said. He raised his stump as though it were all the explanation needed.

"How are the twins going to feel?"

George motioned Hen to rejoin them. "What would you think about asking Madison to work for the family?"

"I thought you already had," Hen said.

"What do you think?" Madison asked. He was going to get an answer from Hen one way or the other.

"I'm not marrying you," Hen said. "I probably won't even see you more than a couple of times a year."

"That's not what I'm asking," Madison said.

"I'd rather have you here than in Boston," Hen said before turning away.

"That's as much of an invitation as you're likely to get from Hen," George said. "What do you think about it?"

"I'll have to talk it over with Fern, but I think it would be better if I kept on working for Freddy. I could gradually start working for the family as well," Madison explained when George started to object. "I'm a very expensive person. I don't think the family could afford me just yet."

"Then it'll be your job to make us rich enough so we can."

"I'm pretty good, but I'm not Midas," Madison said.

"Don't worry. George is," Jeff said. "Everything he touches turns to gold."

"If we had that payroll Pa is supposed to have stolen, none of us would have to work anymore," George said.

"Is there any way we can stop that story?" Madison asked. "I don't want to have to keep getting Hen out of jail."

"I doubt it. People will always prefer to believe they can find a pot of gold at the end of the rainbow rather than have to work for it."

But Madison knew he'd found his pot of gold in Fern. He could hardly wait to get home. He was also anxious to become part of his family again. He couldn't believe how good it felt just to be sitting with his brothers. Even with the tensions that still remained, he felt he had come home.

"I'm going to move to the farm," Fern announced. She and Rose were sitting at breakfast. She hadn't gone to sleep again that night. She sat up till dawn trying to figure out why Sam Belton had killed Troy.

And she did believe Sam Belton was the murderer. Using bits of information she'd gleaned from Madison and what she knew of Troy, she'd pieced together what she thought had happened.

"I thought you were going to stay with us until Madison returned," Rose said. She had been helping William Henry eat his breakfast, but now she let him feed himself. "Madison gave me strict orders not to let you out of my sight."

"I know. He told me the same thing, but I really must get back. I've been here too long."

"You know I enjoy having you. Even William Henry asks about you when you're away."

"I'll miss both of you, but I've got to go."

Rose subjected Fern to a searching look. Fern hated it when that happened. Rose could always discover the very thing she most wanted to keep secret.

"Does it have anything to do with trying to figure out who attacked you?"

"Yes."

"Do you know who it was?"

"Sam Belton."

Rose sat very still for a moment. "Are you sure?"

"As certain as I can be."

"Does he know you know?"

"No."

"What do you plan to do?"

"I don't know."

"How can you be sure he's the man?"

"I wasn't at first. It was dark, and I was too surprised and frightened to think about trying to get a look at his face. I didn't even think about him again because Troy told me Belton had left Kansas and would never come back.

"At Mrs. McCoy's party I saw a man I'd seen once but never talked to. I couldn't figure out why it made me uneasy to talk to him.

"When the man attacked me, he talked the whole time in a soft, whispery voice. He kept telling me how pretty I was, how he liked each part of my body, what he was going to do to me. It was so horrible I shut it out of my mind. I guess hearing his voice dredged it up again. Every time I had the dream, I could hear him more clearly. Last night I knew it was the voice of the man at the party."

"I think you ought to wait until George and Madison return," Rose said. "You have no proof. If he's an important man, I doubt anyone would believe you."

"They wouldn't believe me even if he were a buffalo skinner," Fern said angrily, "but I know he's the man who tried to rape me. I'm also convinced he murdered Troy."

"If that's true, it makes him even more dangerous," Rose said. "Will you be safe at the farm?"

"Safer than here in Abilene. I'm afraid I couldn't meet him without giving myself away."

"Okay, if that's what you think is best," Rose

said, "but I want to hear from you every day. And don't give me the excuse that you were too busy or forgot. If I don't hear from you, I'm coming out to the farm."

"Don't you dare!" Fern exclaimed. "You'd have that baby before you got there."

"Then you remember that. If I find myself delivering what I'm convinced is going to be another male Randolph behind a clump of brush, it'll be your fault."

Rose stopped outside the land office to catch her breath. It was getting more and more difficult to carry her swollen body from Mrs. Abbott's to the center of town. She settled onto a bench and patted the seat next to her for William Henry to sit down.

She guessed she would have to give up her walks until after the baby came, but she hated to think of being cooped up inside the house all day. She didn't think she could stand that much of Mrs. Abbott's chatter. Besides, William Henry looked forward to their walks. He was a good child, but he needed to get out as well. He had grown up with over sixty thousand acres for his back yard and five uncles and a full crew for his playmates.

Here he was confined to a town lot and Ed. Rose found herself looking forward to being home again. The spacious home that George had built after the McClendons burned their dog trot would be a welcome relief from the cramped quarters of Mrs. Abbott's house.

"Are you all right, ma'am?" The man had come up to Rose without her being aware of it.

"I'm just a little winded," she said. "I'll be fine if I just sit here for a few minutes."

"Are you certain? I could send for a buggy to take you home."

"Would you mind?" Rose asked, grateful she wouldn't have to walk back. The way she felt now, she wasn't sure she would make it.

"I'll be back in a minute," the man said and disappeared inside the land office. He returned shortly. "It'll be here soon."

"I can't tell you how much I appreciate this," Rose said, turning so she could see him. "I feel terribly foolish."

"It's perfectly all right."

"I know you're thinking a woman in my condition shouldn't be out, and you're right. I just get so tired of staying at home. And William Henry enjoys the walk too."

"He's a very handsome young man," the man said. "I'm sure you're very proud of him."

"Haven't I met you somewhere before?" Rose said. "I can't recall your name, but your face seems familiar."

"I'm Sam Belton. We weren't introduced, but you probably saw me at the McCoys' party several nights ago."

Rose prayed her face didn't show the shock she felt at coming face to face with the man Fern suspected of murder and attempted rape. "That's where it was," she said, forcing herself to smile. "I should have remembered."

"You didn't have much time to look around. You were occupied with two of the most beautiful women Abilene has ever seen," Sam said, "certainly at one party."

"Yes, there were a lot of introductions to be made."

Rose felt a powerful need to get away from this man. She glanced up the street, hoping to see the carriage, but there was no vehicle in sight.

"I understand Miss Sproull is going to marry your

brother-in-law," Belton said. "Surely she won't want the worry of such a large farm if she's moving to Boston. Is she interested in selling?"

Rose willed herself to an appearance of outward calm. There was nothing unusual in Belton's questions. It was vital that she do nothing to make him suspicious.

"I don't know," Rose answered noncommittally, determined not to let Belton know Fern's whereabouts. "You'll have to ask her."

"She's at the farm," William Henry blurted out. "Her house got busted up, and Uncle Madison gave her a new one."

"She went out to check on things," Rose explained hastily, angry enough at William Henry to tie a knot in his tongue. "She felt uneasy about leaving everything unattended. If you want to talk with her, you could come by Mrs. Abbott's some evening after supper." When George and Madison would be there to make certain Fern was safe.

"Thank you, ma'am. I'll do that."

Rose was relieved when the buggy pulled up in front of the land office. She wasted no time in hustling William Henry and herself into it. She didn't want to have to answer any more questions for Sam Belton.

"You take care of yourself," Belton said to Rose. "I would hate for anything to happen to you while Mr. Randolph is away. And when Miss Sproull comes back, you tell her I'd like to take a look at her farm sometime."

"I will," Rose said as the buggy pulled away.

Once they got home, Rose gave William Henry a stern lecture on talking unbidden to strangers, then put him down for his nap. She went to her own room and lay down, but she couldn't close her eyes. She couldn't stop thinking about Sam Belton. If he really had murdered Troy and tried to rape Fern, he was an extremely dangerous man. Rose ought to do something. But what?

She told herself she might be jumping to conclusions. She had no more proof than Fern. Besides, his business was selling land. It was natural for him to want to see Fern about her farm.

George and Madison were due back tonight. She would tell them and let them decide what to do.

But the more Rose thought about it, the more uneasy she became. Belton had said he was in a hurry to get back to Topeka, so he might come to the house tonight. But wouldn't he want to see the land before he talked to Fern about buying it? That meant he might go to the farm this afternoon. Of course Fern could be wrong, it was all speculation, but Rose wasn't worried about Fern's being wrong. It was the possibility that she might be right that frightened her.

Fern wouldn't be expecting him and might betray herself. Rose couldn't wait for George to get home. Even now Belton might be riding toward the Sproull farm.

Rose's first impulse was to ask Mrs. Abbott to help her, but she decided against that almost at once. Mrs. Abbott would never let her leave the house unless she knew exactly what she intended to do. She couldn't be trusted to keep a confidence. Within an hour, half the town of Abilene would know Rose suspected Sam Belton of killing Troy and trying to rape Fern and that he must be headed out to the Sproull farm right now.

Rose went in search of William Henry. She found him playing rancher with Ed. William Henry was the owner and Ed the ranch hand. Just like his father, Rose thought as she brought the boy back to her room.

"Now listen very carefully to what I'm going to say," she told him after she had made certain Mrs. Abbott was occupied in the kitchen. "Mommy has a very important task for you to do. Do you remember where the livery stable is?"

The boy nodded.

"Do you think you can go there by yourself?"

He nodded again.

"Okay, but you can't take Ed with you. You must go by yourself, and you must not tell Ed or Mrs. Abbott where you're going or what you're doing. Understand?"

He nodded.

"Now, I want you to ask for Tom Everett. You're not to talk to anybody except Tom. Tell him to hitch up a buggy and bring it to the corner of Second and Buckeye. Can you remember that?"

He nodded again.

"Tell me what you're going to do."

"Tell Mr. Tom to bring you a buggy."

"Where?"

"Down the corner so Mrs. Abbott can't see."

Rose hugged her son. "Now hurry. It's very important. And when your father comes home, you tell him exactly what I've done."

"I want to go with you."

"Fern may be in danger. I may have to stay with her. You have to stay here so you can tell your father where to find us. Tell him we know who killed Troy Sproull. Can you do that?"

He nodded.

"One more thing. Tell Mr. Tom it's a secret. He's not to tell anyone."

Rose tried to relax on the front porch while she waited, but she was too nervous to remain seated. Maybe she shouldn't have sent William Henry. He was so young he might not remember what he was supposed to do. But she couldn't have gone herself. After this morning, she knew she would never have made it across town to the livery stable.

"There you are," Mrs. Abbott said, coming out on the porch. "Ed says he can't find William Henry. I thought he was with you."

Rose wasn't one to curse, even silently, but she felt like it now. Mrs. Abbott was a goodhearted soul, a conscientious woman. At any other time Rose would have been grateful she had noticed William Henry's absence so quickly. Today she wasn't glad.

"I sent him to the hotel with a message for his uncle."

"You should have sent Ed with him. A little boy like him shouldn't be wandering about town by himself."

"He's not wandering about," Rose said, "and if he doesn't come back in a few minutes, I'll send Ed after him."

"I'll send Ed to sit with you," Mrs. Abbott offered. "Then he'll be handy in case you need him."

"I'd rather be alone," Rose said. "My nerves are a little thin today."

"It's because your time is so close," Mrs. Abbott said sympathetically. "I'd come sit with you myself, but I've got a cake in the oven and some bread rising."

"I'm fine. I don't mind being alone. The day is so peaceful."

"Well, holler if you need me. I can have Ed here in two shakes of a lamb's tail."

"I will," said Rose, hoping Mrs. Abbott wouldn't linger. She had caught sight of the buggy down the street. She didn't want Mrs. Abbott to see it as well.

She waited until Mrs. Abbott had been inside for a couple of minutes, then she hurried down the steps, across the yard, and down the street.

"You shouldn't be out driving in your condition," Tom Everett said when she reached the buggy.

"I know, but I don't have any choice. Now you make sure you don't tell anybody about this except my husband or his brothers."

"Is there some trouble, Mrs. Randolph? 'Cause if there is, I'll be happy to be of use."

"No trouble, I just don't want everybody in town knowing my business. And the same goes for you, William Henry. When Mrs. Abbott asks where I've gone, you tell her you don't know."

Rose hadn't been more than five minutes on the road when she felt the first pain. She was going into labor.

Chapter Twenty-seven

"And you make sure they don't go anywhere near Claxton's place," Fern told Pike. "I don't want that man on my back just now."

"Something bothering you, ma'am?" Pike asked. "You been nervous as a hen at a coyote reunion."

"I'm just not settled yet," Fern said. "Too much has happened to me lately."

"I hear tell you'll be getting married and moving to Boston."

"Now who told you that?"

"Everybody knows Madison Randolph has asked you. Ain't nobody thinks you're likely to refuse."

"And just who is *everybody*?" Fern asked.

"Mostly Betty Lewis. Folks are saying she says that wasn't you that went to the party. That you hired someone to pretend to be you so he would ask you. She says he's sure going to be disappointed when he finds out who he's marrying."

"And what does everybody else think about that?"

Pike laughed. "They think Betty is so mad she's acting crazy. Seems she figured if there was anybody in Abilene that could catch a fancy man like Mr. Madison, it was herself."

"And what do you think?"

"It ain't none of my business what you do, but I sure would hate to see you go to Boston. There's no way they would appreciate you like we do."

"I don't remember being *appreciated* very much before."

"You didn't give nobody a chance. We figure that since you broke down enough to wear a dress one time, you might do it again. Folks said you was so pretty they didn't believe it."

"Well, I might and I might not, but I do know you'd better be getting out to the herd before Reed decides to come looking for you. Then there'll be nobody keeping those cows from old man Claxton's fields."

Fifteen minutes later Fern stepped out of the house to see Rose coming down the lane driving a buggy. Before Rose reached the house, Fern could tell something was wrong. Rose was bent over in the seat, barely holding on to the reins. Fern ran forward as fast as she could go.

"What's wrong?" she demanded the moment she reached the horse's head. "What are you doing here?"

"Help me inside," Rose said.

"I'm taking you back to town immediately."

"I'll never make it. My labor has already started."

"Piss and vinegar!" Fern cursed, forgetting to curb her tongue in front of Rose. "You can't have that baby here. What about a doctor?"

"You'll have to help me."

No curse in Fern's vocabulary was strong enough

to express how she felt about that.

"George will kill us both," Fern said as soon as she had Rose inside and lying down on the bed. "I'm going for a doctor."

"No, wait. I met Sam Belton in town this morning," Rose said, in a respite from pain.

Fern froze. "What did he want?"

"He wants to buy your farm. I think he may come to look it over this afternoon. I had to warn you. I didn't want you to be surprised and give yourself away."

"It wouldn't have done any harm. He wouldn't have found me here."

"I couldn't know that."

"I don't mean to sound angry with you. I'm just worried. I'm going for a doctor."

"There isn't time," Rose said. "My pains are too close together."

"I know all about calves, but I don't know a thing about delivering human babies."

"It's not very different. Just do what I tell you."

Another pain gripped Rose's body, and Fern blanched.

"Are you sure?"

"Yes," Rose assured her as soon as the contraction passed and she was able to talk again. "Help me undress. And you're going to need all the towels and hot water you can get ready. Some scissors and thread as well. I'm going to make an awful mess."

Fern didn't know how Rose could be so calm. Even though the contractions came faster and harder, Rose never once cried out. And Fern knew she was in pain. She could see the contractions grip Rose's body, encasing her in a merciless vise which turned her white from pain and weak from exhaustion. It made Fern ashamed she had accepted Rose's sympathy over her own pain. Her ribs could never have hurt like this.

After a particularly rough contraction, Fern could remain silent no longer. "How can you bear it?" she asked, unable to understand why Rose would put herself through such agony.

"Can you look at William Henry . . . and not want one just like him?" Rose gasped. "That's worth any amount of pain."

But Fern wasn't sure she agreed. Remembering her own mother, she asked, "Aren't you afraid you might die?"

"No, but people . . . die from many things out here. I figure having a . . . baby is one of the best."

Fern hadn't thought about it that way, but even after she did, she wasn't convinced.

"You're going to . . . have to . . . hold its head," Rose gasped. "Let me . . . know . . . when you . . . see it." Rose's voice was growing weaker. Her words were hard to understand.

Now that the actual birth was about to begin, Fern felt more confident. She had helped with too many births on the farm not to understand the procedure, but it was strange to be helping to deliver a child. Somehow it wasn't the same as delivering a calf or a colt.

"I see its head," Fern said, her excitement beginning to mount. "It's bald."

Rose's laugh turned into a gasp. She managed to say, "Cradle its head," before another contraction momentarily robbed her of speech. "Be ready . . . to catch . . . it . . . as soon . . . as the . . . shoulders emerge."

Fern felt terrified. No sooner did the head appear than it disappeared again. But another contraction, another push, and the head reemerged. Gingerly Fern supported the baby's head. It didn't move. It didn't squirm or cry. It just lay there waiting to be born.

It seemed incredible to her that she was holding a new life. This child was related to Madison. It would be related to her when she became his wife.

This baby was part of her family.

The thought shocked her so much she was almost unprepared when the baby's shoulders emerged one after the other and the infant slid into her waiting hands.

"It's a girl," Fern said, in awe of the tiny human being that now looked up at her with wide blue eyes. "But she's awfully tiny."

"I just hope I'm around when . . . you have your . . . first," Rose said when she managed to catch her breath.

"Madison said I didn't have to have any children if I didn't want to."

But how could she not want to be part of this magical cycle of life? Only a woman could bring new life into the world. Only a woman could create a new human being where there had been none before. How could she possibly refuse this most precious of gifts?

"Well, I want this baby and many more like her," Rose said, trying to twist her tired body so she could see her child. "Hand her to me."

Fern laid the baby on Rose's chest, then cut and tied the umbilical cord and wiped the infant clean.

The child was small, red, wrinkled, and had very thin blond hair. She didn't make a sound until Rose cleaned out her mouth and sharply flicked the bottom of her feet with her finger. Then she started to scream in earnest.

"At least I know her lungs are clear," Rose said, smiling proudly. "You're a beautiful baby, aren't you, sugar?" she crooned. "Daddy's going to be so proud when he sees you."

"I hope he's proud enough to keep from wringing our necks," Fern said. She knew George Randolph well enough to know he was not going to be pleased at his wife's giving birth with only a novice midwife to attend her.

"What are you going to name her?" Fern asked.

"I don't know. I can't decide whether to name her after George's sister—she died as an infant— or after his mother. I think I'll let him choose." Rose looked down at her still-swollen body. "I had hoped to be a good deal thinner when this was over. I guess I've been eating too much. Unless I'm to look like an apple dumpling for the rest of my life, I'll have to start eating a whole lot less."

"Let's see about cleaning you up," Fern said. "You don't want your husband seeing you looking like this."

"You're just full of flattery today, aren't you. I know I'm not looking my best just now, but I— ooowwwwww!"

Fern had turned away to bring fresh water when Rose's cry caused her to spin about. "What's wrong?" she asked, petrified something was wrong.

"I think . . . I'm . . . having . . . twins," Rose managed to gasp.

Though it was no less brutal than the first, the second labor was much shorter. Minutes later, Fern guided a second blond baby girl into the world. Rose could hardly wait until her second daughter lay nestled at her other side.

"Oh my, George won't believe his eyes," she murmured, beaming despite her exhaustion and the perspiration that soaked her body.

"How are you going to tell them apart?" Fern

asked, staring at the two babies held lovingly in Rose's arms.

"Can't you tell?" Rose asked, surprised.

"No. They look just alike."

"Not to me," Rose said. "Nor to George, either, I'll bet. Tie a piece of ribbon around the ankle of the first one. Before the week's out you'll be able to tell them apart, too."

Fern doubted it, but she wasn't about to argue with Rose. While the now-slim mother nestled her two babies, Fern began to clean up. Rose had been right. She had made an awful mess.

An hour later, Fern had cleaned the house, then helped Rose bathe and get into one of the night-gowns she had given Fern.

"I'm going to send Reed for the doctor," Fern said.

"What for?" Rose asked without looking at Fern. She only had eyes for her babies. "We're all doing just fine."

"Because I want to live long enough to marry Madison. Maybe George won't kill me if the doctor says everything turned out fine. I doubt he'll take my word for it."

"But I'm the one who drove out here."

"Do you think that man's going to blame you for anything?" Fern said. "I've never seen anybody as besotted as he is about you."

"How about Madison?"

What about Madison? Did he love her any less than George loved his wife? Did she adore him any less than Rose adored George? Much to her great happiness, she realized their love for each other was just as great. She no longer had to be jealous of Rose or spend hours dreaming of what it might be like to be her. It *had* happened, and one day people would be gazing at her and

Madison the same way she had looked at Rose and George.

Fern smiled happily. "I think Madison loves me just as much, but he never has any trouble telling me when I do something wrong."

"Has it stopped him from loving you?"

"No." And it probably never would. She couldn't imagine him any other way.

"Then don't worry about it. These Randolphs are stubborn as mules, but once they make up their minds, they're made up forever."

"I'll remember that, but I'd better get going. It'll take me about half an hour to find Reed. You sure you'll be all right?"

"I'll be fine," Rose said, crooning to her babies. "I've never been finer in my whole life."

The Pinkerton reached the train before it came to a stop.

"What's wrong?" Madison asked, suddenly fearful. "Has something happened to Fern?"

"No," the Pinkerton answered, relieving Madison's most immediate worry, "but I just found out Belton was in Abilene eight years ago. He came through twice with shipments going down the military road to the Santa Fe trail. The last trip coincided with the time of the attack on Fern."

"What attack?" George asked.

"I'll tell you later," Madison said. "We know who the killer is. As soon as I get Fern somewhere safe, we can close in."

"And don't let him tell you she doesn't need him now that she's delivered," Fern instructed Pike. "Doc Grey is the laziest man alive. He'd starve if he wasn't the only doctor in Abilene."

"What if he won't come?"

Fern

"Hit him over the head and drag him. I'd rather have *him* mad at me than George."

"Or Hen," Pike added as he climbed in the saddle. "The doc don't shoot too straight. Nobody can remember when Hen Randolph missed what he was shooting at."

Fern let her horse canter on a loose rein. He knew the way home from the cow camp without her help. It was just as well. Her head was too full to bother with something as trivial as finding her way home.

She still couldn't get over the birth of Rose's babies. She had known they were coming. Well, she'd known at least one was coming. But nothing had prepared her for seeing Rose lying in that bed, looking down on her newborn daughters as though they were the two most wonderful babies that had ever been born.

Fern wondered if her mother had felt that way about her. She couldn't help but wonder how she would feel about her own baby. About Madison's son or daughter.

She supposed it had been that magic, that basic desire to create life that had caused her mother to try to have a second child when she knew she shouldn't.

She knew Madison wouldn't expect that of her. And she wouldn't expect it of herself, but then she had never wanted to have a houseful of children like Rose. One or two would do. Just thinking about seeing Madison with his own child, being able to hand it to him herself the very first time, made her misty-eyed. Having children was what life was all about, and she wanted to live. She had spent too many years trying to numb herself. Now she wanted to experience it all.

She didn't want to do it in Boston; the idea still

frightened her, but she guessed she could try that, too. She had almost let fear rob her of her entire life. She made a vow never to do that again. No matter what challenges life presented to her, she would not run away again.

Fern's pony neighed, and she looked up to find herself face to face with Sam Belton.

"I don't know where she is," Mrs. Abbott said to George, her hysterical sobs making her words nearly unintelligible. "One minute she was sitting on the front porch, the next minute she was gone, vanished into thin air."

"Well, she couldn't have gone far," George said. "Not in her condition."

"That's what I thought, but she's been gone all day. Surely she would have come back by now."

William Henry pulled on his father's sleeve. Absentmindedly, George picked the youngster up and gave him a welcoming kiss, but his eyes never left Mrs. Abbott.

"Are you certain she didn't say anything about where she was going?"

"Nothing," Mrs. Abbott moaned. Dramatically putting her hands over her face, she collapsed onto a sofa. "I've searched my mind for hours. She didn't say a thing."

"Maybe she went off with Fern," Madison suggested.

"Fern's at the farm."

"Daddy," William Henry whispered in his father's ear.

"Not now, son," George said. "I've got to find your mother. She shouldn't be away from the house this long."

"I think we should notify Marshal Hickok," Jeff said.

"Maybe you ought to check with the doctor first," Hen suggested. "If anything did happen, it's bound to have something to do with the baby. I'll go if you'd like."

"I'd appreciate it," George said.

"And I'll go see the marshal," Jeff volunteered.

"Ask him not to tell anybody," George said. "Rose will kill us if we turn this town upside down only to find she's been next door all afternoon."

"I've asked at nearly every house in town," Mrs. Abbott moaned. "Nobody's seen her."

"Daddy," William Henry said again.

"I don't have time now," George said, setting his son down. "Why don't you go outside and play?"

But William Henry didn't leave. He stood right next to his father.

"What are we going to do?" Madison asked. "I can't sit still waiting for Jeff and Hen to get back. I've got to go see Fern."

"I don't know what else we can do. We don't know where to look." George ran his hand through his hair. "I don't understand it. It's not like Rose to go off without telling anybody where she's going."

"I know where she went," William Henry announced.

"I know you want to help," Mrs. Abbott said, giving the little boy a hug, "but you ought to go find Ed and play. You're daddy's very worried about your mommy."

"Mommy told me where she was going," William Henry said.

"Now, child, you know it's not nice to tell—"

"What did your mother say?" George asked.

"It's a secret. Mommy said not to tell anybody but Daddy."

"You can tell us," George said. "It's all right."

William Henry eyed Mrs. Abbott uncertainly.

"Will you find Ed, Mrs. Abbott?" George asked. "Maybe he knows something as well."

"I've already asked him if—"

"I'm sure you have, but it wouldn't hurt to ask him again."

"If you want," Mrs. Abbott said, clearly unhappy at being sent from the room.

"Now what did Mommy say?" George asked as soon as the door closed behind Mrs. Abbott.

William Henry looked about to make sure Mrs. Abbott had gone.

"Mommy went to see Fern. She knows who killed the man."

"What man?" Madison asked, suddenly alert.

"Mr. Spool," William Henry said.

"Troy Sproull!" Madison exclaimed. "But how could she have found out?"

"What else did Mommy say?" George asked his son.

"To tell Mr. Tom it was a secret."

"Get the horses saddled as quickly as you can," George said to Madison. "I'll be along as soon as I talk to Mrs. Abbott."

"Do you think Fern's in danger?"

"I don't know, but Rose wouldn't have gone to the farm if she hadn't thought so."

"Get your gun," Madison called over his shoulder as he hurried away. "And bring one for me."

Chapter Twenty-eight

Questions whipped through Fern's mind like dry leaves before the wind. What was Sam Belton doing here? Did he know she knew he had tried to rape her, that she believed he had murdered Troy? Did he know Rose was at the house, lying helpless with her babies in her arms? Did he know all the Randolph men were in Topeka and not due back until this evening?

No matter what she did, Fern realized she must not give herself away, for Rose's sake as much as her own. She didn't know what Belton might do, but the thought that he might somehow harm the twins made her sick to her stomach.

"Mr. Belton, what are you doing so far from town?" She spoke first, hoping her voice didn't betray her trepidation. "I thought you would have gone back to Topeka by now."

"I had intended to, but I wanted to talk with you

about buying your farm."

"I don't have any plans to sell."

"This is an awfully big place for one woman to run alone." He waved his hand in a half circle, including more land than Fern owned. "Besides, I heard you're getting married and moving to Boston."

"I'm not sure about that, either."

He didn't look like a murderer, or a rapist. He looked like a sober, middle-class, hard-working businessman. No one would ever believe he had tried to rape her. And with Troy dead, there was no one to support her accusation. They wouldn't believe he had murdered Troy, either. She had absolutely no proof. Neither did Madison.

But she knew he'd done it. She could feel it.

"If you're not doing anything right now, I'd appreciate your showing me anything you might consider selling."

Fern started to tell him to come back another day, but what if, in trying to talk her into selling, he followed her home? Rose and her babies lay helpless in the farmhouse. Fern had to get him as far away as possible. The longer she kept him busy, the closer to the time George and Madison would come looking for Rose. And they would come. They would know Rose wouldn't chance such a trip unless there was grave danger.

"What kind of land did you have in mind?" she asked.

"Homesteads for farmers. Ranchers won't pay for grazing land. They use government grass, then move farther west when things get crowded. But homesteaders will pay well for anything, even marginal farmland. How about the old Connor place?"

Fern didn't want to go to the Connor place. It had too many unpleasant memories and was too far away. However, it was about as far away from Rose as Fern could get and still be on her own land.

She tried to decide if Belton was acting unusual—nervous, tense, watchful, furtive—anything that might help her guess how much he knew. But he seemed perfectly normal. She wouldn't have acted any differently if she'd been in his shoes.

She always carried a rifle in her scabbard, but even though Belton wasn't wearing a gun, she couldn't relax. Like Madison, he wore city clothes. She couldn't tell what he might have in his pockets.

Belton kept up a steady conversation as they rode, asking about the soil, water, grass, the kinds of crops that grew best, all the kinds of questions a land agent would ask. By the time they drew up before the Connor home place, Fern had begun to wonder if Sam Belton even remembered he had tried to rape her eight years ago.

"The house seems to be in pretty good condition," he said. "Looks like a family could move in right now."

"The roof leaks. See for yourself."

Sam smiled uneasily. "This isn't going to make you think very well of my courage, but I don't like going into dark places. One never knows what may be lurking in the corner."

"There's nothing in that soddy," Fern said, trying not to show her scorn. "I've been inside a dozen times. Even at night."

"I'm sure you're right, but would you mind sticking your head inside just to make sure?"

Fern almost snorted in contempt. He may have been a danger to a young girl eight years ago, but she had nothing to fear from him now. He was a coward. Madison hadn't been in Abilene twenty-four hours when he walked into that soddy without a second thought.

But even as she gathered her muscles and shifted

her weight preparing to dismount, some instinct warned Fern to stay where she was. Maybe Belton was acting too much like a coward. She couldn't be sure, but as long as she remained in the saddle, she had the advantage of her rifle and a speedy getaway.

"I don't need to look," she said. "There's never anything inside."

"Nevertheless, I think I'll carry a weapon," Belton said, dismounting with riding crop in hand. "A small protection but better than nothing."

Fern remained alert. "Don't take too long. It's getting late, and it's a long ride back to town."

Fern could hardly believe her eyes when Belton paused to roll up his pant legs so they wouldn't get dirty. Why had she ever been afraid of him?

"I didn't know you still had buffalo," Belton said as he stood up.

"We don't. I haven't seen any in years."

"You've got some now," Belton said, pointing, "a whole herd of them."

Turning her gaze, Fern spied three buffalo lumbering up an incline. "They probably wandered off from the herds in western Kansas," she said. "They—"

She never finished her sentence. While she was turned toward the buffalo, Belton gave her pony a vicious jab in the belly with the but of his riding crop. Squealing in pain, the pony bucked, rising high in the air and twisting his body like a whiplash. Fern, caught unaware and turned in the saddle, was thrown off.

Even as she flew through the air, Fern realized what Belton had done. Landing on her hands and knees, she rolled over in the grass. She scrambled to her feet, but Belton was on her before she could stand up.

Fern

Fern had never been in a fight, but she'd seen several. Being used to doing a man's work, she felt certain she could overpower him. But the moment Fern felt her arm tense against his, she knew Belton was as strong as an ox. And her weeks out of the saddle had caused her muscles to weaken. In a contest of strength, she would lose.

Feinting to the side, Fern attempted to break away from Belton. Not being on her feet, she was too slow. Belton grabbed her leg and threw her off balance. Fern rolled to one side, scrambling frantically to get her feet under her, but Belton jumped on her back, and both of them went down on the ground.

Then Fern got angry.

This man had already ruined eight years of her life. Now he wanted to kill her and deprive her of the rest. She wouldn't let him.

Calling on all her strength, Fern gathered her hands and knees under her. Then pushing with all her might, she rolled over, catching Belton between herself and the ground. He gave a satisfying grunt as her weight smashed the air out of his lungs, but his grip remained unbroken.

Using her elbow, Fern jabbed him in the stomach as hard as she could. Before he could recover, she used her weight to knock the air out of him once more. That broke his hold, and Fern scrambled to her feet.

"Only a coward attacks a woman," Fern said, and drove her fist into his jaw.

Belton collapsed on the ground.

"Now get off my land."

Fern walked over to her horse and gathered up the reins. Obviously still hurting from Belton's jab, the animal didn't want her to mount him. He danced in a circle around her. Out of the corner of her eye she saw Belton come to his knees.

She turned in time to see him throw the rock but too late to get out of its way.

They came out of the night like the four horsemen of the Apocalypse, sparks flying from the hooves of their powerful steeds, their faces set in grim resolve, their eyes cold with rage. They did not carry the sword and shield of conquest, but death rode on their shoulders with vengeance as a companion.

It had been ten years since Madison had ridden with his brothers. Time and fate had conspired to separate them by rivers of life whose turbulence they could not tame, but on this night their differences were forgotten. They rode with one mind, a common goal, a single fierce and deadly determination to defend the women they had chosen as their own.

It was the same single-mindedness that had defied the rustlers and bandits of Texas, the same will to survive that had enabled them to endure a childhood that would have left weaker men crippled and useless.

And now it was focused on Sam Belton.

"Do you think he might be holding them inside the house?" Hen asked as they thundered up to the farmhouse.

"Fern would never let him get inside," Madison said.

George vaulted from his horse ahead of his brothers. He exploded through the door with such force he broke one of the hinges. Madison followed hard on his heels.

"For goodness sakes, George, don't you know how to enter a room?" Rose asked. A baby's soft cry filled the air. It was immediately joined by a second. "Now you've waked your daughters."

"D-daughters?" George stammered. He crossed the room in three strides and, apparently beyond

Fern

speech, looked down at his family.

Not seeing Fern, Madison began to check the other rooms.

"By damn, you swore you'd have a girl," Hen said. He had come through a back window. "But I never expected you'd go and have two of them. What are we going to do with that many females around?"

"You'd better get used to it," Rose said. "Who's to say Fern won't present Madison with twin girls within the year?"

"Where's Fern?" Madison asked, puzzled at Fern's absence.

"She went to send one of the men for the doctor," Rose said, recalled from her preoccupation with her daughters. "She should have been back by now." The beatific smile disappeared and worry creased her brow. She turned to look at Madison. "She knows who killed Troy."

"It was Sam Belton, wasn't it?" Madison asked.

"How did you know?" Rose asked in surprise. "Never mind, you can tell me later. I came to warn her Belton meant to come see her about selling the farm. But my labor started, and I had the babies. Afterwards she went to send for the doctor. I'm worried she may have run into Belton on the trail."

Madison felt as though the earth moved. The hate and contempt he had carried in his heart for Fern's assailant coalesced into a terrible need to kill, a need to kill Sam Belton.

"I'm going after her," Madison said.

"We're going with you."

"Not you, George. You stay with Rose. Someone has to stay," Madison said, when George looked uncertain. "Besides, three of us ought to be enough for one man."

"Come meet your daughters, George," Rose said,

losing interest in her in-laws. "We've been waiting for you all afternoon."

George drew closer and knelt down beside the bed.

"This is Aurelia," Rose said, indicating the baby in her right arm. "She's the older. She's named after your mother. And this is Juliette," Rose said, turning to the other twin. "She's named after your sister."

The brothers tiptoed outside.

Then Madison told them about the time Sam Belton tried to rape Fern.

"But that doesn't explain why he killed Sproull and tried to pin it on me," Hen said.

"Troy had to be blackmailing him," Madison explained.

"So?" Hen prompted.

"So Belton had to get rid of him, but he needed a scapegoat. When you and Troy got into that fight, he had one."

"And I spent three weeks in that miserable jail. Come on," Hen said, spurring his mount into an easy gallop. "I've got a debt to repay."

"She left here more than an hour ago," Reed told them. "Pike left pretty soon after that. I expect the doctor will be at the house about now."

"Where did she go when she left here?" Madison asked.

"Back to the house," Reed told the brothers. "She said she couldn't leave Mrs. Randolph and the babies for long."

"Something's happened," Madison said. "We'll have to separate and look for her."

"I can search along the trail to town," Jeff offered. "At least I won't get lost."

"I can search to the south," Hen said. "I had plenty

of opportunity to study the country the night Belton killed Troy Sproull."

"I'm going toward the Connor place," Madison said. "I know it sounds crazy, but I've got the strangest feeling that if something went wrong, that's where she'd go. If you don't find her, meet me back at the house in two hours and we'll decide what to do next."

But Madison hoped they wouldn't have to do that. If something was wrong, every minute was crucial. Two hours might be too late.

Even only half conscious, Fern was aware of a terrible pain in the side of her head. She tried to raise her hand to investigate the cause of the pain, but she couldn't move her arm. She couldn't move anything.

Fern opened her eyes to find herself tied to the bed. Sam Belton stood at the window. He had wiped one pane clear so he could see any horseman who approached the soddy. Fern's groan of pain attracted his attention.

"You didn't stay out very long," he said.

"Why did you attack me?" she asked. "What are you going to do?"

"You know who I am."

"You're Sam Belton," Fern said, trying desperately to think. "I saw you at the McCoys' party."

"That wasn't the first time we met."

"I saw you get off the train the night Madison Randolph arrived," she said.

"There was another time, eight years ago. I knew the moment you saw me at the party."

So it was useless to try to pretend she still didn't know he had tried to rape her. Even if she hadn't remembered, he wouldn't be able to let her go now.

"I didn't," Fern said.

"Maybe not, but you've remembered since then. I saw it in your eyes tonight."

So she hadn't been able to control her features. If only he hadn't surprised her.

"Why did you kill Troy? Was he blackmailing you?"

"The bastard!" Belton exploded. "My father died a couple of years ago and left me a lot of land. I should have stayed in Chicago and sold everything, but I thought I'd be safe in Topeka. I never planned to come near Abilene. Then a few months ago I stumbled into Troy. He was drunk, but he recognized me. By that time I'd made a place for myself, built a reputation as a solid citizen. But he didn't want to expose me. He just wanted a bottomless source of money for as long as he lived. The job selling farmland was just a cover so he could blackmail me. He never did a lick of work."

"So you killed him. Why did you blame it on Hen?"

"If I could set the town against the Texans, it would kill the cattle market. Without Texas fever, my land would double and triple in value."

"That's what I thought," Fern said.

"You're as intelligent as you are beautiful. I can understand why Madison Randolph wants to make you his mistress."

"Piss and vinegar!" Fern exclaimed. "He wants to marry me."

"Maybe he does," Belton said, looking at Fern more closely, "but it's too late now. He should have taken you to Boston before that party."

"What are you going to do?"

"I'm going to finish what I started eight years ago."

Chapter Twenty-nine

Belton licked his lips, then pulled them back from his teeth like a wolf about to savage its prey. "After that I'm afraid you'll have to join your cousin."

She could see the tightness around his eyes as he struggled to keep himself under control. He smiled, but it was the smile of a rabid coyote before it strikes. Fern felt cold fear in her belly, but she refused to allow it to overpower her wits. She had been a fighter all her life.

He left the window and approached the bed. Fern almost panicked when she saw the bulge in his pants. He had tied her spread-eagled to the bed. She couldn't even twist away from him.

"You could have bowled me over when I saw you the other night. I had no idea what you were hiding under that vest all these years." He stood next to the bed staring straight at her chest.

Fern wondered if Madison and his brothers had

gotten back from Topeka. Certainly they would head
for the farm the minute William Henry told them
where his mother had gone. They would find Rose.
She would be safe, but Madison wouldn't know
where to find her. She was on her own.

"Why did you hide yourself?"

"I hid from people like you," Fern answered.

"Then you never should have worn that dress."

Fern didn't trust the gleam in his eye. But even as
she made up her mind that she wouldn't let him rape
her, that he would not defile an act which Madison
had made so beautiful, she realized it was more
important that she come out of this alive.

The man might be crazy. If so, the wrong word or
movement could cause him to kill her right now.

In a sudden move, Belton's open hand flew toward
Fern's breast. Involuntarily her body became rigid.
His hand stopped just short of touching her. He
smiled cruelly, taunting her, enjoying his kind of
torture.

Fern expected waves of suffocating fear to wrap
her in its coils, but hatred of his touch no longer
had the power to paralyze her. She felt nothing but
fury that this man should think he had the right to
use her body against her will.

She felt his fingers brush her as they moved from
one button to the other. She fought the rigidity that
stiffened her muscles. His gaze bore into her as he
chose a button and undid it. She refused to blink,
to back down, to allow even a trace of fear to flicker
across her face.

With agonizing slowness, his hand moved among
the buttons once more, pausing, choosing, then
moving on. He was deliberately trying to destroy
her self-control. But she was no helpless teenager
now. She was a woman, and more than a match
for him.

Fern

Fern waited.

With a swiftness that caught her completely by surprise, Belton grabbed the yoke of her chemise and ripped it open to the waist. The sound of popping buttons and rending cloth covered her gasp of shock, but she was certain he could see the fear in her eyes.

It took all her willpower not to cry out.

A sadistic smile played across Belton's mouth as his fingers snaked their way across the torn material, brushed her breast.

Belton sat down on the edge of the bed. He didn't move his hand.

The breath caught in Fern's throat.

"Ever since that night I've been thinking about touching you again," Belton murmured, his eyes on her chest.

His expression frightened Fern. She had seen anger and rage many times, but she couldn't be certain she wasn't seeing madness as well.

Abruptly his hand closed on her breast. He squeezed until the pain brought tears to her eyes. "Your skin is so white."

Through the waves of pain, Fern heard a faint sound coming from outside the soddy. Hoofbeats. Someone was coming at a gallop. *Please, God, let it be Madison*. She knew she had to distract Belton. Maybe his head was so full of his crazy thoughts he couldn't hear the rapidly approaching horse, but Fern wasn't willing to take a chance. Swallowing several times, she was finally able to rasp out a few words.

"Why did you try to rape me?" she asked.

At first Fern thought Belton wasn't going to answer her. His grip on her breast loosened; he seemed to be slipping into a world of his own.

"Your skin was so white," he murmured finally.

"Why were you at the Connor place that night?" she asked, afraid that if he stopped talking he would hear the hoofbeats coming closer and closer.

Belton's hand moved from her breast to caress her shoulder. "I knew you had to come home that way. I waited for you. Just like I did today."

"But you didn't know me. You'd never seen me before."

His hand moved down her side and across her abdomen. It took all of Fern's self-control to keep from shivering in disgust.

"I saw you in town, parading about in your pants like no decent woman would do. And I saw all those men panting after you. They were afraid to do more than look, but I wasn't. All I had to do was say I was looking to buy some cattle, and they told me anything I wanted to know. Including where you pastured your herd."

The hoofbeats rang like thunder in Fern's head. Just a minute longer. Even a few seconds.

"You didn't know me. You couldn't like me. How could you—"

"Your skin was so white," Belton crooned, slipping further into a world of his own.

Belton remained so caught up in caressing Fern's skin that he didn't hear Madison until he plunged through the doorway.

Madison struck Belton a vicious blow from behind, but he didn't go down. Screaming like a wild animal, he turned to attack Madison, his fingers curved like talons. Tangled together like two snarling beasts, they lurched around the soddy, crashing into the few pieces of furniture, until they fell through the doorway. In the greater space, Madison was able to use his boxing skills and quickly reduced Belton to staggering helplessness. One last blow sent him crashing to the ground.

"Are you all right?" Madison asked when he reached Fern's side. He began untying the ropes that bound her to the bed. "Did he hurt you?"

"No. I made him so angry he forgot he intended to rape me."

Madison finished untying Fern, and she threw herself into his arms.

"He wanted me because he thought I was pure, untouched. When I told him we had made love, he went crazy."

"He was already crazy," Madison said, holding Fern close.

"One good thing came out of this," Fern said once she was nestled securely in Madison's arms. "I got so furious I wanted to kill him. I wasn't afraid of him at all."

"I'm glad, but—"

"Madison!" Fern screamed as she jumped to her feet and pushed Madison as hard as she could. Belton stood in the yard, his gun drawn, pointing at Madison.

Wrapping his arm around Fern, Madison threw them both into the safety of the shadows. But it wasn't completely dark, and Belton charged toward the doorway, gun drawn.

Madison cursed himself for a fool. In his anxiety to reach Fern, he had failed to tie Belton up and he had laid down his rifle. His years in Boston had caused him to lose most of the survival instincts he had developed in Texas.

"Stay against the wall," Madison whispered to Fern. "I'm going to get the rifle."

"He's just outside the door. He'll see you."

"It's our only chance. He'll kill us like fish in a pond if I don't."

Gathering his muscles, Madison lunged across the space. Guns barked and bullets buried themselves in the walls of the soddy, but Madison reached the rifle. His finger had just closed on the trigger when Belton charged through the doorway, gun blazing. Belton tossed aside an empty gun, drew another from his belt, and turned toward the corner where Fern was hidden.

Madison felt a searing pain in his side. He had been hit, but he had to stop Belton. Even now his gun was pointed at Fern. Bringing his rifle level, he fired into the silhouette in the doorway.

The concussion of the rifle shot nearly deafened him.

The gun dropped from Belton's hand and an expression of incredible agony turned his face into a twisted, horrible mask. Both hands gripped his crotch and Belton staggered backward, screaming over and over again. Stumbling, he fell and lay writhing on the ground; blood stained his pants between his legs.

Keeping a grip on his rifle, Madison helped Fern up. "It's over," he said. "He won't bother you again."

They stepped out into the lengthening shadows of the afternoon. Not fifty feet away Hen sat his horse, an unused gun in his hand.

"Mighty sloppy shooting, brother. What the hell were you aiming for?" he demanded, pointing to Belton's bloody crotch.

"He caught me by surprise," Madison explained. "I guess my aim was off."

"I'm glad you were better eight years ago," Hen said matter-of-factly. "It's probably just as well, though. He'll live to stand his trial, but he won't be bothering any more women."

Fern felt something wet, warm, and sticky oozing between her fingers. She looked down to find her hand covered with blood.

434

"You're hurt," she cried, turning Madison so she could get a better look. She felt terribly guilty. This was the second time she'd caused him to be shot.

Madison grimaced as he twisted so he could look down at his side. "I'm either going to have to head back to Boston on the next train, or learn to shoot again."

"Boston," Fern said quite positively. "I'm not going to have you shot again."

Chapter Thirty

"Stand still," Rose scolded. "You can't get married with your dress half buttoned."

Fern studied herself in the mirror. She was wearing the second of the dresses Madison had bought her, and she didn't like what she saw. "I can't marry Madison in an everyday dress. I bet Samantha would have ordered her dress straight from one of those fancy foreign places Madison is always talking about."

Fern couldn't entirely keep her mind off the fact that Samantha and Freddy Bruce had returned to Abilene for her wedding. She knew people would make comparisons. Try as she might, she couldn't help but worry that Madison would, too.

Not that she worried he would change his mind. Despite a wound that made it very painful for him to get around, he had been positively foolish over her these last several days. Even George had commented on it. She didn't want to remember what Jeff had said. She could easily understand why people didn't always like Jeff very much.

She wasn't even sure that Madison remembered Samantha was here. He hadn't had a thought for anyone but Fern. She had tried to understand it. She'd spent hours cataloging her attributes, positive and negative, and she couldn't figure out why Madison should be so crazy about her. She finally decided there was no reason. He just did, and she would have to accept it.

So she had, and she'd never felt so happy in her life.

"Madison isn't marrying Samantha," Rose said patiently. She had been calming Fern's fears all morning. "And I'm sure he won't care what you're wearing." Rose finished the buttons up the back.

"That yellow dress would have been just perfect," Mrs. Abbott moaned, "but there was a rip right through the bodice. I couldn't do a thing with it."

Mrs. Abbott hadn't ceased to bemoan Fern's destruction of the dress she'd worn to Mrs. McCoy's party.

"I should have gone to Kansas City," Fern said. "Maybe even St. Louis. I knew there was nothing in Abilene I could wear." She had bought six dresses and decided against all of them in favor of the one Madison had bought.

"Stop worrying," Rose said, giving Fern a kiss on the cheek. "You look lovely."

"I'd have ordered a dress from Chicago if my catalogs hadn't been blown away."

"Madison would probably marry you in your pants and sheepskin vest if necessary."

"He wouldn't!" Mrs. Abbott exclaimed, horrified.

"You think so?" Fern asked hopefully.

"You've spent years hating dresses, but here you

are wishing you could go shopping in half the cities of the world just to please him. Don't you think he could put up with your pants for the same reason?"

A blissful smile transformed Fern's features.

"I guess you're right. He doesn't seem to mind a thing I do."

Rose made a last-minute check on her own dress, and turned back to Fern.

"You're going to have to have more confidence in yourself."

"That's what Madison keeps saying, but it's hard. Everything feels so different, it's hard to get used to."

Rose smiled. "I'm sure it is, but you'll have a wonderful time learning."

Fern paused at the threshold of the tiny church. Madison had had a piano brought over from the Old Fruit Saloon and the pianist was regaling the audience with a selection of Stephen Foster's most romantic tunes. She doubted that "Beautiful Dreamer" was the most suitable tune for a wedding, but it exactly reflected her mood. She was living her dream, the most beautiful dream any woman could have.

At the front of the church, Madison stood waiting for her, George at his side. Just like when she'd first seen them. Hen and Jeff were there, too. The boys from Texas had been invited, but they hadn't made it in time.

"See you in a minute,".Rose whispered, then started down the aisle to the front of the church. The babies were two weeks old, and Rose was her petite, trim self again.

As Fern waited for Rose to reach the altar, her gaze narrowed until she saw no one but Madison.

Fern

No one else mattered today. Or tomorrow. Not ever. He was the center and the outer limits of her universe. She still found it difficult to believe she was standing in a church, mere seconds away from starting down the aisle to be married to the man who waited for her.

But it was even harder to believe it was Madison who waited.

"It's time to go," Mrs. Abbott whispered. "Now make sure you walk slow. It'll give everybody a chance to see how pretty you look."

But Fern didn't care about everybody. Only Madison. And as she started forward, it was all she could do to keep from running to him.

"Piss and vinegar!" she muttered. "I'm crying."

At the reception in the churchyard, Fern thought she had never spoken to so many people in her life. They couldn't have all been in the church. It wasn't big enough. Marshal Hickok must have emptied every saloon on Texas Street. She'd have sworn she'd shaken hands with every cowhand in the state of Texas.

"Where are you going on your honeymoon?" Hen asked.

"I have to go back to Boston first," Madison said, "but as soon as I can get away, we're going to New Orleans."

"After he's shown me how proper ladies behave, he's promised to show me the improper ones," Fern said, smiling happily.

"When will we see you back here?" George asked.

"Before winter. I'll let you know."

"And what are you going to do while Madison is hard at work?" Rose asked Fern.

"Go shopping." Fern made a face. "He told me I

could buy all the dresses I want."

"I also told her she didn't have to buy a single one," Madison said. "I fell in love with her in pants. I won't mind being married to her the same way."

"But I will," Fern said. "People might not say anything to me, but they'd say a lot to you."

"It won't matter what anybody says."

"Yes, it will," Fern said. "I can't have you fighting half the people in Boston. It can't be that terrible to wear dresses all the time. Rose does it. But I sure wish I didn't have to find out."

Her new in-laws laughed at her.

"Madison has promised to take me to visit you in Texas. Please say I can bring my pants."

"You can bring anything you like," Rose promised, "hat, vest, or spurs. As long as you're on the Circle-Seven, you can do what you like and nobody will say a word."

Just then three riders turned the corner up the street and headed toward them at a gallop. A smile split George's face.

"Unless I'm badly mistaken, Fern, that's the rest of your in-laws."

"They're a little late," Madison said, sobering. Fern could tell he wasn't looking forward to meeting Monty.

Hen's double practically galloped his horse over the hem of Fern's dress before he threw himself from the saddle. "I rode hell-for-leather all the way from Texas."

Two boys hit the ground close behind him, one a towering beanstalk and one a spitting image of what George must have looked like at twelve or thirteen.

"I been trying to tell him he's got the wrong date," the younger one said, going straight to George, "but Monty never listens to nobody."

Fern

"You said get here the twentieth," Monty said to George.

"That I did, but today's the twenty-first. Madison and Fern were married an hour ago."

"Son-of-a-bitch!" Monty cursed.

"This is James Monroe Randolph," George said, introducing his brother to Fern. "You'll have to forgive him. He's been talking to cows so long he's forgotten how to talk to ladies."

"Sorry, ma'am," Monty apologized, a becoming blush rising in his neck. "I'm just mad as hell at missing the wedding."

"These other two tramps are Tyler and Zac," George said. "Be especially careful of the younger one. He looks harmless, but he's as treacherous as a sidewinder."

"I am not," Zac said, stepping forward. "I like ladies, especially pretty ones."

"Now I know where William Henry gets it," Fern said to Rose.

Monty shoved his little brother aside and stepped up to Madison. "So you finally came home, you son-of-a-bitch!" Without warning he slammed his fist into Madison's jaw, sending him to the ground. Then, to the amazement of his family, his scowl turned to a welcoming smile and he helped Madison to his feet. "Glad you could clear Hen's name. It had George and Rose in a stew." He looked around at the town with disfavor. "This place doesn't look like much. What say I bring the boys up and burn it to the ground?"

"Is that how you show your brother you've forgiven him?" George asked, stunned.

"I didn't shoot him, did I?" Monty responded.

"A little rough and ready," Madison complained, massaging his chin, "but it's quick and to the point. On the whole I prefer it."

"Before you do something else crazy—" Rose started to say but stopped abruptly. Fern had stepped forward and delivered a powerful right to Monty's stomach. The air left his lungs with a loud "ufph" and he doubled over.

"Is that how you greet your brother-in-law?" Monty gasped.

"I didn't shoot you, did I?" Fern replied.

Author's Note

At the close of the Civil War, Texans came home to find their most immediate wealth in the form of millions of unbranded longhorns, which roamed the brush and swampland between the Nueces and the Rio Grande. But a steer that was worth three dollars for hide and tallow in Texas was worth twenty-five to thirty dollars in an eastern market.

Unfortunately Texas longhorns were hosts to a tiny tick that caused splenic fever—commonly called Spanish or Texas fever—to which the longhorns were immune, but which wrought havoc among northern herds. In 1866 Kansas and Missouri quarantine statutes forbidding entry to Texas cattle caused many herds to be turned away at the state line, some by vigilante action. The Texans had a fortune in beef, but no way to get them to market.

In the spring of 1867, The Union Pacific Railway swept along the north bank of the Smoky Hill River in Dickinson County, Kansas. These two circumstances might have remained forever unrelated but for Joseph G. McCoy. He envisioned Abilene as a shipping point for an endless supply of Texas cattle.

Despite the fact that bringing cattle into Abilene was illegal, McCoy obtained a verbal commitment from the Union Pacific officials, built a stockyard, and sent agents south to convince drovers to bring their herds to Abilene. By mid-August Texas longhorns nibbled on the lush upland grasses of Dickinson County.

However, the continued opposition of farmers and local ranchers combined with the advancing agricultural frontier to make 1871 Abilene's last season as a cattle market. The market gradually moved west until it reached Dodge, which remained the major market until 1885. Then the increasing influx of immigrants into western Kansas closed the trails forever.

Thus ended the twenty-year history of the Kansas cattle town, one of the West's most enduring legends.

LEIGH GREENWOOD

"Leigh Greenwood is a dynamo of a storyteller!"
—Los Angeles Times

Jefferson Randolph has never forgotten all he lost in the War Between The States—or forgiven those he has fought. Long after most of his six brothers find wedded bliss, the former Rebel soldier keeps himself buried in work, only dreaming of one day marrying a true daughter of the South. Then a run-in with a Yankee schoolteacher teaches him that he has a lot to learn about passion.

Violet Goodwin is too refined and genteel for an ornery bachelor like Jeff. Yet before he knows it, his disdain for Violet is blossoming into desire. But Jeff fears that love alone isn't enough to help him put his past behind him—or to convince a proper lady that she can find happiness as the newest bride in the rowdy Randolph clan.

_3995-8 $5.99 US/$7.99 CAN

Dorchester Publishing Co., Inc.
65 Commerce Road
Stamford, CT 06902